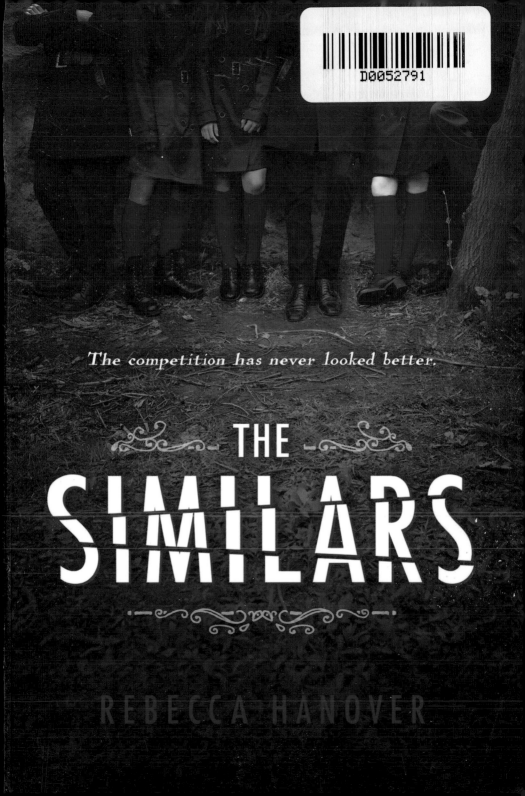

The competition has never looked better.

THE
SIMILARS

REBECCA HANOVER

PRAISE FOR

THE
SIMILARS

"Fascinating. I was captivated."

—Francine Pascal, bestselling author of the
Sweet Valley High and Fearless series

"A page-turner that more than delivers on its premise. Hanover takes on sci-fi and high school with equal wit and understanding. The perfect mix of achingly familiar and completely mysterious, the world of *The Similars* is one we don't want to leave."

—Allison Raskin, *New York Times* bestselling
author of *I Hate Everyone But You*

"A brilliantly imagined near-future world where six clones and their counterparts grapple with profound questions of identity and what it means to be human. Part cautionary tale, part gripping teen romance, *The Similars* is as immersive and fast-paced as it is shrewd, compelling, and heartbreaking."

—Ray Kurzweil, inventor, futurist, and
New York Times bestselling author

"Episodic and fast-moving... Plenty of twists and one very big turn that will delight mystery readers."

—*Booklist*

THE SIMILARS

THE
SIMILARS

REBECCA
HANOVER

sourcebooks
fire

Published by Sourcebooks Fire, an imprint of Sourcebooks
P.O. Box 4410, Naperville, Illinois 60567-4410
(630) 961-3900
sourcebooks.com

The Library of Congress has cataloged the hardcover edition as follows:

Names: Hanover, Rebecca, author.
Title: The similars / Rebecca Hanover.
Description: Naperville, Illinois : Sourcebooks Fire, [2019] | Summary: "When six clones join Emmaline's prestigious boarding school, she must confront the heartbreak of seeing her dead best friend's face each day in class"-- Provided by publisher.
Identifiers: LCCN 2018033682 | (hardcover : alk. paper)
Subjects: | CYAC: Cloning--Fiction. | Experiments--Fiction. | Boarding schools--Fiction. | Schools--Fiction. | Science fiction.
Classification: LCC PZ7.1.H36425 Si 2019 | DDC [Fic]--dc23
LC record available at https://lccn.loc.gov/2018033682

Printed and bound in Canada.
MBP 10 9 8 7 6 5 4 3 2

For Mom and Dad

For Ethan

THE SIMILARS

THE SIMILARS

I DON'T ACTIVELY want to die. Not all the time.

If it weren't for my father, then sure, I'd consider it. He may not be my favorite person in the world, and I am definitely not his, but I don't relish the thought of him standing at my gravesite, hunched over my coffin, racked with sobs. I only think about dying sometimes—like now.

We're almost at Hades Point. In approximately two minutes and thirty seconds, the black Lorax I'm riding in will carry me past the infamous cliff's edge where, historically, twelve students at my school have plummeted to their deaths. I'm not afraid of the point, but maybe I should be. It's deep—Grand Canyon deep. A gaping mouth in the ground that swallows kids who can't handle Darkwood Academy. That's the boarding school I go to in Vermont, where I'm starting my junior year. It's where I spent my first year and sophomore year, too, before *the thing that happened*. But more on that…never.

"Approaching Hades Point!" trills a merry voice, invading my thoughts. You'd think a driverless vehicle would guarantee a person some peace and quiet, but no. When the Lorax picked me up at the Burlington airport two hours ago, the operating system forced me to select a name for its virtual driver. I'd rejected the suggested monikers and typed in one of my own choosing: *Misery*.

"This is Misery, your friendly chauffeur!" the voice had immediately chirped at me. She hasn't stopped to take a metaphorical breath since.

Misery continues her assault on my ears. "If you look to your left, Miss Chance, you'll see we're passing Hades Point, one of the most scenic spots on campus!"

Sure, Misery. I take in the precipitous drop as we round the bend. *If by "scenic," you mean deadly.*

I stare at Hades Point laid out in the distance like a casket. I picture them, all twelve students who tumbled over. I've thought about jumping. I've dreamed of flying through the air and knowing my life would soon end. After what happened, who could blame me? Within hours of my best friend's death this summer, I had faced an onslaught of emotions so intolerable, I felt like a foreigner in my own mind. Grasping for some semblance of order, I began naming my different moods. Example: "A Zombie Just Ate My Body," which is like being frostbitten and stun-gunned and about 94 percent dead inside. At least that one is bearable, unlike "Get That Serrated Knife Out of My Chest," which is as painful as it sounds. I spend entire days walking around with the sensation that somebody stabbed me in the chest and the knife is still inside. Conveniently, there are pills I can take for these afflictions, pharma hybrids that make my life more tolerable. I slinked out of my psychiatrist's office last month, a prescription tube clutched in my fist.

I slide a pill out of my pocket and swallow it dry, then press my cheek to the cool glass window. Sometimes feeling things makes you remember you're alive. And sometimes that is too much to handle.

As we leave the point behind and embark on the last leg of our journey to Darkwood, I imagine it: *Stopping the car. Stepping out. Walking toward the edge of the point. Closing my eyes as the wind whips me, and then, without any fanfare, letting go. Ending it. Just like Oliver did back home in California. In his room. Where I found him—*

"Approaching Darkwood's main campus!" Misery's voice jars me out of the memory. "Established in 1927 by Cornelius Seymour, Darkwood Academy has remained a bastion of intellectual integrity for more than a century—"

"Thank you," I interrupt, pressing my mother's ancient tortoiseshell-framed glasses to the bridge of my nose. "I got it."

"Sorry, Miss Chance. I—!"

"Emmaline," I interrupt again. "But you can call me Emma."

"Big day, isn't it, Emma? Back to school! Seeing friends and starting classes. And, of course—the Similars!"

"Sorry." I shrug. "I'm just not worked up about a couple of DNA copies of some teenage prepsters."

"But, Miss Chance!" Misery sputters. "Have you been watching the feeds? People haven't been this excited since astronauts landed on Mars!"

"Dash," I whisper into my plum, the "everything" device I keep strapped around my wrist so I won't lose it. "Can we turn her off?"

The voice of my genial virtual assistant rings out from the tiny screen on my wrist. "Your simulated chauffeur cannot be muted," says Dash. "But if you would like, Emma, I'll happily report her as spam."

"That won't be necessary. But thanks." I sigh, settling back into my seat and trying to ignore Misery's never-ending monologue. It's not like Misery's wrong. The Similars are *major* news. They've been making headlines for weeks, ever since they arrived in the United States this summer and it was announced that they'd be attending Darkwood Academy, right alongside the kids they were originally cloned from. It's no wonder the whole country is transfixed. Six students at Darkwood Academy are about to sit in class next to their clones, who share their exact DNA, but who they only recently met for the first time. The old me would have shown more interest in the Similars, would have been buzzing Oliver about them nonstop, eager to hear him dissect each new piece of information about their curious upbringing and unlikely existence. But these days, I only care about one thing: keeping the feeling of the serrated knife at bay.

The Lorax reaches the bottom of a hill and turns onto a gravel road that winds through brush and woods to the center of Darkwood Academy.

"I wonder if you'll meet them right away?" Misery muses. "Or later, once everyone has settled in their roo—?"

"Can we turn on the feeds?" I interrupt.

"Of course, Emma! I'd like to hear what they're saying too!"

"I was actually thinking music might be nice…"

But Misery's already tuned to a news station and clearly didn't hear me. I don't feel like repeating myself, so I settle back in my seat to listen.

"It's a pleasure to have you with us today," says a distinguished woman whose image pops up in my view space. She's nearly three-dimensional, but not quite. "For those in the audience who aren't acquainted with his work, our guest today is Jaeger Stanwick, the journalist known for his vocal involvement in the pro-clone movement."

"Happy to be here," says a familiar voice. In my view space, Jaeger's figure materializes, looking characteristically disheveled. I recognize him, and not just because he's made himself famous, or rather, infamous for his views on cloning. Jaeger's also the father of one of my closest friends at Darkwood: my roommate, Prudence Stanwick. Everyone calls her Pru.

"Can you put this momentous day into perspective for us?" the reporter presses.

"'Momentous' doesn't even cover it," Jaeger says. "The arrival of these six teenagers at Darkwood Academy—"

"The Similars," the reporter interrupts. "The teens just

released a written statement to the media sharing their nickname for each other with the broader world. 'The Similars' is what they began calling one another when they first learned the circumstances of their birth."

Jaeger nods. "I believe these teens wanted to take control of how the world views them. By giving us—and the press—a name to call them rather than allowing us to craft our own, they are signaling that they're in charge of their own destiny. And they're doing it with a commendable sense of humor, I might add. But as I was saying…"

"Go ahead—"

"The arrival of these six teenagers at Darkwood is an enormous opportunity."

"How so?"

"It's our chance to welcome them into our lives with open arms. To give them the space and respect they deserve, so they may show the world who they are."

"And that they harbor no evil agendas?" quips the reporter.

Jaeger frowns. "They are boys and girls, just like our children, Demetria. Like every other teenager in America, they have goals and dreams, fears and ambitions. They can be hurt, deeply. They can feel pain and love—and joy. It's time the world acknowledged that."

"Off!" I shout. "Please." All this talk about the Similars is making my head spin.

"Are you finished listening already?" Misery asks. "Do you already know everything there is to know about the Similars?"

"No," I say, trying not to let Misery get to me. She's only

a bot; she can't help it if she's been programmed to be overly eager. "We're here. At Darkwood. See?"

"You're right! So perceptive, Miss Chance."

I resist the urge to roll my eyes as we pull up in front of the main house, a Queen Anne–style manse that looks unbalanced, like it exists on several overlapping planes all at once. As the Lorax inches behind the other cars idling in front of the school, I feel myself tensing. Classmates line the driveway, hugging and gossiping. That would have been me and Oliver. But no more.

The silver car in front of ours stops, and a girl steps out, teetering in high-heeled boots. I instantly recognize her. Tessa Leroy. We aren't friends, but I know all about her—everyone does. Birdlike and petite, Tessa is one of the Ten. She's a year ahead of me, a senior, and her stratum from last year will guarantee her a spot, once again, in that elite group. In spite of her Ten status, no one envies Tessa anymore. Not since the police came knocking on the door of her family's home on Central Park West and arrested her father, Damian Leroy, for fraud.

The Lorax slowly pulls to the front of the line. It's my turn.

"Have a wonderful school year!" Misery calls out as I retrieve my luggage from the trunk. "I'd be bursting to meet the Similars if I were you! I wonder if you'll get one as a roommate. That would be simply—"

I shut the trunk with a *clang* and wheel my bag straight into the throng of students. I pass a girl sporting gorgeous box braids who hoists her cello onto her shoulders, a tenth grader signing up new members for the on-campus LGBTQ+ club, and another girl I don't recognize, probably a first year, who is plugging

7

her bestselling memoir about growing up on the International Space Station. We haven't even unpacked our bags yet, and kids all around me are already raring to go, advertising auditions for the fall musical, *Hamilton*, and recruiting players for several on-campus sports teams. I'm not the extracurricular type—sports bore me senseless, and I've never been good with musical instruments. But I'm like a bot when it comes to numbers, and in eighth grade I wrote a short story that won a bunch of awards, so here I am. Enrolled at Darkwood Academy. Sure, I'm a legacy—my father went here when he was a teenager more than twenty years ago—but that's not enough to get admitted without something "extra." Not that I care about any of that showiness. I didn't before Oliver died, and I definitely don't now.

Classmates block me on all sides, so I'm forced to pause in the driveway, unable to make my way to my dorm. Without meaning to, I've stopped next to Tessa, who's conferring with another campus celebrity, Madison Huxley. The two of them are always together, although Madison—with her silky blond hair and perfectly symmetrical, heavily made-up face—usually outshines her less outspoken counterpart. Personally, I find Tessa's less flashy look far more appealing than Madison's. With long, straight hair like her Taiwanese mother's and a certain elegance to her movements, I'd call Tessa beautiful—except her personality seems lacking. I'm surprised to see Madison's parents standing a few feet away, consulting with Headmaster Ransom, Darkwood's fearless leader. Sporting pleated slacks and an elbow-patched smoking jacket, Headmaster Ransom is a likable figurehead, although I see no sign of his trademark smile today. He's all business.

"Mr. and Mrs. Huxley," I catch Headmaster Ransom saying, "the last thing I want is to upset any of our most prominent families…"

Bianca Huxley smooths her Chanel jacket. "I have never doubted your commitment to Darkwood—not once in all these years. But this time, I'm putting my foot down."

Headmaster Ransom presses his fingertips together, his eyebrows knit with tension. "I will simply repeat what I told the news outlets: I trust these boys and girls, and I believe they deserve a chance."

It's obvious who *they* are: the Similars. Ransom is referring to his decision to invite them to Darkwood, despite the controversial events surrounding their birth.

"Respectfully, we disagree with you, Ransom," Bob Huxley says tightly. "And if I may speak frankly…"

"Please." Headmaster Ransom gestures for him to go ahead.

"My wife and I plan to alert the board that we do not approve of your decision," Mr. Huxley continues. "And we will be adjusting our donation to the school accordingly. I'm afraid there isn't much you can do to change our minds short of sending those boys and girls back to where they came from."

"You know I can't do that. Historically, Darkwood has always placed a great deal of emphasis on inclusion and representation. Students join us here from every socioeconomic background—every race, religion, and sexual orientation. It's the reason I believe these new students will thrive here, of all places. I won't change my mind—"

"Then you leave us no choice. Bianca? It's time to go."

Mr. Huxley slides a protective arm around his wife, and they turn to leave, kissing Madison goodbye before stepping into their waiting stretch Tesla. Did I mention the Huxleys aren't regular people? Robert "Bob" Huxley used to be vice president—*of the United States*. His wife is taking advantage of his former veep status to run for the U.S. Senate in Texas. Early polls indicate she will win.

"I met her," Madison tells Tessa. "A few weeks ago."

"Who?" Tessa rummages through her bag, looking bored.

"My Similar. I've got one, of course. She came to our house. My parents paid her off and warned her not to show her face—*my face*—ever again."

"So she's not coming to Darkwood?"

"Of course not. If the public found out I had a Similar, it would end my mother's political career."

"So where's she going to go?" Tessa asks, finally looking up from her leather tote.

"Who cares? As long as we never see her again."

That's when Tessa notices me standing there, eavesdropping. She stares at me. Tessa and Madison both do.

I feel a nauseating lurch in my stomach. The serrated-knife feeling starts to throb in my chest. I hightail it out of there, pushing my way through the crowd of students toward Cypress, my dorm. It's just beyond a cluster of trees north of the main house. Once comprised of servants' quarters, Cypress is as gloomy as the rest of Darkwood's architecture, what with its gray stone exterior and polygonal tower that looks crooked, as if it might fall at any moment, taking the entire dormitory down with it.

I drag my bags to my dorm room, then flash my gold key in front of the sensor. The lock chimes open, and I slump inside. My room hasn't changed since I was last here in May. It's not much to look at, but even with its plain Shaker-style furniture and lone window looking out onto the depths of Dark Lake, it feels more like home than my real one. Of course, a big part of that isn't *what's* inside it, but rather *who*. Pru. Friend to everyone. But mostly to me.

She drops the book she's reading and jumps up when she sees me. "Emma—"

I don't let her finish her thought.

"Ugh," I say, depositing my bags next to my bed. "I completely forgot Madison and Tessa are still on the transplant list."

Pru frowns. "Transplant list? What transplant list?"

"You know." I slouch down on my sagging twin mattress. "To receive actual beating hearts."

Pru cracks a half smile, her brown eyes lighting up. "What have they done now?"

"Besides contributing to climate change every time they open their mouths and breathe out their toxic fumes of elitism? Everything."

I slip off my shoes and am about to flop back onto my bed when Pru's arms are around me, holding me so tight I can barely breathe. I don't have to ask her why she's squeezing me like a lifeline. I already know. She's thinking of *the thing that happened*, and of the 843 things she wants to say to me but can't. It's okay. She already said them, this summer, in a buzz with the subject line: *Re: RE: RE: RE: FWD: Oliver.*

"You should have let me come to California," Pru says, finally letting go of me. "I wanted to be at Ollie's funeral, Emma. I feel awful that I missed it…"

"You had to take care of your mom. She needed you." There's no way I would have let Pru leave her mother's side, not when she's been decimated by a cancer so rare, even nanobots can't reverse its effects. "How is she? I haven't heard from you in two weeks. I was worried when you went dark…" I don't want to say the words out loud. *I thought your mom died.*

Pru sweeps a strand of her curly black hair out of her eyes. "She's doing okay. They think this latest treatment is going to work."

"Good," I say. I'm grateful to Pru; besides Oliver, she's the one person I can actually stand to be around. Still, I turn away from her, feeling the tears coming hot and fast. The hug from my friend has lodged the serrated knife deep in my chest, and as much as I love Pru, all I want is to be alone.

"So tired," I say, lying back and shutting my eyes. "Must rest."

"I'll see you at assembly," Pru says, as I drape an arm over my eyes for dramatic effect and wait for her to slip out of our room. "And Emma…" she adds, lingering in the doorway. "I'm sorry."

When I hear the door click shut behind her, I sit up. Sleep is my own personal brand of hell, but Pru has no way of knowing that I do almost anything to avoid being unconscious. I never know what, or whom, I might encounter in my dreams.

I slip on my flip-flops and make a beeline for the door, glancing down the hallway to make sure Pru's gone before heading outside. I hurry down a shady path toward a modest clearing by the lake. I picture it in my mind as I walk: the rocks big enough to sit on and the patch of dirt where Oliver and I always convened after our last class of the day. I would tease him for being a flirt, and he'd tell me my sarcasm was going to render me physically incapable of a real smile. I'd shove him, and he'd fall backward... We'd laugh so hard, never imagining our joy would have an expiration date.

Memories of Oliver flood my heart like a vein opening. *Sunlight, gray eyes, floppy bangs, cocky smile, backpacks tumbling, minds daydreaming, fifty years, fifty years—I'll be your best friend for fifty more years. And after that? You have to reapply.*

I stop in my tracks as I arrive at our old spot. I'm not alone.

They're ten, fifteen feet away, at most. Their presence— their existence—sends my heart hammering in my chest. I freeze, watching, observing. I don't think they can see me, not yet—but I can see them.

There are three of them, and one is Tessa. Only, I can tell she isn't Tessa. She has the same long brown hair. The same elegance and fragile features. But her outfit is plain and old-fashioned. She wears a white button-down shirt and a black skirt, both so...*ordinary*, I could never imagine Tessa in them. And her hair—it's pulled back into a french braid, the kind we used to wear in grade school. There's something girlish about her. Something naive. She's a Similar. I'm sure of it.

They talk in hushed tones, and I'm not close enough to make out their words. But I watch as the Tessa Similar addresses another girl. It takes me a moment to process what I'm seeing.

Because the girl the Tessa Similar is talking to isn't simply *any* girl. It's Pru.

No, it's *not* Pru. She was in our room not ten minutes ago, wearing her signature running pants and hoodie. This girl isn't Pru. This girl is her clone, her copy. The Similar standing ten feet from me is willowy and delicate, while my roommate is athletic and lean. Pru's hair is always wild and untamed, while this girl wears her curly locks pulled back in a tight bun. She talks quietly to the others. She doesn't smile.

I shouldn't be surprised that Pru, the daughter of the man who made a name for himself defending clones to the nation, has an identical copy. But I am. Why didn't she tell me? My stomach flips. *Does she even know?* I'm so anxious to find out, I almost buzz her. But this is too big. It can wait a few minutes till I see her in person.

The third Similar is a clone of another boy in my class, Jake Choate. He has the same black hair as Jake, the same dark skin and attractive face. The same build—not too thin, not too muscular. But the devilish expression Jake has spent years perfecting is nowhere to be seen. This boy's face is full of burden, sacrifice, and hardship.

I feel drawn to them. I want to know what they're talking about in hushed, conspiratorial tones. Less than an hour ago, I had little interest in the Similars. Now, I'm more than interested. My mind spins with questions. I want to know everything about them. Where they grew up. What it was like. What they think of Darkwood—

"Are you feeling all right, Emma?" Dash asks.

"Of course," I answer softly, relieved he has no way of knowing that I've been spying on the Similars. I feel like an intruder. As if I'm invading a private moment I have no right to see. "I'm fine," I fib. "Why?"

"Elevated heart rate. I assume you were thinking about Oliver."

"Always," I whisper, my eyes still glued to the clones.

"Assembly starts in ten minutes," Dash reminds me. "You don't want to be late."

"Thanks, Dash," I say, looking down at my plum to swipe away the notification for the assembly and silence my bot.

By the time I look up from my plum, the Similars are gone.

ASSEMBLY

ON THE WALK to the chapel, I think of them. Tessa's look-alike. Pru's look-alike. Both of them so *un*like the teens they were cloned from. And Jake's Similar… He, especially, appeared so markedly different in demeanor from his original just now, it's hard to believe they share the same DNA. I wonder if any of my classmates have spotted them yet, and I wonder what the Similars were talking about with such secrecy. I don't have much time to think about it before I'm surrounded by students, swept into the throng of Darkwoodians convening on the grassy lawn in front of the chapel. We're minutes from learning the identities of the Similars.

But I already know about three of them… Four, if you count Madison's clone.

The thing is, the fact that the clones are enrolled at Darkwood is a big deal. Most of us have never even met a clone. I haven't—at least, not that I know of. The first clones were born in the early part of the century, when scientists started perfecting the technology after that failed Dolly-the-Sheep experiment. Reproductive cloning got really popular among certain wannabe parents who were more excited about copying themselves than using an egg and sperm to have a kid. I guess a lot of people thought cloning was unnatural, because it was eventually outlawed in the United States. But that hasn't stopped people from seeking out reproductive cloning overseas.

The Similars—they aren't supposed to exist. Because of some lab mix-up sixteen years ago, six babies from six high-profile families were cloned without the families' knowledge or permission, using the umbilical cord blood that had been banked after their births. It's fairly standard for modern parents to store their babies' cord blood in case their child needs the stem cells in the future to treat a disease. But in this case, the cord blood somehow got into the hands of an "irresponsible" lab technician. Before anyone knew what was happening, the genetic material from the infants was fused with human egg cells and implanted in surrogate mothers, and voilà—nine months later, six bouncing babies were born. Six "Similars," as they call themselves.

The details came together when the Similars showed up this summer. They'd lived their whole lives up north on some kind of secluded man-made island, and for some inexplicable reason, they'd been sent by the man who raised them to meet their DNA parents...and their "originals." Since the Similars are minors, their identities haven't been disclosed to the public, so nobody knows their names or who their originals are—except their DNA families.

And if all that seems out of the ordinary, here's the wildest part: all six of the original kids are Darkwood students. Which is why the Similars were invited to attend Darkwood Academy. I guess because it's their birthright. But also because Darkwood is progressive. If there's any place the Similars could feel welcome, it should be here, where the administration has focused on inclusion since the school's inception. But who knows. I'm only a junior. I don't really have all the info.

I'm jolted out of my thoughts when I spot him—the real Jake Choate. He's surrounded by his clique, which includes Madison, Tessa, and Jake's roommate, Archer de Leon. Archer, with his winning smile, brown skin, and famously photographed dark locks, hails from sunny Los Angeles and is practically Hollywood royalty. He was a child actor on a successful show I never watched, but I hear it was solidly mediocre.

"Emma!" a voice calls out over the din of my classmates. I spot Pru across the way, waving at me. She pushes against the flow of traffic to get to me, and for a moment, I wonder if this is what life will be like from now on. The people who care about me constantly worrying that I need babysitting. Wondering if Oliver's death has broken me beyond repair. They wouldn't exactly be wrong.

Pru arrives at my side, and I can't help but feel a strange sense of déjà vu. "I saw her," I blurt.

"Who?" Pru asks.

"Your Similar, who else? The jig is up, Pru. She was by the lake just now. I saw her. I know."

"I wanted to tell you, Emma. I swear I did! But the note from the Similars' guardian asked us not to reveal their identities before—"

"I'm not mad! Well, maybe a tiny bit. But start talking. I'm dying to know all the details."

Pru smiles. "Thanks for not hating me. It's the hardest secret I've ever kept, especially from you."

"So what's her deal? What's her *name*?" I ask as we inch our way toward the chapel lobby, following the forward motion of the crowd.

"Her name's Pippa," Pru tells me. "And she spent the last two weeks with us on the farm."

"Two *weeks*?"

"Sorry," Pru says. "It was torture not buzzing you. I had to stash my plum in the freezer so I wouldn't call you."

"So *that's* why I haven't heard from you in forever!"

Pru looks sheepish. "I know! I'm sorry!" She pauses. "Pippa's great, Emma. I really like her, and I think you will too."

"You have the same DNA." I shrug. "She's like, *literally* you. Of course I'll love her. It would be sacrilege if I didn't." A couple of teachers begin directing us into a sloppy line. They hold pen-size scanners that they pass over the plums of the girls in front of us.

"Ms. Chance? Ms. Stanwick? Your devices?" asks Mr. Park, our genial, stubbly-faced American history teacher. I hold out my wrist so he can pass his scanner over my plum, rendering it useless for anything but buzzing across the campus system and sending messages to my father, as well as a few other preapproved contacts. No social media, no live streaming. No one in the country knows the names of the Similars, and we've been told the administration plans to keep it that way. Even the press has been forced to stay silent when it comes to the Similars' identities, due to strict laws protecting minors' privacy. They're just kids, after all. They didn't *ask* to be cloned from someone else's DNA. They didn't ask to be thrust into the public eye. It's only fair to respect their privacy.

"Say goodbye to the cloud for the next nine months," a voice quips behind us. I turn to see Tessa. She's with Madison. They're directly behind us.

"It's like they're stalking us," I mumble to Pru.

Thankfully Madison hasn't heard me, or if she has, she's ignoring me. "They can't do this," she whines. "My channel has a million fans. Who's going to entertain them while I'm gone?"

Pru whips around to face Madison and crosses her arms over her chest. "I, for one, am more than happy to relinquish my live-streaming capabilities if it means a little privacy for our new classmates."

Tessa stares at Pru. "You're taking their side already?"

"She's not taking sides," I answer. "She's *complying* with the request of our *headmaster*—"

"Ms. Huxley? Ms. Leroy? Your plums?" Mr. Park prods.

Madison scowls, tugging her plum off her wrist and hurtling it at Mr. Park's feet. I don't even bother to respond, and neither does Pru. She links her arm through mine and steers us into the chapel.

"I know it's weird," Pru says as we find seats. "She looks exactly like me. I get it. I was freaked out when I first met her. But really, she's a regular person, just like us."

"Define 'regular,'" I mumble, watching as more and more students stream in, the ninth graders all convening in the front rows. Two years ago, I sat next to Oliver in one of those pews on my first day at Darkwood. He'd been my best friend since the third grade, when we'd become inseparable within a few weeks of meeting each other. Oliver and I had applied to Darkwood at the same time, had both been accepted, and had made the trek from Northern California to start our first year together. Back then, I'd been certain that my life was finally beginning. I had no idea that it was the beginning—of the end.

"She wasn't alone," I whisper to Pru. "I saw two of the others. A clone of Tessa and one of Jake. What about the other three? Do you know who they are?" I don't bring up Madison's clone. Who knows if it's even true. She may have made the whole thing up to impress Tessa.

Pru shakes her head. "We got a letter two months ago telling us about Pippa. My parents couldn't believe it, really. We'd heard all the news stories about the Similars—the reports about the lab mix-up, the whole deal. Except we never imagined one of them was a clone of *me*. When we found out, my parents invited her to the farm. Then Pippa showed up at our house two weeks ago. Alone."

"She didn't tell you who the other Similars are? She grew up with them, didn't she?" I press, as Headmaster Ransom makes his way to the podium.

Pru shrugs. "She was so nervous meeting us, I didn't want to pry."

"Welcome back, Darkwoodians," Headmaster Ransom bellows from behind the podium. "I'm thrilled you're all here." He smiles out at us, looking like he's in a far better mood than when I saw him talking to the Huxleys. I wonder how trying this day has been for him. After all, he personally endorsed the Similars, inviting them to Darkwood knowing that it would be a controversial move.

Headmaster Ransom continues his speech. "Whether you're a returning student or beginning your Darkwood career: welcome. You are all here because you are exceedingly intelligent. And you are talented in many ways. Our student body includes world-class athletes, classical musicians, published novelists, and even a successful Hollywood actor."

As if on cue, Archer stands up and gives a little bow. "Happy to represent the school, sir," he says, before popping back into his seat. The student body breaks into applause and chuckles, amused by Archer's bravado. Then the hush settles over us again.

"Some of you come from families who have populated our halls for generations. Your great-great-grandfathers and great-great-grandmothers may have walked these corridors with pride, and now you have that same honor and privilege. You have the opportunity to live up to their expectations. Or, should I say, exceed them. Goodness knows that the bulk of you will try."

The smile disappears from Ransom's lips. "Returning students, you know that in order to thrive at Darkwood, you must not let your talents lie dormant. You must achieve. You must succeed. You must transcend." I nod along, anticipation stirring inside me, in spite of myself. I can't deny that Ransom's hit the core of what matters to him, and to all of us.

"I'm aware that today is important, and that you are all anxious for me to continue with the rest of our program. But before I do, it would be unwise of me to gloss over the implications of this tremendous day in both our school's and our nation's history."

Ransom pauses, and I can feel everyone around me sitting up a tad bit straighter. We aren't eager to hear what he has to say; we are hungry.

"The six upperclassmen joining our junior class today are highly intelligent, talented individuals like you. Do not doubt that they have met Darkwood's standards for admission with flying colors. The fact that these students have come from a different background than your own and that their existence is a scientific phenomenon of sorts has no bearing on how they are to be treated at this school. They deserve every consideration and respect when it comes to their safety and privacy. The media has agreed to keep their identities confidential until they are eighteen, unless they choose to speak out before then. If anyone at Darkwood reveals the identities of these students in any public way, it will be grounds for immediate expulsion. Additionally, there will be serious legal ramifications."

A collective breath is taken. Ransom is asking us to protect the Similars against the outside world.

"We will now begin the key ceremony," Ransom says. "Mr. Park?"

Mr. Park skitters up to the podium, holding a cigar box. The box is closed, its shiny chrome lock tightly fastened, but I know what's inside: six keys, gold in color and old-fashioned, like the ones that used to unlock the doors in Darkwood's rooms decades ago. My hand flies to my neck, where a cord is looped around a key like the ones in the box. Programmed to open Cypress's front door and my dorm room, my key is read by a sensor embedded in the doorknob, verifying my identity through contact with my skin. Keys are presented to each new Darkwood student on the first day of school, along with an ominous warning: they aren't replaceable.

"In this box are six keys to the school," Ransom explains. "Each one belongs to a new member of the Darkwood junior class. You're all undoubtedly aware that transfer students to Darkwood, while uncommon, are not unheard of. However, six new eleventh graders in one year is quite a record, one that's required some creativity on the part of our housing committee. But don't worry, none of you have been assigned to bunk in the outhouses," Headmaster Ransom adds, eliciting light laughter from the student body. Mr. Park opens the box, revealing the six keys. "First years, you will receive your keys immediately following this assembly, so kindly stay in your seats. When you do receive your key, place it around your neck and do not remove it for the first twelve hours, giving the software time to initialize. And now, the first key."

Pru reaches out and grabs my hand, pressing her nails into my palm as she squeezes. I can't tell if she's excited or nervous for Pippa, or simply acknowledging how significant the moment is.

"Welcome to Darkwood, Jago Gravelle. Please come forward

to accept your key." Three hundred fifty-seven necks crane to watch as the first Similar steps out from the very front pew in the chapel. That must be where the clones are sitting.

The boy approaches Headmaster Ransom. It's Jake's Similar who I saw by the lake—the boy with the black hair and the burdened expression. I hear stifled laughter coming from the pew where the original Jake sits. His friends nudge him, elbowing him in the side, no doubt. I can't see Jake's face. I wonder if he's wearing his usual smile, and if so, how forced that smile is.

Jago shakes Ransom's hand, then bends down so Mr. Park can loop the cord with his key around his neck. I let out a breath I didn't realize I was holding. *You knew about the Jake Similar*, I remind myself. *You were expecting this Jago boy.*

"Jago Gravelle," Ransom continues. "Repeat after me. 'I pledge my allegiance to Darkwood Academy. I vow to uphold the school's four founding tenets: Loyalty. Excellence. Inclusion. Identity.'"

Jago repeats the pledge with confidence. As soon as he's done, the student body erupts in applause and chatter.

"He has a British accent?" I murmur.

Pru nods. "So does Pippa. I guess they all do. Hers is charming, but Jago's is kind of hot, right?"

I definitely wasn't expecting the accent. But of course, he wasn't raised in America. He grew up on some secluded island out in the middle of the ocean. It makes sense that he doesn't sound like the rest of us.

Next, Headmaster Ransom introduces Tessa's Similar, and

I make a mental note of the fact that while all the Similars are juniors, the originals, so far, are a mix of seniors and one junior—Pru. Must be because of the way their birthdays fall and the fact that all the Similars are at least nine months younger than their originals. Pru's birthday is in October, so that explains how her clone is a junior and not a sophomore. I bet the clone's birthday is around July. "Welcome to Darkwood, Theodora Gravelle," Ransom says. The girl walks forward, hesitant, like she isn't comfortable in her own skin. On instinct, I seek out Tessa. I locate her three rows in front of me. Madison sits next to her, whispering in her ear. I wonder if Madison's angry that Tessa didn't mention her Similar this morning when they met in the driveway of the school.

Theodora Gravelle repeats the pledge and accepts her key, returning to her pew as unceremoniously as she came. The chapel is no longer hushed. Students can't help whispering. A Jake Similar. A Tessa. *Who else?*

"Their names start with the same first letter," Pru whispers. "Did you notice? Tessa and Theodora. Jake and Jago. Prudence and Pippa. I thought ours was a coincidence, but now… It's like somebody planned it that way."

I hadn't noticed, but she's right. The person who named the Similars—whoever that was—must have wanted them to have another tie to who they came from. Who they were *copied* from. Even their names are a reminder that they share DNA with another person.

Speaking of Pippa, Headmaster Ransom introduces Pru's Similar—Pippa Gravelle.

"I know she's your clone, but I'm still amazed by how much she looks like you," I say, a little awed.

"If I bothered to wear makeup or brush my hair," jokes Pru. She offers her Similar a thumbs-up and a wave.

Next up is Similar number four, a replica of Archer de Leon. As Archer's Similar inches his way up to the podium, I catch sight of Archer's friends clapping him on the back, which strikes me as odd. Archer didn't *do* anything to become the DNA sample for another person, but that's nothing new. Archer gets accolades in life for simply existing.

Archer's Similar is named Ansel, and though he has his original's good looks, that's where the resemblance stops. Ansel shuffles awkwardly to stand next to Mr. Park. He turns his back to us as he recites the Darkwood pledge, which he mumbles so softly we can't hear a word of it. He's clearly shy, or at least suffering from stage fright. Either way, it doesn't help that most of the girls in the chapel are giggling at the sight of him. I'm not surprised. Even America's brightest female students get weak-kneed in Archer's presence. Why would it be any different with Ansel, who's equally handsome, albeit slightly awkward?

Headmaster Ransom introduces the next Similar, and I squint to get a better look. Blond hair. A familiar, symmetrical face… It's Madison, only not. So Madison was telling the truth. She has a clone. But didn't Madison say that her Similar wasn't coming to Darkwood? That her family had paid the Similar to stay away, because if she attended this school and the public found out about it, it would be political suicide for Mrs. Huxley? Then again, Ransom said he'd be introducing six Similars to the school, not five. From the look of things, Madison's clone has matriculated at Darkwood after all.

I turn to stare at Madison the original and catch the betrayed look on her face. Madison jumps to her feet. Tessa grabs her by the arm, pulling her back down to their pew. My gaze returns to Madison the clone. Headmaster Ransom introduces her as Maude, and although she wears Madison's same tight-lipped expression, her eyes—they're different. Hollow. Almost wounded. Yet she has a fierce and determined stance. When Maude takes her oath, she's confident. She doesn't smile, not even a little.

Pru whistles through her teeth. "I feel bad for her. Maude probably had no idea that her original is, well, kind of a bitch."

Maude leans down to accept her key, and I wonder what it must be like to be her. What must it be like to be any of these clones, their very existence an experiment, only to be deposited here at Darkwood for what can only be described as a strange social experiment in itself?

"And now," Headmaster Ransom continues, "our final new student. Welcome to Darkwood Academy, Levi Gravelle. Please come forward to accept your key."

"Where is he?" Pru murmurs. We crane our necks to get a better view of the figure moving toward the podium. I can't make out much from this angle. Nothing about his size or stature jumps out as being remarkable. He's about average height and has longish hair, which covers what I can see of his face. I squint to get a glimpse of his features when Pru tenses beside me. She grabs my arm and squeezes hard—too hard.

"Ow," I whisper, turning to look at her. "Why are you…?"

She looks shocked. Stunned. Like she's seen a ghost. I turn back to the front, confused.

The boy leans down, accepting the key that Mr. Park is placing around his neck. I can't make out which student he's a copy of. Brown hair, medium build—he could be a clone of any number of boys in the junior or senior class. It isn't until he straightens that I see his face.

And it's Oliver's.

LEVI

THE SIMILAR—THE one with Oliver's face—recites the oath, pledging his allegiance to Darkwood Academy. He shakes Ransom's hand, followed by Mr. Park's. He smiles at both of them, and Mr. Park snaps the metal box shut. I watch all of this happening, but it's like I'm looking through the wrong end of a lens. I see it unfolding, but I do not believe it.

The boy is Oliver—only he is not. He is, and he isn't. I find myself trying to make sense of that. I can't.

The Similar has Oliver's chin. He has his floppy bangs, his familiar nose, his cocky smile. He has every feature that Oliver has—*had*.

Only none of the memories. None of the *stuff* of our lives, the stuff that made us *us*. This boy has none of it; he knows none of it. Because Oliver is dead, and this, most definitely, is not him. This person is a shell of my best friend. The same on the outside but not within. He won't know that Oliver and I spent our eighth-grade year watching every movie on the AFI's 100 Greatest American Films list, starting with *Citizen Kane* and ending with *Ben-Hur*. Or that we used to put mustard on our popcorn. He won't know that Oliver understood me so well, he never had to ask how I was. This guy won't know any of it.

Oliver has a clone.

It's impossible. And yet, here this kid stands, in front of me, as real as the rest of the Similars.

"Did anyone know?" Pru asks, her voice sounding hollow. "Ollie's parents didn't mention it to you, did they? At the funeral, or—?"

I shake my head.

The rest of the assembly is a blur. My stare is glued to this Similar, this *not* Oliver, this *Levi*, as he joins the others.

"Before we break for the first-year key ceremony," Headmaster Ransom says, his voice taking a solemn turn, "I'd like to acknowledge the life of a student who is no longer with us. Please take a moment to pay tribute to a beloved member of our community, Oliver Ward. Skilled filmmaker, caring classmate— Oliver will be truly missed. Though Oliver passed away at the beginning of the summer, your return to school may trigger some difficult emotions, given his absence. Because of that, grief counselors will be on-site throughout the first week of school, and we will be holding a suicide-prevention workshop in the coming weeks to raise awareness of the warning signs of suicide, which is the third-leading cause of death among teens—a heartbreaking tragedy. Please know that we—the teachers, administration, and everyone at Darkwood—are here for you if you need to talk. And now, a moment of silence in honor of Oliver."

I feel the serrated knife slide in. I look around at my classmates, all 357 of them, as they bow their heads in silent tribute to Oliver. If you include the Similars, 363. I can't see the clones from where I sit, though I assume they are following Headmaster Ransom's instructions. I wonder what *he* is doing. I wonder if Levi can possibly appreciate the irony of this moment. He is introduced to the school, then we remember Oliver leaving it. It feels like a cruel joke. I appreciate the grief counselors and the steps the school is taking to prevent other deaths—but what would I possibly say to some poor, unsuspecting therapist? My best friend died, but I'll deal? His clone is here instead?

A minute later, Ransom cuts off the tribute. Sixty seconds. Is that all Oliver's life amounted to? Oliver, who was the only kid to talk to me in the third grade when I was the new girl at our elementary school back in California. He was the boy who sat with me at lunch and gave me half of his peanut-butter-and-banana sandwich. He knew my biggest fear in life—that everyone will leave me. He knew that if my house were on fire, the first thing I'd rescue would be my mother's old scrapbooks. Oliver's death was as big a shock to me as to everyone else. There *were* no warning signs that I could see, though I've beaten myself up every day since, wondering if I missed something that could have saved him.

"New transfer students, please follow Mr. Park out the side exit of the chapel to receive your room assignments," Headmaster Ransom directs. I watch as the Similars file out behind Mr. Park, Maude leading the group and Levi bringing up the rear. I barely register what else Ransom says, only that he gives banal instructions for the rest of the day, urging us to unpack and report to dinner. We move to leave, and I push past my classmates. I have to get out of the building as soon as humanly possible. Around me, students dissect the assembly. Some call Ransom a radical for inviting the Similars to Darkwood. Some call him wise and progressive. Others call him a visionary. Still others call him a fool.

I fight my way up the aisle, sliding between clusters of my classmates. I hear Pru calling out to me, but I don't stop. I'm on a mission.

Outside. Air.

I push my way past Jake Choate, and then Madison, who's fuming that her Similar is going to pay for showing up here when her parents explicitly told her not to.

Finally outside, I welcome the fresh Vermont air in my lungs as I gulp in a breath. That's when I spot Madison's Similar—Maude—talking quietly with Jago. Jago, who's nearly a foot taller than Maude, leans down and kisses her.

They're a couple? I'm surprised. I'd thought of the Similars like siblings. But now I realize that was a ridiculous assumption. Why wouldn't they pair off? They aren't genetically related to each other. And with their different hair colors and skin tones, which speak to the diverse heritages of their DNA families, they couldn't look any *less* like genetic sisters and brothers. What they do have in common is their British accents—a product of their secluded upbringing—and their shared childhood.

Archer and Ansel stand together to my right. Ansel looks so awkward next to his doppelgänger. Kids swarm around them, likely trying to get close to Archer. I don't stop to watch. Instead, I run. I dig for the pharma in my pocket and shove it in my mouth, swallowing hard.

Oliver has a clone. Oliver, who died less than three months ago, has an exact DNA replica. And that replica is here, at Darkwood, wearing Oliver's face like he has every right to it. Walking around in Ollie's body, he's a living, breathing reminder of everything I've lost.

I charge to the far side of Dark Lake, leaving my classmates and the Similars behind. As the sky shifts from blue to the gray of an old bruise, I reach a grassy clearing, and my feet stumble and slow. I have no idea how long I've been running, maybe minutes, maybe more. I circle back toward the chapel, trying to calm myself, taking in deep breaths. That's when I sense it—I'm not alone. There is someone else here.

I freeze, the hairs on the back of my neck prickling.

A figure slides out from behind a nearby oak tree.

It is Levi.

The sight of him here, now—it's arresting.

I want to pull him toward me and hold him, letting Oliver's warmth envelop me. Only it would all be false. A ruse. A trick.

This person, this *Levi*, meets my eyes. His white shirt hangs over his muscular frame. He's more athletic than Oliver was.

Oliver was lean, thin. This boy is sturdy. His body is hard. They are different, and yet, they are so achingly the same.

I stare at his face, and it's agony, but I can't look away.

"Don't tell me," he says in the British accent that sounds so wrong in his mouth, in *Oliver's* mouth. "I look just like him."

STRATUM

"YOUR BEST FRIEND, Oliver. I'm a spitting image, aren't I?" Levi speaks so casually, it's as if he doesn't know how painful his words are. "A dead ringer... Sorry. Slip of the tongue."

Before I can stop myself, I reach out and slap Levi across Oliver's face. He stole it, after all. It's not his. He can't have it.

In my peripheral vision, I notice that a cluster of our peers has formed around us. I'm not surprised we have an audience. Kids at Darkwood flock to drama like moths to a flame. I don't know how they found us so quickly, and I don't care. Something's overtaken me—fury, or rage, or insanity. In spite of my audience, I lunge at Levi, scratching, pulling, trying to rip his face off. Levi pushes me away, and I stumble back a few feet.

"I hate you," I spit at him as I stand doubled over, trying to catch my breath. I know the words are juvenile and pathetic, but they're all I have.

Levi observes me like I'm some kind of specimen. "Do you always make snap judgments about people you've just met? Or is it only me?"

"Just you," I respond, letting my eyes drift to the crowd. I don't know most of these kids, but I spot Theodora, Maude, and Jago's faces. I know it's them and not their originals by the way they dress and by their stern, solemn expressions.

"Levi," Maude warns, her voice commanding and in control. Levi doesn't look at her. His stare is glued to me.

"I don't want to see you," I finally say.

"So leave." Levi shrugs. "I doubt anyone would mind." He gestures to our audience, like they're welcome to confirm his statement.

"I don't think you understand me," I seethe. "You can't be here. You can't walk around here with that face. It's not okay."

The corners of his mouth turn up. Levi chuckles a little. It's hard to make sense of how I can simultaneously love and hate one face so much.

"If you're asking me to wear a ski mask, check the Darkwood handbook," Levi says. "Page one hundred thirty-seven. Dress Code. Second paragraph, fourth line. Prohibited item number forty-two: ski masks or other masks that cover the face."

Prohibited item number forty-two? Is this kid serious?

"That's not in the dress code. You're making it up."

"Can you prove it, Emma? Besides, a ski mask is assuredly

inappropriate classroom attire, whether it is against the dress code or not."

"I'm not asking you to wear a ski mask. I'm asking you not to be here. I don't want to see or hear you ever again. So if you have to hide in the shadows or leave this school or jump off of Hades Point, do whatever is necessary. Just. Don't. Exist."

I go. Without a look back at Maude or Theodora or Jago or anyone else, I walk away. As I do, I hear whispers. Some kids are saying I've lost my mind. Others don't blame me for being angry.

"That Levi's cold," whispers one girl to her friends. I push past her, fighting the tears in my eyes. "How can someone be so heartless?"

Another group of students thinks the Similars were abused, or tormented, or at least brainwashed.

"Did you see those two, the ones who look like Jake and Madison? They're a couple," a tall, skinny boy remarks. "They grew up like a family. It's unnatural, if you ask me."

I have to get out of here. To my room, where I can be alone. By the time I reach Cypress, it's nearly twilight. I climb into bed.

"Dash, buzz my father, please."

Dash's voice rings out. "I have buzzed your father, but he is unavailable."

"Shocking," I mutter.

"Would you like to leave him a message, Emma?"

I pause to get my bearings. What do I want to say to my father, anyway? What can he even do about this? About Levi? About any of it? "Sure. Okay." I pull my comforter around me.

I'm shivering. "Dear Dad. This buzz is going to suck, so I'll just come out and say it. It feels like Oliver died again today. He has a clone. A Similar. Some person named Levi. Oh, sh— don't tell anyone. Remember we signed that nondisclosure agreement before school started? We're supposed to keep the Similars' identities confidential. Anyway, I'm sure you're probably going to tell me to be strong, but I can't... Can I come home? Please thank Genevieve for packing my slippers. Love, Emma."

"Oliver has a clone?" Dash chimes in. "Oh, Emma. When did you find out? How did this happen?"

"Dash," I interrupt, more forcefully than I mean to. "I don't really want to talk about it."

"Of course, Emma. I don't mean to pry. This news is unexpected. It's a lot to process. I must admit, it is causing me to feel sad."

Great. Even my plum feels sorry for me. I don't remember when it first started, but Dash has been displaying more and more emotion lately, grappling with a lot of humanlike feelings. Probably all part of his programming, but still. I rely on him to be my rock. I'm not sure I like this new and improved version of my bot.

"Thanks, Dash." I sigh. "That's all."

I pop one more pill and go to sleep, even though it's only six o'clock, and by some miracle, or maybe because the pharmas are doing their job, I don't dream.

❖➤—┤ ├—◄❖

In the dining hall that evening, they sit together: Jago, Ansel, Maude, and Theodora. Of course, Levi's there too. I can't see his face as Pru guides me into the cafeteria, but I burn inside knowing he's there.

This is exactly why I'd wanted to stay in my room, in bed, with the door firmly closed. But Pru had woken me after a measly half-hour nap and dragged me to the dining hall.

"Couldn't you just let me stay in bed till the morning?" My feet feel like lead as I follow my roommate to the food line. For once, I'd actually fallen asleep without tossing and turning. I might have even gotten in a full two hours before waking up in a sweat like I always do, my mind on Oliver...and now, Levi.

"Nope," Pru answers. "They're announcing strata tonight. I can't let you sleep through one of the most important nights of your high school career!"

"Says you," I answer with a sigh. She's right, of course. This night is a big one for the junior class. We'll find out our rank and whether we'll be part of the Ten.

"And excuse me for caring about you," Pru adds, "but you have to eat. Come on, let's get some in vitro steak."

The Darkwood cafeteria harkens back to another time, another world. Vast wooden tables stripe the rectangular space, a chandelier dangling over each one. The only area of the room that doesn't scream premillenium is the eight-by-eight-foot multidimensional view space that hangs high on the opposite wall, projecting feeds, which are our main tie to the world off campus. Of course, everything displayed there is censored by Ransom. He decides which feeds we see and which we don't, so

I'm certain the news story playing now—a recap of the Similars' arrival at Darkwood, or what little the world knows about it—has been thoroughly vetted.

I take my eyes off the feeds and step up to the buffet line. Today's choice: lasagna or stew, both boasting the in vitro meat Pru mentioned. It may be advertised as cheaper and kinder, since it's grown in a lab, but it's definitely not tastier. As I reach for a bowl, I overhear two first-year girls whispering behind me about how I was best friends with Oliver Ward. About how I attacked his clone.

I wonder if Levi sees me. He hasn't turned around or acknowledged I'm here. Surely Maude or Theodora has warned him I've arrived? I hope they do, and I hope he feels bad about it.

"Tell me if there's something I can do," Pru says, scooping lasagna onto her plate. "You know…to help."

"Thanks, but I can't think of anything. Unless you can rearrange atoms. More specifically, the atoms of somebody's face."

"I don't think we'll get that far in honors physics," she hedges. "But I can check my syllabus."

I offer my friend a forced smile. "Thanks. Hey," I say, eager to change the subject. "Where's Pippa?"

I didn't see Pru's clone sitting with the others. My gaze swings back to their table, and I'm right. No Pippa.

"She wanted to sit with me. With us. Is that okay?" Pru asks.

I shrug. "Sure." I don't tell Pru that I'm eager to talk to Pippa and find out how much she and my roommate resemble each other. Not in looks, obviously, since I've already seen Pippa and know that she and Pru are identical, with only a few small differences. But how alike are their personalities? Their interests? Their mannerisms? I scan the room for Pippa, and my gaze lands on the Similars' table again. Only now do I notice that I'm not the only one staring. Kids at nearly every table are looking over at the Similars, though many try not to show it. With the clones seated together like this, it's as if Darkwood gained a second "it" crowd. Their originals—Madison, Jake, Tessa, and Archer—also sit at their usual table, flanked by an entourage of their loyal fans. These four have always been Darkwood royalty, with kids going to extreme lengths to try to break into their group. Though they still have their core followers, everyone else is far more interested in the Similars.

As Pru and I squeeze by the originals' table, Madison's voice projects over the din of the crowd, like she *wants* people to hear her. "They aren't *celebrities*, Archer. They're freaks. There's a big difference."

"Watch it," he teases. "That's my brother you're talking about."

Madison balks. "Your brother? You've got to be kidding me. Ansel isn't your brother, he's a genetic mistake—"

"I don't know, Maddy. I'm pretty excited he turned up. I have three younger sisters. Sure, me and my dads keep things pretty balanced at our house, but I can't wait for Ansel to come visit. We'll totally have the advantage at Casa de Leon."

Jake scoffs. "Speak for yourself. Jago might have the Choate DNA, but he does *not* fit in with our family. He's always reading. It's like he doesn't know the feeds exist."

"Let's go," says Pru, bumping my hip with hers. "Before we catch Jake's nasty attitude."

"Too late," I mumble, following Pru to a table too close to both the Similars and their originals for my liking, and setting down my tray.

"Agreed. I feel fluish," Pru jokes. "Maybe I'll have to skip class." I look up to see her settled across from me. *How did she sit down so fast?*

Except it isn't Pru. It's Pippa.

I watch as Pru—my Pru—slips onto the bench next to her Similar. It takes me a moment to adjust to seeing them together.

"Emma, this is Pippa," Pru introduces us. "Pippa, Emma."

I stare at Pippa. I can't help myself. She is so similar to Pru, and yet so different. While Pru wears her uniform of athletic clothes, Pippa has on a prim gray cardigan, and the gold of her key peeks out from the collar of her trim blouse.

"Hello," Pippa says, her voice even but guarded.

"Top ten crappiest days of your life so far, Pippa," I say. "Go." I feel like a fool as soon as the words have left my mouth. "Sorry," I mutter, staring down at my tray. "I just wondered if today made your list. You know, because it certainly makes mine…" I know I've blown my first impression with Pippa. She probably thinks I mean her and her arrival at Darkwood. How could she know that I'm only doing what I can—*anything I can*—to forget about the boy across the room?

Pippa picks at her bread, and I take careful note of her fingers: slender, neat cuticles, no nail polish. She's obviously the kind of person who takes care of herself, but who eschews current fashion.

"I think it might be one of his top ten most distressing and irksome days," she says.

I almost choke on a spoonful of stew. "I'm sorry. Are you talking about *him*?" I turn in my seat, gesturing toward the Similars' table.

"Levi?" Pippa replies. "Yes, I would assume that Levi is feeling anything but happy today. Having your friend Oliver's face isn't something he asked for. None of us asked for this—"

"Pippa," Pru starts.

"It's okay," I interrupt. "I think Pippa will understand when I say, diplomatically, of course, that whatever Levi is feeling today, or any other day for that matter, I'm going to reserve the right to respectfully not give a damn."

"I do understand," says Pippa, her calm expression never leaving her face. "I wasn't suggesting that you ought to feel differently. I simply bring it up as a matter of context. Whatever vexing day I might be having, Levi's day has been far…crappier."

I'm about to respond when a voice rings out over the dining hall. It belongs to Principal Fleischer. While Ransom, as headmaster, is Darkwood's strategic leader and liaison to the administration, Principal Fleischer oversees our day-to-day operations. She stands at the opposite end of the room, a microphone clipped to her blazer. Thin, bony, unwavering in her authority, Principal Fleischer lives for the sole purpose of disciplining us. Most of us avoid interacting with her at all costs.

"Attention, Darkwoodians," Principal Fleischer announces in her gravelly voice that reeks of inflexibility.

She doesn't have to ask twice. Nearly everyone in the cafeteria drops their conversations. It's clear the moment has arrived. We will find out our strata.

"Three weeks ago," Fleischer continues, "as summer vacation was drawing to a close, the members of the incoming junior class completed a test. The results of that test will determine your individual rank, or stratum as we call it here at Darkwood. Your stratum will fall between one and ninety, with one being the highest and most desirable score, and ninety being the lowest and least desirable score." Principal Fleischer turns to consult with the other teachers who stand in a line behind her, and Pru takes the opportunity to fill in the blanks for Pippa.

"The top five strata are automatically initiated into the Ten," Pru explains.

"The Ten?" Pippa asks.

"Darkwood's elite society. Last year's top five juniors—now seniors—will stay on to mentor this year's new members. Madison and Tessa were in it last year, so that's why they'll be in it again."

"It's also why they think they're God's greatest gift to humanity," I add.

"What do the Ten do? What's it for?" Pippa wonders.

"Good question," I say. "According to the school, the Ten members are ambassadors of the school. They're supposed to model the kind of behavior the administration would like to see in the rest of us...blah, blah, blah. But that's really all I know. Whatever goes on in their meetings is kept *hush-hush*. Unless you nab a spot in the Ten, you won't ever really know."

"You and your friends—should I call them your friends?—took the test, didn't you?" Pru asks Pippa.

"I think so," Pippa responds. "There *was* an exam we had to complete before we left for the States. I guess that's what it was."

I look around the dining room, where every junior is either sweating bullets or trying to act cool. But the truth is, not a single one of us isn't at least a tiny bit curious about the stratum rankings. Even me—though it's not my own rank I care about. I'm simply curious to see how today will play out. For others, this announcement is a lot more significant. Sarah Baxter, a petite girl perched at Madison's table, smooths her hair. She's been vocal about wanting to join the Ten since the day she arrived at Darkwood and looks ready to jump out of her skin. At a table nearby, a junior named Harrison Portwright smiles like he's getting ready to greet a bunch of fans.

"Harrison thinks he's a shoo-in," Pru whispers. "So does Sarah."

"Then I hope they both get it. I don't know about you, but I couldn't care less about being a part of that snobby society." I add, "Plus, they supposedly meet at midnight. Who wants to go to a meeting *then*?"

Pru laughs and turns to her Similar. "Emma is literally the only student at Darkwood who feels that way. Everyone else is dying to join the Ten, but my best friend here would rather *sleep*."

"Funny," I remark. If only Pru knew how little I actually sleep anymore. If I were a part of the Ten, I'd have no trouble waking up for those meetings…

The three of us turn our attention back to Principal

Fleischer. She motions to a few of the teachers, including Mr. Park, who hold boxes of envelopes. My classmates look ready to explode from anticipation. While the first years and sophomores look relieved they haven't had to take the stratum test yet, the seniors appear bored, and some are visibly annoyed they have to sit through this. After all, their fate was sealed last year when their strata were determined. Darkwood was famously one of the first high schools in the country to stop ranking its seniors, a decision that was originally the school's attempt at being different and standing out from the crowd. It was a way to reward students on its own terms, like the founders intended. Since then, many other schools have followed suit. Darkwood didn't get rid of the stratum ranking, though. I guess because the Ten is such a long-standing Darkwood tradition. Determined in our junior year, our strata ranks are the only standing that colleges will see.

"Make no mistake about it," Principal Fleischer continues. "Darkwood's ranking system is based on a highly scrutinized and painstakingly constructed test, one that gives each eleventh-grade student every opportunity to showcase his or her intelligence, talents, and skills. Every single junior has taken the test, and every single junior has the same chance of ranking in the top five."

"Even the Similars?" a guy calls out from somewhere across the room.

"Yes," Fleischer says, her gaze sharpening as she surveys all of us. "Even our newest juniors."

"I wouldn't worry about them," Madison says loudly. We all turn to stare at her, including Principal Fleischer. "Darkwood is the nation's preeminent college preparatory school. Few others even come close to our college admissions statistics or National Merit Scholarships. If you're here, it means you're special. And if you're one of the Ten"—she surveys her captive audience—"then you are part of our legacy. The Similars just got here. They didn't even go to a real *school* before this—they were *homeschooled*," she says with disdain, like it's the worst fate imaginable. "I doubt any of them will make the top five, or even the top twenty, of the junior class."

Madison folds her arms across her chest as reactions ripple through the crowd. Clearly some students agree with her. Others aren't so convinced. I can't even bring myself to look across the table at Pippa. My cheeks are burning, and I don't want her to see how mortified I am. I want to tell her that I don't agree with Madison, that I don't share her opinion in the slightest. But before I can, Fleischer, who is ignoring Madison's outburst, forges ahead. "Your teachers will hand out envelopes with your name marked on them. Inside the envelope is your stratum. Please come up for your envelope when your name is called. Do not—I repeat, do not—open your envelope until every single student in the class has received one."

Not a soul will disobey her. According to Darkwood lore, a student once ripped open her envelope prematurely and was reslotted into the ninetieth stratum, forfeiting her coveted spot in the Ten.

A collective breath is taken as the teachers begin making their way through the maze of tables, calling out names and handing envelopes to the students who jump up to retrieve them.

For a moment, I allow myself to look at Levi.

He's eating. He's slow, almost methodical about the way he organizes his lasagna on his fork, using his knife as a guide. He doesn't look up and is obviously not interested in the stratum rankings.

Then, he moves his head slightly, and our eyes meet. It's exactly like one of those slow-motion moments in a movie. Only in a movie, that's usually the beginning of a relationship, and this is most definitely not.

Neither of us looks away.

"Emma," Pru coaxes me, "you're being summoned."

She's right. Principal Fleischer is calling my name, and I nearly missed it. Because of *him*. I leap up to take my envelope from the principal's hand and sit down again, placing my stratum letter in front of me on the table. *Emmaline Chance* is scrawled across it in crisp, old-fashioned calligraphy. Pru is called a few names later.

As I look around the room, observing the final juniors retrieving their envelopes, I see Levi pull out a book and start reading. I'm too far away to see the cover, but it's a paperback and it's thick. He leans back in his chair, like this is normal, like he's above us all, the clone of a dead boy, who, newly arrived at that dead boy's school, casually *reads* during one of Darkwood's most anticipated and dreaded events. I'm hit with an urge to pummel him until he feels as small as I do.

"Has any junior *not* received an envelope?" Principal Fleischer asks.

No one answers.

"Good. Let me remind you that the five juniors ranked at the top of their class will have the privilege of becoming a part of Darkwood's prestigious Ten. Seniors who were initiated into the Ten last year will remain part of the Ten as mentors, and senior Madison Huxley will serve as this year's Ten leader."

My gaze wanders over to Madison, who beams as students shoot her admiring and envious looks.

"And now," Fleischer says dramatically, "you may open your envelopes."

Ripping is heard across the cafeteria as juniors tear into their letters. I don't open mine yet. Instead, I watch my fellow classmates' reactions. Some are devastated, others ecstatic.

I glance at Levi. He's still reading, clearly unconcerned with anything that's happening around him—especially the envelope sitting in front of him on the table.

"Emma, for God's sake, how can the suspense not be killing you?" Pru teases as she nudges my envelope toward me.

Unable to deny that I'm now nearly as curious as everyone else about how I ranked, I turn my attention to my envelope and slice it open.

Emmaline Chance. Stratum: 5

I am fifth in my class. I am part of the Ten.

DARK LAKE

I STARE AT the card with my name on it. I'm not entirely surprised. On the day of the stratum test, I'd forced myself to banish my grief over Oliver's death and focus solely on the task at hand. Those four hours turned out to be a welcome respite from the feeling of the serrated knife. It's no wonder I did so well on the test.

I suppose I should be celebrating now. At the very least, I should be happy to have some good news to report to my father—but all I can think about is *him*. I don't look back at him. I don't want to see him reading that book so cavalierly. I wonder if he's even bothered to open his envelope, and what his rank is. Then I feel a pang of guilt. Except for the four-hour block during the stratum test, Oliver has occupied my every waking thought since he died. I'm resentful of these questions about Levi that crowd my mind. Resentful of *him*. This is exactly why I told him to get lost. Because his very presence threatens my memories of Oliver.

"Who's going to share?" Pru pipes up, interrupting my thoughts. "Pippa? Emma? Don't everyone talk at once."

"You know the rules, Pru. No one has to share their stratum if they don't want to," I remind her.

"Oh, please. Like you've ever cared about rules. Hand it over," she says, reaching for my envelope.

But I hesitate. It's not that I don't want to tell Pru about my rank. It's that I haven't even processed what it means. And I'm not ready to. Not yet. Then the view space begins flashing, and I'm saved from having to answer her. But my relief is short-lived as I remember from past years what happens next. The names and faces of the top five juniors are about to be displayed. *Great.* Now I have to sit here while my score is revealed not just to Pru, but to the entire school.

Within seconds, a face appears in the view space, a smiling holographic head that rotates in the air above us, giving everyone an opportunity to stare at it.

It's Madison. But she's the Ten leader, so it can't be her... No, it's Maude—her Similar.

The room begins to buzz. I glance over at the Similars' table to see Maude's friends congratulating her, including Levi, who has set his book down and is, surprisingly, engaging. Over at the originals' table, flanked by her fan club, Madison looks ready to murder someone.

In the view space, words scroll across Maude's image in giant type.

MAUDE GRAVELLE. STRATUM: 1

Maude's face dissolves, and in its place comes another familiar one. Not Tessa, but Theodora. I'm starting to feel a strange sense of déjà vu. First Maude, now Theodora? Two clones, holding the top two spots in the junior class?

I watch as Theodora's name scrolls across her image with her stratum.

"Wow," Pru says to Pippa. "Your friends are totally winning at life right now."

Pippa shrugs like it's no big deal, but I see a hint of a smile on her face. She's proud of them. But she doesn't look surprised. It's like she was expecting this all along. Meanwhile, the noise level in the dining hall has risen a decibel or two. The reveal of these first two Ten members has stunned nearly everyone, including Madison and Tessa, who confer at their table, both of them noticeably distressed. I can't help but enjoy seeing them thrown off their game.

As Theodora's face dissolves, another one takes its place. My heart leaps to my throat. It's Levi. He's nabbed the number-three spot.

The whole cafeteria erupts. This is unprecedented. Madison jumps up from her seat, ranting about how the Darkwood board is going to get an earful about this. The Similars can't waltz in and steal top rankings from longtime

Darkwood students. She's convinced the stratum test must have been rigged in their favor.

Up on the view space, Levi's face disappears and another takes its place.

"Pru?" I say out loud, my eyes widening at her rotating image.

PRUDENCE STANWICK. STRATUM: 4

I'm not surprised Pru's scored so well. She's one of the brightest kids at Darkwood.

"I can't believe you didn't say anything!" I chide before swallowing a spoonful of stew, mindful of the fact that I need to eat, even though the pharmas dull my appetite.

"It's been like five minutes!" Pru laughs.

"Five incredibly long minutes," I argue. "And it's the principle of it. Is keeping secrets from me your new MO? First your Similar, now your stratum ranking?" I press.

"Absolutely not," Pru answers lightly. "This is a first-day-of-school anomaly. I promise, if anything notable happens in my life after this, you'll be the first to know. And you too, Pippa," she adds quickly.

"Thanks," Pippa replies, "but you and Emma are roommates. You've been close since forever. I know I can't show up and expect best-friend privileges."

"Trust me, Pippa, you deserve any privileges you want," I say between bites.

"What Emma means is that you and I are practically long-lost sisters," Pru clarifies. "Consider yourself a part of my family. And families tell each other stuff."

From the look on her face, Pippa's touched. She's about to answer when a couple of classmates rush up to wrap Pru in a hug. I watch, happy for my friend. If anyone deserves this accolade, it's Prudence. I'm also relieved she'll be on this Ten journey with me. We'll face it—whatever 'it' entails—together.

I look in the direction of Madison Huxley and her cohorts. If they looked miffed before, now they're downright pissed. They aren't any happier about Pru making it into the Ten than they were about the Similars. It's obvious Madison is threatened by Maude scoring the number-one spot, but what does she have against Pru? Where is this animosity coming from?

"Why has my face been up there for so long?" Pru moans. "What's taking them so long to get on to the next... Oh," Pru says. "*Oh!*"

I look up at the view space, knowing exactly what I'm going to find there, hoping that somehow the outcome will be different. But of course, it isn't. It's me on the screen, my own face projected above the dining hall.

EMMALINE CHANCE. STRATUM: 5

Before I can consider hiding under the table, Pru and Pippa are congratulating—and chastising—me.

"You did *not* just give me a whole speech about keeping secrets when you were sitting on this one!" Pru exclaims. Of course, she's only teasing; I can tell she's genuinely excited for me. I'm glad someone's enjoying this. I haven't come to any conclusions about my rank one way or the other. Sure, the high stratum will complement my college applications next year. But all my dreams of college involved Oliver. With him gone, I can barely think past next week, let alone next year. As for the Ten, is bowing out of that society even an option? No one's done it before, as far as I know. Maybe I could be the first... But then again, my father would probably ground me for life if I gave up this kind of opportunity.

A couple of my classmates rush up to high-five me, but most of the dining hall is quietly staring. I avert my eyes to my bowl. I hate this attention. It's bad enough everyone pities me after Oliver's death. And then with my outburst at Levi's arrival... I'm relieved when my picture dissolves, and the stratum reveal is over. The dining hall returns to its regular decibel level—though each table is having the same conversation about the new members of the Ten.

"I don't know who I'm happier for," Pippa tells Pru. "You two or my three friends. I'll have to remind Levi to look a little bit more appreciative in the future," she adds, glancing at the Similars' table. "His reaction has been slightly underwhelming, don't you think?" As soon as the words have come out of Pippa's mouth, she regrets them. I can tell.

Suddenly it's all too much. I stand, my chair screeching as it scrapes the floor. "I'm going to bed. I'm super tired. Long day. Nice meeting you, Pippa. Congrats again, Pru. See you back in the room. Good night."

I flee the dining hall, hoping I won't run into anyone on my way to Cypress. Tears stream down my face, and the cold evening air accosts me like a stranger.

I consider taking another pharma as I stare at the numerals on my clock: 8:47 p.m. It's a full eleven hours until I have to be up for my first class. The night hours are the worst, because time doesn't move slowly—it ambles to a lazy halt and loiters mercilessly.

There are seventeen pills left. Dr. Delmore gave me enough to get me through the first few weeks of school, warning me to taper them or risk becoming addicted to the comfort they provide. But I've already taken several today. At this rate, they won't last a week. I could go see one of the grief counselors on campus and ask for more pills, but I dismiss that idea immediately. I know they're here to help, but I can't bear the thought of retelling my story. Oliver's story. It would take too much out of me.

If I took one, just one more, then I could sleep without seeing Oliver—without seeing Levi. I swallow the pharma dry. One down, sixteen to go.

When I wake up, I can't breathe.

And it's not a state of mind. I'm choking.

✧—ı—✧

Panic floods my body as I realize I'm not hallucinating. I actually can't breathe. I gasp for air, but instead of oxygen, I get a mouthful of cold water. *What's happening to me? Where am I?* A memory flashes across my mind: the time I fainted as a kid after getting a flu shot. I woke up spread-eagled on the floor of the doctor's office, unsure of my name or how I got there. It was terrifying. It's how I feel now.

My mind races. I'm rational. I can fix this. Can't I?

I can't breathe. I can't breathe because I'm underwater.

I'm submerged.

But where am I? At the bottom of a pool? Then it hits me: Dark Lake.

In Dark Lake. I'M IN DARK LAKE.

Horror builds in my chest as I try, again, to gasp for fresh air. Once again, I gulp in water. *No! This isn't happening!*

Ears pounding, heart thundering against my rib cage, I try to swim to the surface. But something's stopping me. My right leg. It's as heavy as lead. Or maybe it's caught? No, there's a brick tied to it, or something as heavy as a brick. I shake my leg with all the force I can muster, but the weight doesn't budge.

No, no, no. I will not die this way. I can't. I won't!

I grasp for my left wrist, locating my plum by feel and pressing down on the home button, hard. I pray Dash will send out a lifesaving signal. It may be my only hope. Then I angle my head and torso downward toward my leg. The water's pitch-black, and I can't orient myself. Can't see a thing. In desperation, I feel for my right ankle. My fingers fumble around until they rest on a string. There's a string tied around my ankle! And attached to that, the heavy object that's making me sink to the bottom of the lake. The thing that will kill me if I can't get it off.

I can't scream. I can't call for help. I'm trapped, and the seconds are racing by. Precious seconds I need to save myself. *No, no. Please no.* My brain begins to fog. My mind swirls against my will, becoming soft, fuzzy.

But I'm not done. Not even close. Mustering all my strength, adrenaline, and will, I yank at the string. It chafes against my leg. Painfully. I yank again.

The string slips off, and along with it, the weight.

I'm free now. *Free!* But so disoriented. I don't know which way is up. Or which way is down. I make a last-ditch guess as to where the surface is, and I swim, kicking my legs as hard as I can and reaching my arms up with all the fight I have left. But the surface doesn't come.

I must be swimming in the opposite direction. The *wrong* direction. And now, it's too late. My brain clouds from lack of oxygen, and though I try not to give in to it, I close my eyes. I'm so tired... Will it be easier this way? Will I see Oliver sooner? I don't think I believe in heaven, but maybe the universe will be merciful. Maybe I'll wake up on the other side, and he'll be there next to me.

The thing is, I don't actually want to die. Not now. Not yet. Not like this.

Maybe it isn't my time, because someone's pulling me. Someone's *saving* me. I feel sturdy hands around my waist, hoisting me in one direction. Dragging me through the frigid water. To the surface? Or to drown me in the lake's depths? It's impossible to tell, but I have no choice. Nearly gone—nearly unconscious—I do the only thing left. I hold on for dear life, letting my savior guide me.

An eternity later, I'm heaved out of the water and onto the

shore of Dark Lake. Every bone in my body feels like it's thudding against the ground. My head throbs with an alarming level of pain.

I gasp for breath. I cough and choke. I'm alive—I think.

I look up at the figure bending over me. It's Pru. Pippa? No. It's Prudence. She's soaking wet.

"Emma." Pru's voice is ragged. "Emmaline! Are you okay? Tell me you're okay."

I cough for a good thirty seconds before I can utter any words. When I do, my voice sounds choppy and raw, like someone took a grater to my throat. "I'm okay," I sputter. "What happened?"

I'm racking my brain to remember how I got to the lake, but I can't recall anything after dinner. The stratum rankings. The round, white pharma…

"Did I fall in?"

"Not exactly," Pru says, pulling me into a seated position.

"So how did I…?" I stare at Pru's grim face. "Somebody threw me in, didn't they?"

Pru nods.

"But the pharmas." I'm trying to make sense of this. "They aren't *that* strong. Are they?"

Except I took more than one today. It's the only way to explain how I was so dead asleep that I could have been dragged from my bed, never waking until I was submerged under the black water. With a brick tied to my leg. Still, I'm not so sure my pills would completely knock me out like that…

Prudence doesn't explain. As she throws a dry sweater over

my shoulders, I hear stifled giggling a few feet away from us on the shore. Confused, I turn in the direction of the laughter and squint at the figures standing there. In the moonlight, I can see Madison Huxley flanked by Tessa Leroy and a slim girl with jet-black hair to her waist. A senior, Angela Chen. Madison holds a hand up to cover her mouth, and I'm certain she's the one who laughed. Tessa examines the platinum polish on her fingertips, appearing bored. They aren't alone. Off to the side a few paces is Archer, who yawns, barely awake. A few feet from him is Maude. She looks awkward standing there by herself, and incredibly tense. They all stare as Pru helps me to my feet.

"Better grab some towels, you two," Madison lilts. "Wouldn't want you to get sick. It's flu season. Oh," she adds, turning to me and grinning. "Silly me. I forgot to say welcome."

"Welcome?" I pull the sweater as tight around me as I can. I'm shivering and disoriented, and still reeling from almost drowning. Not to mention thankful that Pru is so athletic she could rescue me. "Welcome to what?"

"To the Ten," Madison answers. "What did you think this was, a tea party?"

I look around at the other Ten members, both new and old, who stand there surrounding me, and I have the distinct sense of being circled by predators.

"Let me guess," I say, turning back to Madison, my voice hardening. "This was my initiation. Were you trying to kill me?"

"We weren't going to let you perish, Emmaline." Madison glances back at her entourage. "Were we?"

Angela opens her mouth to speak, then thinks better of it.

"Prudence's task was to save you," Tessa says simply, without further explanation.

I turn to Pru, confused but, once again, immensely grateful. I'm about to thank her for saving my life when Tessa continues. "After she threw you in."

A chill creeps up my body, starting at my toes and ending at the top of my head. And even though my clothes are soaking, this feeling isn't a result of the cold.

"After you threw me *in*?" I turn back to Pru, not believing what I'm hearing.

"We helped, of course," Tessa adds blandly. "You're not that light."

"You tied a brick to my leg!" I protest.

"Kettlebell. But same difference. Pru borrowed it from her crew team."

"That's crazy." I turn back to Pru. "You wouldn't…" When she doesn't answer, I scan the circle. Not everyone's here yet. Not all ten of us. But those who are watch me, especially Madison. She couldn't look more pleased with herself. And Tessa looks exceptionally smug. Prudence doesn't defend herself. Which means it's true. She did this.

"But, Pru. Why would you… How *could* you—?"

I stop. Her face is pure anguish. I can tell that tossing me into Dark Lake was the last thing she'd ever want to do. But she did it anyway.

"Prudence takes her position in the Ten seriously," Madison explains. "You'd be wise to do the same."

"Or what?" I ask, the tremor in my voice nearly betraying me.

"Or suffer the consequences." Madison's voice is cold, and I'm not only chilled now. I'm shivering, and sickened at what Pru thought she had to do. Did Madison and the others threaten her? Is that why she was convinced she had to follow their orders? How twisted *is* this Ten business? The first chance I get, I'll talk to Pru about this, in private.

Tessa hands me and Pru towels from a tote bag. "You're dripping," she says. I take one, still shell-shocked.

"Let's go, everyone," Angela says softly. "It's nearly midnight."

"We have one more stop to make before we commence the first midnight session of the school year," Madison says with authority. "Follow me."

We do, because we're soaked through, and because now doesn't feel like the right moment to defy Madison. Not when we're vulnerable like this. Pru wraps her arm around my waist, and we plod up the grassy hill to school. We keep our distance from Madison, Tessa, and Angela, who walk several feet ahead of us, and Maude and Archer, who follow behind a few paces. Pru grabs my hand and squeezes it. I let her, even though a part of me wants to shout at her and make her explain. How could she bring herself to throw me in the lake? Did she think about saying no?

I check the time on my plum, thankful for its waterproof capabilities up to a thousand feet. There's a notification waiting for me. Apparently Dash was about to send out an emergency alert after my blood pressure increased dramatically from the adrenaline then dropped dangerously low. But I was rescued before the alert went out.

"Thanks, Dash," I whisper. "What would I do without you?"

"I would prefer not to find out," he replies.

"Emma," Pru says, her voice fierce. "You have to know. I would *never* have let anything happen to you."

I'm too overwhelmed to respond. I believe Pru. I do. I know without a shadow of a doubt that she would never hurt me, not if she could help it. She's always been the one person at this school, besides Oliver, whom I'd trust with my life. And tonight, it came to that. I shiver in my wet clothes, reminding myself how Pru worried about me this summer after Ollie died. How she buzzed me that she'd give her right arm to get him back for one last day. One last hour. One last minute. It was the only thing anyone said to me that gave me comfort. It gives me comfort now.

And yet, it doesn't stop the feeling of dread that floods my veins like a lethal injection of black-market pharmas.

MIDNIGHT SESSION

"GIRLS, YOU'LL BE coming with me," Madison dictates as we reach the front steps of Cypress. "Archer, it's time for you to retrieve the guys."

"Roger that, Captain," Archer jokes, moving off toward one of the dorms.

Madison turns to the rest of us—me, Tessa, Prudence, Maude, and Angela. "Up to the third floor. And be quiet," she warns. We follow her silently up the stairs and down the hallway, stopping in front of the penultimate door.

"Left side or right?" Tessa asks Madison.

"Left," Madison replies, but she isn't looking at Tessa. She's staring at me. Madison reaches into her coat pocket and pulls out a pair of gleaming metal scissors. She thrusts them toward me.

"What are those for?" I balk.

"Initiating our final female member of the Ten. Archer is waking up Sunil Bhat, the other senior member, and collecting Levi."

Levi. I'd let myself forget for a second, but now I have no choice but to remember. He's part of the Ten. There won't be any avoiding him, at least not tonight.

"And you're tasked with initiating Theodora," Madison adds.

Theodora. I'd almost forgotten about her rank. Second in the junior class. "If you think I'm going to throw Theodora into Dark Lake, you can think again," I snap.

Madison laughs. "As though any of us would enjoy a repeat of *that.* No, initiating Theodora is only going to take a few minutes."

"What is it we're going to do to her, then?" I ask, though I've never wanted an answer less in my life. "And what are the scissors for? Stabbing her in the back?"

Madison ignores that last comment. "It's not what *we're* going to do, Emmaline," she says, her eyes dancing. "It's what *you're* going to do."

"Can we get this over with?" Tessa whines. "You're cutting off her hair."

"Yeah, right," I say. Except Tessa's face is emotionless. She's not kidding. "You aren't serious—"

"It's Darkwood tradition," Madison reminds me. "Each new member initiates another new member. Prudence initiated you. You initiate Theodora."

"And if I refuse?" I ask.

"You won't," Madison says. "Because then you'd be booted from the Ten. You'd be automatically reslotted into last place. Check the Darkwood handbook if you're shaky on the details."

"That's not in the handbook, and you know it," I snap. I'm certain the administration hasn't given Madison permission for this kind of hazing. They think of the Ten as model students. Whatever hazing goes on without Ransom's knowledge is *definitely* not sanctioned by the school. But I believe her that I'd lose my spot, because who knows what lies she'd tell Ransom about me. And I may not be obsessed with scores and college applications, but I don't want to be reslotted into the ninetieth place of the junior class and have to explain to my father why I discarded my coveted top ranking. He wouldn't understand, and we already have too big of a gulf between us.

"Would you get on with it? It's a haircut, not a lobotomy," Tessa says.

I stare at her, slowly comprehending what she's asking of me. Not just the haircut itself, but the reason *why* she wants me to do this. "You want me to cut off Theodora's *hair*, so she won't look like you anymore. Wow. For some of the smartest kids at this school, you really are an immature bunch. Give me those scissors." I snatch them out of Madison's hand and push my way into Theodora's darkened room. Light from the hallway illuminates the space enough for me to see what I'm doing.

Theodora's sleeping in the left bed. The bed on the right side of the room is empty, and I realize now that it must be Maude's. The two are roommates.

I lean down, picking up a few strands of Theodora's hair. When I'm done, she'll still look like Tessa. There's nothing anyone can do about that, short of plastic surgery. But this move is cruel and hurtful, and I know that, even as I begin my first cut.

"Above the shoulders," Madison says. "A trim won't count."

"Why don't you do it yourself if you're going to micromanage," I snap, but in a whisper. I don't want to wake Theodora. Because once she realizes what's going on... No, I can't think about that. I fight the feeling of dread that settles in my stomach, reminding myself that this haircut might be humiliating for Theodora, but it will grow back. Gritting my teeth, I grab a more sizable chunk of Theodora's hair and lop it straight off. I grab another chunk, and another. Brown locks fall around the two of us as Theodora starts to stir. I'm cutting off the last, uneven chunk when her eyes pop open. I make my final snip then step back, not wanting to give her a heart attack.

Theodora sits up, confused and disoriented as her eyes dart from me to Madison, and then to the others. "What's going on? Is it morning? Is there a fire?"

Madison surveys me. "Nice work, Chance. I didn't think you had it in you."

You and me both, I think. I hate what I've done.

"What's going on?" Theodora asks again more urgently, fingering the chunks of hair littering her bed and finally putting two and two together. Her hands fly instinctively to her head, and she slides from beneath her blankets and runs to the mirror above her desk, flicking on the light. Eyes wide, Theodora takes in her altered appearance, then turns back and zeroes in on me—and the scissors still in my hand. There's no point in trying to pretend. She knows I did this.

"Welcome to the Ten," I say, resigned, and before anyone can do or say anything else, in the only act of solidarity and penance I can think of, I take the scissors to my own hair.

<hr />

Fifteen minutes later, the ten of us huddle around the virtual fire in the turret room at the top of Cypress. We sit in a circle, not talking, staring at the gold-framed photos that line the opposite wall—portraits of past Ten members. I shoot a glance at Theodora, who keeps running her fingers through her butchered hair. Maude sits next to her, but they don't talk. Next to them is Levi. He isn't wet, nor does his hair look any different, so I wonder what they did to him. Maybe I'd rather not know.

Madison sits pin straight in a hardback upholstered chair in front of the door. Legs crossed, her lean body tense with anticipation, she monitors the time on the plum strapped around her wrist. At midnight on the dot, she stands to lock the tower door with her key. Hers must have that extra capability, since she's the Ten leader.

"Welcome, new initiates," she says, clearly relishing her authority. "You survived your first hour as one of the Ten. Like many of your predecessors"—she indicates the portraits on the wall behind her—"you will go down in history as among the most talented students to walk these hallowed halls. Well, some of you, anyway." Madison's eyes land on the Similars. "There are a few of you who may be here for other, questionable reasons, but it is entirely Headmaster Ransom's business if he chooses to weight the stratum test in favor of certain…new transfer students. And scholarship students." Madison looks right at Levi, Theodora, and Maude. "And scholarship students." Then she rests her gaze on Pru. I feel bile rising in my throat. Is she calling out my roommate and friend as a scholarship student? Pru's a legacy— her father attended Darkwood some twenty years ago. And even though he's had a successful career as a journalist, Pru's told me in confidence that her family's finances are strained. Especially since her mom got sick and all the medical bills piled up. From what I can tell, they may never catch up. But I know for a fact that Pru earned that stratum ranking fair and square. By being the smartest and the best. I'm about to jump up, fiercely protective of my friend, but Pru levels me with a look to keep my thoughts to myself.

"As you may already know, being one of the Ten doesn't make you special. It makes you invincible. If you survive your junior year in this coveted club, you'll be automatic members next year, like us." She gestures at Tessa, Angela, Archer, and Sunil. "You'll go on to great things. An Ivy League university. A career in whatever industry you choose. Wealth and connections will be at your fingertips. But all those spoils come at a price— the price of being simultaneously adored and despised. The price of demanding excellence from your peers at all costs. The price of being gifted.

"Darkwood was founded on the belief that our peers are our best critics. It is not solely the job of our teachers to light a fire under us, which is why we must exhort our classmates to be their best, to try harder, to excel. As one of the Ten, you must uphold that vision. You must be ready to make decisions for the good of the whole, not just the individual. You must be ready to surrender to being one of the Ten, even when the agenda does not personally suit you. Does anyone object?"

I object, I scream somewhere deep within myself. *I object to throwing people in Dark Lake and cutting off a girl's hair, and I object to you.*

I start to raise my hand, but before I can fully extend it, Pru grabs my arm, pulling it down and squeezing my forearm so hard it hurts. It's clear she wants me to stay quiet. She must really believe we have to do this, to go along with Madison's agenda. Is that why she threw me in the lake?

"No objectors," Madison responds. "Good."

I shoot my other hand in the air. Madison glares at me. "Yes?"

"Emma!" Pru warns, but I ignore her.

"You must have drugged me," I say, the mechanics of my own initiation suddenly crystalizing in my mind. "To get me into Dark Lake. There's no way I was sleeping that soundly. It was an injective, wasn't it?"

"Go ahead and tell yourself whatever you want, Emmaline. But you and I both know that your little pharma habit took care of our job for us."

I don't have a response to that. She's right, of course. I did take more than the recommended dose of my pills today. Still, I don't believe her. And I'm not done with her. Not even close. I break my gaze with Madison, and my eyes land on Levi, who crosses his arms over his chest. The slight movement catches my attention. As usual, Levi is acting emotionless and unfazed—like this Ten business is just one more item on his to-do list. I don't know whether to be angry or impressed that he doesn't take any of this seriously. I look away, pained that he's taking up my brain space once again.

"Moving on," Tessa pipes up. "Your next action item as Ten members, and this one might be tricky considering, well…"—she indicates the Similars—"you're completely new to the school. Darkwood's esteemed founders wanted the school to be a place of excellence. Historically, the Ten have taken it upon themselves to prune the student body. By doing so, we ensure that mediocrity has no home here. We ask that at the next Ten meeting, you bring us the name of a student who isn't living up to that standard. Have fun."

Fun? As I start to connect the dots, I feel sick to my stomach. Is this what the Ten secretly does, without the school knowing? They make students suffer? They hurt them? Encourage them to leave, or worse? How many students who transferred out of Darkwood midyear were forced out by the Ten? How many kids who plummeted off Hades Point were driven there by their peers?

I won't do it. I can't. My heart tells me to leave. This room, the Ten, and even Darkwood. But no, I'll never do that. Leaving school's not an option, and not simply because my dad would never allow it. I can't leave because of Oliver. This is where we spent two of our happiest years together. Our last two years. It will always be the place that reminds me most of him. Being here with Levi might be torture, but I have to stay. I'll simply refuse to do what Madison's asking.

I stand abruptly. All nine other students turn to look at me.

Madison's voice cuts through the silence. "I haven't dismissed you yet, Emmaline."

"I'm freezing. I want to change into dry clothes and go to bed." I need to get out of here, to go somewhere I can think.

Madison's smile is tight. "I said, I haven't dismissed the meeting yet. Does everyone understand the task at hand?"

The others nod, but I can't bring myself to.

"All right, then." Madison turns to face me. "You are now *officially* dismissed."

Pru and I huddle together as we walk down the dark Cypress hallway. We don't speak until we reach the privacy of our room. As soon as the door shuts behind us, Pru starts talking.

"I had an alert ready to send to the infirmary," she explains. "I cued it up the minute they ordered me to throw you into the lake and pull you out again. You know how strong my arms are from rowing. Plus, I'm certified in CPR. Otherwise, I never would have agreed to it. Emma—I would have died before I let you drown. You know that, right?"

"Of course I do," I say, and I mean it. "I just can't believe the Ten is so...twisted. Although with Madison in charge, I guess I can."

"We could report her," Pru suggests. "There's no way the administration signed off on the hazing stuff she put us through today. The school would be horrified if it knew what their most accomplished students were up to in the middle of the night."

"You don't think Ransom knows about any of it?"

"I doubt it. He'd be in so much trouble if anything happened to one of us…" She pauses. "Emma?"

"Yes?" My heart is pounding as I try to process what went on tonight. And what it means for me and Prudence. And the other Similars in the Ten, including Levi.

"You can't leave. If we quit the Ten…"

"We'll rank in last place," I supply.

"And I'll lose my scholarship," Pru says quietly. "I'll go on academic probation if my rank falls to the bottom. And my mom, she's counting on me graduating. A diploma from Darkwood will make her so proud. My dad too… I want to give her that. You know, in case…"

She dies. That's what Pru can't bring herself to say. My heart sinks. "How'd you know I was thinking about leaving?"

"I consider myself an Emmaline expert."

"We can't do what Madison asked us. We can't bring her the name of a student we want to see fail."

"Then we won't. We'll figure something else out. But if we quit—Madison wins." Pru squeezes my hand, then moves off to her side of our room to get ready for bed, leaving me with my thoughts.

I dig in my backpack for the orange prescription tube, the one that holds the pharmas. I hurry to the bathroom, knowing I won't be able to take back what I'm about to do. When I'm done, I won't be able to escape Oliver—or Levi.

But if I'm going to make it through junior year and this Ten business alive, I can't let my guard down. Or end up at the bottom of Dark Lake, dead this time at Madison's hand. I wouldn't put it past her. I pop the cap off the tube, tilting it toward the toilet bowl. The pills drop into the shallow water, and I flush the suckers down.

Then I step into the shower, letting the heat warm and calm me. After I dry off, I slip on flannel pajama pants and my favorite T-shirt that Oliver gave me, which says "Instant Yo-Yo," and I climb into bed, making sure not to wake Pru, who's already snoring. It's no shock when sleep eludes me. It's hard to stop the never-ending wave of thoughts. About Oliver. About Levi...their twin faces now interchangeable in my mind. Levi has begun to invade my precious memories of Ollie. The ones I rely on for comfort. Those memories are proof that he existed, and that what we had was extraordinary. Now, I see Levi in places where Oliver should be, and I hate him for it.

Footsteps outside the door interrupt the endless loop in my mind. Our room isn't on the way to the bathroom, which is at the other end of the hall. Pru and I have the last room on this end, by the door that leads outside. I briefly wonder who might be out of bed at this hour and what they're doing. The likelihood is that it's another Ten member, still awake. But why would they be heading outside at one o'clock in the morning?

I pull on my gray hoodie and slip into my flip-flops, quietly opening my door and peering down the hallway, where I see a figure opening the door to Darkwood's grounds. The exit sign above the door illuminates her face. *Maude.* It isn't Madison, because this girl's blond hair is pulled back severely. And her face—it looks determined but lacks Madison's detached expression. Where is she going?

Without thinking, I follow her outside and down the path that leads to Dark Lake. She walks quickly, moving with the intention of someone who never questions herself. Is she meeting someone? I'm curious if she's as outraged about the Ten as I am. If what she's doing out of bed has anything to do with Madison's orders tonight. Or if she's meeting the other Similars, including Levi. As much as I want to deny it, I feel compelled to find out more about him, about all of them.

I must be losing my mind. After the emotional and death-defying day I've had, I should be resting for the first day of class, not following a Similar in the dead of night.

Maude takes a turn into the brush. I keep a good ten feet between us, hoping she doesn't turn and spot me. When she reaches the water's edge, I hang back in the trees. I cringe as I take in Dark Lake. Less than two hours ago, I was under that opaque, heavy water, gasping for breath.

I watch Maude approach two figures, and my stomach does a flip. Levi and Jago. Maude takes Jago's hand. He holds on to hers with an ease that says they've done this a thousand times. They are comfortable together. They're an item.

My eyes flick to Levi, glad that it's dark enough I can't be seen and that the trees provide some coverage.

That's when it happens. It's so quick, I almost miss it. It's like Levi flies through the air. It's as if he has wings.

I watch, entranced, as Levi shoots up off the ground, twisting two rotations before landing on his feet with the gentlest bend of his knees, as if the move took no effort at all. He must be doing some kind of acrobatics, and it's clear he's a master of the discipline, whatever it is. I've never seen anything like it.

"Your form was a little off," Maude notes.

"Thanks, Coach," Levi responds, his voice dripping with sarcasm. I find myself simultaneously repulsed by his attitude and captivated by his abilities. I'm eager to hear what he will say next.

"So, have you started yet?" she asks.

"No," Levi says. "I haven't. It's a terrible thing to ask of me—of all of us. What gives him the right?"

"Oh, I don't know…everything? The fact that he raised us? Educated us? That we wouldn't even be here without him?" Maude snaps at him.

Jago snakes his arm around Maude's shoulders. "Maude's right. And even if she weren't, we have no choice in the matter."

Levi paces, clearly disagreeing. He stops and stands in front of the lake, running his hands through his hair. Then he starts talking again. This time, it's harder for me to understand what he's saying. It's like I've suddenly been plunged back into Dark Lake. Levi says something about a task. About not liking what's been asked of him. But his words sound slurred.

But wait. He's not speaking English. He's speaking French. I can tell because it's the language I study at Darkwood. I thought I was pretty fluent, but hearing Levi speak it, I can tell he's mastered it far better than I have. And yet, I can make out most of what he's telling Maude and Jago, and a lot of what they say back to him. Speaking French must be another way the Similars communicate with each other. I'm intrigued, in spite of myself.

They're talking quickly now. I'm sure I'm missing some key details, but I get the gist of their conversation. Levi fumes, declaring the whole thing deplorable, saying that he wishes they hadn't come. Jago stays silent, while Maude makes her opinions known every few moments, reminding Levi that their guardian loves them and only wants what's best for them.

"We're here for a reason, Levi," she insists. "You might be the favorite, but that doesn't mean you can do whatever you want, whenever you want!"

The favorite? Whose favorite? Their guardian's?

"I don't see how I can possibly begin!" Levi explodes, finally speaking in English again. "Forget it. I'm going back to bed."

"Levi..." Jago says. "You know it's more complicated than that."

"I'm done talking about this," Levi responds, his voice gruff. He starts to walk off, right past where I'm standing in the shadows. I take a breath, too loudly, and my heart races. Levi's heard me. He meets my eyes. We see each other. I've been caught.

Is he going to call me out? Tell Maude and Jago that I've been eavesdropping? To my surprise, he doesn't. He walks right past me, without any other acknowledgment.

I let out a breath of relief at Levi's retreating form and try to make sense of what I've heard. Who is their guardian, and what does he expect of them?

"Levi's going to ruin it," Maude says. "For all of us, Jago! It would be one thing if he were acting alone, but he has the rest of us to think about."

Ruin it? Ruin what, exactly?

"It's harder for him," Jago replies. "Accepting our heritage and our purpose. Who we are. Why we're here. But in the end, he can't deny it. It's in his bones, his very lifeblood. It's the reason he thinks and feels and is. And none of us can stop it, even if we do irreparable harm. Even if we regret it till the day we die."

Maude's response is too quiet for me to hear. She leans into Jago, and he embraces her. I step back into the trees, realizing I've overheard something private and sacred, and possibly even terrifying. *Irreparable harm? Regret?* Why are the Similars here? What are they planning? Without another look back, I run through the brush to the safety of my room.

ILLEGAL BEINGS

THE NEXT MORNING, I drag my exhausted self to American history. I assume I'll be the first to arrive, but Theodora's already seated, and as I catch sight of her hair, pulled back into a tight knot and pinned with barrettes, my hand flies to my own head, where I've tried to even out the hack job I gave myself. I'm still ashamed of what I did to her, but if Theodora's angry at me for chopping off her locks, I'd never know it. Like the other Similars, she acts stoic and calm.

It's open seating, so I claim a desk close enough to Theodora to see what she's doing. I watch as she pulls out a notebook and begins writing in it with a neat, steady hand. Her handwriting is crisp and beautiful. She must have made a concerted effort to learn script, unlike the rest of us who were educated at American schools, where cursive is pretty much obsolete. Maybe all the Similars had to learn cursive where they grew up. What was that place like? I haven't given it much thought until now. All I know is what's been reported in the news: the Similars had a wealthy guardian who raised them on his own private island. It was some kind of man-made seasteading property out in the middle of the ocean. The truth is, I really know nothing about the Similars except that they happen to share DNA with a few of my classmates.

I focus my attention back on Theodora. Despite her similarity to Tessa, they couldn't be less alike in their style of dress. And Theodora's hair, now even less like Tessa's, is plainer, less glossy and more brown. Tessa's hair must be professionally highlighted to look the way it does. I like Theodora's natural color better.

Theodora pauses to glance out the window at Darkwood's grounds. I recognize that look. She's homesick. I never felt homesick at Darkwood, not as long as Oliver was here. Without him, it's a different story. I look for him in the hallways where we studied together, laughed together, and ruminated on the meaning of life, and pizza, together. I don't know anything about Theodora, but I can imagine how foreign this place must feel to her. I feel compelled to talk to her. To learn something else about her besides *her hair is brown.*

Before I can, my classmates start piling in, locating desks, and getting situated. Pru sits down and pulls her hair, wet from the shower, into a ponytail. She must have had an early crew practice. I feel bad. After that midnight session, she probably only slept a couple of hours before she had to get up. I only slept a few hours, too, but I'm a different story. Pru and I share a hello wave. Mr. Park is about to close the door when a final student slips inside, claiming the only remaining desk.

Levi. And the desk he claims is right next to mine. I don't look at him. I don't dare. But I feel his presence.

"Welcome back, friends and countrymen," says Mr. Park, running a hand over his gray stubble. "This morning, I'd like to begin a yearlong discussion of current events, one that will be led by none other than…drumroll, please…all of you. Each week, I'll encourage you to bring a news item to the proverbial table for a Monday morning scrum on the topic."

I focus on Mr. Park. Anything to avoid looking at Levi. Out of the corner of my eye, I notice Madison to my left and am instantly brought back to last night's Ten initiation. It feels almost like a dream—or more accurately, a nightmare. This is one of the few classes that juniors and seniors take together, depending on their course schedules. Just my luck to end up in here with *her*.

"Let's not dillydally," Mr. Park continues. "Who would like to begin?"

A hand shoots up. It belongs to Madison. Mr. Park nods. "Go ahead, Ms. Huxley."

"Two clones were detained trying to cross from Mexico into Texas," Madison reports. "It was on the feeds at breakfast. They were college students, and they didn't have updated identification. So, naturally, they were held at the border."

Hearing these words leaving Madison's mouth, my pulse

speeds up. Heat begins to rise from my feet to my head as I take in what Madison's just said. And not only *what* she's said, but the tone in which she's said it. She really believes those college students should have been held at the border? Anger bubbles inside me. But before I can speak up, Mr. Park cuts in.

"Can anyone tell me why the great state of Texas would ask to check the documentation for the two people in question?" he asks.

Another hand shoots up. It belongs to a boy named Henry Blackstone. "Because the government requires it of certain people, if they weren't born here."

"But they *were* born here," Pru interrupts before I can say something myself. She's as incensed as I am. Of course she is. "I saw that story; we all did—"

"I meant conceived," Henry corrects himself. "They weren't conceived here."

"They're U.S. citizens," Pru insists. "They were born here and raised here, like you and me. And they went on a *trip*. A vacation to Mexico. And when they tried to return home, to their home country, they were told they needed extra documentation that other people are not required to carry. It's totally unfair and wrong. It's discrimination, plain and simple."

"That may all be true, but you're conveniently leaving out one key detail," Madison interjects. "They're clones. Their parents used illegal reproductive technology to create them twenty years ago. The documentation is for their own *protection*, because so many people have a fundamental problem with clones."

"I don't know anyone who has a problem with clones," I blurt. "Oh, no, wait. There's *you*."

Madison shoots me a nasty look but doesn't have time to respond, because Pru is reacting too.

"Believe me." Pru crosses her arms over her chest. "That documentation is not for their own protection."

"You're right," Henry pipes up. "It's not *just* for their protection; it's also for ours."

"Why?" I shout, without raising my hand. "What are you implying—that clones are dangerous? You know there are two clones sitting in this classroom, right?" All eyes turn to Levi, who's staring out the window like he doesn't have any vested interest in the conversation, and Theodora, who is furiously writing in her journal. Is she taking notes? I wish I could see. I'm the only one not lingering on Levi. My ears burn thinking about him.

Henry looks exasperated. "I know that. And I'm sure they'll make excellent contributions to this school. We're happy to have them here because Darkwood is progressive."

"Do you even know what that means?" I press, feeling myself getting increasingly worked up. "Darkwood has welcomed students of all races and religions and sexual orientations for decades. We had the first gender-neutral bathrooms and dorms of any boarding school. We have wheelchair access in every single classroom and meeting space. We are inclusive, and we *celebrate* that. 'Inclusion' is one of Darkwood's founding tenets. It's in our school pledge, and it's why Headmaster Ransom knew Darkwood would be a safe space for the Similars!"

"I know that!" Henry cuts in, obviously flustered. "Look, I'm only repeating the facts. Clones are people, but they're different from regular people. It's not an opinion, Emma. It's science."

"We must have a very different definition of what qualifies as science," I say.

"Perhaps it would be helpful if our new students weighed in," Mr. Park says delicately. "Levi? Theodora? Would you like to contribute to this debate?"

Levi shrugs. "Darkwood might be progressive, but your society on the whole has a long history of classifying people by their race or religion or sexual orientation or gender and using those classifications to subjugate particular groups. Is it surprising that a bunch of small-minded government leaders think cloning is the first step onto a slippery slope toward total Armageddon and the demise of the human race as we know it?" He stares at Mr. Park as if he's actually expecting an answer. Again, I look down at my desk. I know everyone else is staring at Levi. I can feel Madison bristling.

"Excuse me," Madison interrupts. "Those government leaders are trying to protect our society from the inevitable pitfalls that come with playing God. Like eugenics. If it's okay to create a clone, what's to stop us from screening embryos for hair and eye color and intelligence, or even more specific genetic markers, and creating a super race?"

"I think we're missing the big picture here," Theodora says with quiet confidence. We all turn to her, surprised she's looked up from her notebook to say anything at all. "We're failing to separate the act of cloning from the product of that act. Cloning itself is not legal in the United States. Whether or not it should be, it isn't. That's something U.S. scientists and lawmakers are going to have to sort through. It really has no bearing on whether or not clones—or people like us"—she indicates herself and Levi—"should be treated differently than anyone else."

"You shouldn't," Pru pipes in, but Mr. Park holds up a hand to silence her.

"Excellent point, Theodora," Mr. Park says. "Is it fair to punish the product of a scientific advancement because we don't agree with the means by which that product was created?"

"Yes," says Madison at the exact same time that Pru offers a vehement "No."

"But, Mr. Park," Pru keeps going, "that's discrimination. It's unconstitutional. Plus, it's cruel and bigoted, and we have to stop that kind of thinking before people start believing it—"

"I beg to differ," Madison responds. "A slew of judges and thinkers agree with me. My father says—"

"Isn't your father's work funded by the National Anti-Cloning Commission?" asks a boy in the back of the class. "And weren't they a big backer of his campaign?"

Madison narrows her eyes at him. "Leave my dad's campaign out of this."

"Should we leave your clone out of it too?" I blurt. "Maude isn't here to defend herself, but I'm pretty sure she'd have a few opinions on whether or not she deserves the same rights as you."

"Maude Gravelle came to Darkwood in spite of my family's warnings," Madison says, barely hiding her fury, "proving her judgment to be questionable."

The class turns to me for a response. "What are you saying?" I ask. "That Maude's intellect is lesser than yours, even though it was formed from the same DNA? Do you think Maude is somehow *lesser* than you, even though the two of you are technically as similar as if you were identical twins developed in the same womb?"

Madison processes what I've said. Then a smile creeps over her face. "Identical twins? Interesting point, Emma. I guess you'd say the same thing about him, wouldn't you?" She nods at Levi. "Should we consider him Oliver's twin, since he and Ollie are so similar? You know, Emma, that's not a bad idea. Then he could be your new best friend."

"That is completely different," I say hotly, every cell in my body on fire. I can't believe she's twisting my words. Clones deserving equal rights as everyone else has *nothing* to do with how I feel about Levi.

"Excuse me. Do I have a say in this?" Levi shifts in his seat, uncrossing his legs. "Because I'm fairly certain I'm nothing like the venerable Oliver."

I'm about to issue a retort when Pru jumps in. "Show some respect. Oliver died less than three months ago—"

"Believe me," Levi says, "I know all about Oliver Ward's death. I am well-versed in all things Oliver. I am his clone, after all. And speaking of respect, what about me? Your friend practically ripped off my face the second I got here."

"Because you don't deserve my respect," I snap, finally looking him straight in the eye. "You're right. You're nothing like Oliver. You're insensitive and obnoxious. Not to mention, a complete jerk—"

"See what I mean?" Levi responds.

"And you're an embarrassment to his memory."

"Mr. Gravelle! Ms. Chance! End of discussion!" Mr. Park exclaims.

But Levi doesn't stop. "Do you think I want to have this face, Emma? Do you think I wake up every day pleased with myself for looking like this?"

"I don't know," I say honestly. "Maybe you do."

"Well, I would tell you if you ever thought to ask me. Instead, you make snap judgments, assume the worst about me, and punish me the minute you meet me."

I'm beginning to return the onslaught when, apparently, the decibel of my voice pushes Mr. Park over the edge.

"That's enough!" he barks. "Both of you. Headmaster Ransom's office. Now."

DUTY

"SIT," PRINCIPAL FLEISCHER instructs us, ushering me and Levi inside Ransom's office. She leaves without another word, and I'm relieved. The look on her face as she walked us in here was not a pleasant one.

Levi and I settle into twin upholstered chairs facing Ransom. I make sure not to look sideways, at Levi. Instead, I sit perfectly straight, my gaze on our headmaster, who's perched behind his desk, his brow furrowed.

"I see," Ransom says.

I'm about to ask, "See what?" when I notice he's talking to someone on the phone, not us. He isn't using the video feature, so from my vantage point, I can't see or hear the person he's talking to.

"Yes. I understand," Ransom replies in a conciliatory tone. There's a pause as he listens to the person on the other end. Then his brow drops into a frown. "As a matter of fact, she's here now."

Goose bumps prickle up my arms and down my spine. *She?* Does Ransom mean me?

"Certainly, Colin. I'll relay the message," says Ransom before pushing a button on his touch screen, abruptly ending the call. I straighten in my chair as though branded on the back with a hot iron. Colin. As in Colin Chance. The headmaster was talking to my father.

"Ms. Chance," says Headmaster Ransom, surveying me. He turns his head to glance at Levi. "Mr. Gravelle." Neither of us breathes a word in response. "As I'm sure you're aware, Emmaline, that was your father on the phone."

"I picked up on that, yeah," I say begrudgingly. I hate that my father answered a call from the head of the school before responding to a buzz from his own daughter. But I don't say that.

"He was not pleased to hear that you had already found yourself in my office. I assured him that whatever happened today in Mr. Park's class was an anomaly. This is an uneasy time in our school's history. Tensions are running high." His gaze leaves mine and lands on Levi. "Wouldn't you agree, Mr. Gravelle?"

Levi shifts in his seat, shrugs.

"Just give me my detention, please," I say flatly. "Or whatever the punishment may be. It can't be worse than sitting here with him."

Ransom leans back in his chair, the leather squeaking as he reclines. "You know, Emmaline, I would encourage you to consider the well-known phrase 'Be careful what you wish for.'"

"And why is that?"

"At three o'clock this afternoon, the two of you will start your weeklong duty for today's infraction."

"The two of us?" Levi chokes out.

"At the commencement of class each day, you will hike down to the boathouse, where you'll repaint it over the course of the next five days. Together."

"Is that all?" Levi asks tightly.

"You are dismissed."

<hr />

I've been waiting for the call ever since I left Ransom's office, and sure enough, my father finally buzzes me. When his face pops up on my plum screen looking appropriately concerned, I'm not in the mood to talk.

"I know you're having a hard time, Emmaline, but detention? Already? A fight in front of your teacher?"

"It wasn't a fight—"

"Maybe I should have Dr. Delmore reach out to you."

"Why, so he can prescribe more pharmas?" I answer hotly. My father's the CEO of a pharmaceutical company. Leave it to him to think prescription drugs are the answer to every problem. If I've learned anything these past few months since Oliver died, it's that pills don't take away your grief and pain on their own. They can mask it, briefly. But it's all the worse when you emerge from the pharma haze and realize your best friend is still gone.

"I'm only trying to help," my father says. I know he means

well, but it feels patronizing. "Emma, if I could change this, all of it, I would…"

"No offense, Dad, but I'm pretty sure even you aren't powerful enough to bring back the dead. But thanks. You know, for offering," I add.

His voice softens. "Emmaline, honey. What can I do?"

I sigh. If my father's emotionally unavailable, it's not his fault—not entirely, anyway. He had to raise me alone all these years.

"Nothing, Dad," I answer. "We're survivors, right? It's what we do. First Mom, now Oliver."

"You've been through more than any sixteen-year-old should have to deal with," he says. "And for that, Emmaline, I am truly so—" His voice cuts out.

"Dad?" There's only silence on his end. "You still there?"

"Honey, it's work. I have to take this. Can I call you later?"

"You know where to find me." I don't let on that his abruptness makes me feel even more alone than I already do. I'm used to it, though that doesn't make it any easier.

I say goodbye and start down the dirt path that leads from the main house to the boathouse, where I'll do my duty. I'm not familiar with the route, since I rarely visit this part of campus, but it's scenic. As I descend the hill to the shoreline, I glimpse a stark cement-block building that looms over the other side of Dark Lake. Rumor has it, the building was once home to a scientific research facility that was closed down years ago. I trip over my own feet as I try to get a better look at it, but then trees encroach on the path, and the building shifts out of my view.

When I arrive at the boathouse, I get why Ransom asked us

to paint it. It needs a major renovation. I'm doubtful Levi and I will be able to turn it into a thing of beauty, but as long as we get our duty over with, that's all I care about.

Out from under the canopy of the trees, the sky is very blue. Sunlight reflects off the waters of Dark Lake, rendering it almost beautiful. I approach the dilapidated boathouse and am about to peer inside to see if I'm alone, when I hear a rustling of cracked leaves.

Levi has arrived.

As I turn to watch him approach, it's like I'm suddenly on autopilot. *Must not talk to him. Must avoid.* I'm angry at him, and I'm heartbroken. But mostly, I'm afraid. I'm not afraid that he'll hurt me, and I'm not suspicious of him for being a Similar, as so many people in our country and at Darkwood are. I'm afraid of the way my pulse quickens when I stare at his face.

I wrench open the boathouse door and step inside. The interior is lined with close to fifty racing shells, stacked upside down on racks that run from floor to ceiling. A few canoes sit right-side up on the floor, and next to them is a tall ladder. To my left lie paint cans, brushes, and other equipment, loosely covered by a drop cloth. I walk straight to the painting supplies and begin sifting through them.

"Dash?" I say. "You there?"

"Always," Dash responds in a familiar voice that I can almost imagine is connected to a real human. "Where else would I be... Paris?"

I laugh, even though I feel like crying. "I think you made your first joke, Dash. Nice work," I tell him.

"New operating system, new me," Dash says. "Soon I'll be mastering sarcasm."

"Can you play *The List*?" I instruct him.

"Queuing *The List*," says Dash. The playlist Ollie made me last year floods the buds embedded in my ears.

A few moments later, I feel Levi's presence. I quickly mumble, "Volume, up," then add, "Background noise, silenced," hoping to drown out every last sound that's not the music. I look at the paint cans. They all appear to contain the same drab, mossy-green color, so I grab two cans by their handles and lug them outside, taking a second trip to gather brushes, rollers, and tools. Levi follows my lead. I don't look over my shoulder, but I sense him behind me, gathering paint cans and tracing my steps outside.

We work in silence, though it's not silent for me. I have Ollie's playlist to keep me company. I'm mixing some of the green paint with a wooden dowel when a hand touches my shoulder, and I startle.

"What?" I snap, ruder than I intended, as I turn to face Levi.

He speaks, but I can't hear what he's saying, since I've silenced all background noise. Once his lips stop moving, he stares at me, waiting for a response. I shrug and go back to my work.

Levi taps me on the shoulder again. It's clear he's not going to leave me alone.

"Pause music," I say reluctantly. As the sound of the world returns, Levi speaks again.

"Primer," he says. "You can't start with green paint. You need a base."

I stare at him for a second, standing there in front of me in the bright daylight. He's wearing the same jeans he had on yesterday, plus a white short-sleeved T-shirt. I wonder if he's cold. He doesn't look it. His muscular arms look like they'd be warm to the touch. I don't respond, I simply head back inside the boathouse to fetch the cans of primer.

"Emma," he calls out. I turn and look at him again. "I'm sorry you had to find out about me like that."

For one fleeting moment, I don't hate him. That moment vanishes as quickly as it came.

"What should I have done?" he presses. "Skipped the assembly? Blindfolded you during my induction? Would that have even helped?"

"No."

Levi's eyes pierce mine. "Then what? This isn't my choice, Emmaline. None of it is."

"Can we please not talk?" I ask. "It was better when we didn't talk."

I grab the primer and carry it outside, where I pry open the paint can with the end of a screwdriver, pouring paint into a flimsy aluminum paint tray. I like this task. I like the way the paint spills into the metal pan in a puddle. I like using my hands and not thinking. I turn up the volume on my plum and try to lose myself in Ollie's favorite tunes.

As we continue to work side by side, not talking for at least an hour, the sun dips into the horizon. It turns downright chilly, and I zip my hoodie to my chin. My plum eventually runs out of battery—stupid thing keeps glitching on me, probably because I keep forgetting to update the software—and there's not enough sunlight to recharge with solar, so we work in true silence. I feel empty and spent without the music Ollie loved coursing through me.

I've only managed to prime one small area, but the distraction is more than welcome. I won't mind doing it every day—trudging out to this abandoned spot and running this same brush over this same wall for the foreseeable future. The thought is comforting.

I'm enjoying the peace when we hear the scream.

Levi and I both freeze. Our gazes meet.

"Did you—?" I start.

"Where was it—?"

I point to a far corner of the boathouse. "It came from inside."

I start toward the direction of the scream. Suddenly his hand covers my mouth and his other arm is around me, holding me close. His mouth is at my ear. I feel his breath. My own breathing hitches at his closeness, my pulse racing in my ears.

"Don't talk," Levi says. "It's not safe. Please."

I nod, and he lets go of me, though my heart doesn't slow. Summoning all my confidence, I step toward the wide double doors, aware that Levi is following me. Inside the boathouse, the rows of racing shells look formidable in the dim afternoon light. It's nearly dark in here now, but we can't turn on a light.

Levi pads toward the far end of the boathouse, carefully stepping so as not to make the ancient floorboards creak. I follow quietly. We move to the other side of the rack of racing shells. This part of the boathouse is even darker, since little light makes its way between the stacked boats. I step over a few loose rags, noticing a rowing oar on the ground—but nothing else is amiss. Levi and I exchange a glance, and we both shrug. We heard it, didn't we? That piercing scream? Someone else must be here.

Levi stands amid the canoes and runs his fingers through his hair, stumped. But I'm not ready to give up. I know what I heard, and it came from inside this boathouse—I'm sure of it. I start peering into the canoes. Cushions, a crumpled old lunch sack—I'm about to concede that we're alone when I see it.

There's a dark form inside the canoe in the corner. At first, I can't tell what it is. I have to bend down and get my face up close to it to make sense of what I'm seeing. And then I scream.

It's a body.

PRUDENCE

WE LEAN OVER the canoe, Levi and I. In my mind, I'm taken back.

Oliver in his bed, not waking up. Oliver, not breathing. Oliver, dead.

Looking at this body, at the person lying in this canoe, I'm overwhelmed by the same paralyzing fear I had then.

I take a deep breath and reach out to the body, my hand trembling, and sweep the hair from the person's face.

It's *her*.

I gasp.

Levi recognizes her at the same time I do. "Is that...?"

"Pru." I'm sure it's Pru and not her Similar. These are the athletic clothes Pru was wearing a couple of hours ago. I'd recognize them anywhere. "It's not Pippa. Pru's on the crew team," I say, my voice frantic. "That must be why she was here."

"I can't find a pulse," Levi says, all business, but I can only think one thing: *Not Pru. Not Prudence too. No, no, no.*

"Maybe you're not doing it right," I snap as I watch Levi search Pru's wrist for signs of life. A part of me wishes this *was* Pippa lying here, and that Levi was feeling this pain instead of me. I know it's wrong, but still—I hate him for it.

"Got it," Levi mumbles. "There's a pulse. She's alive. For now."

"Dash," I bark. "Call the school nurse." When Dash doesn't respond, I remember. My plum's dead. I wasted my last bar of battery listening to *The List*, and now when I need it—*when Pru needs me*—I can't help her.

"Your plum," I say to Levi, pushing the panic out of my voice. "Can you signal the infirmary?"

Levi nods, pulling his plum from his pocket and scrolling over the screen. He fumbles like he doesn't know how to work it.

"Hey," I say, my voice cracking. "Quickly! Do it already!"

"I just got this thing," Levi explains as he searches for the emergency icon. After what feels like forever, but is only a few seconds, he finds it and presses. "First phone." He shrugs.

"Your first…" I struggle to absorb that thought. "You mean your first Plum 5000?"

"No, first phone. We didn't have them growing up."

"Hurry," I say. "She can't… I won't let her…"

Tears balloon in my eyes. I lean over and lace my fingers through Pru's. Her skin feels ice cold.

"What happened to you, Pru?" I ask, even though I know she won't answer. Was it an accident? Did Prudence trip? Was she climbing to get some gear and fell, landing in this canoe?

"It's not going through. Bad signal out here," Levi interrupts my train of thought. "We need to move her."

"No," I say. "You're never supposed to move an injured person."

"I could run to the school," Levi offers. "Find someone to help us. But that might take too long. Plus," he adds, "I don't want to leave you here alone."

"I can take care of myself."

"No doubt," says Levi coolly. "But what if your friend loses her pulse? Goes into cardiac arrest? The quicker we get her out of here, the better."

"Fine," I relent. "You can move her. But please—be careful."

Levi lifts Pru into his arms, and we start back toward the main house Levi hurries with focus, his eyes serious as he carries my friend gingerly along the uneven path. I wonder briefly if shouldering the weight of her body is a struggle for him. From the look of his biceps, he's strong enough to manage.

When we're about five minutes from the center of campus, I ask Levi for his plum. "I want to try the infirmary again. If we get through, they can have an ambulance waiting for us."

Levi tosses me his plum, and I press the emergency icon again. One ring and someone picks up. I nod to let Levi know we've made contact.

"Am I speaking with Levi Gravelle?" clips the voice on the other end.

"No," I answer quickly. "This is Emmaline Chance. I'm with him. I'm using Levi's phone."

"What is your emergency?"

"There's been an accident. Prudence Stanwick. She's unconscious. We heard a scream by the boathouse. We don't know what happened. She has a pulse, but she isn't responding."

"I've secured your GPS," says the woman on the other end, probably one of the Darkwood nurses. "Help will meet you at the clearing. Do not leave that location."

"Okay," I say. "Do you want me to stay on the line?"

"Yes," the nurse responds. I imagine her busy behind her desk, setting off a whole command chain—contacting the hospital. Headmaster Ransom. The administration.

"Her pulse has held steady," says Levi. "That's a good sign."

"Was medical training part of your education at your old school?" I snip as I dodge a knobby tree root.

"There wasn't a school where I grew up," he murmurs.

I step over some rocks, remembering what Madison said. "So it's true, then? You were homeschooled?"

"In a sense. We had tutors. Teachers were brought in via videoconference. They never met us in person. Never even knew our real names."

"What was it like?" I ask, unable to help myself.

"It was cold and lonely. The island was secluded, so it felt like a floating city. Glass and steel buildings sitting atop sand."

I report to the nurse that we are almost there, and to please hurry with the ambulance. I hear Levi's breath growing more ragged as we get closer to the school. He hoists Pru over his shoulder like a sack of potatoes. I keep willing her to open her eyes. She doesn't.

Finally, we emerge from the woods. I stop short as the scene unfolds before me. Paramedics transfer Pru's limp body from Levi's arms to a stretcher. They shout medical terms I don't understand, except when they threaten to intubate.

While that is happening, two police officers arrive, armed with lasers. I imagine they'll sweep the boathouse for evidence to run through their DNA database. Headmaster Ransom steps up to talk to them, and I wonder when he arrived. But my gaze returns to Pru, as if it's being pulled by a magnet. The paramedics load Pru's stretcher into the back of the white van. I follow to climb in beside her when a hand clasps my shoulder.

"Where do you think you're going, young lady?"

I turn and come face-to-face with Principal Fleischer.

"To the hospital. I'm riding with her."

"We both are," adds Levi.

Within seconds, Headmaster Ransom is at my side. "The two of you have been through quite an ordeal," Ransom says to me and Levi, though his words sound far away.

I'm not the one who was faceup in a canoe, unconscious! I want to shout, but I don't. My voice isn't functioning.

"I suggest you both head to the infirmary, then to your dorms for some rest," Ransom continues. I sense Fleischer wants to add something, but Ransom silences her with a look.

"There's nothing wrong with us," Levi responds. "We don't need to see the nurse."

Ransom surveys Levi for a moment before answering. "That

is your prerogative, Mr. Gravelle." He pivots on his heel, returning to the police officers. I overhear Ransom urging the officers not to question us, not now. Even if they wanted to, they can't—not without our parents or guardians present. Ransom tells the police that we're in no state to talk about what just happened, and that the lasers will confirm what Ransom already suspects—this was all an unfortunate accident.

Levi and I watch as the ambulance's engine purrs to life, and the vehicle begins to drive off with Prudence and Principal Fleischer inside.

Something inside me springs to life, and I turn to Levi. "This is wrong. We should be with her. Pru needs us!"

"She doesn't even know me," Levi points out, his voice quiet.

"I'm her *best friend*," I respond. "Her *roommate*. What if she wakes up and doesn't know where she is? She'll be alone," I say, unable to keep the panic from my voice. Suddenly, I feel light-headed. I sway.

Levi reaches out to steady me.

"When was the last time you ate?" he asks.

"Yesterday," I admit as I shrug off his hand.

"Let me walk you back to Cypress," Levi says, but I want no such thing. I begin walking in the direction of the main house. If Ransom doesn't want me going to the hospital with Pru, I won't fight him. I'll simply find a way to see her on my own.

"Hey," Levi says, trailing me. "Emma! Wait! Just wait up for a second, okay? I know. I know."

"Know what?" I croak, hoping if I move fast enough, I'll lose him.

"I know seeing Pru like that must feel like losing Oliver all over again. I know a person can only handle finding so many bodies in the span of a lifetime."

"Try a summer," I say.

I'm flooded once again by the memory of Oliver. I miss him so much. Seeing his face without having access to the person he was only makes that worse.

"Hang on," I say. "You said I found bodies. Plural. How did you know I found him? Oliver, I mean."

Levi shrugs. "Everyone knows, don't they?"

"I guess."

Levi pulls his arms across his chest. It's only then that I notice how scratched they are from carrying Pru through the brambles. On instinct, I reach out. He yanks his arm away as though burned.

"Ransom was right. You should see the nurse," I offer. "She could clean and put something on those."

"I'm fine," he says, shrugging off my suggestion.

"Do you think it was an accident?" I blurt.

Levi stares at me, and for a heartbeat I am grateful to him. He carried Pru to safety. Without him, she might still be lying there... *Not dead!* I scream in my head. *Not Prudence too...*

"I don't know," he answers. "What if someone did this to her? Hit her over the head. Left her in that canoe."

I nod, because answering him would be too painful. I suddenly feel like I might throw up. I start striding toward the main house again, and Levi calls after me.

"Emma?"

I don't turn around, and Levi doesn't say anything more.

THE ORPHAN

THAT EVENING, I'M surprised that Prudence is at dinner. She's sitting by herself at a long, otherwise empty table. My heart leaps as I rush to her.

"Pru?"

She looks up at the sound of her name, and her eyes are puffy and red, no doubt from crying. Though it is Pru's features I see—same eyes, same small chin, same nose—I deflate. It's not Pru.

It's Pippa.

Of course it is. Because Pru isn't here. She was taken to the hospital. After her accident, or…whatever it was.

"Pippa," I say, my voice hoarse. I wish I could go back and correct myself, because I'm certain I've made her pain a thousand times worse by calling her Pru like that. Reminding her that she looks exactly like the girl who was attacked in the boathouse. Her original.

"It's okay," Pippa says. I want to hug her and never let her go, but I don't. I don't know this girl. This isn't my friend. This is her DNA replica. Not Pru at all.

Pippa has heard about Pru's accident—everyone has—and she's full of questions for me. *What happened? What did I see? What was I doing when I found her? Do I know if Pru is going to be okay?*

I tell Pippa what little I know, and Pippa tells me she buzzed her DNA father, but Jaeger hasn't responded. She explains that she doesn't feel close enough to the Stanwicks to call them. I see Levi nab a tray and step into the buffet line with his friends. He doesn't look in my direction. He doesn't notice me. I, on the other hand, notice everything about him. He's changed his clothes. Now he wears long sleeves, and I wonder if this clean shirt is strategic, to cover up his scratches from carrying Pru through the woods. He's stuffed another paperback book into his back jeans pocket.

Before I can wonder what book he's reading, that boy from American history—Henry Blackstone—approaches the Similars, and all thoughts of Levi's reading habits vanish. I can't hear what he's saying, but it looks like Henry is making an animated proposal, one specifically focused on Theodora.

"I wonder what that's about," I murmur. I'm not the only curious one. Plenty of our classmates have stopped their conversations to stare. The Similars have stayed so insulated in their own little group, with the exception of Pippa sitting with me and Pru...

"He's asking Theodora to go on a date with him," says Pippa.

"Really?" I ask, momentarily thrown. "That's...bold of him." Then something occurs to me. I turn to face Pippa. "How do you know that's what Henry said? Do you read lips?"

Pippa nods.

"Let me guess. You learned how to do that as a kid?"

Pippa shrugs. "Where we grew up..."

"On the island," I supply.

"Yes. There wasn't a lot to do besides study. We each mastered a sport, a variety of skills in various disciplines, and languages. I speak five."

"And you learned all that from private tutors?" I press.

"That's right," she replies.

"Levi told me it was like those seasteads I've read about, a floating city out in open water?"

"Essentially," Pippa says. "It is its own micronation, governed by its own laws. It's four square miles and had everything we needed—food, shelter, caregivers. All the basics," she adds wryly.

"Why do you all have British accents?" I blurt. "Was the island near England?"

"We had British nannies," Pippa explains. "They took care of us, made sure we were adequately nurtured: read to us, hugged us, that sort of thing."

Now I'm even more fascinated about the Similars' lives before Darkwood. Still, I'm wary of bombarding Pippa with too many questions about her home, so I turn my attention, instead, to her friends. "Well," I prod. "Did you see what Theodora said? Did Henry seal the deal? He looks pretty happy."

Pippa neatly folds her napkin in her lap. "She said she'd think about it."

◇──┤ ├──◇

The next afternoon, I receive a buzz saying that duty has been relocated to the library. Not surprising, given that the police are still using their laser technologies to scour the boathouse for clues about what happened to Pru.

I'm sick with worry over her. Every time I close my eyes, I see her lying there in that canoe. But I still have to show up for detention, so I wrench open one of the doors of the library and scan the browsing room, searching for some instruction. I have no idea what I'm supposed to do, and I don't see Levi, so I wander. First, through the tables in the center of the main room, where the windowed dome in the ceiling lets in wedges of afternoon light. I circle back through some of the stacks. The beautiful spines of the old books offer so much promise. I pull a book at random. *War and Peace*. It's heavy. Digital books have no weight, no heft. This is part of why I love physical books.

I slide *War and Peace* back into its spot and round the corner, then stop short. Three students are huddled over a table in the far corner, oblivious to my presence, and to everything besides whatever it is they're concentrating on.

Jake, Tessa, and Madison. I'm sure it's them, and not their Similars, from their outfits and the way Jake tilts his head back as he laughs, his leather satchel slung carelessly on the back of his chair, grazing the shiny wood floor. He's leisurely, like someone who's never had a care in the world, which definitely doesn't fit Jago's demeanor. I shift my position, but I still can't tell what it is they're looking at.

"It isn't funny, Jake," I overhear Tessa saying. "Madison didn't show up for her blood work yesterday. Principal Fleischer said she won't be able to participate if she doesn't keep her appointments."

"Please," Madison says, waving off Tessa. "My mother would never let her disqualify me."

"Madison skipped because she can't stand the sight of blood." Jake chuckles. "You should have told me, baby. Next time I'll come with you. Hold your hand."

"Never happening," Madison retorts. "And I'm not afraid of blood. I had something more important to take care of yesterday afternoon."

Tessa looks annoyed. "I don't care what you were doing. I showed up for my appointment yesterday morning. I never would have dreamed of missing it. This affects all of us, you know. It's not a game!"

I've never seen Tessa so impassioned about anything before. From the looks on Madison and Jake's faces, they haven't either.

"Jeez, Tessa," Jake says. "I'm sure Madison can reschedule. Right, babe?" He throws an arm around the back of Madison's chair.

Madison glares at him. "Call me babe again, and your arm will be permanently dislocated from your shoulder."

"I'd like to see *that*," Jake responds, laughing. As he leans back into his chair, I catch sight of some papers on the table. It looks like a printout.

"She isn't interested," Tessa says. "Maybe you'd have better luck with her Similar."

Jake scowls. "Like Henry Blackstone? What a loser. I wonder if Theodora's desperate enough to go out with him."

Madison scrolls through her plum. "She's probably never gone on a date before. I suppose Henry's better than no one."

"Do you think any of them have ever...you know...?" Tessa shrugs.

"Please stop," Madison says, finally looking up from her plum. "I don't want the image of *that* stuck in my head all afternoon." She looks pointedly at Jake. "It's bad enough my Similar is dating yours."

"Did your parents adore him?" Tessa cuts in, changing the topic.

"Who?" asks Jake. He snaps a rubber band between his fingers.

"Jago, obviously."

"What do you think?" asks Jake. "Jago's the son they always wished they'd had, except he's dull as a freaking subterranean rock. You couldn't pay me to switch places with that kid."

"But you could," says Tessa. "You look just like him, share his DNA and everything. Don't you think that could be...useful?"

Jake smiles. "Obviously. Did you know our keys are interchangeable?"

Tessa stares at him. "What do you mean?"

"Exactly what I said. I heard Ransom and Fleischer talking

about it. Because the key system is set up with our DNA, the keys can't distinguish between two students with the same genetic makeup. It's never been an issue before because Darkwood's only had three sets of identical twins in its history, and they've always shared a room. And the administration made sure the twins all logged in manually for exams, but it wasn't a problem aside from a few test-taking snafus."

Tessa leans forward. I can tell she's more than a little interested. Madison too.

"So, in a nutshell," says Tessa, "if you had Jago's key, you could get into his room. Even take his exams…"

"Fascinating, but we should go," Madison cuts in. "I have a planning session for DAAM in twenty minutes."

DAAM? What's that? Some new extracurricular she's taking on to impress colleges? Not that she needs it—being leader of the Ten is enough to secure a spot at any university she wants.

"It's weird," says a hushed voice behind me. Levi. Of course. He's here for duty too. "They look like my friends," he says. "Only…"

"Only they aren't," I say flatly.

For a moment, I consider how ironic it is that I view the Similars as copies of my classmates, and he views my classmates in the same way.

That's when we notice Jake, Madison, and Tessa staring at us. They quickly stand, gathering their papers and stashing them in their bags.

"Oh, look," Tessa says. "It's one of them. And he's made a friend."

Madison smiles at me. "I'm impressed, Emmaline. You took my advice and adopted Oliver's clone. Good for you."

I want to slap her, but I stay where I am. "Don't worry," I mutter to Levi. "I won't make a scene."

"I wasn't worried," Levi says, as Madison, Tessa, and Jake turn away from us. "Have you heard anything? About Prudence?"

I shake my head. "No." My frustration comes through in my voice. "I'm her best friend, and no one's told me anything."

"We could go to the hospital," Levi suggests. "See her. Find out—"

If she's dead. I finish the sentence in my head, but not out loud.

"We can't leave. We have duty." I gesture to a cart of textbooks, handing Levi a note that I found on top of the stack. "It says we're supposed to sort and reshelve these, Dewey decimal–style."

"Most of these books look like they get checked out about once a century. Don't you think they can wait?"

Though a voice in my head warns me not to make more trouble for myself by skipping out on duty, my heart is with him. He doesn't have to ask again.

"Let's go."

◇─┤ ├─◇

We walk together down the wooded path that leads to the highway. Levi directs us, consulting the map on his plum.

"How long till we're there?" I ask, breaking our self-imposed silence.

"Thirty-seven minutes," Levi answers. "But add an extra

seventeen hours to that. The map doesn't account for how slowly you walk."

"Funny," I say.

"Anytime," he replies.

We lapse back into silence. As the afternoon bleeds into twilight, I zip my hoodie to my chin, wishing I'd worn a coat. Levi is wearing another long-sleeved shirt, but no sweater or jacket, yet he appears unaffected by the temperature. I trip over a rock and bump into him. His arm is solid beneath his sleeve.

"How did you do that thing?" I blurt.

Levi knits his brow. "What thing?"

"The other night, by Dark Lake. You flipped through the air. You were practically flying."

Levi shrugs. "It's called tricking. I learned it on Castor Island where I grew up."

"I've never seen anyone do that before," I say. "You know, in California. Where *I* grew up."

Levi looks thoughtful. "California, huh? What's that like?"

Levi's legs are longer than mine, and I have to add an extra step every few yards just to keep up, so my voice is a bit breathy when I respond. "I thought you knew everything, Mr. Stratum Three."

"I'd never been anywhere until this summer. Surely you've read the tabloids? I've lived my whole life within a four-mile radius on a compound made of steel and glass. One of the perks of being the DNA mistake of the century, remember?"

"I've read the articles," I say. "And the blog posts. And the in-depth exclusives. Everyone has."

"So you know my existence is a complete and total fluke. I'm only here because some lab technician implanted cells that were taken from your friend," he says, eyeing me, "and all the others."

"Was it really an accident?"

"An accident or a mistake," Levi answers. "Either way, we were created by a lab tech who had no idea of the ramifications of what he was doing."

I consider this. Levi's right, of course. According to every report on the incident, the lab tech was suffering a psychological breakdown when he cloned the originals. It wasn't clear he truly comprehended what he had done. He was fired and transferred to a private facility for mental evaluation. That was sixteen years ago. No one's heard anything about him since.

"So. What was he like?" Levi asks.

"What was who like?" I whisper, though I know with every atom of my being who he's talking about.

"My original. My doppelgänger. My...clone, if you will."

"Well, for starters, Oliver wasn't a jerk."

Levi actually laughs. "I forgot how much you love snap judgments. I suppose I could see how that might be endearing. To some."

He carried Pru all that way, I remind myself. *He isn't a jerk, Emma.*

"Oliver is—was—my chlorophyll," I say simply.

I wait for Levi to make fun of what I said. But he doesn't.

Then a moment later, it comes. "Oliver helped you produce oxygen which you then released as a waste product?"

I sigh. "No. He converted light into energy."

I can tell he's intrigued because he doesn't ask any more questions.

We come to the highway and walk side by side on the shoulder. A few lonely cars whoosh past us.

"You're not an easy person to get to know," Levi says. "We spent hours together yesterday. During duty and after..." He shrugs. "I still know nothing about you. Not to mention Oliver, whom you only described using a pretty tenuous metaphor related to botany."

A high-pitched shriek sounds above us as a hawk circles overhead. I tremble at the sound and the chill. I'm suddenly acutely aware of the boy walking next to me.

"I don't want you to pity me when I say this," Levi explains. "But I've spent my entire life knowing that I looked exactly like a person I'd never met. Now that person is dead, so I'll never have the chance to meet him—and I always thought I would." He clarifies, "I didn't think we'd be instant brothers or anything. I just thought someday we'd meet. And since we can't... Learning about him—it helps."

"Helps with what?" I ask, my voice barely audible.

"Making sense of my life," he replies. "Of my seemingly random, and for the most part, useless existence."

We're silent for another minute as our steps accelerate.

"You want to know something about Oliver?" I offer. "Something real?"

Levi doesn't respond, but the mood shifts between us. I can tell I have his undivided attention.

"There are physical differences between you and him. Your

hair is longer than his was. Also, I don't know if you're more muscular or he was just leaner, but…" I stop myself. The last thing I want to discuss is Levi's body. "Oliver was smart. He had a geeky love of learning. He would talk to me about the most random and irrelevant stuff. Only, it wasn't random or irrelevant, not to him."

"What kind of stuff?"

"Astronomy. History. Politics. That's why he loved filmmaking. He thought everything in the world was worth documenting, even the most mundane stories. But the real reason Oliver was my best friend was because he was so freaking genuine. He was funny, you know? Not in a sarcastic way, like me…or you," I add. "He was so optimistic. So *earnest*. The truth is, I would have hated him if he weren't my favorite person."

Levi considers this, then: "What are Oliver's parents like?"

My heart leaps at the mention of them. "Who, Jane and Booker? Jane is…" I feel myself tearing up. "Jane is not describable. At least not in words."

"Try charades, then," Levi offers.

I scowl. "I guess you could say she is real. If 'real' means kind and perceptive and funny and forgiving. And Booker— technically, he's Oliver's stepfather, but he raised Ollie from when he was really little. He legally adopted him and everything. Ollie doesn't even remember a time when Booker wasn't his dad." I correct myself, "Didn't."

"Let me guess. He's 'real' too?"

"Very" is all I can choke out.

Levi's brow furrows, like something's bothering him. It's clear he doesn't like the answer I've given him.

I stop walking. "I'm confused," I say.

"What about?" Levi asks, stopping too.

"I don't understand why they didn't tell Jane and Booker about you. The other parents—Madison's, Tessa's, Pru's mom and dad, the others... They were all told that their kids had Similars."

"How do you know they didn't tell Jane and Booker about me?" Levi asks, his voice tight.

"You haven't met them, have you?"

"No."

"If they knew about you, they would want to meet you."

"Oliver's parents *were* told. The Wards sent a note explaining they weren't interested in meeting me." The emotion drains from his voice. "Mrs. Ward said I 'wasn't to consider myself a part of their family.'"

"But they're your parents!" I exclaim, before I can stop myself.

Levi's gaze locks on my own. "Jane and Booker Ward are no more my parents than they are yours."

"Of course they are. You're a clone of their son, aren't you?"

"You just said Mr. Ward is Oliver's stepdad. Which means I don't share his DNA. Only Mrs. Ward's."

"But Booker loved Ollie like a son. That is *not* up for debate."

"Either way," Levi says. "I'm a stranger to them, a science project gone wrong."

"I don't believe for one second that Mrs. Ward wouldn't want to know you or want you in her life. Did you see that note they sent? Actually see it?"

"No—"

"Then maybe it's not true. Maybe your guardian lied to you."

Levi throws up his hands. "Fine," he says, as he starts walking again, quickening his pace. I scramble to catch up with him. "They'll be on campus after fall break. We can settle this debate then."

I give him a blank look. Levi continues, "The dedication ceremony? The one honoring Oliver Ward? Some of the teachers were talking about it yesterday. I assumed you already knew. They're building an arts wing in his honor. Donated by the very 'real' Jane and Booker Ward."

"They're coming to Darkwood?" I can barely get out the words. "Jane and Booker?"

"I've been considering ways to introduce myself. 'Hey, how's it going?' probably won't suffice."

"And when you meet them, it will be obvious they've never heard about you," I say quietly. "You'll see. Jane could never reject you."

Levi responds by lengthening his strides. I try to keep up. We're nearly there.

"I don't know why no one told Booker and Jane about you, or why you were lied to," I go on, dogging Levi's steps. "But once they meet you…"

"I'll replace the son they lost?" Levi's face is so sad, it's more than I can take. "Don't you get it, Emma? Maybe they could have been something more than strangers before, but now that their son is gone, I'll never be anything to them but a slap in the face. A reminder of everything that's been taken from them. Look, it's not like you were happy to meet me either." He laughs. *Does he find this funny?* "Don't worry. I've managed for sixteen years

118

without parents. From what I hear about curfews and nagging, why would I want to start now?"

He strides off, and I let him go as I consider the weight of what he told me. For all intents and purposes, Levi is an orphan. Worse than that—he is parentless. An orphan is someone who's lost their mother and father. Levi never had parents to lose.

JAEGER

AT THE HOSPITAL, a receptionist informs us that Prudence Stanwick is no longer a patient. She was checked out on the same night she was admitted.

"Checked out?" I stammer. "How? Who took her?"

"Doesn't say."

"But that can't be right. She was unconscious. She couldn't have just left!"

The receptionist sighs, more interested in her plum than giving me answers.

"I can't help you, miss. The patient was released."

And just like that, my world crumbles again.

No Prudence? If she's not at the hospital, where is she? I wonder. *She'd call me if she was okay.*

I'm not a runner, but I run now. There are rocks along the edge of the road. I pick one up and pitch it into the woods that line the road. Then another rock and another. And with each one, I yell.

I sense Levi next to me as I pick up a fist-size stone and toss it, hard, like a shot put. It feels good. I don't want to hit anyone or anything, but I need to move, to channel my anger into something physical. Levi hurls one too. I'm surprised, but also grateful. Maybe he understands, at least a little bit, how I feel.

"They must have transferred her to another hospital," I say as I throw another rock. "It's the only answer that makes sense."

"Maybe she went home. If she was well enough to travel, they might have sent her home to her family," Levi suggests.

"No. She would have buzzed me—"

"Not if she isn't on your approved list of outside callers," Levi reminds me.

I forgot about the blocks on our plums. But Pru's dad is on my approved caller list. Wouldn't Pru borrow her dad's phone to get in touch with me? I pick up another rock, squeezing it in my palm. Something about this feels wrong and unsettling. *Where is Pru?*

I let the rock slip out of my hand and hit the ground. I'm done with this. I'm ready to go back. I start down the road, back to campus. I hear Levi toss his rock, and then his footsteps follow me.

After a few minutes, Levi interrupts the silence. "If she were dead, we'd know."

I stop in my tracks. "Excuse me?"

"I said, if she were dead—"

"I heard you." My voice is low.

"They would have told us," he explains. "There'd be no reason not to."

I'm so tense, I feel like a rubber band about to snap. "Prudence Stanwick is my best friend. Oliver Ward *was* my best friend, but he died. So aside from my *bot*, Pru is pretty much the only person I have left in my life. Which means her being dead is the worst thing you could say to me. Ever."

"I didn't mean—"

"What's wrong with you, anyway?" I lash out. "Any normal person would say something reassuring."

"Haven't I told you enough times, Emma? My upbringing didn't make me normal."

"And you think I am? My mother died when I was three. I have no memories of her outside the ones I've recreated from old photographs. I live with my dad, which is essentially like living with a corpse. We aren't that different, you and me."

Levi stares at me.

"What?" I snap at him. "What now?"

"You think you know anything about what my life has been like?" Levi breathes deeply. "Try living in near isolation for sixteen years. Try never meeting or hanging out with any kids your age except for five other clones who you have nothing in common with, besides the fact that you're all genetic mistakes." Levi stands quite close to me now, so close I can practically feel his chest heave up and down.

"Try living a life so lonely you thought you might never

122

know what it's like to have a friend you've chosen yourself. Try getting sent away, at age sixteen, to attend the prep school of the dead kid you were cloned from." It's the first time I've ever heard him express this much emotion or intensity. I don't know if I'm afraid, but I'm definitely unnerved.

Sick over Prudence and aching to be back in my dorm room, I continue down the road. Neither of us says another word the whole way back to campus. My thoughts and his breathing are all I hear.

Back in my room, I find a pensive Pippa outside my door. For the second time, my heart leaps, thinking it's my roommate. Still, seeing Pippa here is both comforting and disorienting. It's not a new sensation. It's how I feel whenever I see Levi.

"I—I waited for you. I hope you don't mind," Pippa says quietly. "You got a package." She hands me a letter-size envelope, but with something bulky inside. My eyes immediately dart to the return address. *J. Porter, Palo Alto, CA.* My heart does a flip-flop. That's Jane Ward's maiden name. A package from Oliver's mom? I ache to open it, but not now. I unlock the door and we go inside, where I stuff the package under my mattress for later, when I can be alone.

"Have you heard anything else?" Pippa presses. "About Pru?"

"She's gone," I choke out before I can stop myself.

Pippa sucks in a tight breath. "Gone? You mean—"

"Not, *gone* gone." I let out a sigh that's more like a sob. "Levi and I, we went to the hospital to see her. We skipped out on duty," I explain. "When we got there, they said she checked out the same night she arrived."

"But that doesn't make sense," Pippa says, agitated.

"What if they've taken her someplace else. Home? Or—" I stop before I give Pippa the same terror I felt envisioning Pru's lifeless body being slid into a coffin.

"This must all be a mistake," Pippa goes on. Her voice pleads with me—or the universe?—to make Pru okay. It's like she's even more shaken by what's happened than I am. Suddenly it makes sense. Of course she's distressed. She may not have known her for long, but Pru is quite literally Pippa's other half.

"There has to be some other explanation for this," Pippa continues. "Right?"

I nod because it feels like the right thing to do. The truth is, I have no idea.

◇—┤ ├—◇

In American history the next morning, Mr. Park projects a holographic world map in our view space. Countries are color-coded: some blue, some orange, some red.

"Blue countries," Mr. Park's voice booms, "are countries where cloning is currently illegal."

If the class wasn't paying full attention before, we are now. Out of the corner of my eye, I catch Theodora stiffen.

"Red countries are safe spaces for clones. Orange countries are nations where a law has not been put in place one way or the other."

Five hands shoot into the air, and as the discussion turns into another debate on cloning, its history, and the most recent

Supreme Court case on clones' rights, I do my best not to look at Levi. Things were tense when we parted ways yesterday. I don't want to talk to him, and I'm sure he doesn't want to talk to me.

I'm snapped out of my reverie when the discussion turns to Albert Seymour, the young American scientist who took cloning to the next level, helping couples and individuals around the world conceive children who would be genetic replicas of one of their parents.

"Who is familiar with Dr. Seymour's famous primate experiment?" Mr. Park asks.

Silence. Apparently none of us have heard of it before. Mr. Park scans the room. "Theodora? Levi? Is it safe to assume you know about it?"

I allow myself to glance over at Levi. After getting so emotional yesterday, Levi looks nothing short of bored this morning. Arms across his chest, hair in his eyes, he shrugs. "Albert Seymour created us. We know everything about him," he says, standoffish.

"What Levi means," Theodora chimes in, "is yes, we know all about his monkey experiment. But that's classified information."

"Wait a second. Go back," Henry, the boy who asked Theodora on a date, interjects. "What do you mean, Albert Seymour created you? I thought that lab technician created you. And that you were an accident, of sorts."

"What he *meant*," Theodora clarifies, "is that Dr. Seymour's technology brought us into this world, though he did not directly supervise the procedure. You're right, that happened at the hands of Evan Soto, the lab technician."

"The one who was later sent to the mental hospital," Henry confirms.

"Yes," says Theodora.

"Emmaline Chance?" a voice rings out, interrupting Henry and Theodora's dialogue. It's Principal Fleischer. "Come with me."

My heart sinks. What could this possibly be about? Prudence? I don't ask questions; I simply follow her across campus. Thankfully, she doesn't speak to me. I can tell she'd rather be doing anything other than escorting me on this errand, whatever it is. When I arrive at the front doors of the library, Pippa is already there. My heart aches at the sight of her—so like Pru, and yet so not.

Except my heart lurches twice, because Pippa is standing close to someone I haven't seen since watching the feeds the day the Lorax brought me to school. Pru's father, Jaeger Stanwick. Though he's still as lean and athletic as ever, Jaeger looks more frail today than I've seen him before. His scrabbly gray hair is unkempt, and his clothes look rumpled and neglected.

Pippa pauses their conversation at the sight of me, and as Jaeger turns to acknowledge me, I get an eyeful of the weariness played out on his face. It's as if he's aged a million years since the last time I saw him. He reaches out to grab my hand, and it's like he's moving through mud, not air. Every move looks painful.

"It's good to see you," he says simply.

"Is Pru...?"

"How is she?" Pippa adds. "*Where* is—?"

"Can we take a walk?" he interrupts. "I hate standing still. Always have."

126

"Of course," Pippa and I answer, following Jaeger down the steps. I notice Principal Fleischer leave as we walk along the path that leads to Dark Lake. The wind whips at us, and my heart pounds in my ears as I imagine what he might be here to tell us, in person: *Pru is dead.*

"Emma, before I forget," Jaeger says, pulling a paperback book from his coat pocket and handing it to me. "This is for you. Prudence always said you love the classics. I thought you'd like it." I take it and thank him. *To Kill a Mockingbird*. I've read this novel for class, but I don't have my own copy. I slip this one into my coat pocket as Jaeger stops to take in the lake. "Prudence loved it here," he mutters. "I told her this school had its pitfalls, but she never believed me. Was always saying Darkwood was her favorite place in the world."

"Was?" Pippa asks carefully. "So it's true, then? She didn't make it?"

Tears prick my eyes. I bite my lip to keep from crying out.

Jaeger turns to Pippa. "Make it? Oh, no, Pru didn't die. She's struggling, but she's alive. They didn't tell you?"

I shake my head. So does Pippa.

"We had her transferred to a hospital in Massachusetts so she could be near her mother. Pru's mom is too immuno-compromised to fly and too sick to make the drive."

"Can we buzz her? Talk to her? When can we see Pru?" The questions fly out of us like rockets.

Jaeger rubs his temple, then squints as though he has sun-light in his eyes.

"She's in a medically induced coma," he says. "I thought

you knew. The attack left her with multiple skull fractures and a brain bleed, which the doctors were able to stem with surgery. They induced the coma afterward so her body could rest."

My voice feels divorced from my body, but I'm pretty sure I say, "The attack?"

Jaeger looks from me to Pippa, and then out at Dark Lake. Pru's father nods. "The severity and nature of her injuries suggest that it wasn't an accident."

GUARDIAN

THAT AFTERNOON, DURING duty, I tell Levi about Jaeger's visit. Though things are still tense between us, I feel I owe him that. After all, he was the one who carried Pru to safety.

"Thanks for letting me know," he says, distant.

"You're welcome."

We get to work reshelving books. All I can think about is Pru lying in that canoe, and the fact that she didn't fall. It wasn't an accident. Someone hurt her. Deliberately. Someone might have been trying to *kill* her.

But who? And why?

My gaze falls on that corner table, empty now, where Tessa, Madison, and Jake were sitting yesterday. That's when it dawns on me: maybe I know more than I think. I remember overhearing Tessa. *Madison didn't show up yesterday for her blood work.* I have no idea what this blood work business is all about, but what matters is that Madison missed an appointment the same afternoon that Pru was attacked. Tessa didn't mention what time that appointment was. Still, I can't help but wonder if Madison wasn't getting her blood work taken because she was in the boathouse, knocking Pru over the head with a rowing oar. Madison's made it clear from the beginning that she hates Pru and resents her being in the Ten.

Did Madison attack Pru?

I don't have any answers, and I won't until I can find some proof Madison did this. So I turn up *The List* and dive into organizing books until it's nearly dinnertime. Alone with my thoughts, I remember the package Jane sent me. Suddenly I really want to open it.

Once duty ends, I race back to Cypress, fetch the package from under my mattress, and slit open the envelope with the beveled edge of my key. My hands tremble as I pull out the letter. It's written in the bot-generated handwriting I recognize as Jane's.

Dear Emmaline,

This letter has taken me weeks to write. I hope you are well, though I know it's a loaded term. I hope you are better than I am. That's not saying much, I suppose.

The days are long, and each one makes me feel

like I've lost him a little more. I'm sorry I haven't seen you since the funeral. We haven't forgotten about you. You were always like a daughter to us.

Have you heard about the dedication ceremony? Booker and I donated a sizable fund to Darkwood for a new arts building in Oliver's honor. We will be there after fall break when they break ground. I look forward to seeing you.

This is for you. There is a note enclosed...from him.

All my love,
Jane

A note from Oliver? My pulse thuds in my throat as I fish in the envelope for the hard object I felt when I first picked up the package. I pull out a gold key, and with a rush of emotion, I realize it must be Oliver's. It was on a chain around his neck when I found him in his room, not breathing. Jane must have removed it before he was buried. And now, it's mine.

The note is a folded scrap of paper. I weigh it in my hands. Whatever's written there will be the last words from Oliver that I'll ever read. I can't open it. Not yet. I stuff the note in my hoodie pocket and make my way to the dining hall, suppressing tears.

One day passes into the next, and when I arrive at the library for my next duty, Levi isn't sorting yet. He's reading another paperback. I get close enough to glance at the cover. Mary Shelley's *Frankenstein*.

"It's not what you think," he says, snapping the book closed.

"I wasn't thinking anything."

"You were feeling sorry for me. The sad, test-tube clone. I don't think I'm Frankenstein's monster, you know. I don't believe I'm a freak of nature. Though part of me has been struggling to figure out why I'm here, ever since I understood that I was different."

Levi looks at the worn pages of his book. "Of course, Frankenstein's monster wasn't a mistake at all. He was quite wanted by his master, at least when he was first created. I can't say the same for myself." He pauses. "I'm sorry about your mother," he says. "You really don't remember her?"

"No." I turn to the book cart. "For a lot of my childhood, I told myself I did. But when I was about ten, I realized I'd been recreating who I thought she was from old photographs. They weren't memories at all. The mind can be quite convincing when it wants to be."

"But you had a mother...once," he says. "That means something, Emma. Not all of us can say the same."

"So you didn't...?"

"Have a mother?" he asks, turning to face me. "No. We had artificial wombs, motherless births. I believe we were the first babies to be successfully gestated outside a human body."

I have to admit, I'm taken aback. "I always assumed a surrogate carried you," I say softly.

"You and everyone else," Levi quips. "But aren't you lucky! You've got a real Similar, here in the flesh, to set the record straight. Go ahead—what else do you want to know?"

For some reason, I feel shy now—like I'm afraid to ask. "Um, if you didn't have mothers or surrogates, did your guardian give you super formula?"

"Naturally. No one was there to nurse us, were they?" He adds, "But super formula is considered nutritionally superior to human breast milk, so it's not like we were deprived." The sarcasm in his voice is hard to miss.

I press on. "What was homeschooling like?"

Levi laughs sharply. "You could call it that. We had lessons from top specialists in every subject. They taught us everything from math and science to archery and forensics, but we never met any of them in person."

"Forensics? Why would you learn *that*?"

He shrugs. "Our guardian thought it might come in handy."

"And the martial arts?"

"I learned a mix of aikido, kung fu, and jujitsu with acrobatics and gymnastics."

"You know all of those?"

"We each had to master a sport. That was mine. Surely you didn't peg me as a basketball player."

I ignore his joke. "Your guardian. Pippa mentioned him too," I say as I stack some history books into a pile. The conversation is easier if I don't look at him. "Who is he? What is he like? That night by the lake… You and Maude and Jago were talking about something he asked you to do. You called it deplorable," I whisper.

"His name is Gravelle," Levi says simply, ignoring the second part of my question.

"Gravelle," I repeat. *Levi Gravelle.* "Like your last names?"

"He gave us his surname, and legally, he is like a father to us. He's paid our expenses, educated us, raised us. In a sense."

"Did you—? Was he—?" I stop, at a loss for how to pose this next question.

"Did he love us?" Levi finishes for me. "It's okay. You can ask me."

"Oh," I say. "Well, um… Did he?"

Levi lets that sit for a few seconds, considering, and then responds. "In his own way, yes, I think he did love us. *Does* love us. He's still my guardian, you know, until I turn eighteen. He's still the only family I have. And according to him, the only family I will ever have."

"What does that mean?" I press.

"Isn't it obvious? Who knows what our lives will be like, whether we'll ever be accepted in normal society. I don't know if I'll ever get married, have kids, live the American dream. That might not be possible for me."

I don't know what to say to that. How could I? So I change the subject.

"I got a letter from Jane," I blurt. "Jane Ward. Oliver's mother. Your DNA mother…"

"So what?" Levi says, his voice tight.

"She has to mean something to you," I insist.

"She doesn't," Levi replies. "Besides, I thought we were tabling this topic until further notice."

"Until the dedication ceremony," I suggest. "Then we'll see what Jane has to say when she meets you."

"I will await the moment with bated breath," Levi mutters.

I freeze. I've hurt his feelings. "I'm sorry…" But the words sound worthless, and I know my attempt to make it better has only made it worse.

◇─┤├─◇

That night at dinner, gossip in the dining hall is at a record high. From what I can gather by eavesdropping on the table next to me—they're obnoxiously loud, so it isn't hard—a sophomore chatted up a couple of locals when she went into town. She heard the police had pinpointed a suspect in Pru's attack. The incident is no longer being treated as an accident.

My eyes immediately fly to Madison, sitting with Jake, Tessa, Archer, and the other senior Ten members, who are all talking animatedly.

The suspect they should be pinpointing is Madison…

I think about the other day in the library, when Tessa, Madison, and Jake referenced their blood work. If I could find out what that's all about, I'd be closer to learning why Madison wasn't there that day, why she missed her appointment. And if she missed it because she was attacking Pru…

"Attention!" a gravelly voice calls out. Everyone quiets down reluctantly as Principal Fleischer takes center stage. Pippa slips into a seat next to me, and I notice her friends across the room also listening attentively. "I have an announcement. It will not come as a surprise that one of our junior members of the Ten is, at this time, taking a leave of absence from the school."

I tense in my seat; Pippa does the same. This is clearly about Pru. *A leave of absence?* I think. *That's what they're calling it?* I meet Pippa's gaze. She looks as pained as I feel.

"The rules governing the Ten are quite clear. In order to participate, students must be on campus for the duration of the school year. Given that, we have moved Emmaline Chance up to the fourth spot in the Ten, and another student will be taking the fifth slot."

Murmurs ripple across the dining hall. Another student is being slotted into the Ten? Someone new will be part of Darkwood's prestigious group?

"The student with the sixth-highest score on the original stratum test is…" Principal Fleischer pauses. The entire school waits with bated breath. "Pippa Gravelle." Fleischer holds up a hand, heading off any vocal reactions at the pass. "I assure you, the fact that Prudence and Pippa bear a unique resemblance has nothing to do with this decision. It was based purely on test scores. You may finish eating."

Fleischer walks off as everyone in the dining hall starts processing this development. I look over at Pippa. She isn't celebrating—how could she? We both know, without saying it out loud, what this means: the school doesn't expect Pru back anytime soon.

COMMITMENT

AFTER THE ANNOUNCEMENT, I buzz Jaeger about Pru's condition when I'm back in my dorm room, growing more and more anxious. I can't reach him. I don't know much about medically induced comas, but I imagine they're like missing persons, and a patient is far more likely to recover in the early days, not the later ones.

The more my mind races, the harder it is for me to fall asleep. I don't have enough concentration for homework, so I try to get through a few pages of *Pride and Prejudice* but keep rereading the same paragraph. Finally, I give up, turn out my light, and stare at the ceiling. Maybe I shouldn't have flushed those pharmas after all.

A few weeks later, I still haven't heard back from Jaeger. I'm so worried about Pru I've been sleeping even less than usual, and I'm bleary-eyed when I walk into the dining hall for breakfast to find the walls plastered in multicolored flyers. They're all over every available bulletin board.

DAAM
The Darkwood Academy Anti-Cloning Movement
Not human...
Not like us...
Not right!
If you believe clones have no place at Darkwood, you are not alone. Join us in fighting for our rights, as humans, against those who commit hubris against God and man. Visit DAAM.darkwood.com to sign up for our weekly newsletter.
Help us make the world right again.

"Who would do this?" Pippa asks as she rips down a flyer and studies it.

"I'll give you one guess, and she looks just like one of your friends," I say grimly. "Madison's had it out for you guys since you got here. But this is totally unacceptable." I grab the flyer from Pippa and rip it to shreds. "Speaking of Madison, did I ever tell you she missed an appointment?" I ask Pippa under my breath. "The same day Pru was attacked."

Pippa stares at me, incredulous. "You think Madison had something to do with what happened to her?"

"I don't know. But I wouldn't be surprised," I mutter as Madison walks past us, shoving a flyer at a couple of ninth-grade boys and, from the look of it, winning them over with her charm. "Would you?"

"It's okay," Madison tells the boys. "Most of us have been uncomfortable since the day they arrived, what with having our values so blatantly attacked, and in such a public way. DAAM is here for you."

Sarah Baxter appears at Madison's right side. "We'll be holding office hours and organizing rallies," Sarah says. "Stay tuned."

"Sarah's only doing this because she's bitter she didn't make the Ten, and she blames your friends," I tell Pippa. I sit at a table nearby, and Pippa follows me.

"There's a lot we can do, individually and as a group," Madison continues loudly, the first-year boys hanging on to her every word. "My mother's already apportioning millions to the cause. All legally, of course." She laughs, and the boys laugh too. Sarah snickers.

That's when the other Similars walk in.

Levi and I have barely had reason to speak to each other these last few weeks. We haven't spoken since our last day of duty in the library, where we didn't talk. We used the mountain of books to shelve as an excuse to ignore each other. My pulse quickens as I watch him sit down and open another paperback book. For a reason I can't possibly understand, I want to know what he's reading.

One table over, Madison starts into her DAAM pitch again.

"Excuse me," I say to Pippa, getting up from my seat.

"Emma? What are you—?"

I don't really know myself, but before I can talk myself out of it, I walk up to Madison and grab a flyer out of her perfectly manicured fingers. I scan the paper, then hand it back. "Interesting concept. Have you registered this club with Headmaster Ransom? Last I heard, he has to sign off before organizations are allowed to meet on this campus."

Madison narrows her eyes. "That's none of your business."

I shrug. "It's everyone's business if you don't have a charter and you're meeting in school common areas. But I'm sure you'll have no trouble getting Ransom's approval, since he personally invited the Similars to attend Darkwood and all."

"I'm sure I'll have no trouble at all," she says, a smile playing on her lips. "But thanks for your concern."

"When's the next midnight session?" I ask casually. "We've only had one since the school year started." I lean in and whisper, "I'm sure everyone would understand if you canceled the meetings altogether. It can't be easy to accept that Maude scored better on the stratum test than you did last year when you were a junior."

"What are you talking about?" Madison demands.

"Maude's score was higher than any recorded in Darkwood's history."

Sarah's jaw drops. She turns to Madison, mouthing her next words: "Even higher than yours?"

Madison crumples the flyer in her hand. "Emma's making that up. It's not true. It can't be. And anyway, that information is never revealed to the student body."

I shrug. "I'm only reporting what I heard."

"Midnight session tonight," Madison growls. "Tell your friends." I know she means Maude, Theodora, Pippa, and Levi.

"Happily," I respond as Madison grabs Sarah by the arm and storms off.

◇>—⊢—<◇

"Oliver's mom sent me his key," I tell Pippa. I've kept Jane's letter to myself these past few weeks, but now I feel the need to tell Pippa about it. We've arrived early for the Ten meeting at the Tower Room. Neither of us could sleep or wait in our rooms. "Jane, I mean." I finger the key, along with my own. The twin gold objects never leave my neck. "There was a note from Ollie. I haven't let myself read it yet."

"She was one of the Ten, you know," Pippa says, indicating the wall of portraits of past Darkwood Ten members. The last time I was here, after initiation, I was too wet and disturbed to get a good look at them. I walk over to look closer.

"Jaeger was one of them too," Pippa says. "See?" She points to a group portrait that was taken about two decades ago. It hangs eye level on the wall, near the right side. Like the others, it features both the junior and senior members of that year's Ten. I lean in. She's right. It's Pru's father.

I skim over the other names on the frame's plaque. *Colin Chance. My father* was a Ten member too?

"I had no idea. He's never mentioned it," I tell Pippa.

Even more curious now, I scan the other names to see if I recognize any of them. I can't quite believe it when I see a few more that I know. *Bianca Kravitz*—Madison's mom. *Luis de Leon*—Archer's dad.

Pippa points to some of the other captions. "There's Booker Ward and Jane Porter," she says. "Oliver's parents."

They look so young in the photograph; it's almost painful to see them so carefree.

"And look who else," Pippa says. "Ezekiel Choate. Jake's father."

I move to another photo, still scanning the names. Damian Leroy, Tessa's dad, was in the Ten too. Of course, there are lots of other names I don't recognize. *John Underwood. Camila Garcia. Albert Seymour.* Wait, I know that last name, don't I? But from where? I'm too distracted to wonder long. I keep returning to look at my father's image, and Booker's and Jane's.

"I knew my dad and Jane and Booker were friends when they went to Darkwood, but I never knew they were actually in the Ten together," I say.

The door opens, and the rest of the group starts streaming in. First Maude and Theodora, followed by Madison, who saunters directly behind them, not even acknowledging her Similar. She perches herself by the door and checks her plum every five seconds as it ticks toward midnight. I try not to stare at the door, but I can't help it. When Levi finally slips through it at the last minute, I let out a sigh of relief.

"Welcome to the second midnight session of the school year," Madison announces as we grab seats around the circle. "We have a new member to usher into our fold today." She looks about as excited to welcome Pippa as she would be to get a root canal. "Since one of your classmates has had the nasty luck to be otherwise occupied."

"In a coma." Tessa stands in the doorway. She repeats, "Prudence is in a coma."

"You're late," Madison grumbles, though Tessa acts like she hasn't heard her. "As I was saying, welcome, Pippa. This really is an unexpected development. It certainly isn't the group I envisioned when I agreed to be this year's Ten Leader."

Maude raises her hand.

"Yes," Madison answers. "Did you have something to say?" I notice she doesn't address Maude by name.

"It was never our intention to disturb your vision for this year's Ten," Maude says steadily, offering up a weak smile. "In other words, we come in peace."

"Did you come in peace when you defied my parents' orders to never show your face at this school? Did you come in peace when you stood on stage at assembly, throwing their generosity in their faces? Did you come in peace when you cheated on the stratum test so you could outdo me?"

"If that's how you see things," Maude says quietly, "I'm sure I won't be able to convince you otherwise."

"It's midnight," I interrupt. "Can we get on with whatever tonight's agenda is? And no, I didn't bring the name of a student who isn't 'living up to your standards,' like you asked us to last time. I refuse."

Madison glowers at me before responding. "That's a shame, Emma. But I'll give you a pass—for now. Because tonight, we have something different planned for you. For all of you."

Tessa nods, jumping in. "It's time to test your commitment to Darkwood and to the Ten."

Test our commitment? What does that even mean? Did we not do this before our last meeting? I shoot a look at Pippa. She shrugs. We don't have time to wonder long. Before I know what is happening, Tessa is standing over me, and I feel a tingle in my upper arm. And then—blackness.

The darkness only lasts a minute, maybe less, though it's hard to tell. When I open my eyes again, I'm still sitting in the Tower Room. The other Ten members are in their chairs. Nothing's different, except I *feel* different. So loose, almost comfortable.

"New Ten members, the seniors took the liberty of giving you an injective," Madison says. "Don't worry, it's completely harmless. Tessa and I have taken it ourselves before, and we can guarantee that it will have no lasting effect on you."

Like I believe a word she says about anything. But I've heard my dad talk to his colleagues about pharmas my entire life. It's unlikely that Madison and Tessa have procured an injective so powerful it could kill us. At least, I hope that's the case.

"You drugged us?" Pippa asks. Her voice sounds far away.

"Think of the injective like a dear old friend. One who will simply guide you through this next exercise."

"Which is?" I ask. My voice is calm. I feel like I should be angry. Furious, even. But I'm not. I'm relaxed. Too relaxed.

"Divulging your most hidden secrets," Madison says. "By sharing them with us, with each other, you'll form a bond. One that can never be broken or cast aside."

"You'll trust each other implicitly," says Tessa. "By virtue of knowing each other's deepest thoughts. The thoughts you never share with anyone. The sentiments you might not even realize are buried in the recesses of your minds."

I glance over at Pippa again. She doesn't look concerned. Neither do the others. I stare at Levi. He is still and his face is expressionless. I want to run, but I remain seated. It must be the injective.

"We'll start with you, Theodora," Tessa prompts. "It's time to reveal the secrets of your heart."

We all watch Theodora, who, like the rest of us junior Ten members, is neither agitated nor upset by what's being asked of her. She speaks.

"I never experienced homesickness until I came to Darkwood. There is something in the air here that is so foreign, it makes my bones ache. Even though I know how limited my life was on the island, I miss it with every atom of my being. I miss when it was just the six of us. I do not think I can stand it here much longer. I feel like I might turn to dust and the wind will carry me away. I thought I could love the Leroys, but they are not my family. I do not think we are made from the same cloth, even though we share the same genes. Even though Tessa and I share the same DNA, it is like we are different species, and that makes me unbearably sad."

When Theodora stops speaking, we all sit in heavy silence. I look over at Tessa to see if Theodora's words have moved her, but Tessa appears indifferent.

"Thank you," says Madison, moving on abruptly despite Theodora's raw confession. "Pippa? You're next."

Suddenly, I feel so sleepy, it's difficult to keep my eyes open. I don't quite drift off, but I slowly slump in my chair, hearing what Pippa says, but as though through a wind tunnel.

"I'm so worried about Prudence. Her health keeps me up every night, frozen with fear," Pippa confesses. "I understand why Theodora feels no kinship to the Leroys, but when I met Pru, I finally found a sister. And now that sister may be gone. It is more than I can bear."

An ache swells in my chest. I want to reach out and embrace Pippa, but the fogginess of the injective holds me back.

"Thank you for your honesty, Pippa," Madison says, looking smug. "Maude?" Her eyes narrow. "You're up."

Maude takes a moment before speaking.

"Coming to Darkwood, defying your parents' wishes?" Maude addresses her words directly to Madison. "It's the best decision I've ever made in my life. I think I've been doing a pretty fantastic job of tolerating you, Madison, because that's what my guardian asked me to do. But the truth is, I despise you and everything you stand for."

Madison squeezes her hand into a fist. It's like she's holding herself back from doing or saying something she'll regret. Instead, she plasters a smile on her face.

"I assure you, the feeling is mutual. But before we move on..." Madison muses, pacing in a tight circle. "Why do you think, Maude, that your guardian instructed you to tolerate me?"

"Because it's what I'm here to do," Maude says quickly.

"*What you're here to do?* Aren't you here to attend school? To get an education at the best institution in America?"

"In part," Maude responds.

"And the other part?" Madison presses. The tension between these two is palpable, which isn't lost on any of us, even in our drugged state. I shift uncomfortably in my chair.

Maude stares her down. "Isn't it obvious? My guardian wants me to destroy you."

No one speaks. No one moves. Madison pauses, standing in front of Maude like she's ready to pounce on her.

"She comes with a sense of humor," Madison says, crossing her arms over her chest. "I didn't think you had it in you."

"I don't," says Maude, her voice tight. "You and I... We're alike in so many ways, aren't we?"

"That's debatable."

Maude rolls over her words. "We're both focused. Intelligent. Detail-oriented. But no, neither of us is particularly funny."

"Is this your way of telling me that you aren't kidding?" Madison asks. "That you really came to Darkwood to ruin me?"

"I guess that will remain open to interpretation," Maude says lightly. I glance between the two of them, certain one—or both—is going to snap.

"Excuse me." It's Tessa. "As much as I'm enjoying this conversation, we haven't gotten through everyone."

Madison clears her throat. "Thank you, Maude, for that touching confession. Levi?" she says. "You have the floor."

Even in my altered state, my heart quickens as he begins to speak. I don't know why my pulse races. It's not as though he's going to say anything about me.

I wouldn't even want him to.

"The time I've spent at Darkwood has been the most thrilling of my life," Levi shares, his voice steady and even, "and the most miserable. I've never felt this free. To roam, to read my favorite books, to just be. I've also never felt so shackled. I'm tethered to all the parts of myself I despise. At Darkwood, I'm held back by who I am. It's simple, really. I am both myself here and not myself at all."

I take in a shallow breath. Will he say more? Will he *reveal* more?

"I don't wish to go back. There is nothing left for me there. But here... It's difficult to say what might become of me. I may, eventually, thrive. Or I may drown."

We all stare at him, waiting for more, but that's all he shares.

Madison shifts her weight, looking antsy. "Poetic. Emmaline? Go ahead."

I look around at my classmates. Some watch me, but others stare at their hands. The senior Ten members—Angela, Sunil, and Archer—observe me awkwardly. They must have helped Madison and Tessa drug us.

"Oliver and I weren't really speaking when he died," I hear myself say, unable to stop the words from tumbling out. It's a strange sensation, like I'm talking without my permission. The words flow on their own without my consent. "We weren't *not* talking. We weren't angry at each other. But something had happened. He'd told me something, a few months before, back in March. He said..." I pause. A tiny voice in the back of my mind urges me to stop, not to tell this story. For half a second, I listen to it. The urge to keep going is stronger. So I do.

"Oliver said that he loved me. Of course, I knew that. I loved him too. He was my best and oldest friend. He was my person. But he meant he *loved me* loved me. I told him that couldn't be true. He couldn't *love* me. Not like that. That would ruin everything. And I was right. It did. Because things changed between us. And three months later, he died. And now, all this." I gesture at the room, as though that will mean something to any of them.

Nine pairs of eyes stare at me. I meet Levi's gaze, then quickly look away. "That's all," I mutter.

"Well, I believe that's everyone." Madison smirks. "The injective certainly works like a charm. Don't fret, it'll wear off in a few hours. But isn't it great how well we all know each other now? Bonding moment!" she practically squeals.

If I weren't totally drugged, I'd punch her in the face. And with that, we're dismissed.

By the time I make it back to my room, the injective has started to lose its strength. I feel the heaviness of my body again and what my heart "revealed," or whatever nonsense Madison called it.

I told everyone about Oliver's confession. Including Levi.

As my mind returns, my pulse quickens.

This doesn't change anything, I tell myself. It doesn't matter. However Oliver felt about me, Levi is still Levi and Oliver is still gone.

Oliver.

The serrated knife slowly slides into my chest again, and I wince. God, I miss him. I squeeze his key at my neck as if that would make him reappear.

His note! I dig in my hoodie pocket for the scrap of paper that Jane sent me with Ollie's key. I open it, hungry for Oliver's words.

Emma,

I'm sorry. The key is for you. It will explain everything. Especially about him.

Love always,
O

I sink onto my bed, willing the note to say more than it does. My hand goes to my neck again, to the two keys hanging there. I'd assumed sending me Oliver's key had been Jane's idea, that she had wanted me to have it as a keepsake, a reminder of him. Turns out Ollie himself had wanted me to have it. I look over to Pru's empty side of the room, her bed still unmade, her athletic clothes scattered on the floor. If only she were here. She'd probably have a million ideas about what Ollie meant…

I focus on the note. Oliver obviously wrote it in haste, or he would have been more explicit. But why was he in a hurry? *Why* was he rushing to the end—*his* end? The tears come hard and fast as I imagine him in his room, writing this note for me. Pain and anguish must have roiled through him, leading him to take that handful of pharmas…

Why did he want me to have his key? And how could it possibly "explain everything"? Is there something in his old room he wanted me to find? It's not even *his* room anymore.

And even more cryptic, who is the "him"? Did he mean Levi? Did Oliver know he had a Similar before he died?

I scroll on my tablet to this year's room assignments. I find Oliver's room from last year. It's empty. Oliver's old roommate, Arthur Wong, has been assigned to a new room, and no one's living there now—even with the influx of new students.

It's weird, but I bet none of the parents wanted their kid to live there after Oliver's death. Which will make it easier to search Oliver's old dorm room. It's what he wanted. I owe it to him. I might not have been ready to love him the same way he loved me, but I can honor his last request.

But to search Oliver's room, I will need Levi's help. It's not enough to have the key without Oliver's DNA. It was Tessa, after all, who said it that day in the library. *Jake could take Jago's tests if only he had his key.* And Levi will be able to unlock the door of Oliver's old room. The thought of approaching him after what I revealed about myself, about *Oliver*, makes my skin flush with embarrassment. And yet, I have to do it. Now, before I lose my nerve.

I'm already slipping on my boots and grabbing my coat, then looking up Levi's room assignment. He and Jago are roommates. I hadn't known that. Their dorm is in the same building as Oliver's old room. It's called Nightshade. I steel myself for what I'm about to do. Returning to Oliver's dorm—without Oliver— will take all the strength I can muster.

◇⟶┤ ├⟵◇

Standing on the fire escape that runs up the side of Nightshade, the wind groans, threatening to blow my small, insignificant body right off. I'm having second thoughts. Why did I think it was a good idea to climb up here and ask Levi's help right this minute?

But it's too late. I'm already rapping on the window to get his attention. His hair is messy, and he's shirtless and barefoot, wearing only jeans.

He comes to the window and opens it. "Emma?" He surveys me, and I detect the hint of a smile on his lips. "Are you out of your mind? It's two in the morning."

"I know how to tell time. Are you going to let me in?"

Levi holds out a hand, and I take it, noting his firm grip as he helps me inside. As I jump down from the windowsill, I brush against his bare chest. A shiver runs down my spine. Levi lets go of my hand and grabs a T-shirt from the back of his desk chair. That's when I notice Jago standing to the side, looking ready to murder me.

"Hi," I say.

Jago doesn't say it back. "You realize you're breaking pretty much every Darkwood rule by being here, and by association, so are we?" Jago rants. "So unless you're on fire—"

"Do I look like I'm on fire?"

"You have to leave. Now."

"Oliver left me his key," I blurt.

"So?" Jago presses, and Levi levels him with a look.

He says something to Jago I can't understand. For a moment, I'm puzzled. This doesn't sound like French—I would understand that, or at least some of it.

"What language was that?" I ask.

Jago stares at me. "Portuguese. Why?"

"I thought you spoke French to one another."

"We do," Levi starts. "We did. Until…"

I suddenly understand and supply the rest of the sentence. "That night by the lake."

Levi nods. "I didn't realize until the other day, when you told me you understood us and what we were talking about— *privately*, we thought."

"Let me guess," I say. "You switched to Portuguese because it's not taught here?"

"She's a smart one," Jago says before grabbing his jacket. "I'm going to Ansel's room. The two of you can do what you want. Enjoy detention again, expulsion, whatever. It's not my problem." Jago slams the door behind him.

"Light sleeper," explains Levi. "He was working his way toward his REM cycle when you so unceremoniously interrupted him."

"Oh." I'm not sure what else to say, so I switch gears, thrusting Oliver's note toward him. Levi reads it.

"This tells us nothing," he says.

"Thanks, Sherlock," I snap, grabbing the note from his hand. "He wanted me to look for something in his old room. I checked the housing assignments. It's empty. I know it's a long shot, but maybe there will be some answers about why Oliver did what he did. The key won't work for me, not if the room's locked—"

Levi smiles wryly. "Enter me. And my genetics, to be exact.

Who is *he*? I mean, 'him'?" Levi asks, brow scrunching as he looks at the note again.

"I don't know," I say quickly. "The only person I could come up with was—is—you."

Levi takes that in, walking over to the window and staring at the dark grounds below. "There's not a lot of moonlight tonight. You weren't scared climbing that thing?" He gestures at the fire escape.

I shrug. "Should I have been?"

Levi turns back to face me. "You think Oliver knew about me before he died?"

"It's the only explanation that makes any sense. Otherwise, who is he talking about? I think somehow he knew. Even if Jane and Booker didn't," I add, since Levi and I disagree on that point. "And whatever's in his room, it could explain everything—how he knew he had a clone, why he has a clone, why he…died. For God's sake, Levi. This is your life we're talking about too. Don't you want to know?"

"Of course I do," he says quietly. "I've wondered, no *hoped*, all of my life that there was a reason why I exist besides a mistaken lab experiment. That somebody actually wanted me." He's quiet for a moment, then makes a decision in his head and grabs a pair of sneakers. "Let's go now. Unless you feel like scaling that fire escape again tomorrow night?"

"The next time we break and enter, you can come down and let me in," I reply.

"Next time?" he ribs.

We are off. It doesn't take long to get to Oliver's old room.

154

I try the doorknob, but as I suspected, it doesn't open for me. "Here," I say, handing him Ollie's key. "Put it on. You should probably wear it around your neck, like you would, you know, if you were actually him."

Levi nods, slips Oliver's key around his neck, and holds it in front of the doorknob. There is a faint *beep* as the door unlocks. It worked. With a steady hand, Levi turns the knob, and just like that, we're in.

I don't know what I was expecting, but the room doesn't scream "Oliver!" in any profound way. It's empty, except for twin beds pushed to opposite ends of the room. There are the standard-issue dressers and desks, and a closet, bare except for a few wire hangers dangling from a metal rod.

"I'll take the right side. You take the left," Levi says matter-of-factly. As we scour our respective sides of the room, I have three thoughts. The first is that working side by side like this, me and Levi, like we did during duty, feels easy and familiar. The second is that I'm grateful to him for helping me. And the third is that I must've completely misunderstood Oliver's last message because after twenty long minutes of searching, we've come up with nothing that could even begin to qualify as a clue or a message.

Levi yawns and asks me if I'm ready to go, and with one glance back as if I'll spot the ghost of my best friend, we walk out together.

We are silent as we approach the front doors of Nightshade.

"I'm sorry we didn't find anything," Levi says softly.

"I'll live," I reply. What I don't say is that I need to know why Oliver *didn't* live. And I won't stop trying until I figure out what his note meant.

"Levi?" I whisper.

"Yeah?"

"The midnight session. The injective. What I said back there..."

Levi doesn't respond. He simply stares at me with those gray eyes, the ones I love, or used to, anyway.

"Oliver meant the world to me. I didn't mean to push him away."

"I get it," he says. "You were scared. You didn't want to risk a relationship. You didn't want your friendship to change. If there were someone I cared about that much..."

"What?" I ask, my heart in my throat.

Levi shakes his head. "Nothing."

There's something I've been meaning to ask him, but it was never the right time, until now. "Levi? You said before, when we were in your room, that you've always hoped there was a reason you were created. I think you know more about that than you're telling me."

He hesitates before answering. "What makes you say that?"

"In American history, when Mr. Park dedicated that whole class to discussing cloning, there was talk of an experiment. Something about primates. Theodora said she knew all about it, but that it was classified."

"It is."

"But you know about it too."

Levi shuts down all at once. He stiffens and his jaw locks. If

I've had any window of insight into him tonight, I don't anymore. It's been closed. Maybe indefinitely. "You should go to bed, Emma. Stop thinking about Albert Seymour and his primates. I can assure you, you're better off not knowing the details."

Without so much as a goodbye, he turns and leaves me alone in the darkened hallway.

That night, as I toss and turn, drifting in and out of a fitful sleep, I startle awake. That's it, the piece of the puzzle that has been eluding me. *Albert Seymour.* I remember where I last saw the scientist's name. He was in the portrait of the Ten, the one from my father's senior year. Albert Seymour was the man standing between my father and Jane Porter.

THE WARDS

"DASH," I ADDRESS my plum, "who was Albert Seymour?"

"Researching Albert Seymour," Dash responds. "Is there anything else I can assist you with, hon?"

"Hon?" I tease. I'm not used to this sass in the middle of the night.

"It's something I'm trying out," Dash quips. His response makes me smile.

Over the next week, I eagerly read all Dash can collect about Albert Seymour's life. I devour a biography of the man, discovering that he was born into an influential family in Boston. Seymour's only sibling was a half brother, John Underwood, who shared the same father. Little is said about Underwood, or the brothers' childhood, except that they lived apart, and Underwood took his mother's last name. The book skips to Seymour's days at Harvard, where he graduated early, then began studies for his PhD, completing his dissertation on reproductive cloning by the age of twenty-two. Seymour wasted no time starting his own cloning lab in Boston, eventually moving it abroad when laws in the United States barred him from continuing his research.

The book glosses over Seymour's Darkwood days in a few sparse paragraphs, so I trek to the Tower Room to study the portrait of the Ten from Seymour's year. I scan the names, lingering on the familiar ones—my father; Oliver's parents, Jane and Booker; Prudence's dad, Jaeger's family. There along with Albert Seymour is John Underwood. I'd read the name before, but I hadn't realized the two were half brothers. I make a mental note to ask my father about both of them if he ever answers any of my buzzes.

As I take in the picture, I match each name to a figure in the photograph. My father, Jaeger, Bianca Kravitz, Booker Ward, Ezekiel Choate… Albert Seymour is the scrawny guy near the end with oversize glasses. His clothes are wrinkled and look too big for his narrow frame. I look again. Something isn't adding up. Where is John Underwood? I count the people in the photograph. There are only nine. John Underwood is listed, but he isn't in the photo.

That night, I read the book a second time, thinking maybe I missed references to Seymour's primate experiment, but it's not even mentioned. That strikes me as odd. If the experiment was so groundbreaking, why can't I find any information on it? Theodora called it "classified," but Mr. Park knew enough about the experiment to bring it up in class. Where did *he* learn about it?

A week later, I linger behind in American history to find out. "Mr. Park?"

"Hmm?" He stacks textbooks on his desk, clearly preoccupied.

"That day you brought up Albert Seymour's primate experiment...sir," I add politely. "You were going to say more about it, only the class's discussion got sidetracked. I can't find any information about it anywhere. Can you tell me more?"

Mr. Park sighs. "I appreciate your scholarly interest in the topic, but I'm in a rush, Emma. My next class starts in two minutes in the annex across campus."

"I understand," I say quickly. "You must have a book you can point me to? Some articles?" And for good measure: "I'm trying to learn more about the issues, Mr. Park. Expand my base of knowledge." I cast my most winning smile.

"I'll try to locate some material for you," he answers hurriedly before making a beeline for the door.

"I thought I told you to let that go," a voice says from behind me. I turn, taken aback, to find that Levi is still in the room. I'd thought Mr. Park and I were alone.

"You did. I ignored you."

Levi sighs, and I almost welcome that sound. It's been almost two weeks since our sleuthing in Oliver's room, and with class and homework, we've barely spoken.

"Albert Seymour went to Darkwood," I blurt.

Levi doesn't react, though his gaze hardens. I don't flinch or look away.

"And so did his half brother, John Underwood," I add.

"Your point?"

"They're both in a portrait of the Ten, from my father's year. Actually, Seymour's in it. Underwood isn't pictured."

"I've seen it," says Levi tightly.

"Of course you have," I answer. "Because you know legions of things you plan to never tell me, and in fact, hope I never think about again."

"Why are you doing this, Emma?" he asks quietly. "Why can't you let this go?"

"Let this go? You want me to let go of my questions about Oliver's death? Let go of what he said in his last note to me? Let go of the fact that the man who *invented cloning* went to this school?!" I'm so angry, I could slap him. But I don't. I hold in my fury. "When you feel like telling me whatever it is you know about Albert Seymour, you know where to find me."

I storm off like a petulant child.

Weeks pass, and now Levi and I don't even say hello to each other. There have been two midnight sessions where we avoided each other's gaze. For once, I was happy that Madison rambled on about our duty to uphold Darkwood's founding tenet of excellence. At least she didn't make us participate in any more "exercises." Of course, I noticed him at the sessions. Anytime we're in a room together, I look to see what he's doing. In the dining hall, I crane my neck to see what he's reading. I can't help it.

Meanwhile, more and more students inquire about DAAM. I can't help but notice that the general mistrust of the Similars on campus is mounting, and it makes me furious. Where is this coming from? Darkwood students are supposed to be inclusive, which is the whole reason Headmaster Ransom felt he could invite the Similars here. So why does it feel like he completely missed the mark?

One November morning at breakfast, Pippa slaps a stack of paper on the table. She explains that it's a printout of an essay that's gone viral around the nation—and our dining hall—called "The Case for No Clones."

"Apparently it got more than twenty million page views. And they had to turn off comments because the site kept crashing."

"Where did you get this?" I ask as I scan it.

"A girl in my calculus BC class."

"But how did she get her hands on it? There's no way Headmaster Ransom would ever let this through his firewalls."

"A junior hacked the system." Pippa shrugs. "I've heard it's not that hard if you know what you're doing. Anyway, the essay says we were abused. This author thinks our unconventional childhood on Castor Island altered us irrevocably."

"Abused? That's—*How?*" My gaze leaps to the Similars' table, where Ansel and Theodora talk quietly, and Levi and Jago absentmindedly play a game of tic-tac-toe. My heart hurts considering the possibility that this could be true.

"We were treated well. But according to this article, what happened to us there made us dangerous," Pippa offers in a barely audible voice.

"If anyone's dangerous, it's not any of you," I tell Pippa. "It's Madison. She's the only person who could have attacked Pru…"

"But we don't have any proof," Pippa reminds me. "And Jaeger isn't returning my buzzes. I feel like an intruder, like the last person he wants to hear from is me."

I grab Pippa's hand across the table and squeeze it. "You aren't an intruder. Jaeger's just dealing in his own way with what happened. It's got to be why he hasn't called either of us back. When Pru wakes up…" I fight my own tears. "Everything will be different. You'll see." But I don't know if I believe that myself.

◇—┤ ├—◇

Fall break passes in a blur. I stay on campus with a handful of other students, plunging into a wormhole on the history of cloning, on Seymour, and also on Gravelle, the Similars' guardian. Not much is known about his personal life, only that he's a self-made billionaire who funded the lab that made the big mistake when they created the Similars. He then took responsibility for raising the six clones—and according to "The Case for No Clones," brainwashed and abused them.

Though I don't believe the author of that article has all the facts, I'm still gutted to think that what transpired at the compound might have hurt Pippa, Levi, and the other Similars. I know their childhood was unconventional. I know Levi said he'd never traveled off the island. I know they didn't have real parents. And I suppose that could be considered abuse in its own right.

Not surprisingly, the Similars stay on campus during break

too. Pippa and I spend the holiday together. I buzz Pru's father on our behalf, leaving him message after message. *We want to visit Prudence. Please tell us a good day to come.* When he finally contacts us, he says Pru is still in a coma. *She wouldn't want you to see her like that,* he insists. *Please don't come. Not yet.*

I don't talk to Levi over the break. I have nothing to say to him, and it's clear he feels the same. But I won't back down from what I said. I need to know more about Albert Seymour, and if Levi won't tell me, I'll find out another way.

As the long weekend draws to an end, I'm filled with a growing sense of unease. In only a few short days, Oliver's parents will be arriving for the dedication ceremony—when they won't be able to avoid meeting Oliver's Similar. I haven't seen Jane since Oliver's funeral, and the idea of watching her grieve all over again is nearly more than I can bear. If I could spare her from this, I would. But I can't stop them from coming. And even if I could, they will have to meet Levi eventually. They can't avoid the inevitable. Levi exists. Hard as that is for me to process, it's a fact.

I remind Levi on the first day back after American history, "Oliver's parents will be here on Saturday. Do you know what you're going to say to them?"

"Do you?" he shoots back.

During lunch, Headmaster Ransom makes an announcement. We're all being issued new keys.

"First," he explains to the hushed crowd, "let me acknowledge what you're already thinking—that a midsemester key replacement is, indeed, a first for this institution. The old key system has served the school well for nearly two decades. Yet it has come to our attention that there are certain security limitations that we cannot overlook. Your new keys are outfitted with updated software that can track your whereabouts via GPS and serve other important safety functions. Many parents have clamored for these changes in light of the unfortunate incident that happened in the boathouse in September. With that in mind, we ask that you not, under any circumstances, remove your key from your neck."

Several students start to protest, but Headmaster Ransom holds up a hand and continues, "Each and every one of your parents has already signed a privacy waiver, giving Darkwood permission to virtually track your movements to keep you safe."

There are whispers all around. Though I don't say it out loud, I am sure that one of the current keys' "limitations" is the very loophole that allowed Levi to enter Oliver's old room.

"Once your key is initialized," Ransom continues, "during the first twelve hours you wear it, it will learn to recognize you via your DNA, as well as several other markers that are distinctly yours and yours alone." He doesn't have to say it, but I'm certain that the Similars will no longer be able to swap keys with their originals, and vice versa.

After we deposit our old keys into a metal box, new keys that look identical to our old ones are looped over our heads. I run my finger along the beveled edge of my new key, along with Oliver's. I haven't turned his in. No one except Levi knows that I have it, so the administration can't ask for it back. And I'm certainly not ready to give it up, not when I haven't discovered what Oliver was trying to tell me.

That Saturday, with two keys rattling together under my shirt, I walk down to the field where the dedication ceremony will be held. Principal Fleischer instructed me to meet Jane and Booker fifteen minutes ahead of the ceremony to welcome them to campus. When I asked her if anyone had told them yet about Levi, she said it was none of my business.

It's not hard to interpret what that means. It's up to me. For whatever reason, I've been left with the job of breaking the news to them. Maybe this is what Ransom wants? Maybe he thinks I'm best equipped for this heartbreaking task? I have no idea.

When I arrive at the empty field, I'm bowled over by the beauty of the day. The sky is azure and cloudless, the expanse of grass still green in spite of the mounting cold that nips at my hands and face.

I walk over to where a wooden stake has been hammered into the ground with a sign. OLIVER WARD HALL: DEDICATION CEREMONY. There's a podium set up next to it, flanked by a few folding chairs.

"Emmaline?"

I turn and see two figures walking toward me. Booker has one arm around Jane like he's holding her up. Her familiar face comes into view, and I'm instantly filled with love for her and for Oliver—and an intense longing for a life that will never be, not ever again.

"Jane," I say quietly, and before I know what's happening, her frail arms wind around me in a hug. A few moments later, Booker clears his throat, and we pull apart.

I finally get a good look at Jane's face, and I'm stunned by how much older she looks now than before her whole world cracked and shifted like tectonic plates. Her forehead is lined and weary, and dark circles shadow the skin beneath her eyes. I don't know how I'm going to do this—adding to her pain feels wrong on so many levels.

"I'm so glad you came," I say, and I give Booker a cursory hug as well. We've never been close, he and I, but I can see the toll the past few months have taken on him too.

"Oh, Emma," says Jane, blinking back tears. "I never thought... This isn't..."

"Maybe you should sit." I pull up folding chairs for them. "Were you traveling all day? You must be exhausted."

Jane shrugs, and Booker rests a hand on her shoulder. "It's hard being back on campus, knowing how happy Oliver was here," he says as an explanation.

"Tell us, please, Emma, about your junior year so far. We want to hear everything," Jane says. "We love you like a daughter. That won't ever change. Not because—" She stops, unable to say the words out loud. *Not because our son has died.*

"Jane, Booker, there's something I have to tell you." I take in a halting breath. This is it, the moment of truth. I'm about to launch into my prepared speech when I see him in the distance, walking toward us. My heart stalls in my chest.

Levi.

I want to yell at him to go. *Not yet!* I want to shout. *They're not ready. I'm not ready.* Levi meets my gaze, and it's like he reads my mind. He pauses a couple of yards off, standing still as a statue.

"Emma? Are you okay?" Jane asks. She starts to turn to follow my gaze, and I lower my eyes.

"There isn't an easy way to explain this," I say.

Jane and Booker stare at me quizzically, not understanding what I am trying to say. How could they?

"The clones at Darkwood," I say. "The ones who joined the junior class this year?"

"We heard," Jane says. "Three of their names were leaked. It's all over the feeds. They were—they are—clones of Tessa Leroy, Jake Choate, and that other girl? The Huxleys' daughter?"

"Madison," I supply.

Booker whistles. "Her family can't be too happy about that. I keep telling Jane, I wouldn't be surprised if the National Anti-Cloning Commission got involved and petitioned the school against having them here."

Jane squeezes Booker's hand. "Let's not bore Emma with unsavory politics. You were saying, dear?"

My mouth gapes.

"Emmaline, honey," Jane starts, then glances over at her husband, who nods. "What is it?"

"As you know, there are six Similars," I blurt. "Except one of the students was cloned and his parents weren't notified, not like the others. At least, I don't think they were," I add quickly. "I would like you to meet Levi. The sixth Similar. He's your son."

DEDICATION

I DON'T WAIT to hear Jane and Booker's reaction. I motion Levi over to us.

I don't tell Levi *I told you so*, though I know in my heart of hearts I was right. Jane and Booker had no idea he existed. It couldn't be any clearer from their faces. Oliver's parents look lost, confused. Worse—they look torn apart.

Levi approaches, and as Jane and Booker get their first look at him, at his Oliverian face, his too-long hair, and his gray eyes, I'm plunged back into the memory of when I first laid eyes on Levi. I know how Jane feels. Seeing Levi is like seeing a mirage or a cruel optical illusion. He is so exactly like Oliver, and yet, he is not.

"I don't know why no one told you…" I feel like I'm babbling. I don't know what else to do.

"The school left us some messages," Booker says, his voice hollow. "We didn't listen to all of them…" He and Jane continue to stare at Levi. Levi holds out a hand for them to shake. When they don't move, he retracts it and slips it into his coat pocket.

"Hey, no worries," Levi says with a shrug. "If I were you, I probably wouldn't want to meet me either."

"This is Levi," I jump in, because he deserves a proper introduction. "Levi Gravelle. He grew up…up north. He's smart and really good at martial arts." It's a bit random, but we're all just trying to make it through this moment. "I'm sorry. I didn't know how to tell you. When I first met him, when I first saw him…" My eyes meet Levi's in a silent apology. I'm bad at this, but I'm trying. I hope he knows that. "At least now we know. Your guardian lied to you. Jane and Booker never knew you existed."

"Is it wrong that I hoped?" Jane asks, her voice warbled and strained. Levi and I both turn to her, surprised. "Is it wrong that I dreamed this would happen?" she says to Booker. "When I heard about the clones coming to Darkwood, there was a part of me that wanted Oliver to have one. A Similar. Because after he died…" Her words melt into sobs, and Booker embraces her. "After he died, I did too."

Out of the corner of my eye, I see Levi sag. I get it now. This is his worst fear, that he'll only be seen as a copy. A replacement for a dead boy.

Before any of us can say more, students begin convening on the grassy pavilion. It's time for the dedication ceremony. Kids are filing in, teachers too. The hush in the air is gone, and our serene, quiet space fills up with chatter. I notice Headmaster Ransom arrive and snag Principal Fleischer for what looks like an intense discussion. I watch Madison, Tessa, Archer, and Jake filter in out of the corner of my eye. Madison looks angry about something. The others look amused.

"Will you have lunch with us, Levi? After the ceremony?" Booker asks. "Please forgive our initial shock. We would very much like to get to know you."

Levi nods, and then Principal Fleischer interrupts, leading Jane and Booker to the podium to speak about their son.

⟡⊶⊷⟡

In the dining hall, I park myself at a table with a plate of pasta. It sits untouched in front of me. Across the way, I watch Jane, Booker, and Levi, who are eating together. Pippa pulls up a chair next to me, and though I haven't had a chance to tell her about the Wards' meeting with Levi, it isn't hard for her to figure out what happened. Anyway, Levi probably already filled her in.

"How did they take the news?" she asks, her voice solemn.

"I think it's the first time someone could say they saw a ghost and mean it literally."

"I've never understood why there weren't told..." Pippa says.

"The Wards had just lost their son." I shrug. "Maybe whoever was supposed to inform them couldn't bring themselves to do it."

"Maybe," Pippa says. But she doesn't sound all that convinced.

Then her eyes widen. I follow her gaze to the feeds, where there is a picture of a familiar-looking man projected with a headline below it: MEDIA MOGUL—GUILTY AS CHARGED.

Pippa shakes her head. "Tessa's father, Damian Leroy. A jury found him guilty this morning on seven counts of securities fraud."

I'm not surprised. We'd all seen this coming, what with the media coverage of the evidence presented at trial. Yet, as I stare up at the feeds, the headlines are shocking, nonetheless: DAMIAN LEROY: BILLIONAIRE CROOK and THE LEROY DYNASTY—THE MAKINGS OF A FRAUDULENT EMPIRE.

A slideshow of photos sweeps across the view space. Damian and his wife. Damian and their two children—Tessa and her little brother. I scan the cafeteria for Tessa, but I don't see her.

Then another familiar face pops up in the view space. It's Jaeger, looking as careworn as ever, but suited in a spiffy blazer. Next to him is a young anchorman I recognize from the feeds. Pippa stiffens at the sight of her DNA father.

"Jaeger Stanwick, thanks for being with us today," says the anchorman. "You were the first to break the story of the FBI's investigation of Damian Leroy's financial reports."

"It wasn't a job I relished," Jaeger says. "Damian and I were schoolmates back in the day. He's an old friend."

"And now, a convicted criminal," the anchorman points out.

Jaeger sighs. "Facts are facts. It was my journalistic duty to expose his corruption."

"Some say that your personal connection influenced your report."

"People say a lot of things," Jaeger responds darkly. "That doesn't make them true."

"Up next," the anchorman says, "'The Case for No Clones.' Mr. Stanwick, you have a lot to say about that essay, I presume?"

"Only that it's indefensible," Jaeger replies.

"So you don't believe the Similars are a danger to society?"

"Absolutely not."

"More on that when we return. First, a word from our sponsor," the anchorman says before the feeds cut out. I let out a heavy breath. Seeing Jaeger always makes me think of Pru.

"Jaeger didn't look so good," I tell Pippa.

She shakes her head. "No." Then, "I wonder where Tessa is?"

"Hiding in her room?" I do feel sorry for Tessa. Even she doesn't deserve a father with a prison sentence.

A burst of voices comes from across the room, and I spot Levi getting up abruptly from his table. He looks rattled, which is unusual for him. He's always so impassive. Jane scoots back her chair to get up too, and she moves to fold Levi into her arms. Though Levi reacts stiffly, he allows her to hug him. Once Jane lets go, he takes a step back. I can't quite tell what's happening, but it's clear he's not happy. He picks up his tray of food, barely eaten, and walks out the door.

I don't bother to bus my tray. I ask Pippa to take care of it for me and run after Levi. He's walking toward the woods. I hurry to catch up to him.

"Levi!" I shout.

"Can I help you?" he asks distantly when I reach him at the edge of the brambles. It's quiet as a morgue out here, and there's not a soul in sight. A voice deep down warns me that I shouldn't be out here alone with him. What if that report is right and the Similars are dangerous? I shut the voice out of my head as quickly as it came.

"What happened?" I ask. "What did they say?"

"Let's see," says Levi. "Once they got over the shock of meeting me, they called their family lawyer. They decided to name me a beneficiary in the family will, along with their twin daughters, Chloe and Lucy. They called them my little *sisters*," he says, emphasizing the word like it's terrible. "Here's the best part. Their lawyer is planning to shift equity in the Ward family business, so that as soon as I sign some paperwork, I'll be gifted a large grant of super voting shares of Ward, Inc. stock. It is stock Oliver would have held...if he'd lived."

"I don't understand," I say. "They're doing everything in their power to make you a part of their family. To be like a mom and dad to you. Why are you so upset?"

"A mom and dad? To me? Are you delusional?"

"No," I say, trying not to sound too defensive. *He's in pain*, I remind myself. "All I know is that if Jane Porter wanted to be my mother, it would be the best thing to ever happen to me."

Levi storms into the woods. I follow. He's walking fast, as though he's trying to outrun it all, and I hurry to keep up, my heart pounding in my chest.

"Levi," I cry out. "Wait!"

He wheels on me, his breath shallow, his cheeks red. Something in his eyes makes him look lost, as though he could breathe fire. A shiver runs up my spine.

"I would have thought you of all people would understand," he seethes.

"Understand what?"

"The look on Jane's face when she was telling me she wanted me to be a part of their family's legacy. It was the same look you had on your face the day I met you."

I flinch. I remain silent as I follow him deeper into the woods. When Levi reaches a small clearing, he kicks at a bed of leaves, sending them flying. I move past him and sit on a rock, wrapping my arms around my knees.

"You could get surgery," I suggest. "Remake yourself."

"Don't think I haven't considered it."

"Would you? Change your face?" I ask. Before I can stop myself, I reach out to touch his cheek. As soon as I do, I pull back as though singed.

"In an instant," he says, looking directly into my eyes. "I've told you that already."

"And now I believe you," I say quietly. Because I am quite certain that being Levi Gravelle and living in Oliver Ward's body isn't something I'd wish on anyone.

⋄⊷—⊶⋄

It's Sunday morning, and I'm meeting Jane and Booker outside the main house to say goodbye.

"Emma?" Jane asks as I approach. If she was exhausted and emotional yesterday, today she looks wrecked. She clutches her purse, and Booker wheels a suitcase behind them.

I pull Ollie's letter, now careworn and wrinkled, from my pocket. "Oliver's note, the one you sent to me? I don't understand it. I've been trying to work it out, but nothing makes sense, unless..." I am not sure how to say this. "You read it, right? Who is 'him'? Who is he talking about?" I hand Jane the note to jog her memory. "Did he know? About Levi? Did Oliver know he had a Similar?"

"How could he have known?" Jane asks. "We didn't know ourselves."

"Could someone have tried to contact you, and Ollie intercepted the message?" I know it sounds far-fetched. But still, I can't think of any other explanation for Oliver's note, for Oliver's leaving.

"Emmaline, please," Booker jumps in. "Don't start this—" He stops himself, his harshness dissipating, when he sees the hurt in my eyes.

"I'm sorry, Emma," Jane says. "We've been through an untold amount of stress. Booker didn't mean..."

I get it. I nod. Still, there's something else I want to say to them. "Levi was upset yesterday. What you offered him, it was very generous. I've gotten to know him the past few months. He's a good person. I know what everyone says about the Similars, but it's not true. They aren't dangerous, and I don't think they were brainwashed—" I stop myself as Jane starts to get emotional again. "Levi deserves to be a part of a family, of *your* family."

Jane and Booker exchange a look.

"What?" I press. "What's going on?"

Jane clutches the strap of her bag. "Emma, that's part of the reason we're leaving this morning. Levi—"

"What about him?"

"He signed the paperwork yesterday afternoon. We gifted him, in a custodial account, the shares of Ward, Inc. that would have been Oliver's, including the super voting rights that would give him quite a bit of influence over the company. The only other shareholders who have that kind of power are us—Booker and me. We did this on faith, you understand. We did this because of everything you just said. Because the Similars, all of them, deserve a chance. And because he is my son."

"That's a good first step, isn't it?" I say tentatively.

"We also did it because we are grieving. And we were fools. Early this morning, we received a call from our lawyer. As soon as the proverbial ink was dry, Levi's guardian—as custodian of the account—sold Levi's shares on his behalf," Booker supplies.

"He sold them? But...why?"

"We don't know why his guardian agreed to sell them, but we do know to whom." Jane looks over at Booker. He nods. "Himself."

"What?" I respond. "I don't understand."

"No, you wouldn't, because it's so hard to believe. But Levi's guardian transferred the stock from Levi's account to his *own* personal account, on Levi's orders. Which means the man who raised Levi and the other Similars, Augustus Gravelle— whatever kind of person he may be—is now a key stakeholder in our family's company."

THE TASKS

THE DAY PASSES in a blur. All I can think about is how Levi handed his shares of Ward, Inc. to his guardian. There must be more to the story than that. Surely there is an explanation or justification for what he's done. Before she left, Jane told me that they plan to fight this with a lawsuit. What Gravelle did was a gross violation of his custodial duty. I asked her not to blame Levi for what his guardian likely made him do. I don't think Levi is a bad person, though I can't say I agree with his actions. Still, it's not enough to make me distrust him—or the Similars—like the students on campus signing up for DAAM do. Not since I've gotten to know them. Pippa misses Pru as much as I do. And Levi saved Pru's life. All of that has to mean something. It must.

At lunch, I look for Levi in the dining hall, but he isn't there. Neither are the other Similars, except for Pippa. I'm relieved when she sits next to me. She makes it feel like a part of Pru is still here, and not in a coma, or worse. Plus, in the time I have gotten to know Pippa, I have begun to think of her as a good friend. I don't tell Pippa what I've learned about Ward, Inc. For now, it feels like my secret. Mine and Levi's.

Madison sends alerts to our plums about a midnight session, and Pippa and I wonder if Tessa will be there. No one's seen her since her father's guilty conviction, but we doubt she'd miss a Ten meeting.

That night, as I climb into bed at ten o'clock, fully clothed, with no intention of dozing off, I think about how much Jane and Booker are suffering. I keep running what they said through my mind, that the Similars' guardian is now a key shareholder in their company.

I ask Dash to run a search on Augustus Gravelle, and he finds article after article about Gravelle's accomplishments in the business world, but none of them share a thing about his younger years. It's like he didn't exist before the age of thirty.

Restless and feeling like I'll lose my mind if I stay in my room any longer, I slip on my boots, leaving my key on my bed. Now that our keys can track our whereabouts, it's risky to carry it while wandering the grounds at night. I don't really want to invite the company of campus security. Though we've been warned not to ever take our keys off, and I have no way of knowing what will happen if I do, I take that chance and leave it behind, putting a piece of masking tape where the bolt would meet the doorjamb, so that the door to my room looks closed but doesn't actually lock. It's a silly trick, but it's better than being tracked.

I still have Oliver's key around my neck. It can't be traced, and I'd never dream of leaving it unattended. It's my only remaining connection to Oliver in his last moments. Well, besides his note, which I can't for the life of me decipher. As I walk out the front door of Cypress and into the biting night, I run Oliver's note through my brain again. *It will explain everything. Especially about him.*

I'm so caught up in my own thoughts, I walk all the way to Dark Lake. I'm almost to the edge of the woods when I see six figures illuminated in the moonlight. They stand in a row on the bank of the lake with their backs to me. They are so still—too still. In a way that's almost inhuman. It's them. The Similars.

In one perfectly synchronized motion, they dive into the lake, their sleek bodies slicing though the onyx water. The water around them ripples, and their bodies disappear under the surface. The lake stills again.

I gasp, amazed and impressed by their orchestrated motion, the way in which they all moved as if choreographed.

I inch closer, expecting them to pop out of the water at any moment. I wonder if it will be all in one fluid motion. As I walk toward the lake, careful to stay in the shadows of the trees, I look at my plum, noting the time. It's been about twenty seconds since they dived in, and the water hasn't rippled since. It's as still as an obsidian mirror.

I watch, then glance at my plum again. It's been more than a minute since their initial dive. I'm no expert, but I'm pretty sure most people can't hold their breath underwater for much more than two minutes, though I suppose they may have trained for this on their island, like Olympians. Maybe holding their breath was a daily exercise there.

Still, a feeling of dread washes over me as I wait for them to emerge, the seconds—and minutes—ticking by. At the back of my brain, I recognize the beginnings of panic. Are they in trouble? Should I call for help? Dive in after them? I can't imagine what could be keeping them under for so long. *Come on, Emma. They're fine. They're simply skilled at swimming, like everything else.*

I check my plum again and can hardly believe what I'm seeing—it's been more than four minutes since they first went in. I'm sure of it. My heart racing, I scroll to the Darkwood emergency icon. Something is wrong. No matter how trained they might be, no one holds their breath for *that* long. I haven't seen the slightest disturbance on the surface of the lake. If they aren't swimming, what are they doing under there?

I'm about to click the emergency button, my pulse hammering in my throat, when it happens. In one clean motion, the figures cut through the glasslike lake, bursting into the air like dolphins at a show.

I let out a breath as I watch them swim toward the shore. Each strong, lithe movement is synchronized. The Similars climb out of the lake onto the bank, shaking the water off their clothes as though what they did was perfectly normal. Seeing them lined up like this, I am enthralled by their athleticism, their beauty. None of them have the same body build, and yet, they all share the same physical strength and skills from training on Castor Island.

As the Similars head away from the lake toward campus, it dawns on me that the water they climbed out of must be freezing. A week ago, I dug out my heavy coat from the back of my closet, and I'm wearing it. Even so, I'm cold. And here they are, soaked through, none of them the slightest bit bothered.

Theodora and Maude sprint toward a nearby tree. Theodora starts climbing, and Maude follows right behind her. In what feels like seconds, Theodora has reached a branch about ten feet up. She stands slowly, meticulous with her movements as she steadies herself by holding onto a branch above her head, and then she lets go. I watch her creep away from the trunk. My instinct is to be afraid for her. But as she steps one foot in front of the other, arms out like a gymnast on a balance beam, it's clear she's an expert with little, if any, fear of falling.

Her friends cheer her on. Not one of them shows any worry as she walks farther out onto the branch, gaining speed and confidence as she goes. I'm quite certain there's no way it will hold her weight. *Are they going to let her fall?* I wonder. *Would they do that to one of their own?*

Just as the branch is beginning to give way under her, she leaps off and lands steadily on her feet on the sand. The Similars hoot and holler, clapping her on the back. Maude follows suit. I watch her climb the tree—only she ventures higher, to a branch above Theodora's. Her ascent is quick, and her descent is even quicker. She jumps down from what must be twenty feet in the air. This time, her fellow clones catch her in their arms.

I'm bowled over by the sheer physicality of what I'm seeing. The synchronized diving, the climbing, balancing, leaping. I'm also disturbed by it. Normal teenagers wouldn't be able to do half of what the Similars just did. Normal teenagers couldn't hold their breath for that long or balance on a branch that high. I'm certain of it. Something is not right. The Similars are beautiful and lithe and fiercely confident. But they are also, somehow, inhuman.

I have to go. I can't let them spot me, not after what I've seen. I don't know why exactly, but I know in my gut that I can't let *them* know what I know. I spin on my heels and start back to Cypress. I move faster the farther I get from the lake and the Similars, with their eerie middle-of-the-night routines.

A hand clasps my arm.

I spin around, ready to defend myself, but when I face my attacker, I'm staring into familiar eyes. Levi's eyes. I move to slide out of his grip when I notice the blood in the moonlight. Levi has a gash on his bicep, maybe four inches long. It's bleeding.

"Your arm—" I exclaim as I reach for him. Levi pulls back.

"I must have scraped it on a rock when I was coming out of the water. I thought I felt something sharp."

"It's deep," I say firmly. "You might need stitches."

"I'm fine," he says, crossing his arms over his chest, dismissing my suggestion. "I know you saw us, Emma. Diving into the lake. Climbing that tree."

"Yes," I say carefully. "I did."

"I can explain."

"Oh, I'm sure you can," I seethe, suddenly furious at him. "Just like you can explain how you helped your guardian dupe Booker and Jane out of shares of their own company."

Pain flashes across Levi's face, but not physical pain. He hardly acknowledges the gash on his arm. But inside, it's a different story.

"They told you," he says.

"Yes. And I've been racking my brain to understand how or why you would do that. But I've only been able to come up with one explanation: you did it to hurt them."

"Is that what you believe?" Levi asks.

"I don't know," I answer honestly. "If you'd asked me this morning after I said goodbye to them, I would have said no. But now…" I falter. "I don't understand any of it. You. The other Similars. What I just saw."

"There are things I can't tell you, Emma, but that's not my choice—"

I don't give him a chance to finish. "Then you won't mind if I do. I'm happy to tell everyone about your extreme sports."

"That took years of practice. You'd be amazed what you can do if you're relentless. Some of the kids at Darkwood want to be world-class concert pianists and athletes. That takes talent, but mostly, it takes persistence. Hours doing nothing else. We swam on the island. Every single day. Sometimes for hours at a time. And Gravelle, he would time us. At first, we could only hold our breath for thirty seconds. It took years to learn how to do that, Emma."

"Why were you out here in the middle of the night?"

"Same reason you were." He shrugs, his wet T-shirt clinging to his chest. "Couldn't sleep."

"We should go," I say. "The midnight session starts soon.

Madison won't like it if we're late," I turn to leave. He reaches out and grabs my arm again.

"Emma, please," he says. "Hold on. Wait."

That's when I notice his arm. The gash. The one that was bleeding moments ago is almost entirely healed.

I must be seeing things. Was it on the other arm, the cut? But no. The skin on Levi's other arm is smooth and unblemished. The gash is still there, the same shape and size, only it doesn't look fresh anymore. It looks like it's a few days old, with blood dried around it.

Levi glances at his arm, then at my face. In a heartbeat, we both acknowledge how strange and *not right* this is. I'm suddenly aware of how alone we are on these dark, desolate grounds. Where are the other Similars?

Levi lets go of me—thank God, he lets go of me—and I step away from him. If I were to scream, no one would hear me but Levi's companions. And they are just as "other" as he is.

"I can't do this," I say. "The Wards are like my family. I can't know what I know and not do something about it. If they get hurt, or someone else I love..."

"Then what?"

"I could never live with myself. Levi, you have to explain it to me. Why you did that to Booker and Jane. Why your skin healed so fast. It's almost like you were never cut in the first place. Tell me or I tell everyone what I saw," I say, and I hate myself for threatening him, but there is too much at stake.

"You want to know, Emma?"

"Yes!"

"You want to know what happened with Jane and Booker's company? You want to know what my guardian has planned for them, for *all* the originals' families?"

I freeze. *What he has planned for them?*

"We were all sent here with tasks," Levi says quietly. "Me, Maude, Jago, Ansel, Pippa, and Theodora."

"Tasks?" I ask softly.

"Yes. We each have one."

"I don't understand."

"No," he says, scanning the horizon. "How could you. You think we're just kids. Teenagers attending Darkwood to get a top-notch education and prepare ourselves for the most prestigious Ivy League universities."

"Aren't you?" I ask, but I think I already know the answer.

Levi laughs. "We learned calculus at ten and biophysics at thirteen. We've read every classic and written our own. Maude's an expert computer programmer. Pippa could be playing flute at Carnegie Hall. Trust me, we don't *need* a Darkwood education."

"But your strata," I insist. "If you're all more advanced than us, Ansel and Jago should also be in the top five. You and your friends would have taken all *five* spots."

"Come on, Emma—think about it. Wouldn't that have been a tad suspicious?"

"What are you saying?"

"Jago and Ansel didn't—how should I put this?—'try their hardest' on the test. Frankly, none of us did. Though Maude, Theodora, and I still ended up with the top spots."

"You threw the test." I feel like an idiot.

"All part of Gravelle's plan, Emmaline. All part of his plan."

"What did you mean when you said you had tasks? What kind of tasks?"

"Isn't it obvious? Mine was to make sure Jane and Booker accepted me into their family and into the family business, so that Gravelle could seize shares of Ward, Inc. He's wanted to be a major stakeholder in their company for years."

"But why?"

"He says it's for my own good." Levi shrugs. "He told me I'd be reclaiming what was rightfully mine. He says I deserve it, that they owe me, as my DNA parents."

"But why would you need to sign your shares over to *him*?"

Levi shrugs again. "He thinks I might make emotional decisions as I get to know my DNA parents. If he owns the shares himself, he can act on my behalf."

"So you knew about this," I say, trying to comprehend. "You knew about this plan all along—this, this *task*, and you were always planning on going through with it?"

Levi stares into my eyes. "Yes." He has no shame, no remorse. "I did. And I played my role well," he says wryly. "You've wanted to hate me from the minute I arrived at Darkwood, but you never had a reason—except for the fact that I look like your dead best friend. Congratulations. Now you have all the justification you need. I'm going to get changed."

Levi walks away, and I'm left standing in that desolate field, wondering if everyone has been right all along. The Similars can't be trusted.

THE SUSPECT

THE WIND WHIPS at my cheeks and ears as I hurry back to Cypress, walking as briskly as I can without running. For the first time, I'm afraid of him, of the Similars. He explained about the stock, but he failed to tell me how his cut disappeared like that, so quickly. *Are they human?* I ask myself, the cold starting to pound in my head. *Who—no, what—are they?*

Pippa stands outside Cypress waiting for me. I check my plum. It's 11:55. How did she change and get here so fast? She holds out my key.

"You weren't in your room when I went by to get you for the session," she says as an explanation, and she puts the key around my neck. "If I were you, I'd be a little more careful where I left this. I walked right into your room and saw it on your bed."

For the first time, I cringe being so close to Pippa. She is one of them, after all. I don't know if I can trust her, or any of them.

I say nothing about what I saw as we walk together up the creaky stairs to the Tower Room. I never thought I would look forward to spending time with Madison, but at least in this group setting, I will be safe.

What are you afraid of, Emma? That they will hurt you? I run the first day of duty over in my mind again: both of us working, Levi and me. Both of us painting. Hearing Pru scream. Entering the boathouse together.

Is that what happened, or is my mind playing tricks on me? He carried Pru to safety, didn't he? Of course, there's the possibility that he did that to cover his tracks. But Levi couldn't be that fast, that devious, that disturbed as to have hurt Pru…could he? He shares Oliver's DNA. Oliver, who wouldn't hurt a fly. And yet, their upbringings. They were so drastically different. Oliver was so loved, Levi… I don't know. Abused? Brainwashed? Pushed to extremes or simply neglected? The way he dove under that water… It scares me to think how strong he might be. How easily he could have grabbed Pru.

It's the same with Pippa. She shares Pru's DNA, after all. *Surely she can't be dangerous*, I think, as I sit next to her, not taking off my coat. I'm shivering. I take in a sharp breath when Levi enters the room followed by Theodora and Maude. He doesn't meet my eyes as he sits between his fellow clones. The others arrive, all except Tessa. I wonder if she'll show, if anyone's seen her since the news about her father. Madison shuts the door. The click of the lock makes me jump.

"Welcome to the fifth midnight session of the school year," says Madison. I tune out her voice as I stare at Levi's arm that was bleeding only thirty minutes ago. I want there to be some explanation that doesn't scare the living daylights out of me, but I can't find it. My heart pounds, urging me to do something, *anything*. After all, the Similars are plotting to hurt the originals' families. Levi practically admitted it. How far will they go to get what they want?

There's a rapping at the door. We all watch as Madison walks over and opens it with her key. Tessa stands in the threshold. She looks thinner than ever, no doubt from skipping a few meals to avoid the dining hall.

"What did I miss?" she asks, breezing past Madison and taking a seat.

"I was about to tell the group there's good news," Madison announces. She turns to us, beaming. "My mother's been helping the National Anti-Cloning Commission push through new legislation. It'll go into effect this month."

"What kind of legislation?" I ask, my voice dull as I sneak a look at Pippa. She tenses. So do the other Similars, try as they might to appear calm.

"Good question, Emma. Too bad you weren't at the latest DAAM meeting or you'd already know."

I stare at Madison. I may not be the Similars' biggest advocate after what I've learned tonight, but that doesn't mean I'm going to let her steamroll me—or them.

"Clones will be required to obtain special visas to enter this country," Tessa declares, sounding pleased to deliver this news. I look over at her, puzzled as to how she can feel so little empathy after what happened to her father. "And parents who smuggle into the U.S. a child who's been produced via cloning technology— even a fetus in utero—may face fines or prison time."

"That will never happen," I say.

Madison shrugs. "Most people agree that clones pose a threat to America's core values. They're all dangerous."

"That's an incredibly broad generalization! And you're wrong. Most people do *not* think that way. I don't. I know they aren't dangerous—"

"Are you sure about that?" Madison presses.

I'm not. Not after tonight. In spite of wanting to believe the Similars are well-meaning, I can't ignore that they have come to Darkwood with an agenda. They are hiding things from us and from their DNA families. But why should that be reflective of all clones?

"Why do you hate them so much?" I ask, ignoring the voice in my head that tells me Madison might be right to be suspicious of our newest classmates. All kinds of people scheme. Look at Madison. And she has no excuse to be so cruel. She had everything she could have wanted growing up. Loving parents. Friends, a community. Opportunities to see the world. All the things the Similars were deprived of.

"Excuse me, Emma, but I don't have the slightest idea what you're talking about." Madison sounds so dismissive I could scream.

"Is it because of your parents? Have they taught you to fear what you don't understand?"

"They've taught me to fear people who are a threat."

"Was Prudence a threat?" I snap. "Is that why you attacked her?"

"Emma!" Pippa cries out.

I don't take my eyes off Madison. I assume she's going to be furious at me, lash out. Instead, she laughs. "Prudence Stanwick isn't even on my radar. I barely know who she is. I mean, *was*."

My blood boils. Madison turns back to her announcement, and it's clear that in her mind this conversation's over. *Not for me*, I think. I feel even more certain in my gut that she had something to do with Pru's attack.

When Madison finally releases us, I walk with Pippa back to our rooms in silence. I can't take it anymore, this avoidance.

"I saw you," I say as we approach my door. "Tonight. In the lake. Maude and Theodora climbing that tree."

"I thought so," Pippa says quietly.

"I know about the tasks. Levi told me."

"Emma, I wish I could explain…"

"But you can't. Of course you can't. Good night, Pippa." From what Levi said, she's charged with some task too, whatever it might be. I want to lash out at her for that, but there's been enough confrontation tonight.

I slip into my room and take a few deep breaths, trying to calm myself. But I need a distraction—anything. My eyes land on the book sitting on my desk. *To Kill a Mockingbird*. It's the book Jaeger gave me when he visited and told me and Pippa about Pru's medically induced coma. I haven't opened it yet, but losing myself in its pages is the perfect solution. I need to escape my own head.

I open the book to the first page and am surprised to find a note scrawled there.

Stop looking. You won't find her.

It's signed *JS*—Jaeger Stanwick. Pru's father. My heart plummets to my feet.

There's no denying he wrote this note for me. He gave me this book, brought it all the way here and made a point of encouraging me to reread it. It's also clear who the "her" is: Prudence.

I glance at Jaeger's note again. *Stop looking. You won't find her.*

Why, I want to shout, *because she's dead?*

I can't think straight. There's too much to process. The Similars' physical feats. The gash on Levi's arm. The tasks. Madison's mom's legislation.

And now this.

My heart races as I consider the implications of Jaeger's cryptic note. He's been ignoring my buzzes; Pippa's too. I tuck *To Kill a Mockingbird* under my arm and head back into the cold night.

There's only one person who can help me now. It's time to find him.

◇—◇—◇

Ten minutes later, I arrive at Headmaster Ransom's house on campus. I'm breaking curfew and a million other rules by being here, but that's far from important. I ring Ransom's bell.

Moments later, he opens the door in his robe and slippers, looking bewildered. "Emmaline Chance," he says. "It's the middle of the night!"

"I know. I can assure you, sir, this is urgent."

"By all means, then, come in." Ransom gestures for me to follow him inside. "You look pale. Sit. Let me get you some water."

I sink onto his couch, trying to calm my racing heart, and look around. His home is cozy and sparsely decorated.

He returns and hands me a glass. "I won't ask why you're out of your dorm room..." Ransom says as he settles back into a tufted leather chair, his pajama-clad legs crossed at the ankles, his house slippers in plain view.

"I'll get right to the point," I say, taking a deep drink of the water to fortify myself for what I have to do. "Headmaster Ransom, sir, I received some very unsettling information tonight." I pull out the copy of *To Kill a Mockingbird* and flip to the front page. "It's a note. From Prudence's father—Jaeger Stanwick. He told me and Pippa that Pru's in a hospital in her hometown, in a medically induced coma. Only this message..." I hand the novel to him so he can see it. "This message would suggest otherwise. He gave me this book the day he visited. I only noticed the message tonight."

As Ransom takes in the note, his face sags and then hardens. "I agree, this is unsettling, Emmaline."

"Jaeger told us the police think someone attacked her. Can you help, sir? Do you know why Jaeger would tell me not to look for her? Do you know who might have done this to her?"

"Oh, Emmaline, I'm afraid the investigation is up to the authorities. You see, as headmaster, I have power over my students," he says with a small, sad smile, "but little power when it comes to the law. Once Prudence left campus, she was no longer under my charge. I'm afraid I know as much about her condition and whereabouts as you do. As for who attacked her, perhaps I should ask you that question. After all, you were there that day at the boathouse when the incident occurred."

"Yes," I respond quickly, "but I would have told you if I knew anything. I don't. I was listening to music. Putting on primer. Levi and I were working side by side when we heard Prudence scream. When we got inside, when we found her lying in that canoe, it was too late to catch whoever hurt her. We were all alone. Though, if I may speak freely, sir…"

"Please do."

"There is only one person at Darkwood who hates Prudence enough to want to hurt her."

Ransom raises an eyebrow. "Go on."

"Madison Huxley," I say. "She's made it clear from our first Ten meeting that she didn't think Pru deserved to be there."

Ransom no longer lounges across from me. He sits at attention.

"That's quite an accusation, Ms. Chance. What proof do you have that Ms. Huxley is capable of committing such an egregious crime?"

"I don't have any, not exactly. But she missed an appointment, something about getting her blood work taken? And it was the same afternoon Prudence was attacked—"

"Without proof, accusing Madison Huxley of such a crime would be pure speculation. Madison is the leader of the Ten. She has never acted unworthy of that role—no matter how you might feel about her," he adds pointedly.

"But who else would have done this to her? If this was an attempt to hurt Prudence, or worse, to *kill* her, then who is responsible? The only people there, at least as far as we know, were me and Levi!"

Ransom studies me. The lines crinkling around his eyes make him look sad and burdened. "The answer may be right under your nose, Emmaline."

"You aren't suggesting I did this."

"Obviously not. Prudence was one of your best friends."

It hits me like a ton of bricks. "Then Levi?"

Ransom nods.

"It couldn't have been him." I shake my head. "That doesn't make sense. He was standing next to me the whole time."

"Are you sure about that?" he presses. I remind myself that I can trust Headmaster Ransom. He has no reason to suspect Levi, and all the reason in the world to prove the students he invited to Darkwood deserve our trust.

"Absolutely," I say, though deep down I question myself. "My plum ran out of battery just before we heard Pru scream. Otherwise I wouldn't have even heard her," I say, running the events of that afternoon through my mind. "Levi was right next to me when it happened. I'm sure of it because we looked at each other," I add. "I remember when our eyes met. We were both shocked."

"But suppose Levi went into the boathouse, attacked Pru, then returned to your side. He could have been back beside you in an instant," Ransom suggests.

I shake my head. "No. Even if that's possible, he didn't know Prudence. Why hurt her?"

"That's not entirely true, Emmaline," Ransom says. "Don't forget he has a friend who shares Prudence's every feature."

"Pippa? You think Levi attacked Prudence because of something that had to do with her Similar?"

Ransom sighs, leaning back against his tufted chair. It squeaks from his body weight. "Is that so out of the question?"

I tense, remembering everything I've learned about the clones today.

"Sir," I say, breathless. "Do you still trust them? The Similars, I mean?"

Ransom studies me. If my question has ruffled him, he doesn't let it show. "I invited them to Darkwood, didn't I?"

"Yes," I say. "But..." I stop myself. *Should I say this? Is it the right thing to do?* "But, sir, what if I told you they are not as they first appear? They have special abilities..."

Ransom doesn't answer me immediately. Finally, he speaks. "Emmaline, excuse me if I'm overstepping, but would I be wrong to point out that you've had quite a challenging year? First Oliver's death, then Prudence's attack..."

I nod.

Ransom continues, "Let me give you some advice, if I may. Go back to your room. Get some rest. There isn't anything you can do for Prudence that her father isn't already doing. As for who did this to her, it is not your job to identify the perpetrator. Leave that to the police. Or to Prudence, when she wakes up from her coma, God willing."

I want to heed Headmaster Ransom's advice. I want nothing more than to return to my room and sleep like my peers. I look at the empty glass in my hands. I'm suddenly so incredibly tired and so strangely calm. Ransom walks me to the front door, exhorting me to return to Cypress safely. When I get back to my room, I fall straight into bed. I sleep soundly. I don't dream.

The next morning, I am inexplicably lighter. My talk with Ransom has made me feel, in some way, less alone. I'm still worried about Pru and more than a little disturbed by what I've learned about the Similars, but having Ransom in my corner is a relief. I'm not expecting it when two police officers corner me on my way to breakfast.

"Emmaline Chance?" asks a female officer. I recognize her from the clearing, from the day Pru was rushed to the hospital. A male cop is with her. He is silent, middle-aged, balding.

"Yes?"

"In light of new developments in the case, we've received permission from Headmaster Ransom to question you about the events of September fifteenth. The day you found Prudence Stanwick unconscious in the boathouse."

"You are not a suspect in the case," the male cop reassures me. "But we'd like to get your perspective on the events of that day."

"To help us piece together what happened," the female cop adds gently.

"There's nothing to tell," I say, feeling my cheeks flushing with heat. "I was priming the side wall of the boathouse. Levi and I were working together when someone screamed. We ran inside and found my roommate, Prudence."

"We'd like to walk down to the boathouse with you," the female cop says. "Have you take us through that afternoon, step by step. It is your right to have a parent present—"

I stop her right there. No need to call my father. I know what I will tell them: the truth. My father being here won't change that.

Still, dread begins in my toes and travels up my spine. There can only be one reason they are here asking me these questions. One of us is a suspect. And if they say it's not me, then it's Levi.

❖──┤├──❖

Returning to the boathouse is painful. It brings back memories of that afternoon. I expected yellow police tape to circle the canoe where I found Pru's body, but apparently the police have collected whatever evidence and photographs they needed. It is no longer a crime scene.

Still, the officers interrogate me for nearly an hour. They ask where I was standing, where Levi was standing. What we were doing and when. Where exactly I stood when I discovered Pru. How Levi reacted. I remind them that Levi carried Prudence all the way to safety. All he wanted was to help her, I explain.

And yet, when they ask me whether it's possible that Levi could have slipped away while I was lost in thought, and—by my own admission—avoiding talking to him because of his resemblance to Oliver, I have to confess that yes, it was.

"So you admit that you couldn't see Levi the entire time you were painting?" asks the male cop.

"I was looking at the *wall*, so no, I wasn't looking at him the entire time."

"He wasn't always in your line of sight, then?" the female cop prods.

"I already told you. No. That doesn't mean he had time to go and attack Prudence…"

"It might not be probable. But if it's at all *possible*…"

"Then what? You'll arrest him?" I say, my voice hot.

"Not without proper evidence, no," says the male cop. "Both of your fingerprints were all over this boathouse. But that's not enough for us to go on—not yet."

"This has been helpful, Ms. Chance," the female cop says with finality. "More than you know. We'll spend a few more minutes here, but you are free to go."

On the walk back to campus, I can think of nothing except the police twisting my words. They weren't interested in the truth, only in the holes they could poke in my story. It's so frustrating, especially because I know that, based on the facts, he couldn't have done it.

By the time I reach the main campus, I've missed breakfast. I'm ragged, dragging my feet through the morning routine and my first three classes. By midday, I'm starving. I practically burst through the doors of the dining hall. I don't care what they're serving, I'll eat it.

The cafeteria is uncharacteristically silent. There's no bustle, no gossiping. Every single student has their eyes glued to the Similars. They're huddled at the side of the room with three police officers. Two questioned me a few hours ago, but the third I don't recognize. I can't tell if the officers are trying to make a show of it, but their conversation is center stage.

"Levi Gravelle," says the male officer who interrogated me. "New information has been brought to light in the attempted murder of Prudence Stanwick, and we have permission to escort you back to the police station for questioning."

My breath catches in my throat. *New information? Is this because of what I told the officers this morning? What have I done?*

Whispers ripple through the room. My classmates are saying Levi must be a suspect, that the police must believe he did it. I search Levi's face for some sign that he's okay or some sign that he isn't—but his face is blank. Pippa and Theodora stand by his side, their faces betraying their worry. Jago and Ansel confer quietly with each other, while Maude stands silently behind them, her arms crossed over her chest.

"You have the right to call an attorney and to have an attorney and your legal guardian present during questioning," the cop continues.

Cold air floods in as the door by me opens. "Is this really necessary?" bellows a voice, and everyone turns to see Headmaster Ransom charge in, his silver hair standing up on end, his tie crooked.

"Evidence suggests that Ms. Stanwick's injuries were not the result of an accident," says the female officer. "Mr. Gravelle was present at the time of the attack."

So was I! I want to shout out, but they don't think I did it. And they're right. *But neither did Levi,* I tell myself.

"Are you arresting me?" Levi asks.

"No," answers the female cop.

Theodora inserts herself into the conversation. "Then he doesn't have to go with you."

"He doesn't," the female cop agrees. "But things will go a lot more smoothly if he cooperates."

"He needs a lawyer," Theodora insists. She turns to Levi, grabbing him and whispering something in his ear.

Levi runs a hand through his hair. "I'll go," he says to the officers. "But Theodora's right. I won't talk until I have a lawyer present."

"Our guardian will call one," Theodora announces.

"One of us should go with you," Maude says.

"No," says Levi quickly. Then he says something in a language I don't understand but the other Similars do. Probably Portuguese again. All I can make out is the name of their guardian. *Gravelle.*

"What are we waiting for, then?" Levi addresses the officers. "Let's go. I'd prefer not to miss all of my afternoon classes."

The police officers guide Levi across the dining hall to the double doors where I am standing. My heart jackhammers in my chest as they approach. I try to make eye contact with Levi, but he doesn't look at me, just stares straight ahead. It's not until he's about three feet from me that his eyes meet mine—those gray eyes I've tried for months to interpret, like some sort of ancient rune. The look between us is brief. I try to tell him that it's going to be okay. That I'm sorry. That I know he didn't do it. An instant later, the officers steer Levi past me, and he's gone.

Within moments, the entire room is abuzz. One of our own—one of the Ten, no less—is a suspect in an attempted murder case. I hear my classmates going back to eating, gossiping, and speculating over their lunches, their voices drenched in shock and judgment. But I'm frozen by the door. My stomach churns. There's no way I can eat lunch now.

Headmaster Ransom strides toward the exit. "Sir," I say hoarsely.

He stops to survey me, his face giving away no emotion. "Yes, Emmaline?"

"What happened? Last night, you told me to stop thinking about it. About who might have attacked Prudence..."

"I did, didn't I?"

I find the lack of emotion in his voice troubling. "Then what, why—?"

"After you left," Ransom says, "I could not deny that there was, in fact, an opportunity for Levi to have attacked Prudence. I placed a call to the police this morning, suggesting that they question you. You understand, of course. I have the safety of my students to consider. Don't blame yourself, Ms. Chance. You came to me because you care. So do I. About Prudence, and the entire student body. Now, if you'll excuse me..."

He walks off, leaving me standing there watching his retreating form.

PROPERTIES

NO ONE TALKS about anything except Levi for the rest of the day. When I spot Madison in the dining hall that evening handing out fresh new DAAM flyers, I make a mental note to find some proof that she did this to Pru, as soon as humanly possible.

At least Levi has returned to school. He sits with the other Similars at dinner, and for maybe the first time ever, he's not reading a book. He talks quietly, an untouched tray of food in front of him. Pippa puts an arm around him. The others huddle in close.

I wonder if they're talking about me. Word has gotten out that I gave a statement to the police—my version of the events surrounding Pru's attack. I feel manipulated and foolish. Why had I let myself panic, tracking down Headmaster Ransom in the middle of the night? Why hadn't I kept my mouth shut? Though the Similars can make me uncomfortable, I don't believe, deep down, that Levi would have hurt Prudence. But Levi doesn't know that. If he's heard the rumors, he knows I had something to do with him being questioned. And Pippa must know too, which would explain why she hasn't walked over to sit with me or even waved hello. Our last interaction was tense, to say the least, but we both care about Pru. I'm still dying to show her *To Kill a Mockingbird* and Jaeger's note. Now doesn't feel like the right time.

When I see Levi get up from the table and bus his tray, I excuse myself and follow him outside. He must not see me because when I call out his name, he turns, surprised. We're standing on a lit path outside the dining hall. Students shuffle past, some sneaking glances at us before moving on. We aren't completely alone, but we're alone enough to talk.

"What is it, Emma?"

"I did something."

Levi doesn't respond. I can't tell if he looks betrayed, heart-broken, angry, or all of the above.

"I went to see Headmaster Ransom last night. I told him I thought Madison attacked Pru," I say, forcing myself to act more confident than I feel. "I wanted to get his help. Ransom said he trusted you. He never would have invited you and the other Similars here if he didn't. But then he asked the police to question me this morning. They tried to poke holes in my story. I defended you! Please, Levi. You have to know I didn't say anything to hurt you. I love Pru. The idea of her in a coma, or dead—it's killing me."

I take a deep breath before continuing. "The thing is, Levi. Maybe if you had explained it all to me: The cut on your arm. The tasks. Maybe I wouldn't have felt so completely in the dark. Maybe if something in my life made sense—"

"You want to know what it all means?" Levi interrupts me.

"Yes! God, yes. I want to trust you. I don't *think* you attacked Prudence. I don't *want* to believe you would do anything to hurt anyone—but how am I supposed to *know* that? Particularly when all of your secrets make you seem dangerous."

"Our bodies don't work like yours, Emma. Sure, we have the same organs and bones and cells. But there are properties," he says softly, almost reverently, not looking at me. It's almost like he can't. "Ways our bodies function that no one can explain."

We've wandered over to a bench, away from the other students. It's quiet, so quiet I can hear my own breath as it leaves my body.

"It was Seymour," Levi continues. "His famous primate experiment, the one I asked you not to question. Albert Seymour cloned some monkeys in his lab using a slightly different technique than his tried-and-true protocol. Later, when Seymour was studying them, he discovered that they were impervious to certain diseases, far less likely to get sick than the original monkeys they were cloned from. He eventually figured out that their wounds healed faster, and that their bones were about forty times harder to break."

"So if they fell," I start, "like from a tree…"

Levi nods and finishes my thought, "They wouldn't be harmed."

"And you and the Similars..."

"We were created using this same technique."

"But why?" I ask.

"We believe someone in Seymour's lab knew about his results with the monkeys and chose to re-create the experiment."

"So most clones aren't like you. They don't have special attributes."

"No. Every other clone, at least that I know of, has been conceived in the traditional way. Somatic cell nuclear transfer. After Seymour had those surprising results with the primates, he wrote a paper on it—the one Mr. Park referred to—but it was never published in any journals. He buried it in his files. I think he was worried about the implications of being able to clone people with 'atypical' capabilities."

"So you're saying someone who worked for Seymour defied his wishes and cloned you and your friends using this alternate method—without Seymour's knowledge?"

"Yes."

"Or maybe Seymour did it."

"I suppose that's possible. But why does it matter?"

"It matters because whoever did so must have had an agenda. And maybe that explains why you and the other Similars were created. Are you all the same?" I ask pointedly. "You, Pippa, Jago, and the others? Do you have the same capabilities? If they get wounded, do they heal quickly too?"

"Not exactly," he says. "We're all different in that respect.

I don't bleed for very long. It has to do with the way my blood clots. Jago, for example, is stronger than me. He can lift twice as much as you'd expect from someone his size. Theodora doesn't bruise, ever, but I do. Our bodies can withstand more trauma than the average human, but we're not unbreakable. And if we're like the monkeys, we won't age like regular people. We'll plateau. The monkeys did, anyway."

"What do you mean, you'll plateau? You won't get older?"

"We're not totally sure." He shrugs. "It's simply one more way in which we're different. That's the polite way of saying we're freaks. It's the reason our guardian told us we'd never lead normal lives."

"You don't know that," I insist.

"Don't I? Look, Emma. Do you understand why I didn't tell you all this earlier at the lake? You were never supposed to see that. You were never—*are* never—supposed to know."

"Of course not," I say hotly. "Because I'm never supposed to know anything about you. About your life. About what you feel, or think, or believe. I knew nearly everything about Oliver, but you're not him!"

"Is that really how you see me?" he asks. His voice sounds so painfully sad.

A sudden guilt washes over me. I know he's kind. I know he's the most infuriating person I've ever met, and also the most insightful. I know he's suffered. I know he shares Oliver's DNA, and yet they are not the same. But I can't. I don't…

"Yes," I say instead. "Yes, that's how I see you—"

"It's for your own good!" he shouts, then lowers his voice.

"You have to trust me, Emma. I've just told you the one thing that is very much in my self-interest—and yours—for you to never know about." He gets up and starts to walk away.

"What?" I ask, my own voice coming out violent. I get up too. "That I can't hurt you?" I follow my question by pushing him, hard—hard for me, anyway. Levi isn't expecting my sudden outburst and trips backward a step before finding his footing. I see something in his eyes engage. I'd never win against him in a fight, but what I'm doing isn't logical; it's primal. I push him again, even harder this time. "That you're the only one who has the power to hurt me? And not the other way around?"

Levi doesn't say anything. I think he's too stunned. I keep pushing him, over and over, until my pushes turn into punches. "I can't hurt you, right? I can't cause you pain because of your 'special properties'?"

I treat his torso like a punching bag, hitting harder with each blow. "You said Theodora never bruises? Well, I'm glad you do!" I shove at him with all my strength, then collapse into myself.

Levi catches me in his arms. He holds me so tight I almost can't breathe. Leaning against his body, I can feel his every breath as his chest rises and falls, rises and falls. We don't speak. He keeps his arms fixed around me, and I let him.

Oh my God, I think. *What did I do, lashing out at him like that?* I start to apologize. "Levi—" Suddenly, his lips are on mine. Our mouths meet, and heat rushes from my head to my outer extremities as I kiss him back.

I can't explain it. I can't control it. But we are both hungry and desperate. Our kiss is anything but soft or sweet. It is hard, raw. Ugly, even. Yet inexplicably tender too. The heat from our bodies merges. Somewhere in the back of my mind I register that this is inadvisable, not good for either of us—*is it?*—and yet, all I want is in front of me, right now. *Don't stop.*

But he does. Abruptly. He lets go of me, and we step back. I feel the absence of his touch instantly. It's cold and unwelcome. I dislike it.

Levi runs his hands through his hair. My heart thuds so loudly in my chest, I'm sure he can hear it.

"Did we just—?" Levi asks.

"Yes," I answer softly, finally meeting his eyes.

"We don't even like each other," he says.

"No," I answer. "We don't."

For a minute, we're both silent.

"Emma?"

"Yes?" I answer quickly.

"Please forget everything I told you. I'm not saying this for my sake. It's for yours too."

Is he serious? "I'm not a bot," I snap. "I can't reboot myself and pretend I don't know that you and the Similars have special *powers.*"

"They aren't powers! For God's sake, Emma. What I told you—"

"You told her?" asks a bleak voice. We both turn to see five figures standing behind us in the lamplight. It's Maude, Jago, Theodora, Ansel, and Pippa.

Did they see us? Did they see…everything?

I'm nearly certain they did. I have no idea how long they've been standing there, but it's not like we're particularly hidden.

"She knows?" Maude asks as she looks from Levi to me and back again.

"Yes. I told her, but not on purpose…"

"Irrelevant!" Maude shouts before regaining her composure. "It doesn't matter why you told her. She knows. That changes everything."

"She knows about the tasks too," says Pippa. The others turn to look at her.

"You told her about those?" Theodora asks, incredulous.

"She found out when Jane and Booker's shares of Ward, Inc. were transferred to our guardian," Levi says in explanation. "It was bound to come out. It's not as though she knows the details…"

"Just that we have them," says Ansel. Levi nods. I cross my arms over my chest, ignoring the chill running up my spine. I feel cornered. Surrounded. *They're just like you, Emmaline. Human beings with super strength*, I remind myself, then push that thought out of my head.

"I'm standing right here, you know," I say, finding my nerve. "You don't have to talk about me like I'm not here."

Maude turns to face me, her features stern. "I suppose you think you're going to tell the whole world about us, then," she says. "About our capabilities. All of it."

"No," I answer. "I wouldn't. There's only one thing I care about, and that's finding out who attacked Pru. She deserves justice. And—and I want Levi to get his life back to normal."

"Normal," says Maude. "That's something none of us will

ever know, though it's sweet of you to suggest it. Love can do that to a person. I get it. When I fell in love with Jago, the rest of my friends didn't speak to me for a month. They said I was impossible to be around." She smiles at Jago, who laughs and walks over to kiss her. But I barely process any of that—I'm too mortified as I look over at Levi, embarrassed by what Maude's implied. Only he's leaning close to Theodora, talking to her. No, not just talking to her—he has his arm around her. After a moment, they look over at the rest of us, as though they'd forgotten we were here.

I stare at Levi and Theodora. No one says a word, especially not me.

"Emma and I—we got caught up in the moment," Levi finally explains. "The kiss, it didn't mean anything. We don't even like each other. Right, Emma?"

I stare at him and Theodora. He's still got his arm around her. I'm so confused I can hardly speak.

"Right," I say. They're standing there, so close, like a couple. *Like a couple.* That's exactly what they are.

A couple.

Levi and Theodora. Tessa's look-alike. She and Levi have some kind of history. They're an *item*. I'd always thought their relationship was platonic, not noticing there was anything more there than familial love. But Maude and Jago are a couple. Why shouldn't Levi and Theodora be one too? I look from Levi back to Theodora. I can't believe I didn't see it, that I never realized.

Then why the hell was he just kissing me?

"Can we wrap this up?" Pippa offers, and I'm so relieved to

hear her say this, it's all I can do not to hug her. "Emma isn't going to tell anyone what she knows about us. I trust her."

"Thank you," I mouth to Pippa.

"Fine," says Maude. "Let's go. You coming, Levi? Thea?" Maude calls in their direction as she turns and starts walking back toward the dorms.

Levi sighs and starts after her, holding Theodora's hand as they walk. He doesn't even glance in my direction. Pippa shoots me one last look before following the other Similars, and I am left behind, feeling like a fool.

THE RALLY

FOR THE NEXT two weeks, I avoid Levi. How could I have felt close enough to him to let him kiss me, yet have had no idea that he and Theodora are a couple? *That kiss was a mistake*, I remind myself as I stuff my feet into my slippers and shuffle to the window, staring out at Dark Lake.

Then why did it feel so entirely wonderful?

I don't let my mind go to the million places it wants to—like wondering how long he and Theodora have been dating, wondering why I was so clueless, and if Levi ever planned to tell me.

It's not only him I want to avoid. It's all of them. I can't deny I felt like prey, the Similars ringed around me, so troubled, so melancholy. And I've never been as mortified in my life as when they caught me and Levi kissing.

Thankfully, I have studying for winter exams to distract me. And though I dread going home for the mandatory winter break, I make plans to interrogate my father about Albert Seymour and John Underwood. Even in my humiliation over what happened with Levi, I can stay focused on figuring out what Oliver was trying to tell me, and proving Madison's guilt.

The last day of school before vacation, I'm bussing my tray when Levi and the Similars walk into the dining hall. I hurry toward the door. I don't want to risk seeing Levi and Theodora with their arms around each other.

"He didn't mean to hurt you," Pippa says before I can escape.

"I know that," I respond, even though I don't. Not really. But I can't talk to Pippa about that. Not now or maybe ever. "I'm going home tomorrow," I say as the Similars call her over. She starts to walk off. "Pippa, wait. About Pru…"

She turns. "What about her?"

"Jaeger left a note for me the day he visited. In that book he gave me. He said… He said I should stop looking for her." I feel tears pooling in my eyes and don't try to stop them. "I still don't know what he meant, but I thought… I thought you should know."

"I have to go," she says, giving me a quick hug, "but thank you. For telling me." I watch her walk off, then run smack into Archer and Ansel on my way out of the dining hall. Archer's clapping Ansel on the back, telling him how psyched he is about Ansel's first Christmas in California.

"It's going to be sweet, dude. My dads have a Malibu crash pad. It's sick."

"And you're sure they want me there?" Ansel asks.

"'Course. You're one of the family now. Look, let me give you a couple of tips. My dads are exercise freaks, so bring sneakers. First thing we do Christmas morning is hike up to the Hollywood sign. Ansel, buddy. Don't look so worried."

I walk off before I can hear the rest, wondering vaguely what task Ansel was given by his guardian, and if he's going to get started over the holidays.

◇―┤├―◇

"Genevieve," I call out from the sofa in my father's living room, my voice initializing our household bot. "What do you know about Albert Seymour?"

I'm back home in San Francisco. Normally Oliver and I would spend our breaks binge-watching movies together, but now I'm determined to learn more about Seymour's time at Darkwood. He is, after all, the reason the Similars are who they are—special attributes and all. That alone compels me to dig up everything I can about him.

"Looking him up now," Genevieve responds. Unlike Dash, Genevieve isn't my *friend*. Blunt and to-the-point, she gets things done, scanning documents and articles faster than any bot I've ever interfaced with.

"Thanks—"

"You know about his cloning lab, I assume," she cuts in before I can say more. "His pivotal research…"

"Yes," I say, sitting up a little straighter. "Everything

about his days at Harvard and beyond has been thoroughly documented—except for his primate experiment. That's not in any of the literature I've found. And there's hardly anything about his years at Darkwood. He was there at the same time as my father, and the parents of several of my classmates. Plus, his brother was there…"

"His half brother, you mean? John Underwood?"

"Exactly. I can't find anything on him either."

"He was expelled," Genevieve says briskly. "Underwood, I mean. At the end of his junior year."

"Really?" This is news to me. "Why? What did he do?"

"Seymour was working in a research lab on the Darkwood campus. Something to do with animals. A precursor experiment to cloning, I presume. Underwood let the subjects loose on some kind of ill-advised dare."

I stand and start pacing the room. "Underwood got kicked out of Darkwood?" I stop by the fireplace in front of an old photograph of my parents. In it, they look young, happy. "Where are you getting this info from?"

"The source is a bit shady," Genevieve admits. "I might have hacked a few personal emails…"

"Is there anything else?" I ask, ignoring that last part. If Genevieve did something untoward, I don't want to know about it.

"No," she answers. "That's all I've got."

I spend pretty much the entire vacation alone, with only my research and Genevieve and Dash to keep me company. When I tell Dash about Underwood's expulsion, he sounds hurt that I asked Genevieve for help instead of him. I remind him that I have so few actual friends, he has nothing to worry about. I still need him.

I miss Prudence so much it hurts, but short of showing up at the farm and demanding to see her, I don't know what else I can do. Jaeger hasn't responded to any of my buzzes, and the last thing I want is to upset her parents, particularly not with her mom so ill…

I try to keep my mind occupied, thinking about Seymour's brother. I'm still reeling over the fact that Underwood was expelled in his junior year. Could Seymour have had something to do with it? I don't know how or if it is relevant, but something in my gut tells me it is.

I only have to endure one awkward dinner with my father on Christmas Day—the one holiday where even he can't claim to have work obligations. I slip in a few questions between bites of in vitro steak. There's no easy way to start a conversation with my father, so I just come out with it. "You never talk about being in the Ten. How come? Is there a reason you don't want me to know about it?"

My father looks up from his plate. If he's surprised, he doesn't show it. "It was a long time ago, Emma. A lot has changed since then." He sighs, carefully separating his vegetables from his meat. "Why are you interested?"

"For starters, *I'm* part of the Ten this year, or didn't you get the memo?"

"And I'm proud of you, honey, though not surprised. You always manage to do well academically, in spite of… Well, you know."

"What?" I ask, my cheeks growing hot. "My best friend dying? Or do you mean Levi? Is this your way of acknowledging that Oliver's clone showed up at Darkwood? Since I got home, you haven't mentioned two words about Oliver, or Levi, or your call with Headmaster Ransom at the start of the semester."

My father opens his mouth, maybe to apologize, though I sincerely doubt it. Whatever he's about to say, he never gets the chance. The view space above our dining table beeps with a news alert.

"Protestors gathered today in Sacramento on the capitol's steps," the automated voice booms out over us, "to rally against a recent ruling that allows couples to seek out reproductive cloning in the state of California. Many believe this ruling is a slippery slope toward clone assimilation and clones' rights."

I stare at the feed, horrified as I watch thousands of Americans brandishing anti-clone signs, pumping their fists in the air and crying, "Say no to clones!"

The reporter continues, "California is the first state to rule in favor of clones' rights, arguing last month that clones should receive equal protection under the law, and that border checks are unconstitutional. But many do not agree with the ruling—"

There's a click, and the room goes silent. My father has turned off the feed.

"Why did you turn it off?"

My father adjusts his napkin in his lap. "Because that protest is abhorrent. Because the idea that clones aren't people like us, people who eat and breathe and feel the same emotions that we do... I couldn't stand to watch another second of it."

"Oh." I'm chastened. I had no idea he felt so strongly about clones' rights. The way I do. But of course, he raised me. Distant as he is, he's shaped what I believe. And when it comes to clones and the Similars... I feel sick, thinking of Pippa, and Maude, and Ansel...and, of course, Levi. He doesn't deserve that. None of them do.

My father interrupts my thoughts. "Are you friends with him? With Levi?"

"No, Levi and I will never be friends. Or anything else," I mutter. We finish our meal, and I don't ask my father about Underwood's expulsion. I'm sure he won't give me any useful answers, anyway. I'll have to find them some other way.

Returning to Darkwood, I spend most of the flight trying not to imagine what I will say to Levi when I'm eventually forced to talk to him. Maybe I can avoid him forever. *Yeah, right.*

When I step out of the car that delivers me to the main house and see all the warm reunions among my classmates, it's not lost on me that nearly everyone I love is no longer here at school. I feel a pang of longing, wondering where Pippa and the Similars—including Levi—went over the holiday. They all couldn't have gone home with their originals like Ansel.

I'm so caught up in my thoughts, I barely notice the flyers plastered across campus about the first rally for DAAM, the Darkwood Academy Anti-Cloning Movement. Of course, I'm not out of the loop for long. Not with the entire campus buzzing about it, and Madison talking it up to anyone who will listen.

"It doesn't make sense," a couple of sophomores say. "Why is Ransom allowing this? Why's he giving that evil group a charter?"

I don't tell them that I don't trust anything Ransom says or does anymore. Still, it's hard to imagine why Ransom would allow a rally like this to take place at Darkwood. I feel like the founders of the school would turn over in their graves if they knew this kind of discrimination was happening on their beloved campus. The *only* positive to this rally is that Madison seems to be too preoccupied to call any midnight sessions lately, and for that, I'm relieved.

That evening, I head to the rally. Boycotting it, I reason, would only make me ignorant to whatever Madison's planning. I head out of my dorm, following the crowd to the athletic center, where nearly the entire school has convened. From the look of it, not a single student is missing this.

A first-year girl shoves a leaflet into my hands as we funnel into the gym. Soon, I am surrounded on all sides. There are DAAM supporters and potential supporters, who are chanting the club's slogan, while others are wide-eyed and hushed as they prattle on about how horrifying, and simultaneously fascinating, this is. I scan the gathering for the Similars. I don't see them. I can't ignore the ache I feel when I think about what it would be like to be Theodora, Pippa, Maude, Jago, Ansel, or Levi. I would hate there being a rally to protest my very existence. It cuts me to the bone, on their behalf, and I have to suppress the tears that form in my eyes as I consider how wrong this is. How unfair.

Someone taps on a microphone, and a moment or two later, Madison Huxley walks up to a makeshift lectern and smiles at the crowd.

"I'm so pleased by the turnout." She basks in the spotlight

while Sarah Baxter plays the role of assistant, fiddling with Madison's microphone. I notice several of the boys, the ones Madison was charming in the dining hall, up front, waving and whooping their support. "First, I'd like to thank Headmaster Ransom for granting us our charter." Madison flashes her signature grin at Ransom, who's standing to the side of the staging area, watching the rally unfold, his arms over his chest, his face unreadable. A few other teachers dot the sidelines. They look serious, like they're here to stop any inappropriate behavior before it can start. But hasn't it started already? Isn't this entire rally, by its very existence, inappropriate?

Madison beams at the crowd. "I'd like to thank all of you for coming. From the look of it, most of Darkwood is in attendance, which means you're all here to listen to, and accept, the truth." There's a smattering of clapping from the audience. Madison waves off the applause. "No need for all of that. I'm not here because I get personal satisfaction out of public speaking. I'm here because I'm following in my parents' footsteps, taking on the mantle, the burden, if you will, of righting a huge wrong in our society. One that affects all of us—at Darkwood and beyond.

"Today, I would like to challenge you to look inside yourselves and ask an all-important question: Do you think it is right for your fellow citizens to be able to tamper with natural order, with biology, simply because they are vain or narcissistic or selfish enough to want to make an identical copy of themselves?

"Now, I'm sure you're thinking, 'Maybe it *is* vain or narcissistic or selfish to clone oneself, but what does that have to do with me?' Everything, my friends. Imagine a future world, one in which you have no control over your DNA. Imagine that scientists want to clone you—to take your DNA and make ten copies of you. A hundred copies. A thousand, even."

"No one wants a thousand copies of you!" someone shouts from the crowd.

"Maybe not," Madison says, maintaining her cool demeanor. "But if they did, would I—*should I*—have a say in it? Who owns my DNA, anyway? Scientists? Other people who want to play God? Or me?"

The crowd grows quiet as everyone contemplates that thought.

"Some people believe DNA is the window into the soul. I happen to agree. I believe it is the only thing each of us possess that is purely, uniquely ours. If we don't have control over our own DNA, we have no control over our destiny. And if that day comes—or should I say, *when* that day comes—we will have crossed an invisible barrier into a world where anything is permitted. Like stealing someone else's genes and using them for one's own gain. Or choosing embryos from a petri dish based on intelligence, or looks, or talent. Eugenics isn't a concept from a science fiction novel. It is a real possibility unless we take a stand, unless we stop those who wish to destroy the very essence of what makes us human and distinctly American: our individuality."

A few people start clapping. Others storm out of the gym, the door slamming behind them and echoing across the room. Madison holds up a hand to silence the applause.

"Who will you be if there are others exactly like you? What will make you special? I would argue—nothing. Because there *is* no point in being you if you are replaceable. If you are disposable. There's no point in earning that high stratum. No point in practicing those extracurriculars. No point in falling in love. Because someone else could do it for you. Someone else could take your place..."

My pulse quickens as I think of Levi. Madison's wrong. He and Oliver *aren't* one in the same.

Madison stares out at all of us. The crowd is hushed, completely rapt—even those who think she's totally off base are still mesmerized by Madison's audacity. And even though I don't agree with any of what she is saying, there is no denying that Madison is a very compelling speaker.

She lowers her voice. "When I found out I had been cloned—against my will, without my parents' permission—I was devastated. Someone had taken what makes me *me*, and shared it? Watered it down? Made me...irrelevant? I'll be honest. It took me weeks to crawl out of the emotional hole I dug for myself. Then I realized what I needed to do.

"My calling from this point on is to protect all of you, so that you never have to go through the same experience that I have. So that you never have to live with the reality that I wake up to every single day. The reality that I am not unique, and—as long as *she* exists—I never will be again.

"That starts with the Similars. We must make it clear to the world that their existence will not be tolerated. That we won't freely welcome clones into our homes and our schools. That they shouldn't have the same rights as the rest of us. Recent events have shown us that we can't trust them, not when one of them has allegedly attacked a fellow student."

I gasp. She means Levi. She is making this witch hunt about him. I feel sick to my stomach. This is not okay. Everything about what Madison just said is so completely twisted and unjust.

"Obviously, the Similars were not taught proper ethics or morals where they grew up. The truth is they should be sequestered from the rest of society, because of the threat they pose."

I stand, my blood boiling, and scan the crowd for teachers, for Ransom, someone with authority who can rein in Madison. But Ransom's gone.

"Read the leaflets. Think about what I've said today. You can buzz me or Sarah Baxter, my copresident, with any questions. In the meantime, I implore all of you to help us make the world safe again. Say no to clones. Say no to clones. Say no to clones!" she shouts, raising a fist in the air, echoing the chant I heard on the news during Christmas break.

Pockets of students begin to chant after her, quietly at first, then louder, and with increasing conviction. *No!* I want to shout out, but I know my voice would be lost in the din. Tears fill my eyes, hot and wet, as I drift to the back of the crowd to leave. I'm not the only one who is disturbed by Madison's message, but it's hard to push my way out of the throng. The battle cry grows stronger as more students shout, "Say no to clones! Say no to clones!"

I grab a student's arm—a girl who is chanting along with Madison. "Why are you doing this? What did clones ever do to hurt you? To make you feel this way?"

The girl meets my eyes, surprised I've addressed her. "They existed." I feel a lurch of nausea, and that's when I see them.

Madison, Tessa, and Jake are at the side of the gathering, forming their own little circle. They are joined by Ransom. And he doesn't look angry. He looks pleased.

THE LAB

I INCH THROUGH the crowd, wishing I could move faster as I make my way closer to Madison, Tessa, and Jake. I wonder what they're discussing with Headmaster Ransom. Why does he look so happy after that cringeworthy display of bigotry and intolerance? He was the one who invited the Similars to Darkwood in the first place. Has Ransom known about Madison's ill intentions all along? Has he been bought by her parents? Did he use Levi as a cover-up for the crime *Madison* committed? I know it's a long shot. Ransom might be weaker than I thought, but would he go so far as to frame one student to protect another whose parents are important financial donors? I don't know. All I know is that my conversation with him about my suspicions led him straight to the authorities.

I watch from a distance, unable to get close enough to hear what Madison, Tessa, and Jake are saying. From the look of it, the conversation is ending. They smile at Ransom. He walks off, and then the three of them start to leave, still conversing in their tight pack. I follow them outside, still brushing away the tears that fill my eyes. I am so upset at what I witnessed at that rally. But more than that, I feel disappointed on a cellular level. Most of those students have no reason to join in a chant like that except to fit in. It must make them feel momentarily good about picking on another group, one they don't or can't understand. But that feeling won't last. And kids at Darkwood are supposed to be above all that. Enlightened, even...

I feel even more motivated to follow my targets as they head toward the lake, walking in a close little formation, talking quietly among themselves. Tessa looks bored as always; Jake looks jovial enough. I notice that he brushes his fingers against Madison's as they walk, but she doesn't reciprocate the gesture. *So, he's still trying to win her over...*

The three keep walking, and so do I. I'm not too worried about being discovered. It's eight thirty and dark. If I'm quiet, I won't be noticed. We approach the brambly path that leads down to the boathouse. But instead of turning left, Madison, Tessa, and Jake turn right, heading farther into the brush. Now I'm perplexed—and on guard. Where are they going?

I follow them, but it's becoming difficult to keep my footsteps quiet on the rougher ground. I pause for a minute or two, letting them get farther ahead of me before I continue. Up in the distance is the research facility of cement-block construction. Is that where they're headed? That building hasn't been a working science facility in years, and it's definitely off-limits to students.

My curiosity is piqued. I follow them toward the stark building. I tense, every nerve ending in my body alert as they pause at the front door. Madison pulls out her key and flashes it in front of the door. Then she grabs the handle, turning it. It opens, and Tessa and Jake follow her inside. I have mere seconds to react. Without thinking, I run and shove the toe of my sneaker to catch the door. I've done it. I've kept the door open, and now I can get inside. I make sure not to let the door bang shut behind me, closing it softly.

How do they have access to this building? Did they get it from Ransom?

I stand alone in what looks like a lobby. Madison, Tessa, and Jake have already headed off, leaving me by myself. There's a desk and a couple of old couches. A lamp stands lonely in the corner, a stash of equipment next to it. On the desk are a couple of outdated computer monitors.

Directly in front of me is an elevator bank with two elevators. Did they go up? I'm about to start for them when I hear voices coming from around the corner. Cautious, I walk down the hall toward the voices.

"I'm not supposed to tell anyone yet. It could trigger a catastrophic ripple effect among the student body," Madison is saying.

"Harvard and every other Ivy League school, plus Stanford and Oxford?" Jake asks, sounding dazed.

"All of them. I got my acceptance letters over Christmas

break—plus running scholarships at every single one. They all want me for their track teams."

"But I didn't think you could even *get* early admission to more than one school at a time," says Tessa.

"You can't, unless you're me. It's going to be a tough decision..."

I stealthily peer into the classroom where they are sitting.

"We feel incredibly sorry for you," Jake says dryly. Tessa laughs. Madison scowls.

I scan the room. There's nothing too interesting in there, just old desks and blackboards stripped of any materials.

"Where's Fleischer?" asks Madison. "She said eight forty-five."

Fleischer? I wonder. *They're meeting Principal Fleischer here?* Does this have to do with that mysterious blood work they were talking about that day in the library after Pru's attack?

"She'll be here," Tessa says. "Ransom said she would be."

Prickles go up my back at the mention of his name. *Ransom. Headmaster Ransom knows about these meetings too?* Of course he does. He's the head of the school. He must know everything that's going on at Darkwood...good and bad. I have a feeling this might fall into the latter category.

"He seemed happy, don't you think?" Jake says. "After the rally?"

"Happy to keep up his charade as long as possible," Madison replies.

Charade? What *charade?*

I hear footsteps coming down the hall and realize it can only be one person—Fleischer. I turn to leave. As much as I want to know what these three are up to, and what Fleischer and Ransom have to do with it, she can't find me here. I don't have access to this building, and I'm certain Fleischer will punish me for it. The last thing I need right now is more duty. Or worse.

I bolt to the end of the hall, away from the sound of the clacking shoes, where I'm met by another elevator bank. I jump inside and press the button for the top floor. I have no idea where I'm going or what I'm doing, but some inner drive propels me upward.

Ding. With a lurch, the elevator stops on the fourth floor, and the doors open. I walk out into a corridor lined with maybe ten labs. The doors to each are metal with plexiglass. The rooms are locked, but I peek inside. Everything looks hospital-grade white and sterile, with all the requisite equipment: hoods, test tubes, beakers, and elaborate computer systems.

At the very end of the hall is a massive room, a loftlike space with exposed beams and steel panels on the walls. I try scanning my key over the doorknob. It remains locked. Absentmindedly, I finger my key and run it through my hands, rubbing it like a talisman of sorts. Hoping it will offer some kind of answer. Something, *anything.*

I nearly gasp when a figure appears on the other side of the glass.

I am looking at myself.

I'm flummoxed as I stare at my mirror image. The figure has the same harsh bangs that need trimming, the same small frame and gray hoodie. For half a second, I think this girl must be my clone—my DNA twin, *my* other—but after a second, I realize she's not real.

She's a hologram.

I can tell by her feathery appearance, by the way she stands, eerily still, yet waves a little back and forth, like a reed in the breeze. Her eyes don't focus on anything. She smiles vaguely, but her expression stays constant. I'm certain that if I were standing in front of this virtual Emma, I'd be able to swipe my hand right through her.

I pull on the doorknob. Where did this Emma hologram come from? I grab my key. That's what made the hologram appear; I'm sure of it. And now I wonder if there's a hologram for every single student at Darkwood. I don't have access to this room, and I don't know how to get it either. From what I can tell, Madison is the only one with clearance to this building, because she's working directly with Ransom and Fleischer...

That's when it hits me. Madison's key is my best shot at getting into this room. If she has access to the front door, she likely has access to this room too. I need to steal her key. And then I need Maude and her identical DNA...

Then I remember: the new keys have been fixed to solve that loophole. Maude won't be able to make Madison's key work. I'll have to think of another solution.

I race down the hall, toward the stairs next to the elevator bank, down the few flights to the first floor, and out the back door of the building. I don't spot Madison or the others on my way out. I hustle to the main campus, back through the brush, and up to Cypress. It's late now, ten o'clock. But an idea is forming.

The next morning at breakfast, I walk straight to the Similars' table.

"Hi," I say. I meet all their eyes—Maude's, Ansel's, Jago's, Theodora's, Pippa's, and Levi's—feigning a confidence I don't really feel.

"Can we help you?" Theodora smiles at me diplomatically. I push thoughts of her and Levi out of my head.

"I need to talk to Maude," I blurt.

Maude looks surprised but shrugs and scoots her chair back. She follows me to a quiet corner where I begin my pitch. I start from the beginning—overhearing Madison, Tessa, and Jake that day at the library and Madison's missed "blood work" appointment. I tell her my suspicions about Madison. I tell her about Oliver's note and how he left me his key. I conclude with my latest stunt—sneaking into the research building and confronting my own hologram.

"I'm not sure why you're telling me all this," Maude says finally. "The only logical conclusion I can draw is that you need my help."

"I don't know what it's all about," I admit. "But I think if we can get into that room, it could help Levi. Maybe even prove Madison attacked Pru, not him."

"Then I'm in," she says simply, before walking back to join her friends.

⋄⊷⊶⊷⊶⋄

The next week flies by as we set our plan in motion. What Maude and I are about to do is extreme, but we don't have any other options. I have to know what's going on in that research building and what that hologram of me is for. Maude's programming skills are sure to be useful. I don't know what other expertise might be necessary when we get into that room, but I want Maude with me when I face it. The truth is, I don't even know how much I trust her or the other Similars, not since Pippa and I stopped hanging out together, and Levi and I...well, kissed. But I'm willing to take that gamble.

I fake a migraine and visit the Darkwood infirmary. When the nurse leaves the exam room to tend to another patient, I open the cabinet behind me and grab three syringes. They're labeled First Class E, which means they're stronger than an over-the-counter pain reliever but not strong enough to warrant being properly locked up. I've heard my dad talk about these before, and I'm pretty sure these are the same injectives Madison and the other senior Ten members used on us. I've done my research with Dash's help. I know they make the user especially forthcoming, as well as lethargic and compliant. I sneak the needles into my pocket, and the nurse is none the wiser. Then I lie back on the cot and pretend to rest.

◇→─┤├─←◇

Maude and I wait for Madison by the track at dawn. There's a reason she was offered all those running scholarships. She's dedicated. When Madison approaches the bleachers in her running gear and bends down to stretch her legs, I slide from the shadows and inject her. She screams, wheeling on me, but Maude grabs her arms before she can hurt me.

Within moments, the injective starts to take effect. Maude gingerly lets go of Madison's arms, and she doesn't make a move to run or fight us. She stands perfectly still, looking confused.

"What are you guys doing here?" she asks. It's the first time I've ever seen Madison like this—not in control.

We tell her to come with us, and she shrugs, doing exactly as we say. It's a quiet walk to the abandoned science building. Madison's sufficiently dazed and doesn't question us when we ask her to flash her key in front of the door. It opens.

A few minutes later, we're on the fourth floor, standing at the end of the long white corridor. I take in a breath as Madison holds up her key at the entrance to the hologram room. The lock clicks. We're in.

"Keep your key in your hand," I tell Madison. "Roll your palms over it." Madison does as I say, and within seconds, a hologram appears—Madison's hologram. She stares at it like it's a daydream.

"You'll have one too," I tell Maude. "If you get out your own key."

Maude's one step ahead of me. Her hologram pops up next to Madison's. I pull out my own key and make mine appear as well.

Maude mutters as she walks around them, surveying the three holograms. "Flicker hologram technology."

I remember reading about that once. "The latest advancements in lasers?"

"Exactly," says Maude.

It's fascinating stuff, but I don't dwell on it. Time is of the essence. If anyone finds out that we aren't in our dorm rooms or that Madison is missing, they'll be able to track us by our keys—and not only have we gained access to a restricted room in a closed facility, we've stolen injectives and kidnapped Madison. We have to hustle.

"What's stored in these?" I ask Maude, indicating the holograms. "We know the new keys track our GPS. But is there more?"

Maude doesn't respond, but I know she's heard me. She's focused, pacing the room, murmuring something I can't hear. Before I know what's happening, she's pulled a virtual control panel out of thin air. I stare as she keys commands into it. I have no clue how she did that, but then again, that's exactly why I asked her to come with me.

I circle my hologram, studying this uncanny "Emma" in front of me. I clutch my key again, squeezing it—and that's when Emma the hologram starts to flicker and glow bright red.

"Maude," I say quietly. "Come look at this."

She's instantly by my side, and we both watch as Emma the hologram rises into the air, ghostly and ethereal. With her tight-lipped smile and her half-awake, half-asleep demeanor, the hologram is a strange, unsettling sight. Hovering a few feet in the air, she morphs from red to a deep, bruiselike purple.

Next to her, words and numbers begin to flash in the air.

NAME: EMMALINE KATHARINE CHANCE
STATUS: JUNIOR
BIRTH DATE: MAY 26

On and on, statistics scroll about me. About my parents, Colin and Katharine Chance. About my record at Darkwood: my attendance, my test scores, my grades, even the results of my stratum test. They are all here, stored in my hologram. And it was my key that triggered it, unlocking this digital file. Then a map of the Darkwood campus flashes in the air, and on it, a dot. My location, labeled "Research Lab."

Within moments, Maude is activating the data on both the Madison and Maude holograms, so that they, too, are rising in the air, flashing statistics about each girl. I read the data as it speeds past. Maude was born on Castor Island. The parent listed on her birth certificate is A. Gravelle.

"Why's it called Castor Island, anyway?" I ask Maude.

"Our guardian named it when he first designed and built the place, some twenty years ago. Have you heard of the Gemini twins? Castor and Pollux?"

"Like the constellation," I say.

"That's right. Castor and Pollux were immortalized by Zeus in the stars, where they are together, for eternity."

"Twins," I say, thinking how strange and yet fitting it is that Gravelle raised the Similars on an island named for the world's most famous twin brothers. I'm distracted from the thought when more of my own stats cycle past—all of my report cards, before Darkwood, and my birth certificate. It lists my parents as my parents, naturally, and is stamped by the State of California. I start to wonder if my driving record is in here too, when Maude and I are surrounded.

I gasp, startled, as the bodies of several hundred Darkwood

students fill the room. They are scattered throughout the space like players on a massive chess board. These aren't my flesh-and-blood classmates, of course. From where I stand, they look entirely real, but as soon as I move left or right, forward or back, I see that they have no substance. Like the other holograms, these figures are made of light.

"How did you do that? You called them all up without their keys!" I say, amazed.

"T2X command," Maude answers.

I'm too awed to question this. Instead, I walk from hologram to hologram, peering at the faces of students I know, and some I don't. It's eerie, the way they stare at me as I walk past. Some have permanent smiles on their faces. Others frown. Still others look zoned out.

"Is there one here for every Darkwood student?" I ask.

"Yes—every *current* student. My hunch is that every student who's ever had a key is logged in the system somewhere, but I haven't figured out how to call up past students yet."

I turn to her. "So even my dad would have a hologram? Pru's father? Jane and Booker Ward? My father said that when he was in school, they had primitive versions of the keys we have now. They must have improved them significantly in the last two decades..." Then I ask quietly, "Can we pull up Oliver's hologram? I think this might have been what he wanted me to see when he left me his key."

Maude nods as she operates the control panel, and I brace myself when Oliver's hologram steps forward.

But I'm not gutted. I've been sitting in class with Levi for months, so the sight of Ollie's face isn't jarring. Still, the hint of a smile on his lips makes me ache for him.

"Okay," Maude says, all business. "What information do you want to see first?"

"Is that a serious question?" I scowl. "If I knew, we wouldn't be doing this!"

Maude laughs. "Point taken. Let's scroll through Oliver's data and see what we find. Maybe something will jump out at you."

"Thanks," I say. "And sorry. I'm a little on edge."

Maude starts reading as data pops up. "Oliver Elliott Ward. Born September twenty-third. Parents Jane and Booker Ward. Oliver attended the Nueva School in Hillsborough, California, until eighth grade. He came to Darkwood as a first year, two and a half years ago. Here are all of Oliver's exam papers and test scores. His class schedule for his ninth- and tenth-grade years. And his junior year…"

"The schedule he would have had if he'd lived," I finish.

Maude nods. "Does that mean anything to you?" she asks.

I shake my head. That's when I notice Madison looking from me to Maude curiously, like she's starting to question what's going on.

"Time for round two," I tell Maude, pulling a second syringe from my pocket.

Maude nods, taking the syringe from me and injecting Madison's arm with it. "I'd feel bad," she says, "except she did the same thing to us, didn't she? At the midnight session?"

"Yep," I say, turning back to Oliver's stats. "Wait a second. Can you go back to Ollie's birth certificate?"

"I think so," Maude says, pressing a few keys. "There it is. Why? Did you notice something?"

"The names! Look at that. Oliver's mother is Jane Porter. And his father is listed as John Underwood. As in, Albert Seymour's half brother." I can't believe what I'm reading. I'm certain my eyes are playing tricks on me, but after blinking a few times, the document remains the same. "John Underwood is Ollie's dad?"

DARK WEEKEND

I SCRAMBLE FOR words, trying to explain this to Maude. "They were in the Ten together. Porter and Underwood. Damian Leroy, Jaeger Stanwick…and Seymour. The man behind the science that created you." I'm so taken aback, I can barely think straight.

"So?" asks Maude.

"This says Underwood was Oliver's dad. His DNA father."

"I thought Booker Ward was Oliver's father," Maude says.

"He's his stepfather. Adopted him when Ollie was two or three. Oliver never knew who his biological father was. His mother, Jane—she never talked about him. If his dad's Underwood, Seymour's half brother…and Seymour's the reason you and your friends exist…"

Maude gives me a look, and I backpedal. "I didn't mean he's the *only* reason you exist…"

"Whatever. It's fine," Maude says, waving me off. "But this must be what Oliver meant in the note he left you."

I rack my brain. Oliver always told me he didn't know his biological father's name. He said Booker was his dad, regardless of whether they shared DNA.

"Emma?" Maude prods.

"Yeah?" I say, distracted by this new information.

"Look what else the keys are storing. Medical records." Maude's back on her own hologram. "Blood pressure, height, weight. And look at *this*. Resting heart rate. BMI. Bone density. It's all here."

"So the school is tracking stats related to our health? Aside from being invasive and a gross violation of our privacy, is that a big deal?"

"It is if anyone studies these numbers closely. Emma, these stats prove that our bodies—mine and the other Similars'—don't run like a normal human's. They reveal our unique properties." Maude looks noticeably distressed.

"But who would look for variants? If someone didn't know what they were looking for, the data wouldn't look all that suspicious, would it?"

Maude shrugs. "If these stats are run through a statistical analysis, an alarm bell might go off. Maybe it already has."

"Then what?" I wonder out loud.

"No idea. But we should get back," she says, switching gears quickly. "It's almost seven. Breakfast starts in ten minutes."

"Wait," I say. "Before we go. Madison?"

"Yeah?" she says, still dazed from the injective.

"Did you attack Prudence?" I ask, the words catching in my throat. "Was it you?"

Madison stares at me, her blue eyes unfocused. "Attack Prudence? What do you mean?"

"Where were you?" I press. "The afternoon Pru was attacked? Tessa said you missed an appointment for blood work. Why?"

Madison blinks, then frowns. "I had a meeting with my virtual tutor. If I get another A minus in calculus, my mother will kill me. Don't tell anyone. I'd rather fling myself off Hades Point than have anyone in the Ten know."

I sag. I don't want to believe it, but Madison's telling the truth. She must be. The injective doesn't lie.

"Madison," Maude says loudly.

Madison looks at her. "Yes?"

"We're leaving."

The three of us walk silently back to campus, the morning light threading through the trees. I can't believe I was so certain Madison was Pru's attacker. It was such a sensible solution. Now, I'm no closer to figuring out who attacked my friend, and that means Levi's still a suspect. I fight off the tears ballooning in my eyes as I reassure myself that I've learned something useful today. I wonder if I've finally found it, the thing Oliver wanted me to know when he left me that note. *Especially about him.* The "him" in the note must refer to Ollie's biological father, John Underwood. I feel a shiver creeping up my spine as I consider what this could mean, what it *does* mean for all of us.

I'm dying to return to the research lab. Thinking of what I could learn by studying all those holograms—it's taking everything I have not to steal more injectives from the infirmary and kidnap Madison again. But I know I can't. We risked enough doing it once; surely we'd be caught a second time.

I run down to the research building one evening after dinner, hoping to think of something, *anything*, that could get me access besides Madison's key. When I reach the building, I see a figure standing outside the door. When I move closer to get a better view, I realize who this person is—a guard. I deflate as I move back into the shadows, not just because the door is being guarded, but because this guard has never, to my knowledge, been here before. Someone must know Maude and I were here. And now, that person wants to keep us out.

I have no choice. I can't go back to the lab, not without permission. Instead, I visit the Tower Room every chance I get, studying that photograph of the Ten from my father and Underwood's year. Now that I know about Underwood's expulsion, I assume that's the reason he isn't pictured. Still, his name is listed. Was the photograph taken after he was forced to leave the school?

I don't talk to Levi. I'm sure Maude has told him what we learned in the research building, both the revelation that Underwood is his DNA father and the fact that the Similars' properties are being recorded and tracked. Plus, Madison's "confession" of her innocence. I find myself sleeping more than

I have in a year, but there's a dark truth to it. In my dreams, there is no Theodora, and Levi isn't off-limits.

I'm momentarily surprised when I get a notice on my plum from Headmaster Ransom, saying he's suspending our unofficial midnight sessions for the time being—there have been too many students out of their rooms, roaming campus in the middle of the night. I know he's referring to me and Maude and perhaps is even warning us to toe the line, but still, I'm relieved, and I hope he'll suspend the midnight sessions for the rest of the year.

It's a cold weekend in February when the parents arrive. Dark Weekend—our school's version of a parents' weekend—is an annual tradition, and classes are canceled on Friday. Normally I hate this obligatory "holiday," but this year I have a goal in mind: finding out as much about Underwood as I possibly can.

We convene outside the main house after breakfast to await the arrival of the students' parents, legal guardian, or grandparents. The Huxleys step out of a long black limo, waving across the yard to the Choates, who've also arrived. It's always strange seeing parents here, so out of place. This year, it's exponentially strange. It's not lost on me, or anyone, that the Similars don't have parents. Sure, they have their guardian, Gravelle. But I haven't seen him arrive, and I doubt he'll show. Meanwhile, the originals *do* have parents. Parents they don't or can't—or won't—share. I hear whispered conversations all around me, students wondering if the Similars' guardian is coming, and if they will be invited to eat lunch with their DNA families, or whether it'll be "too weird." I think back to the day when I first really understood that Levi was parentless. *It's not weird*, I want to shout. *It's heartbreaking.* It makes me think the Similars really were created by mistake. Who would do that to a child, creating him with no real family to love and raise him? In that moment, I long to support Levi so much, it hurts.

I notice Jake Choate sidling over to greet his father. Ezekiel Choate slaps his son on the back before waving at someone across the way. "Jago!" Ezekiel calls out, gesturing for him to join them. Jake doesn't look too pleased, and Jago looks even less comfortable.

Seeing the Choates and Huxleys makes me wonder if the Leroy family will attend this weekend. We learned last week from the feeds that Tessa's father has finally been sentenced—fifteen years in federal prison. He reports in one week. I spot Ansel chatting with the de Leons, more at ease with Archer's dads since they all spent Christmas break together. He's telling them a story, and Archer's laughing. I wonder if Ansel's making any headway on his task, whatever that might be.

I look for Pippa, and I'm momentarily thrown to see her waving to someone walking up the lawn, a rugged walking stick in his hand. It's Jaeger. He's here for Dark Weekend? To spend it with Pippa, not the daughter who he raised? While I'm thrilled he would come to support Pippa, I'm gutted by thoughts of Pru—of her still in a coma, lying in a hospital bed. That's when I'm reminded of his cryptic note, the one that I haven't been able to make any sense of, that led me to go to Ransom in the middle of the night. I will corner Jaeger about that the first chance I get.

My own father arrives in time to attend the all-school

assembly in the Darkwood chapel. We sit together, and as I get a whiff of his scent—lemon and soap—a dull, unwelcome ache settles in my chest. He and I weren't always so distant. We used to have fun together when I was a little girl. It's hard for me to grasp exactly what happened between us as I got older, but we became more like roommates than family. He's always sad when he is with me. *I could never make him happy*, I remind myself. I could never fill the hole left by my mother when she died.

Ransom gives a speech much like the one he gave at the start of the school year, and I zone out, scanning the room. This is the only day students sit with their parents or other family members instead of their preferred cliques. I look for Levi, but I can't spot him from where I sit. I wonder if Jane and Booker flew out to support Levi like Jaeger has Pippa. Given everything that happened with the stock of Ward, Inc., I highly doubt it.

With Jane and Booker in mind, I feel for Oliver's key around my neck. My own father and I have been invited to a dinner at Headmaster Ransom's house. It's for current members of the Ten and their families. It's another Darkwood tradition, and one of the "perks" of being a Ten: exclusive events and a chance to socialize with the other Ten members' families. For me, it's the perfect opportunity to find out more about John Underwood. After tonight, hopefully I'll finally figure out the significance of "him"—Ollie's biological father.

In the fading light, my father and I walk to Ransom's house. We are joined by Pippa and Jaeger. I'm surprised when my father leans in close to his old schoolmate, resting a hand on his shoulder.

"How is she?" he asks, skipping over the formalities to inquire about Pru.

"The same, old friend." Jaeger's voice is tight. "But we continue to be optimistic."

I can't wait. "Your note," I blurt. "Why did you tell me to—?"

Jaeger silences me with a look. I'll have to find him later.

Ransom greets us at the door and ushers us inside, where we hang up our coats and convene in the living room. I'm instantly reminded of my foolish night seeking Ransom's counsel.

We are the first to arrive but are soon joined by the Huxleys, who exchange pleasantries with my father and Jaeger, and by Maude and Theodora, who arrive together, parentless, of course. Madison and Maude don't speak to each other. They stay on opposite sides of the room as the Huxleys whisper loudly that Ransom should have held a separate dinner for the clones. My father mumbles something about how the Huxleys always were bigots, and I feel a surge of pride standing next to him.

The other Ten members and their families drift in—Angela and Sunil with their families, and Archer with his dads—and, finally, Levi. As he shakes Ransom's hand and joins Maude and Theodora by the fireplace, my heartbeat quickens. I wonder if he'll reach for Theodora's hand or, worse, put his arm around her. I'm relieved that he does neither of those things. I force myself to look away, toward the door, instead. That's when I see Tessa stride in with her mother, Frederica, and her father, Damian.

"Ransom," coos Frederica as she sweeps in, air kissing him on each cheek. "Pleasure, as always. Can someone take my coat?" Flinging her stole at the nearest waiter, she blows past Ransom.

I take one look at Tessa's father and am stunned by what I see. Though he still wears an expensive suit and gold rings, dark shadows circle his unfocused eyes, and his skin hangs on his haggard face. He no longer projects the appearance of a powerful media mogul. My gaze turns to Jaeger to gauge his reaction, given their history. He adjusts his jacket collar, unfazed.

Frederica greets the Huxleys, but from what I can tell, it's all pleasantries, and her husband's impending time in prison isn't part of their conversation.

After some mingling and a few more passed hors d'oeuvres, Ransom announces dinner and we filter into the dining room, where several round tables have been set up for us, complete with formal place cards. The Huxleys are thick as thieves with Headmaster Ransom, which strikes me as odd. Weren't they angry with him at the beginning of the year for inviting the Similars to Darkwood? What's changed? I try to listen in on their conversation, but there are too many people talking and I can't hear.

The Leroys stick to themselves in a corner, hovering near their table. Damian turns white as a sheet as he scans the place cards. I can't figure out why until Theodora approaches the same table. She's been seated with her DNA family. I have no idea how they feel about Theodora, since Tessa's never said anything about her Similar one way or another, but from the look on Frederica's face and from Damian's ghostly pallor, they are not pleased.

Taking my eyes off the Leroys, I follow my father, who has found our table and gestures me to the seat next to him. I glance at the card to see who will be sitting to my left. It's Levi.

THE LAST SUPPER

"RANSOM MUST HAVE a sick sense of humor," I mutter as I pull out my chair and sit.

"I was just thinking the same thing," Levi responds.

Does he look *amused*?

Pippa and Jaeger are across from us. I'm relieved. Maybe the two of them will talk enough for the whole table.

"Look," I say to Levi. "I'm sure you'd much prefer I were Theodora, but she's sitting over there, and I'm here, so…" I shrug.

"Emma, about that…"

"Dad?" I say, an idea forming. My father turns to me. He's been listening to the two of us; I'm sure of it. "We're switching seats." I grab my father's place card and trade it for my own. "Meet your new neighbor, Levi Gravelle."

"I'm Emmaline's father," my dad says vaguely to Levi. As confident as he usually is, I can tell he is thrown to see Oliver's Similar up close. "Colin Chance."

"Pleasure," Levi says, holding out a hand for my father to shake. But my father keeps his own hands by his side.

"You're the one who allegedly attacked Emma's roommate, Prudence," my father says, unsmiling.

"Allegedly," Levi says, not breaking my father's gaze, but lowering his hand.

I feel obligated to explain. "Levi was questioned, but—"

"Welcome to the fourteenth annual Darkwood Ten dinner," booms Ransom, interrupting my impassioned defense of Levi. "You are here because you have climbed to the top of Darkwood's ranks." I notice Bianca leaning over to Bob, whispering something in his ear, while Madison glares across the table at Maude. Wait—Ransom has seated Maude at her DNA family's table too? Just as Theodora is with the Leroys? Why would he do that? Does he think a single dinner might change the Huxleys' minds about their daughter's clone? Or the Leroys' about theirs?

"We also have a great many Ten alumni in our presence," Ransom continues. "Colin Chance, Bianca Huxley, Damian Leroy, Jaeger Stanwick, and Ezekiel Choate were all Ten members when they attended Darkwood. And Sunil Bhat's mother was also a student here, though not a part of the Ten."

"A failure that has haunted me every day since," she chimes in. I zero in on Sunil's mom—a petite lady with shiny black hair and flawless skin—and I wonder if she's joking or not.

Ransom smiles politely. "Oh, and I must not forget Luis de Leon, but he probably doesn't need introducing, given his visibility on the Hollywood scene as a renowned TV producer. Nor does the esteemed former vice president, Bob Huxley. Though he didn't attend Darkwood himself, his wife and daughter have convinced him of the school's many virtues." Ransom chuckles. "As you can see, being a part of the Ten is not to be taken for granted. It is the highest honor at Darkwood, and some would say, in the nation. The Ten alumni are an influential group, serving as arbiters of taste and culture in our society. They have historically been highly respected patrons of the arts, technology, and education, as well as avid philanthropists." I look over at my father. I've never once heard him speak of the connections he's made because of this society. Is that normal?

"I hope you keep that in mind as you take advantage of tonight's company. Here in this room are some of Darkwood's finest. Please, enjoy your dinners and a night that is sure to be memorable." Ransom sits back down, and waiters bring soup to the table, leaving us to our own devices.

It's awkward as we all pretend to be fascinated by the soup. I'm uncomfortable, and not only me—Pippa is too. I don't know why I thought she wouldn't be. She's clearly not comfortable sitting next to Jaeger, not when Pru isn't here. I notice Pippa exchange a look with Levi. He nods, then says something across the table to her, probably in Portuguese.

I can't take the weirdness any longer.

"Jaeger? Have you met Levi? He and Pippa are, well... They grew up together."

"We're quite close," Pippa says. "We've known each other our whole lives."

"Just like you and my father," I say to Jaeger. "Or nearly, anyway. You were in the Ten together, weren't you? Along with Jake's parents, and Oliver's mom and stepdad... Speaking of. There's a classmate of yours. A member of the Ten, actually, who I'm curious about. John Underwood."

I glance at Levi out of the corner of my eye, certain Maude told him about Oliver's birth certificate. It affects him too; after all, it's where half of his DNA came from. From Jane and from Underwood.

Jaeger shrugs. "Nice fellow. Kept to himself. Maybe Colin remembers more." He breaks off a piece of roll from his bread plate and starts chewing.

My dad sets down his soup spoon. "We talked about this, Emmaline. That was years ago. Decades in the past—"

"But surely you remember something about his expulsion."

As soon as I say it, it's like a bomb has gone off in the room. It can't be a coincidence—or perhaps it is—but at that exact moment the room goes silent. Everyone has heard me.

"How do you know about that?" Headmaster Ransom asks quietly from his table.

"Doesn't everyone?" says Frederica Leroy. "It was a huge scandal. Underwood was disgraced. Damian told me all about it." She pats her husband's limp hand.

"We remember," says Bianca in a strained voice, sharing a look with Ransom. Again, I'm perplexed by this sudden closeness in their relationship.

"We were dismayed to see Underwood go," says Ransom. "He was so sharp. Came here on a scholarship. We hate to see any student make a misstep, particularly those who would not have otherwise had the opportunity to attend Darkwood. Sadly, he passed away. Thirteen years ago, I believe."

"How did he die?" I ask, feeling all eyes on me.

"Car accident," Ransom answers. "Tragic."

"I didn't know he died, Damian." Frederica turns to her husband. "Why didn't you tell me?" she asks accusingly.

"Jesus, Mom!" Tessa suddenly explodes. "Would you stop talking to Dad like this high school drama is important? He's going to prison next week. For fifteen years. This is his freaking Last Supper, for God's sake!"

Every eye is on the Leroys. Before anyone knows what's happening, Frederica reaches out and slaps Tessa across the cheek. Tessa gasps. Theodora cringes. Damian recoils.

Ransom stands, flummoxed. "I'm sure this must be a difficult time for you and your family, Tessa. And perhaps our timing here tonight was ill-advised—"

"Don't ever talk to me that way again, Tessa Caroline Leroy," Frederica says, ignoring Ransom.

"I don't know why you're so mad at me. Not when she's the one who did this!" Tessa points to Theodora. "*She* betrayed our family. After we invited her into our home. After we accepted her. That's right," Tessa says, addressing the whole room. "We didn't try to pay her off, or get rid of her, like the Huxleys did to Maude." Tessa eyes Madison, who scowls. "We told her she was welcome to join our family. We knew people might judge us.

But we believed it was the right thing to do." Tessa turns now and faces Theodora directly. "I thought you cared about me. We talked like we were sisters. And then you did *this* to us?" Tessa's fighting tears. "You went into my father's office, you broke into his computer, and found those files. You gave them to the FBI. And then you helped *him*"—she points at Jaeger—"write a story about our family. An exposé that millions of people read."

I'm floored. Theodora was the one who exposed Damian Leroy for fraud? She was the one who tipped off the authorities? Gave the FBI the information to indict him?

"I didn't break in," Theodora says evenly. "Those files were on his tablet for anyone to see."

"*That's* your excuse?" Tessa hiccups. "That you didn't do anything wrong…?"

"He's a criminal, Tessa. I know he's your father, but he cheated thousands of people out of their money. It was wrong."

"And I suppose that's for you to decide. Who gets caught and who doesn't. Who's guilty and who isn't."

My stomach sinks.

I turn to Levi. "That was her task, wasn't it?"

"In part, yes," he answers under his breath.

"Why? Why does Gravelle want to do this? Break up families…"

"He wants to right wrongs. Recalibrate the scales of justice to their proper positions."

"I don't understand."

Levi shakes his head. "Not now, Emma."

"Then when?" I demand. "Stop brushing me off."

"Emmaline?" my father says. His face is tight, anxious. "I thought we discussed this over the holiday. I thought we came to an agreement. But clearly," he adds, eyeing Levi, "I was wrong."

"Wrong about what?"

"You assured me that you and Levi were not friends."

"We aren't," I respond quickly.

"It doesn't look that way to me."

"I moved our place cards so we wouldn't have to sit next to each other. How much clearer could I be?" I grumble.

"What your daughter means to say"—a trace of a smile plays on Levi's lips—"is that we don't like each other."

No, we don't like each other, I think. *What we feel, or what I feel, anyway, is far more than that juvenile word could ever convey.*

"I'm sorry, Levi. This is a family matter between me and my daughter," my father says. "I cannot emphasize this enough, honey. You know I completely support clones and believe they deserve the same rights as everyone else. But for other, personal reasons I don't care to get into here… It is not a good idea for you to spend time with Levi or any of the other Similars."

"Don't worry about it," I snap. "Levi has made it clear that we mean nothing to each other. That he has other…people he'd rather spend his time with. It's fine, Dad. I will stay far, far away from the Similars. Indefinitely."

THE HOLOGRAM

THE REST OF the dinner passes with a strained tension. My father and I don't utter another word to each other. Nor do I talk with Levi or Pippa. Ransom starts making his way from table to table during dessert, thanking us all for coming. I notice that he hugs Bianca and shakes Bob's hand before leaning in to consult with them. I have a feeling this isn't idle chitchat. Compelled to hear what he's saying to Madison's parents and eager to escape my table, I head to the Huxleys' table under the guise of pouring myself some water from a pitcher on the nearby sideboard. Madison is deep in conversation with Angela, complaining about how hard it is to choose between so many Ivy Leagues. Maude is discussing stock market trends with Angela's mother. I strain to tune out Maude and Madison and focus on Ransom and the Huxleys.

"It's nearly complete," I catch Ransom saying to them. "Months. Possibly even weeks. I couldn't be more pleased with the data thus far."

"And it's all being completed in the research lab?" Bianca asks under her breath.

"Yes," says Ransom. "We are almost ready. Thanks to your generous donation, of course."

The Huxleys made a donation? To what? I wonder.

Before I can overhear more, Madison appears next to me.

"I know what you did," she says simply.

"I don't know what you're talking about," I say.

"The injective. The science building. I remember it all."

"So what? You did the same thing to me, to all of us, at the midnight session. Looks like we're even." I walk off, a lot less calm than I am trying to project, leaving Madison glaring as Ransom clangs on his glass for everyone's attention.

"It's been a pleasure hosting all of you here tonight. Thank you again for coming. Please, make your way back to your dorms and hotel rooms safely. I look forward to the rest of our weekend eagerly."

I try to catch Jaeger as we collect our coats and head out into the cold night, but Pippa blocks my way to say good night, her voice strained. Jaeger shakes my father's hand, promising to keep him posted on Pru's continued recovery. I want desperately to ask him about his note, but when I make eye contact, he shakes his head.

Levi and Pippa start down the path back to the main campus, followed by Jaeger. I excuse myself from my dad and catch up with Jaeger. "Please. Tell me what your note meant! Why do you want me and Pippa to stop searching for Pru? Where is she? Is Prudence—" I force myself to say the words out loud. "Is she dead?"

Jaeger sighs like he has the weight of the world on his shoulders. "Pru is not dead. She is doing much better, in fact."

I'm stunned. *She is?* "Then where is she? Why isn't she back at school? Why hasn't she buzzed me?"

"It's not safe for her at Darkwood. Not after she was attacked. Her mother and I want to keep her home where we're sure she won't be in danger. Rest assured, Pru is recuperating nicely, and she sends her love. But we would prefer that she and her health not be the center of conversation on campus. You should get back to your father." He leaves me standing on the paved walkway. I watch as the Huxleys, the Leroys, Maude, Theodora, and all the others stream by.

It's only me and my father now.

"I'll walk you to your dorm," he offers. "I'm leaving in the morning. I hope you understand that I can't stay for the rest of the events."

"Fine," I say quietly. We begin to walk, efficiently, quickly.

"I have no choice but to be firm on this issue, Emmaline. The Similars aren't good friends for you."

I wheel on him. I can't hold in my fury any longer. "With all due respect, Dad—if you even deserve to be called that, given how distant you've been—you can't tell me what to do. Make whatever recommendations you like, but I will make my own decisions about whether or not I associate with the Similars."

My father stops in his tracks, looking bewildered. "You

agreed with me at dinner just thirty minutes ago. Are you in love with him?" he demands.

"What?" My voice catches. I can hardly breathe.

"Is that what this is about? Was that some kind of lovers' quarrel back there?"

"Jesus, Dad! No."

He says quietly, "I've been contemplating whether to have you stay at Darkwood or come home. Continuing your education here with the opportunities it affords you has been the better choice, I was sure of it. But now... Dammit, Emmaline. This isn't going to end well."

We stand there in silence.

"I'm sorry, Dad," I finally say. "I know you never wanted to raise me alone. I know it's not what you signed up for. You thought Mom would be here. But she isn't." I force the tears back, not wanting him to see me cry. "I know you never would have agreed to this if...if you'd known what it would be like."

His voice is gentle. "Agreed? Emma, honey, agreed to what?"

"To being a dad. To being my father," I say.

"Is that what you think?" he asks quietly. "That if I could go back in time, I wouldn't have had you? Emmaline. You were—you are—the best thing that ever happened to me."

I shrug my shoulders, toughening up like I always do. "Then why were you so cold when Ollie died this summer? My best friend dies and you practically ignore it. No offense, but I think I'm good on my own."

I continue to my dorm, and he doesn't call after me or follow me. In the morning, he's gone.

The rest of February is gray and gloomy. After the Ten dinner, I have little contact with any of the Similars, even Maude. Ever since our discovery of the holograms in the research building, I've felt closer to her. But she remains radio silent. I don't talk much to Pippa either, and she sits exclusively with the Similars in the dining hall. I've gotten used to eating with my textbooks, but I still miss Pippa. My friend.

Even with as much work as I have for my classes, I can't get the holograms out of my head. I'd give my right arm to get back in the research lab, but as far as I can tell, there's a security guard stationed there twenty-four seven. So I hole up in my room outside of class hours with only Dash to keep me company.

As February drifts into March, it starts to feel like at least half the school is not just avoiding the Similars—they're outwardly shunning them. Even though there's been no arrest, in the absence of an alternate theory, everyone still thinks Levi attacked Pru. And after the Ten dinner at Ransom's house, word got out that Theodora was behind Damian Leroy's arrest. There are pockets of kids who remain loyal to the Similars, but, overall, skeptical curiosity has turned to downright suspicion and hostility. As more reports of discrimination against clones surface on our feeds from the outside world, support for DAAM has increased. Madison rotates different anti-clone petitions on a sign-up tablet in the dining hall, and they overflow with signatures. I am devastated and angry. I consider starting an organization to counter DAAM, but I don't know if the Similars would want me to. They are so fiercely independent. I'm not sure they'd want me to speak on their behalf.

I miss spending time with Levi, even though it's painful to admit it. I remind myself that he has Theodora. And even if he didn't, we aren't an "us," and we never will be.

I fall asleep every night clutching Oliver's key in my hand, trying and failing to figure out what he was telling me in his note and what it means that Underwood was Ollie's father.

One morning, I'm headed to my first class of the day when I hear Mr. Park is leaving Darkwood. At first, I don't know why I'm disconcerted. Mr. Park and I aren't close. He shooed me away when I tried to ask him for help. And yet, a voice in the back of my head reminds me that he knew—*knows*—about Seymour's primate experiment. For that reason alone, I seek him out.

By the time I make it to the American history classroom, Mr. Park's cleaning out his desk.

"What happened?" I ask quietly as Mr. Park slides books into a canvas sack.

Mr. Park looks up and stares at me like I'm an alien.

"I'm leaving," he says, then goes back to packing. "Isn't that obvious?"

"Did they fire you?" I ask.

Mr. Park frowns. "I can't disclose my reasons for leaving Darkwood. They're personal."

"Fine. But before you go—please, Mr. Park, I need your help."

Mr. Park raises his eyebrows. "I'm trying to catch a noon train. But go ahead."

"I know," I say flatly.

"About my train?" He sounds puzzled, but doesn't look up from his sorting.

"About the Similars. About their capabilities. How they're stronger, more resilient than other people. And I know it all stemmed from Albert Seymour's primate experiment. Is that what you were getting at when you mentioned it in class? Did you *want* us to find out about the Similars?"

Mr. Park finally looks up from his desk. "I have only wanted one thing since the Similars arrived at Darkwood: to protect them," he says simply. "Now that I can no longer do that, I'm leaving."

I don't know what to make of that—how could I?—but it's clear from his tone that he isn't going to volunteer anything more.

Still, I press. "You know how the keys work, don't you? You know about the holograms. You know about all of it."

"And if I do?" he asks, guarded.

"Then you have to tell me," I insist. "Oliver left me his key and a note. Maude and I, we found the room with the holograms. She figured out how to unlock each key."

"Sounds like you don't need me, then."

"Yes, I do! Oliver's father was John Underwood. And I know that means something, because Underwood was Seymour's half brother. And Underwood was expelled. But... What else? There's got to be more to Oliver's message than that, Mr. Park." I know I sound desperate; I don't care. I am.

Mr. Park sighs. "The keys don't simply store data, like GPS tracking and test scores. They're receivers. They can hold recordings from their owner."

"The key is a receiver?" I repeat. Receivers are like the flash drives of the past. They store data, and they can transmit it. "Why don't any of us know about this?" I demand.

"There was a scandal, years back. Students took advantage of the keys, recorded inappropriate information. The administration stopped advertising this feature, but I believe the keys still hold that capability, if you know how to use it."

"So what do I do? How do I unlock Oliver's key to get the message he left for me? If he even left a message for me there?"

"You'd need to know his passcode." Mr. Park returns to his sorting.

I take in a breath. "Okay, imagine I *could* somehow figure out Oliver's passcode. You're skipping about fifty steps. What do I *do* with it?"

"How did you break into the hologram server?"

"Maude helped me."

"Then I suggest you enlist Maude's help again. Now, if you'll excuse me, Emmaline," he says. "I need to catch my train."

◇>⊣ ⊢<◇

I corner Maude between classes and tell her everything. About the security at the research building. About my conversation with Mr. Park.

"A receiver," she repeats. "Brilliant. Give me Oliver's key."

I spot Levi coming down the hallway. "Not now. Tonight. Come to my room."

I try to focus on my classes for the rest of the day, but it feels like an eternity until Maude's gentle knock sounds at my door that evening. "Come on in," I say. Then, in case anyone is within earshot, "Thanks for coming by to study." I close the door behind her, then take Pru's chair and wedge it under the doorknob. "We don't want anyone walking in on us." It's study hours. It's not like I have other friends who would want to borrow my notes or cram for our upcoming calc exam, but still.

"Hand over the key," Maude says.

I do, relinquishing it to Maude's confident grip. I feel a slight pang at letting it go, like I'm letting Oliver go too.

Maude takes out her plum and sets it on the rug. She places Oliver's key next to it.

"You're the expert," I say, "but I'm guessing we need to get on the server. Does the key have an internal tracker that runs on Wi-Fi?"

"Hopefully," Maude answers. She fiddles with some commands on her plum until she finds a screen that looks promising. "Okay. I found the right setting. Now we need the code that connects it to our keys," she says, concentrating as she hits a few buttons on the plum.

"Is it working?" I press.

"Give me a second." She pauses. "I'm entering the Darkwood transmitter codes—done," Maude says as the key begins to glow orange.

"That's it? You did it?" I stare at the key and at the plum.

"Almost," she says. "Now I need his passcode." She holds up the plum to show me the screen. It says OLIVER WARD. Underneath is his birth date and four blank spaces for a four-digit passcode.

"Right," I mutter. I knew this was coming. "How many tries do we get?"

"Not sure. It could shut us out if we miss too many times, so...let's not. Figure you've got three at the most."

I begin to pace. What would Oliver have used as his passcode? It must be something I'd know. Otherwise, he would have left me a clue. Did he? I take out his note.

> *Emma,*
>
> *I'm sorry. The key is for you. It will explain everything. Especially about him.*
>
> > *Love always,*
> > *O*

There aren't any hints in here, are there? Only one four-letter word stands out...

"Can the digits be letters? Or only numbers?" I ask Maude tightly.

"Either," she says. "It's an alphanumeric system."

I sigh. "What about 'love'? L-o-v-e?"

She types in the letters. "Error message. Any other ideas?"

I rack my brain. What on earth would Oliver use as his passcode? I read the note again. There's *nothing*. "W-i-l-l? Try that."

Maude keys it in. "Nope."

I think a moment. "'Emma,'" I say quietly. "It's four letters.

It's the first word in the note he left me. I didn't think of it at first because it seemed, well, like *nothing*..."

Maude is already punching it in. "Bingo," she says, a smile spreading over her face. "We're in." Maude presses a few buttons on her plum, and the key glows again, turning from orange to dark purple. A figure materializes over the key. It's Oliver—his hologram, anyway.

Oliver's hologram looks just like the one we met in the research lab. Same familiar face. Jovial, but strangely inhuman.

"Um," I mutter, staring at him. "Hi?"

Maude rolls her eyes. "Hold on. I have to key in a few more commands. There," she says finally. "Go," she tells the hologram.

Now it's my turn to roll my eyes. "He can't hear you. What makes you think he's going to talk, anyway?"

But just like that, he does. "Hi, Emma."

UNDERWOOD

I KNOW THIS isn't the real Oliver. It's a hologram, a figment. And yet, hearing him say my name like that, like he used to— it's disarming. Oliver's body doesn't move as he talks, only his mouth. I shake off the strangeness of it all. His message is what matters. Oliver, the real Oliver, recorded it, knowing, or hoping, that I'd hear it.

"Sorry to be so cryptic," Oliver's hologram continues. "But if you are listening to this, it means I'm not there to tell you what I have to say in person. I'm sorry about that."

I look over at Maude. *Is she as entranced as I am? Yes.* My eyes flit back to Oliver's, staring into them like they hold all the answers to my many questions. I hope they do.

"Back in the spring, I fell into one of my filmmaking worm-holes," Oliver explains. "I'd decided to make a documentary about all of Darkwood's hidden gems. The places on campus most students know little about. Did you know that the Tower Room was once the hiding place of a wanted criminal? It was decades ago, but I digress."

I exhale. This hologram—this flimsy version of Oliver—sounds like he did when he was narrating one of his films.

"That's what brought me to the old science building by the lake. It's been vacant for years. It took some digging to learn about what had happened there. Nearly twenty years ago, when the lab was a fully functioning research center, a couple of students set some laboratory animals loose, and the media got wind of the incident, stirring up negative press for the school. Darkwood's students were painted as irresponsible and its administrators lax."

Underwood, I think. *He's talking about his expulsion.*

"The research center was brought under scrutiny for many years and, eventually, was closed to students and mostly shut down. I was determined to film inside and thought I'd have to break in, but my key opened the door. Which is how I discovered our holograms. A room full of stored holograms, accessible via each student's key? Talk about an exposé! I wanted to uncover everything about how the keys worked and expose the Darkwood administration for keeping this from us. For tracking us—our GPS, our medical stats, our pasts—without our explicit permission."

It takes me a moment to process what I'm hearing. Oliver

was in the hologram room. Oliver saw what Maude and I saw. GPS data. Medical stats. *Last year. Before the new keys were issued.* Which means that wasn't a new feature of the new keys. Our old keys must have had all that tracking too. We just didn't know about it. And neither did our parents, if they only recently signed waivers permitting the school to keep tabs on our whereabouts. The administration was spying on us without anyone's knowledge. I look at Maude, and we both raise our eyebrows.

I turn my attention back to Oliver.

"I had a coconspirator. A teacher who knew what the administration was doing and agreed that it was wrong, who would have been pleased to see Darkwood's underbelly exposed."

A teacher? I wonder to myself. *Was it Mr. Park?*

"This teacher gave me the technical help I needed to get started, as well as a pass to access the hologram room that couldn't be traced to my key. I went there nearly every night, after everyone else had gone to bed. I spent hours there, trying to break into the system. It took me weeks to crack the code. I'm not a programmer. Sure, I took computer science as an elective and could dabble in JavaScript, Rust, and Julia. But the hologram system was complex. It took me some time to get in and unlock my key, and, subsequently, all the others."

I don't have to wonder why Oliver never told me he was doing any of this. For the last few months of school, we were barely speaking. After his confession, after he told me he wanted to be more than friends, I shut him down.

"Imagine my surprise, when—after gaining full access to the system—I saw my birth certificate and discovered that my father was John Underwood. I recognized the name instantly. I knew he had been in the Ten with my mother and stepfather. I also knew he was Albert Seymour's half brother. What I didn't know before was that Underwood and my mother had had a relationship. My mother had never spoken about it, nor had my stepfather. I grew up thinking of Booker Ward as my father, and I never really questioned who my biological father was. It had never mattered. Maybe I was afraid to ask questions that could hurt my mother or Booker. I don't know. But that changed the moment I saw the name on my birth certificate.

"So I tried to access Underwood's hologram. I hadn't tried calling up the hologram of a *former* student, but I could tell that the data was in the system. That every student, past and present, who ever had a key, had a hologram stored there.

"It took another week before I could gain access to other people's profiles. But my assumptions were correct: Underwood had a hologram in the system, even though he hadn't attended Darkwood in more than two decades. I was nervous to call up my biological father's hologram. He wasn't pictured in the Ten portrait, so I had no idea what he looked like. My searches online had been futile, almost as though someone had erased all evidence of him. And then, when the data appeared—there was no image. No 'John Underwood' hologram, only words and numbers streaming across my view space.

"I assumed it was a limitation of the old system and didn't give it any more thought. The data was what I needed. I dove into my father's medical statistics and his test scores, which were top-notch. All that digging, and I learned something about the man, but not nearly enough. Test scores didn't tell me who he was. Why was there so little information about him, and no photographs? That's when I made the discovery that changed everything."

I stiffen. Is this when he will reveal the secrets behind his note? Behind why he left us? He's so in control, so alive in this recording. What happened?

"I was scrolling through the reams of Underwood's data when I came across a stat I hadn't noticed before. Vital signs. *Current* vital signs. Blood pressure, resting heart rate... These weren't stats from Underwood's childhood or even his early adulthood. They were current. They were from the present."

I tense. *Current* vital signs? How could that be?

I turn to Maude, flabbergasted. "Underwood is *alive*? If what he's saying is true, the keys keep recording our information even after we leave Darkwood. How?"

Maude considers this. "It could be a signal transmitted from an implanted chip in our bodies. One that continues to send data back to its base..."

"Even decades later?"

"It's possible."

"It became abundantly clear," Oliver goes on, and I focus my attention back on him, "that my father was—*is*—still alive. And yet, every article I could find reported that he had died in a car accident. That was the story my mother had told me. But these vital signs could only mean one of two things. They were either fake, or the man had never died.

"I had what felt like a million questions, from how this

technology worked to the people it kept tabs on. I decided not to go to my mother, for a whole host of reasons. Instead, I decided to confront the one person who might actually know the truth about Underwood's story—his half brother, Albert Seymour. My uncle."

"After some sleuthing, I discovered that Seymour lived in Cambridge by his old stomping grounds at Harvard. So, I found a summer film conservatory I could attend in Boston for three weeks. It took some real work to find a program that had a last-minute open slot, but when I did, it was the perfect cover, and it even included housing. My parents were thrilled for me to go.

"Seymour was an odd fellow—reserved, brilliant, socially awkward. He was surprised when I arrived on his doorstep, but he didn't turn me away. We quickly formed a bond. Seymour liked me. Or maybe just felt guilty about the many years we'd lost. I suppose I was using my uncle, forging a friendship, taking advantage of our familial ties to gather information. I did attend the film program, but during my breaks, my uncle and I met for lunches. I got to ask many questions, but never let on that I thought my father might still be alive.

"I began to feel the pressure of time as my film program was supposed to end, and I was due back home. I arrived early for one of our lunches, which was when I overheard a phone conversation that stopped me in my tracks. I was waiting in my uncle's living room, studying the stacks of scientific tomes, the strange objects on his shelves. He had various skeletons, glass jars with small preserved creatures inside, and other pickled, unidentified remains. Seymour was in the other room getting his keys and wallet when the phone rang. Among his artifacts, he had a land-line. He must have assumed I couldn't hear him.

"'I've tried to send him home. He isn't taking my hints,' Seymour whispered urgently. He went on to tell this person on the other end that I was 'tough to get rid of.' That's how he put it. He wanted me gone, which made me more determined to find out everything he was hiding. I was done not knowing.

"I watched Seymour carefully, how he locked his brownstone by key code. How he enabled and disabled the alarm. I sneaked into his house two days later. I was used to exploring, when you look for things you don't know you're trying to find.

"I poked around and discovered a locked box, which used the same code as the alarm, and in it, a binder of documents that held every answer I could have ever needed. It was simple, really, once I saw the fake death certificate. There was even a handwrit-ten receipt tallying what cash had been paid for the forgery, the notary to sign it. I have no idea why my uncle saved all this—maybe to use as blackmail against his brother? Who knows. But whatever the reason, it was clear that John Underwood—my father—had faked his own death and reinvented himself as a new man. Augustus Gravelle."

Oliver's hologram pauses. His words linger in the air—*that name* lingers in the air. *Augustus Gravelle*. The Similars' guard-ian. The man who raised them on Castor Island.

"It was all in that locked box. I had no doubts about the truth of it. It all made perfect sense. Gravelle's wards—the six Similars he'd been raising from birth—were created using

274

Seymour's technology. After all, Underwood, I mean, *Gravelle*, and Seymour are *brothers*.

"I left town without saying goodbye. I had to go home so my mom wouldn't get suspicious, but then I knew what I had to do. Travel to my father's private island. Talk to him. Learn the truth about him, and, ultimately, about me. The rest, as they say, is history."

The hologram flickers and disappears.

"Come back," I protest feebly, but I know there's no point. That's all Ollie recorded.

I think I'm in shock. I turn to Maude, who must be as stunned as I am. *Her guardian is Oliver's father?*

"He died only a few weeks after he recorded this," I tell her, my voice sounding disconnected, cold. "Oliver, I mean."

"I know," Maude says.

"Do you think—"

"He went to see him? To confront Gravelle? Like he said he was planning to?"

I nod.

"Maybe."

"What did Gravelle do to him?" I whisper. "Hurt him? Threaten him or his family? *What?*"

"I don't know, Emma," Maude says. "We can't know…"

"Tell me," I say resolutely. "Is your guardian a good man? Is he evil?"

"I don't know. Emma, you have to understand—he never let us in. Never let us know him. He is distant. Aloof. He's intimidating. He has burns across his face…"

My stomach drops. "Burns? What kind of burns?"

"There *was* a car crash when he was younger. It ended in a blaze. He said as much. That's probably how he faked his death. Everyone must have assumed he burned along with the car."

"Did you know who he was? Or suspect?"

"That he and Underwood were one and the same? Of course not. I had no idea before tonight."

I'm flooded with conflicting thoughts and emotions; I can barely get ahold of them. Oliver, his suicide, his note, the hologram. The fact that he *knew* Gravelle was his biological father.

"He must have killed himself after he met Gravelle. Which means something that man said or did to him must have been so traumatic, it messed with his head." I look at my hands. They're trembling. I feel sick. And yet, I'm so relieved there is some clue to help make sense of Oliver's death.

"We don't know that, Emma," Maude says, fixing her plum around her wrist. "I wish we did, but..."

"We have to tell Levi," I say. "He needs to know that your guardian is his father, that he shares DNA with that man."

"No."

"Excuse me?" I'm sure I've misheard her.

"It's a bad idea," she says. "One that will only hurt him."

"It's the truth," I sputter. "Doesn't he deserve to know where his DNA came from?"

"That's arguable. Isn't it enough he knows that Underwood was his father?"

"So you're planning to keep this massive secret from him

forever? Let him live his life never realizing that Gravelle is his flesh and blood?"

"You don't know what our childhood was like for us," she responds. "You can't. I helped you, Emma. Please trust me when I say this is not what Levi needs right now. I will tell him when the time is right."

EXPERIMENT

I SPEND THE next week replaying the hologram message over and over in my head. Underwood didn't die. He reinvented himself as Gravelle—the secretive, self-made billionaire who only made the headlines when the Similars arrived at Darkwood. I think of Oliver's note. *Especially about him.* He meant Underwood; he meant Gravelle. I see that now. Beyond that—what it meant for Oliver, how it's tied to his death—is still a mystery, one I'm compelled to solve.

I think of the keys, and what the administration—Ransom himself?—has been hiding from Darkwood's students. They've tracked students' whereabouts for decades. They have our medical records, our current vital signs. It's a gross invasion of privacy. And they don't stop taking our data when we graduate.

Classes pass by in a haze, and I'm eager for spring break. It's not like my dad will be around, so I'm staying on campus for the week. I figure it will be the perfect opportunity to get back in the research lab, to figure out the building's security and break in to study the holograms of the past Ten members who knew Seymour and Underwood. My father, Pru's dad, Ezekiel Choate…all of them. I corner Maude in the dining hall after the last day of midterm exams.

"We have to go back to the hologram room," I say under my breath as I catch up to her in the line to bus our trays.

"We can't—the security guard," Maude reminds me.

"We can get around him."

"How?" she asks as we walk outside. It may be spring, but it's still freezing at Darkwood. I stuff my hands into my coat pockets.

"The guard has seen Madison go into that building dozens of times…"

"We still don't know why," Maude interjects.

"No. But if you can convince him that you're *her*, and that you've forgotten your key…then you could let me in a back door." I shrug. "It could work."

Maude sighs. "And when do you want to do this?"

"You're staying here for break, right? You and your friends? How about Wednesday?"

Maude nods. "But why Wednesday?"

"Everyone should be gone—or bored. Maybe the guard won't even be on duty."

"I doubt that," Maude says wryly.

"Meet me behind Cypress. Wednesday. Midnight." I make

Maude promise she won't bail on me and then head back to my dorm room.

The Darkwood campus is eerily quiet this holiday. At meals, only a smattering of students trickle through the dining hall. That Wednesday night, a few hours after dinner, I can't sleep, but I'm so used to my own brand of insomnia that I hardly even notice it anymore. I stare at Pru's side of the room, missing her so much, it hurts. I haven't pulled the sheets off her bed or moved any of her things—that would feel like sacrilege. I still wonder why she hasn't buzzed me. It feels wrong that all I have to go on is Jaeger's word. And yet, I want, and need, to believe that she's okay.

Pru and Ollie aren't the only ones I miss. If I'm honest with myself, I miss Levi's company too. It's strange to miss someone who isn't dead or gone, but is simply across the room. It's a new sensation, one I categorically dislike. Like there's a hole inside me, an empty space I can't fill.

I glance at the clock. It's 11:45. Time to meet Maude.

I slip on boots and a coat and head out to the patio behind Cypress. Tonight, I gaze out at the grounds. It is a beautiful campus.

"I don't know what you're expecting to find," says a voice. I turn to see Maude, her eyes bright even in the darkness.

"I want to call up my father's hologram. Jaeger Stanwick's. All of them—"

"It'll be useless data. No hologram. You heard what Oliver said in his message. Underwood's hologram wasn't a hologram at all, simply random stats about his life. Is knowing someone's resting blood pressure really going to help you?"

"No, but—"

"But what?"

"I don't *know* what it is I'm looking for. I just need to see if we've missed anything. I've got to study all the parents' holograms. Then, once I've looked at every Ten member's stats from my father's year, I want to look at Underwood's."

"What for?" Maude asks, frustration rising in her voice. "We already know he's my guardian. We already know he faked his death and took on a new identity and played a role in cloning us from our originals..."

"But why?" I know I sound desperate, and desperately sad. That's because I am. "Why would Underwood—I mean, Gravelle—do that? Why would he clone Oliver and the others? And what did he do to Ollie that drove him to suicide?"

"You won't find that out from the holograms."

"How do you know that? I might. I certainly have to try. Maude, I need your help. I did what you asked. I haven't told Levi what we found out." I let out a sigh that leaves me empty. "Please?"

"All right," she relents. "What do you want me to do?"

"Walk to the research building. Explain to the guard that you're there per Fleischer's instructions, but accidentally left your key in your room."

"So play Madison Huxley to the best of my ability?" Maude supplies.

"Yes. The real Madison Huxley left for Texas three days ago. It would never work if she were on campus. She could have real plans to visit the building. But this will work. It has to."

Something occurs to me. A new wrinkle. "You can do it, can't you? Act like her? What about your accent?"

"What accent?" Maude replies, all traces of her British inflection gone as she impersonates Madison. I'm momentarily taken aback. She's good.

"I'll follow in five minutes. If I'm there with you from the get-go, we'll look suspicious. I think if you're alone, you'll have a better chance of getting in."

"What if security lets me in and you're not there yet? You should be right behind me. Otherwise, I won't be able to wait."

"I'll be there," I say resolutely. "But if I'm not, pull the holograms. Read the data. Take notes. Memorize it. Whatever you have to do. You ready?"

"Ready to pretend to be her? I suppose so." She sighs.

"See you there. And Maude…"

"Yes?"

"Thank you."

She nods before slipping off into the dark. I wait for only a few seconds before following her. I will watch from the trees while she talks to the security guard. Then I'll join her. I take in a sharp breath. I hope this will work.

Suddenly my plum rings. I go to silence it, but then I see who is buzzing me. It's Jaeger Stanwick. I accept and his face appears on the plum's small screen.

Pru's dad's gray hair is long and unkempt. His eyes look glassy and exhausted.

I stop in my tracks. "Jaeger," I whisper. "Is Pru okay? What's happening? What's wrong?"

"I lied before," he says quietly. "When I told you Pru was recuperating at home. She *was*—that wasn't entirely untrue. But now… I couldn't risk you asking questions before. That's why I wrote you that note, to try to make you understand. We couldn't share our plans with you, not yet—"

"What plans?" I ask, feeling so frustrated I could scream. "Is Pru okay? What aren't you telling me?"

"Pru's mother and I, we're part of an underground organization called the Quarry," Jaeger says. "It's a pro-clone group started nearly a decade ago to fight for clones' rights. Mr. Park is also a member, as are a handful of other politicians and activists. The Quarry's membership has grown in numbers exponentially recently."

I take that in, trying to comprehend. Pru's parents are in an underground organization? I had no idea. "What does this have to do with Pru's attack?"

Jaeger sighs. "I'm afraid whoever attacked her may have had a bone to pick with me and what the Quarry stands for."

My mind is racing with this new information, but all I can think about is Pru. "So, her attack didn't have anything to do with the Similars? Where is she? Can I speak to—"

"Augustus Gravelle harbors an agenda that isn't entirely dissimilar to the Quarry's. It runs parallel to what we believe—that clones should be treated equally and fairly. His agenda is more about domination than clones' rights. But that's not important right now. When Prudence recovered from her attack, she was insistent on joining the Quarry. It was premature, in my opinion. I had always planned on her finishing her education first. But I have been preoccupied. Her mother, you see—" Jaeger's voice cracks at this. "Prudence made contact with Gravelle and traveled to his island a week ago to try to form an alliance with him. She and I lost communication a few days ago, and I'm afraid… I'm afraid she may be in danger."

I feel my throat constricting. *Pru is on Castor Island? Meeting with the Similars' guardian?*

"What are we supposed to *do*?" I ask, all too aware that Pru is in danger and I'm supposed to be meeting Maude right this minute at the research building.

"I would go after her, only Prudence's mother… She's dying, Emmaline. I'm afraid she doesn't have much time left. Days, possibly weeks. I need your help."

"Oh, God. I can't right—I have to run," I stammer, looking one last time at Jaeger's grief-stricken face before clicking off my plum and running at a sprint down the path. I'm overwhelmed with a million questions, but I have to focus. It's the middle of the night. I'm not going to be able to help Pru at this very moment—but the information in the hologram room might be a step in that direction.

When I reach the research building, I'm out of breath. I slink as close as I can to the door, where I spot two figures. One is a large, bulky man—the security guard. The other is petite. It's Maude, I can tell from the outline of her coat. She's talking to him. I let out a breath of relief. I haven't missed them—or my window of opportunity. I move closer.

"I know it's asking a lot," Maude says a little too loudly, but likely for my benefit. Her voice is smooth as silk, with a slight

Southern twang, her British accent completely gone. "But it's late. Principal Fleischer wanted me to check in right at midnight. If I go back to get my key…"

I can't hear what the security guard says, but the next thing I know, the door is opening. He's letting her in. Heart thumping, I run toward them.

"Wait!" I say breathlessly, but Maude doesn't turn around. The door closes with a thud behind her as I reach the guard. "Sorry!" I choke out. "I'm supposed to be with her."

The guard stands in front of the door with his arms crossed. "Who are you?"

"Emmaline Chance," I say quickly. "I'm helping Madison with…" I lower my voice, thinking fast. "Well, it's confidential, of course. We've both been ordered by Principal Fleischer not to leak any details. But it's important. Surely you know what I'm talking about?"

"Of course I do," the guard says, though I get the distinct sense that he knows nothing and doesn't want to let on.

"Madison forget her key," I say, an idea forming. "I grabbed it before I left our dorm. Here. Look." I pull my key out from under my T-shirt along with Oliver's. "See? I put hers on before I left. Didn't want to lose it in the dark. I'm a scatterbrain like that." *Will it work? Will he let me in?* "I'd open the door myself, but Maddie's the one with privileges, and you know I can't use her key. Wrong DNA." I flash a smile.

The guard doesn't move.

"Please," I plead. "My dad'll kill me if I get in trouble with Principal Fleischer. You know how scary she is."

He looks at me for a moment, then shrugs. "Go ahead." He uses his own key to open the door for me.

"Thanks so much," I say as I hurry inside. "I owe you one!"

I hustle to the bank of elevators when I hear a door at the end of the hallway close. It happens so fast, I don't see who did it. My heart pounds. Is someone else here in this building, at midnight? Someone besides me and Maude? Or *was* that Maude? And if so, what's she doing on the first floor?

I quickly walk down the hall. I need to know if it was Maude. If it was someone else—Fleischer, for instance—I want to know so that we aren't ambushed.

This door is solid—there's no window to see who, or what, is inside. I steel myself, listening at the door for a few minutes. Nothing. I try the door handle. It opens easily. Blood pulsing through my veins, I push it open gingerly, aware that I'm breaking a million rules.

The room is large, not unlike the hologram room, and the lighting is low. The space is virtually bare—except for medical equipment and five chairs all in a row.

Each chair is hefty like an armchair, though these chairs don't look comfortable. There is a figure in each chair, and each person is hooked up to a bank of wires and IV tubes. I'm immediately reminded of when Pru and I visited her mother during one of her chemotherapy sessions. Is that what this is? A treatment center?

I step inside to get a better look. My eyes focus. And my heart stops.

The people in the chairs are students. And not just any students. The Similars.

I'm stunned. What are they doing here? What is *Maude* doing here? Why is she here and not in the hologram room as we planned?

My gaze leaps from face to face. Levi is not here.

The more I stare, I realize it's not a matter of what they're doing. No, the question is what's being done *to them*.

Each Similar is perfectly still and has his or her eyes closed. When I look more carefully, I see that blood runs from them through tubes to the bank of machines and monitors. A light reddish substance runs to them through another series of tubes.

"Maude?" I ask hesitantly as I approach her chair. "Are you awake? Can you hear me? What's going on?"

She doesn't respond. Fear courses through my body. "Maude!" I shout this time. "Theodora. Pippa?!" I say, facing the Similars. No answer. They can't hear me.

Panicked, I back toward the door. My instinct is to free them. To start pulling out those IVs and needles and tubes. But what if I hurt them? What if yanking out a tube is dangerous, even deadly?

"How nice of you to join us." I whirl, my heart beating in my ears like a metal drum. It's Fleischer in a white lab coat. She stands in the doorway, not two feet from me.

"Principal Fleischer," I say. "You have to help! What's happening? Why are the Similars—? What is—what is this?"

"Nothing of your concern."

"Is this safe? Are they hurt? What are the tubes for? What is this treatment for? Are they unconscious?"

She replies calmly, "As a matter of fact, they are. One of

the tubes is delivering a sleeping injective. You have nothing to worry about, Emmaline. They can't feel a thing."

"But you *know* about this," I say.

"Of course I do." She smiles. The look on her face sends shivers up and down my spine. "Run along, and I won't have to inform Headmaster Ransom about you breaking curfew again."

"I don't care about curfew. What are you *doing* to them?"

"I won't repeat myself, Emmaline. Go." I don't know what it is about her voice, but I worry she is going to hurt me.

That's when it dawns on me. Maude had minutes to get to this room before I entered the building. And from the look of things, she knew exactly where she was going, what she was doing. She told me she would let me into the building, but she didn't. She let the door shut before I got in. She played me.

But why? To come here to be hooked up to machines? It doesn't make any sense. Unless she wanted me to see what was happening here. To see the truth.

"This is what Madison and Jake and Tessa were talking about," I say, as a thought occurs to me. "The blood work. The appointments they had with you…" My thoughts spill out before I can stop them. "The Similars' special properties. You know about them, don't you? The Similars' unique vital signs and what they mean. You've been tracking them. From the keys."

"This is my third warning, Emmaline. I've reached the end of my patience."

I barely hear her. I walk around the chairs, studying the motionless faces of the Similars. Are they in on this? Or are they unwilling participants? Did Maude play me so that I'd find out?

"You're doing research," I say, my voice breathless as I grab a bag of what appears to be Theodora's blood. I'm not usually squeamish, but I have to fight the urge to gag. "Research that the Huxleys funded. Research to find out how their bodies work. Is that why Headmaster Ransom invited them to Darkwood in the first place?" It's an epiphany. "Did Ransom admit the Similars so he could turn them into his own personal science experiment?"

"You are a very imaginative girl," Fleischer says, her voice frighteningly even. "One who should go back to her room, and go to bed, and forget she ever saw any of this."

Fear courses through me as I begin to comprehend what I've discovered and what Fleischer might do to keep me from telling anyone what I've seen.

My mind churns. I have to protect myself. "Don't you want to hear what I think about it? The Similars are dangerous. Levi Gravelle attacked my best friend. If you can find out what makes them so…inhuman, I support your efforts one hundred percent."

Fleischer studies me for a second. I can tell she's trying to decide whether or not to believe me. "Bed, Emmaline. Now."

I nod, not risking another word as I sprint out the door, down the hallway, past the elevator bank, and outside into the cool night.

The security guard watches me run out, offering a weak good night that I don't return as I race back up the dirt path.

Fleischer is researching the Similars. Fleischer knows about their properties.

I'm sure of something else too: this was all Ransom's doing. He's been planning this research, whatever it is, since the

Similars arrived. Before. This was all part of a greater plan. I am sure of it.

The next thing I know, I'm standing at the top of the fire escape outside Levi's room as the wind needles me. I rap on his window, just like I did that night we searched Oliver's room. And just like last time, he opens it for me, then holds out a hand. I take it, his warmth rippling through me as I notice he's shirtless again too.

We're alone. After all, Jago isn't here. He's back in that room in the research building with the others.

"Emma?" Levi asks. I squeeze his hands. He doesn't let go. I don't want him to.

I tell him everything.

CONFESSIONS

I TELL HIM what I saw: his friends held hostage by Fleischer. I tell him about Oliver's hologram, leaving out the part about Underwood and Gravelle being one and the same person. When the time is right, I will tell him that too. I also tell Levi about Pru, how she's gone to Castor Island and is possibly being held there by Gravelle. She's my roommate and one of the only people in the world I'd do anything for—and I need to help her.

Levi throws on a T-shirt and paces the room. I wish we could hold each other, support each other, but I remind myself about Theodora. He is with her, not me. *Snap out of it, Emmaline. Focus.*

"Maude and I discovered something when we found the holograms," I tell him. "The keys have had GPS tracking for ages; the old keys were recording our vital signs too. Like our resting heart rates. Data that, if looked at carefully, would reveal your special attributes. I think Ransom knows. I think he's taking advantage of the Similars with the Huxleys' help. I think he's conducting research on them, probably on some sick quest for enhancement or immortality... Levi? Are you listening to me?"

Levi nods. "I knew the others were going somewhere. I noticed Jago slip out a couple of nights, and then I started putting two and two together. But why wouldn't Ransom want to study me?"

"I know why," I say carefully. "Only five Similars are being studied because their originals are still alive."

"And mine is dead," Levi says.

"Yes. I may be wrong—although I don't think I am. Ransom wanted the Similars, all of you, here at Darkwood to study you. To compare you to your originals. He's taking samples or blood or plasma or *something* with all those tubes and needles, and he's examining it. Madison and Tessa and Jake, they've been giving blood. Probably so Fleischer has a control to compare their blood to. I bet Archer was asked to give blood too. And Pru— well, I don't know. She'd never agree to that, but maybe Ransom got her blood some other way, without her consent, before the accident."

"I'm not as useful, then, am I?" Levi says.

"Obviously Ransom still wanted you here at Darkwood. He couldn't invite your friends and not you..."

There's a long moment as we both process the gravity of that.

"We have to tell someone," I say quickly. "This isn't right. What he's doing to them is criminal."

"Not if they've agreed to it," Levi reminds me. "We won't be able to ask them till tomorrow, but I wouldn't be surprised if they'd signed away their rights."

"Why would they do that?" It makes no sense, none at all.

"They have to play Ransom's game if they want to stay here," Levi says simply. "And they need to stay here to accomplish their tasks, remember?"

"Tasks that could hurt the originals' families," I remind him.

"That depends on how you look at it," Levi says. "Is it wrong for my friends to want to claim their rightful places in their DNA families? Was it wrong for Maude to defy the Huxleys? Or Theodora to expose a criminal?"

I tense at her name.

"Of course you'd defend her," I find myself saying, sounding far too antagonistic. "She's your—whatever she is."

"I'm not with Theodora."

"What? Yes, you are. I saw you two…"

"You saw an illusion."

I study him, those gray eyes. I've missed those eyes. First Oliver's, then his.

"I don't know what you're talking about, but I'm sure you won't explain it, so…"

"I asked her to pretend," Levi says. I can't tell if there's pain in his voice, or sadness. But I cling to his every word. "I asked her to make you think we were dating because I knew that you and I… It wasn't good for you. Or me. To do what we did."

"You mean our kiss?"

"I mean all of it." Levi sighs. "Theodora and I have never been more to each other than close friends. We are like family; we are not what you think. What I *made* you think."

My mind is reeling. My throat feels dry. "Then why…?"

"I wanted you to believe we meant something to each other, Thea and I, because at the time I thought it was best for everyone. Do you remember when you first saw me?" Levi asks, the urgency thick in his voice.

"The day I practically attacked you? Yes, it comes to mind."

"That was the day I fell for you."

I feel my breathing speed up. *The day he what?*

"I knew it would never work between us. You are, after all, the only living girl in the universe who will never be able to separate me from the memory of her dead best friend, who she also loved. Can you?"

"I don't—" I sputter, not even finishing my thought before he interrupts.

"Why did you kiss me that day? Why do you watch me across the dining hall? Why do you want to learn everything there is to know about me and my friends? Is it because I am uniquely interesting to you? Or because I look like *him*? And if we ever were, well, an *us*…" There's an intensity in his eyes that I've never seen before. "How could I ever be sure that you loved me for the right reasons?"

I don't even hesitate. Answering that question is as easy as stating my own name. "Because when I look at you, I don't see him. Not anymore. I see the person who carried Pru to get help.

I see a person who is well read, and athletic, and has no idea how compelling he is. How brilliant, and captivating, and sometimes infuriating. But also kind. I don't see Oliver. I see that. I see you."

"Nice speech," Levi whispers.

"It's the truth." I breathe out. "But..."

"What?" he asks, gently taking my hand in his.

"You still lied to me. About Theodora."

"I'm sorry," he says, his face dropping. "That was a regrettable mistake, and I hope you can forgive me. There's no good explanation for it, except that I thought it would be better for me, and for you, if we stayed out of each other's way. I honored what you asked of me the first time we met. I steered clear of you. Let you live your life."

"But that's not what I want anymore," I say quietly.

"Me either." He pulls me into his arms and presses his lips to mine. This time when we kiss, it is unbounded, turning every inch of me inside out.

When the kiss is over, I stare into his eyes. I have to say this now. If I don't, I'll lose my will.

"Did Maude tell you?" I blurt.

"Tell me what?"

"About Underwood. About your father."

"I don't have a father."

"Your DNA father, then. He is..." I have to tell him. "He's Gravelle."

The words hang in the air between us. As soon as I've said them, I'm filled with regret. Will anything ever be the same again? Can it be?

"Underwood faked his death. The car crash, it didn't kill him. Oliver left me a message, in his hologram... He discovered all of this. He wanted me to know. I had to tell you," I say with conviction. "Maude didn't want me to. She's going to be angry at me, furious even. But I can't keep this from you. Not anymore."

Levi is quiet for a moment.

"Levi? Please. Say something."

"I've suspected for a while now." I can tell he's trying to hide his hurt from me. But he can't hide it, not entirely.

"You have?"

He nods. "I denied it, for years, because of what it meant. Sharing genes with Gravelle... It would mean that I was the worst of us. The one related to our guardian by blood. The one with an inescapable tie to the man who had kept us isolated all those years. I didn't want to believe it. But I think I've always known."

He knows. He's always known. I haven't ruined his life with this news. "When Oliver left me that note," I explain, "I was so desperate to understand his message, it never occurred to me that it would affect you too. I'm sorry, Levi. I didn't want to make your life more complicated. Not that it would be the first time," I add. "I have a bad habit of ruining people's lives."

Levi studies me, and I'm certain he can see past my hardened exterior to the girl inside, the one who was lonely and sad long before Oliver died. He steps back from me, pained. "Why would you say something like that?"

"Because it's true, isn't it?" I shrug. "It's my fault my mother died. I was sick. I had leukemia. My parents thought I would die; the doctors were sure of it. For a year, my parents went through hell. Chemotherapy, drugs that made me so weak I couldn't keep my eyes open.

"When I was on the brink of death, my mother couldn't stand it anymore. She couldn't cope with the thought of losing me. She had wanted a child so badly. It had taken her years of fertility treatments to conceive. She loved me so much that, in the end, she couldn't bear to watch me die." I pause. I've never told anyone that except Oliver. "My mother overdosed on pharmas. And then, within weeks of her death, the miracle happened," I say bitterly. "My father found an experimental treatment in Sweden. Nanobots. He whisked me there against everyone's advice. And even though the doctors thought the treatment would never work, it did. I survived. Except my mother was already gone. My whole life, I've been aware of the irony of my existence. I shouldn't have lived; *she* should have. My father's never been able to stand looking at me because of that. I took her away from him. So that's it. My whole sad life story. Everyone around me, and I mean everyone, leaves, or dies, or gets attacked in a boathouse. If I were you, I'd watch your back."

Levi doesn't answer me. He gently reaches a hand to the small of my back and pulls me toward him. As our bodies merge, I press my lips to his with a hunger that is matched only by his twin desire. And even though there is so much that scares me—Prudence's safety, whatever Levi's friends are enduring at the hands of Ransom, the truth behind Oliver's death—I sink into Levi's arms, and for a few stolen moments, I allow myself to forget.

◇➤━┥┝━◀◇

Reeling from the events of the day, I climb into bed. We sat on the floor, Levi and I, and I traced my fingers over his bare arms. Over the spot where that wound healed at warp speed after his dive into Dark Lake. Touching his skin like that, electricity coursed through my veins. I felt supercharged, amped, like every nerve ending in my body had been prodded and awoken. I also felt terrified.

What were we doing? What were we thinking? I'd never kissed a boy like that before. I'd never wanted to. And this boy I used to hate with every fiber of my being, was now the only one I would ever want to kiss. We could stay up all night, every night talking, and it would never be enough. We could never be close enough.

We'd considered it—me staying over in his room. In the end, I left. It went against every impulse I had, and yet I knew it was the right thing to do. What if Jago came back and discovered me there? What if—?

I hadn't allowed myself think about it.

"Dash," I whisper, as I slide deep under the covers, still dressed in my jeans and hoodie.

"Yes, Emmaline? Is there something I can assist you with?"

"Oh, you know," I say, my voice trembling. "Everything."

I know Dash can't smile, but I feel the comfort of his presence anyway. "Good night, Emmaline," are the last words I hear before I drift off to sleep.

The next morning, Levi and I find each other at breakfast. I scan the dining hall for the Similars. They aren't here.

"Have you seen the others? Did Jago come back last night?"

"Yes, but he was still asleep this morning when I got up. I'll talk to them," Levi promises. "About Ransom and the research. I'll find out why they didn't tell me…"

"To protect you," I guess.

"Or to make sure I didn't try to stop them," he offers. I nod in understanding. We stand next to each other, but we don't touch. Whatever closeness we shared last night is outside of this moment, though I'm sure he's thinking of it as much as I am.

Or maybe he isn't. Maybe he didn't dream about me all night, the way I dreamed about him. The thought is sobering. It dawns on me that Levi didn't grow up like I did, hasn't attended high school until this year. His declaration of…whatever that was, might not mean the same thing to him that it meant to me.

"Levi," I say, "I didn't exactly sleep well last night, after…" My cheeks flush.

"Me either," he says, his eyes focused on mine.

I could get lost in those gray eyes for good…

I force myself to focus. "I couldn't stop thinking about Prudence. And her father. Pru's mom is sick. *Really* sick. She's probably going to die soon, and, and…" I pause, willing myself not to cry. "I have to go to Pru. Find her. Bring her home."

"Emma, I know how much you care about her, but what do you think you're going to do? You know nothing about Castor Island. How would you even get there?"

"That's where you come in," I say quietly. "You have to tell me everything you know about it. Where it is, how to find it, how to get her out."

"No," says Levi. "Absolutely not."

"Excuse me?" I say, wheeling on him.

"It's too dangerous. You don't know what that place is like," Levi says. "What *he's* like."

"What's the worst thing that could happen?" My eyes are bright with tears now. "Would joining my best friend in death be so terrible if it helped me save another friend?" I meet Levi's gaze and see the recognition in his face. He gets how serious I am. That I will not, cannot, be persuaded to stand by and do nothing. "This is Pru we're talking about. Levi—I don't have a choice."

"Then I'm coming with you," he says. "The island is off the grid and Gravelle is dangerous. If you're going to have any chance of success... You need me. I can get us in. But we'll need to prepare."

"Fine," I relent. "You have two weeks."

THE JOURNEY

LEVI IS RIGHT. I do need him. I'd have no chance of getting to Castor Island without him. It was ridiculous of me to think I could. Still, I worry I'm putting him in danger by asking him to return to his home. I feel the unfairness of it with every atom of my being. I have the privilege, the freedom to leave Darkwood, the state, the country without fear that I'll arouse suspicion. Levi, as a Similar, enjoys none of that safety. And yet, he's determined to join me.

Gravelle is twisted, a self-made lunatic, Levi reminds me. And though I feel sick at the thought of putting Levi in more danger with his guardian, part of me thrills that we'll take this journey together. If I'm heading on a kamikaze mission, I want it to be with him.

We make our plans carefully. We will leave in two weeks, after our next science exam. With prep and study sessions before, our teachers would know something was wrong if we weren't there. Missing a few classes afterward will be less noticeable, and we need a head start. We don't want to tip off our teachers too soon.

Levi warns me that anyone who enters the island without Gravelle's express permission faces consequences. I am nervous but undaunted. Oliver went to Castor Island, and Prudence is there now. She needs us. I buzz Jaeger, leaving a message to tell me if he hears from Prudence. I don't let on that I'm planning on going after her. I have a feeling he already knows.

Dash finds me the times of the early morning buses out of town. Levi and I plan to walk the three miles to the bus station, then take the most inconspicuous bus to Bar Harbor, where we'll catch our ferry. We will tell no one besides Maude what we're planning. We'll give her our keys to hold, hoping we'll be long gone before the school, or anyone, realizes we've left the Darkwood campus.

Levi and I plot routes and strategies, anticipating what Gravelle might say or do to us when we arrive on the island. We haven't mentioned our kiss again. It's like neither of us wants to acknowledge what we said, what we did, for fear the memory of it will burst.

While we plan, Levi confronts his friends. They confirm what I had suspected—that Ransom is behind the research. They agreed to play his game because they felt they had no other choice.

"We have to do something. We can't let Ransom treat them

like lab rats. Like *specimens*," I tell Levi. It's late afternoon, and the April landscape is starting to bud as we stand by Dark Lake, staring out at its glassy surface.

"Ransom isn't well. Maude said he suffers from a host of autoimmune diseases. He's counting on his research to provide him longevity. A guarantee that he will not die before his time."

"I still can't understand why they agreed to it. Why Maude lied to me—"

"She didn't lie. She kept the truth from you to protect you, Emmaline. What good does it do you to know about this?"

"I can help," I insist hotly. "I can stop him…"

"And Gravelle too? It's bad enough you want to travel to Castor Island. You can't fight Ransom. Leave that to my friends. When the time is right, they'll expose him. Maude swore to me that ever since they signed Ransom's waiver, they've been planning to take him down. In their own time."

Though I don't like staying silent, I do, but only because I don't know what good it would do to confront Ransom now. Levi and I are focused on the big picture: Gravelle.

It's a dismal Thursday morning when I grab my small backpack and place the straps securely over my shoulders. I meet Levi outside Cypress. I've left Pippa a vague note telling her not to worry about us. I don't want her to know too much and have to lie to Ransom. Levi and I say little during the walk down the path to the edge of campus, and then to the bus station on the outskirts of town.

Boarding and finding seats next to each other on the self-driving bus, we look like any other teens setting out on a road trip. Only we aren't enjoying the view of the Vermont countryside as it rolls past our window—we have work to do. Levi pulls out a tablet and begins sketching a map of the island, as much as he can piece together from memory. Using an app that allows him to configure hallways, doors, and windows, he puts together a sophisticated blueprint and talks me through it. I don't have to lean far to see it, sandwiched together as we are in our cramped seats.

"The island is several miles off the coast—you can't see it from the mainland. It's completely man-made and ecologically sound; it doesn't interfere negatively with marine life, and the entire foundation of it is made up of materials recycled and ground into sand. The compound where we lived is composed almost exclusively of glass and steel. Everything that happens there is guarded, planned. Every delivery, every visitor—they have to arrive via boat or helicopter. The keepers are not allowed to bring devices on the premises, and it wouldn't be in their best interest to tell anyone what they know; they're desperate to please him. Gravelle pays them well for their silence."

"How big is it?" I ask.

"The actual structure? Big—but I don't know square footage. I know the layout of the entire place like the back of my hand; every hallway and passage, even the restricted ones. But it's difficult to have a sense of scale when you're *inside* it. The only word I can think of to accurately describe it is that it's floating, which in some ways, it is—the whole island is like some sea monster jutting out of the surf. But that much glass, I don't know if that's ever been done anywhere else. Gravelle paid the architect who designed the compound to keep the whole endeavor as top secret as a CIA initiative."

"That's why there aren't any photos of it."

Levi nods.

"So if it's glass everywhere, does that mean you never had any privacy?"

"It's only glass on the perimeter. Once you're inside, unless you're in one of the outer chambers, you could get completely lost in darkness. Our lessons were held in windowless rooms for hours at a time. There were days when I didn't know if it was midnight or noon, morning, night, or something in between."

"He kept you locked up like prisoners?"

"We had outside time. But it's an island—where would we have gone?"

Levi pauses for a second, looking at his tablet. He zooms in on a corridor.

"We shared rooms—my roommate has always been Jago. Our bedrooms on the compound weren't all that different from the setup at Darkwood, though they had every technological advance, whereas the Darkwood dormitories are, shall we say…"

"Primitive?" I supply.

Levi nods. "Our rooms had touch screens to operate every function, from the lights to the toilets. I never knew anything different. Now I see it was a little bit like living on a ship or a space station."

Levi highlights a section on his drawing. "Here's where all the classroom areas were clustered: an art room, a room for martial arts, a dance studio, a theater, a science lab."

He hovers over another block of rooms.

"What's that area?" I ask.

"Gravelle's quarters. They were strictly off-limits. Code Purple, he called them. None of us ever saw the inside of where Gravelle lived and worked. Code Yellow rooms—the library, for example, which was glass on all sides, including the ceiling—were always open to us. That was my favorite room," he adds, highlighting it in yellow on the floor plan. Levi fiddles with a setting, and suddenly the whole drawing changes perspective, from a flat, two-dimensional rendering to a 3-D view of the space. Even as a sketch, it's beautiful. "Every book you could imagine was contained within those walls. The ceiling was twenty feet high. If you wanted to read a book that was shelved at the very top, you could request it, and the entire room would shift like a factory assembly line to bring the book down to you."

"Why weren't they all just digitized?"

Levi shrugs. "Gravelle valued physical books."

We spend the rest of the bus ride planning the next leg of our journey. I fall asleep with my head on Levi's shoulder. I dream of the compound, of intricate mazes of hallways, and of Gravelle, towering over us, his face twisted and ugly. When I wake up, we're at Bar Harbor.

The bus ride has taken much more time than anticipated—most of the day, in fact. It's getting dark now. We have to stop for the night. I find a nondescript hotel in town and pay for a room in cash. There's only one queen-size bed that takes up most of the space. For dinner, we eat snacks from the hall vending machine—chocolate bars and chips.

"Can I tell you a secret?" I ask Levi as I take a bite out of a candy bar.

"Depends what it is," he quips as he pops open a bag of pretzels.

"Ha," I say, allowing myself for one miniscule second to appreciate the simplicity of this moment. Us, here in this room together, acting, for all intents and purposes, like regular teenagers.

"So? What's this big confession?" Levi asks, lying back on a pillow, his hands behind his head. My heart hammers as I look at him, lying there, and imagine all the things I would do…if I could…

"My dad never let me eat this kind of stuff growing up. I think I was fourteen before I ever tasted soda."

"Wow," says Levi, his whole face lighting up. "And to think, I almost went my whole life without knowing that critical fact." I toss a pillow at him, and he ducks, laughing. After our sugar-laden meal, Levi sets up a cot in the corner, spreading out a blanket and rooting in his bag for his toothbrush. We get changed for the night without talking. I pull on a tank and shorts in the bathroom. It's what I usually sleep in, but tonight, it gives me pause. The shorts feel short, and my shoulders feel bare. I climb into the bed; Levi takes the cot.

"Levi?" I say, as I lie there in the dark.

"Yes?" he answers back from only a few feet away.

"Can you come lie next to me?"

I don't even know I've asked it until it's too late for me to take it back. I hold my breath as I hear him move from the cot to the bed, where he lies down next to me, on top of the covers. I can't pretend I haven't been waiting for this moment, for us to be alone like this with no one to interrupt. No roommates, no curfews, no rules. Just us.

"What did you mean," I ask, my voice barely audible, "when you said you fell for me?"

Levi turns on his side to face me. I expect to see lightness, a smile, or the hint of one. Instead, he is focused and intense. A fever builds in me, starting at my toes and traveling up my spine as he takes my cheek in his hand and leans in, pressing his lips to mine with fervor. I kiss him back, hungry, as he pulls me toward him, the full weight of his body against my own. It's like I'm melting into him as we continue to kiss, arms and legs entwining, sparks traveling from his body to mine and back again like static electricity.

We pull away, letting our bodies detach only as much as is necessary to look at each other. I am momentarily flustered.

"So that answered my question," I mumble. Levi laughs, the humor back in his voice as he brushes a strand of hair out of my eyes. The action is so tender, it's hard to reconcile with the raw strength I know he possesses.

"I'm glad you found that response acceptable."

I rest my head on his shoulder, suddenly tired. "Levi?"

"Yes?" he answers back, his voice thick.

"If something happens to us tomorrow…"

"Yes?"

I look in his eyes. He hasn't tried to reassure me. To promise that I am safe with him. I am glad for his honesty.

"I will never regret that you came to Darkwood."

The next morning, we catch the ferry that will take us through the ocean to Queen's Harbor. It's a four-hour ride, but we don't talk much. We're both nervous—we've made it this far, but the last leg of our journey will be the hardest.

We spend most of the ferry ride on the outside deck, our coats bundled around us as the wind of the open water whips at us. We leave the bay, lined with trees and dotted with houses. It feels like we're entering another world, leaving behind New England for uncharted waters. It feels like we're barreling toward the edge of the planet.

"Will he be expecting us?" I ask Levi, as I shove my hands into the pockets of my down coat. "The fisherman who can take us there?"

"Yes," Levi says. He's explained that this man knows Castor Island well, and that based on Levi's previous encounters with him, he won't tip off Gravelle.

At Queen's Harbor—a quaint little fishing town untouched by time—we find the fisherman down at the docks. He's ready to take us the two hours to Castor Island, but he warns us we're in for a bumpy ride.

Grateful for this man's help, we climb aboard his weather-worn motorboat. I cling to the edge of my seat the entire time, biting back seasickness as we pound through the choppy water.

When I finally see the island, I'm staggered. In all his descriptions of the place where he grew up, Levi never once mentioned its sheer beauty.

Jutting out of the water like a majestic, if small-scale, city, Castor Island is a work of art. Wrought out of steel and glass, the compound where Levi and his friends spent most of their waking and sleeping hours glows in the sunlight, its steel hinges and supports sparking colors like a kaleidoscope. The angles of this structure are unexpected and somehow defy logic.

"It's stunning," I say.

"It's home," Levi responds. "If home is the place where you're locked up without a key."

"Was it that bad? Always?"

"Not all of it," he admits, as the fisherman steers the boat toward the shore. "I had the others, and they cared about me. We were a team of sorts. A motley crew. But a team, nevertheless."

"So." I stare, entranced, at the compound before us. "How are we going to do this?" After all the travel, all the planning, I suddenly feel foolish. The compound mocks me with its grandeur and otherworldliness, and the truth is, I'm afraid. *Can we do this? Is it even possible?*

Levi doesn't answer. He reaches out a hand, and I take it. Clasping his in my own gives me an instant boost of confidence. We disembark from the boat, paying the fisherman generously for helping us. He wishes us luck—we're going to need it—before he turns for the mainland.

As my feet hit the sand, I notice that the beach doesn't feel at all man-made. It's like a vacation destination. Well, except for the fact that the Similars were never allowed to leave.

"I know the security codes," Levi explains, as we make our way toward the main building. "It took me years to figure them out, but I had a feeling they might come in handy someday, so I memorized them. They have a regular rotation, but Gravelle won't have changed them. So as long as no one's tipped him off that we're coming…" He shrugs. "We'll be able to walk right inside."

"That's it?" I ask, losing all my bravado. We're minutes from entering the lion's den.

"That's it," he says. I detect fear and panic in Levi's voice, even though I know he's pretending, for his sake and mine, that he's in control. Before I can respond, he kisses me. Our lips mash together, our teeth banging. It's not a kiss, really, so much as a last, desperate connection.

"Let's go," he says. I take his hand, and we do.

THE COMPOUND

WE RACE DOWN the labyrinthine halls in the compound. I follow Levi, trusting him implicitly.

"I'm hoping Pru's in a dorm room," Levi says. "Or in the dining hall or study. Otherwise—"

"What?" I ask, watching carefully as he tries the handle of a door, finds it locked, and peers into a small, squat window at the top.

"Nothing," he answers. I don't press him.

Declaring the room empty, Levi moves on, peering through the window of the next door. I do the same with the one across from it. We repeat this pattern all the way down the hall, until I find a door that's ajar and cautiously push it open. Inside is a bare bed and the touch screens Levi described on the bus ride here. There are countless machines and 3-D printers, a wall completely covered in steel cabinetry, and a glass shelf filled with needles in hard plastic cases.

"What's all this for?" I wonder.

"Most of it was for me and my friends." Levi glances over a couple of readouts from a printer. "But with us gone, I can't imagine what Gravelle will use it—"

"Surely you have some idea," says a voice. I turn to see a figure standing in the doorway. It only takes me seconds to realize who it is.

Sagging skin covers 80 percent of his face. His forehead is traversed by a deep and abiding scar. This is the man formerly known as John Underwood. This is Augustus Gravelle.

"Emmaline Chance." Gravelle lifts a hand to his face and rubs his chin. "You're as beautiful as you were as a little girl. Please. You need sustenance and rest." Gravelle claps his hands, and in what feels like no time, two guards appear behind him. Under their identical white uniforms, they have stocky, hard bodies. Their faces, free of any lines or expression, look almost inhuman.

"Show our guests to the lobby," Gravelle orders the guards. Levi and I have no choice but to oblige as we are led forcefully by our elbows into the heart of the compound.

A guard pulls me along, and my breath catches as I notice that he wears a gun in a holster. We reach a vast, minimalistic lobby, decorated tastefully with sprawling modern sofas and low glass coffee tables. A million things are rushing through my mind: I'm terrified that we'll never find Prudence, that this man has already done something terrible to her, that he'll do terrible things to us. But I try to stay present and keep my bearings.

"Sit," Gravelle says as he directs us to a couch. A tray of cheese, crackers, and sparkling water waits on a nearby side table. "Eat. As your host, it's my job to keep you fed, watered, and laundered."

I do as I'm told, and so does Levi. We sit. We eat. We are starving, not having eaten anything since last night's candy bars. For a moment, I wonder if the food is poisoned or drugged. I guess we'll know soon enough.

Gravelle leans back in his chair, his cane on his knees, and watches us eat. "You were a beautiful child, Emmaline," he muses. "But you've grown to be quite stunning."

"You keep saying that," I say between bites. "But when did you see me as a little girl?"

"Your father and I were roommates at Darkwood, Emmaline, or did you not know that?" He's still staring at me. I meet his gaze and immediately want to look away from his intensity. But this last bit of information gives me pause.

"No. I didn't know that."

"I see," says Gravelle. "We were close, your dad and I. I would have loved to have known you more as you were growing up. Now, I am nearly too late…"

I meet Levi's gaze with wide eyes. *Too late? What does he mean by that?*

"The two of you have a lot to learn. That can be easily remedied." Gravelle smiles to himself.

"Where's Prudence?" I demand. "We know she's here somewhere—"

Gravelle holds up a hand to silence me. Then he reaches for a bell on a side table and rings it. Its sound fills the vast, impersonal room. Moments later, a diminutive man rushes in. Unlike the guards, he is neither muscular nor intimidating. He bows to Gravelle and speaks in a foreign language I don't understand. Gravelle responds in the same language. I look to Levi for some explanation. Predictably, he lets no emotion show in his face. He is as stoic as ever. My eyes flit to the door. The two guards stand directly in front of it, their bodies forming a blockade.

Gravelle grins at the diminutive man—a servant, I assume—and the man bows.

"Wonderful," Gravelle says in English now, looking from me to Levi with a pleased expression. "Dominic will show you to your accommodations. Dominic?"

Dominic reaches for my hand. Does he think I need help off of the couch? I stand, bewildered, looking to Levi for some guidance. The next thing I know, Dominic's sliding a needle into my forearm. Suddenly I feel nauseous, like I'm back on that motorboat.

"What are you doing to me?" I manage to ask.

"You requested answers." Gravelle smiles. "And I aim to please."

After that, everything goes blank.

⬦⸻⸻⬦

I wake up disoriented. I'm in a windowless room, so I can't tell how long I've been out. As my mind starts to work again, it occurs to me that I must be in an inner chamber of the compound, in a room like the ones Levi and I searched when we first got here. I'm in a bed with white sheets, and nearly everything around me in this small, impersonal space is white. There are a few machines in the corner, and tubing…lots of tubing. It takes me a moment to realize the tubes are connected to me. I stare at them, not quite processing what I'm seeing. What are they for?

I look down at my body. There's an IV stuck in my inner arm. Screens and monitors buzz softly around me. Panic builds in my chest. My first instinct is to run. I try to push myself up to a sitting position, but I can't. I slam back against the bed. It's like there's a force field around me. I can't see or feel this invisible barrier when I reach out to try to touch it, but something is holding me back.

I lie in bed, breathing in and out, trying to conjure the meditation exercises Dr. Delmore taught me from when Dad sent me to therapy after Oliver died. They don't help. My mind is racing. *Where is Levi? Is he being held like this somewhere too?*

I fight the invisible barrier again, and I'm slammed down against the bed. My panic morphs into dread. *Surely Gravelle won't keep me in this bed forever—will he?* The thought makes my stomach lurch.

There's a tablet next to me. I can just reach its screen beside my bed, which I know is by design. *He wants me to look at it*, I tell myself. Gravelle has put it here, with me a captive audience. He knows I'd rather see what he has to show me than lie here with only my thoughts, bleak and desperate as they are.

I reach for the screen, scrolling through the different icons. There are encyclopedias full of information on everything from botany and calculus to politics and languages. I click on "Botany," and beautiful images of flowers pop up, not on the small screen, but in the air in front of me. They are luscious and three-dimensional, as if the plant is growing right before my eyes. Born of what is obviously the latest in virtual reality technology, the blooms are so vivid that I want to reach out and touch them. But they are just out of my reach.

I continue to flip through the topics on the screen until I notice another folder on the main home page. It's labeled "Personal." Inside, I find hundreds of other folders, each one labeled "Memory" with a descriptor beside it. I've read about this somewhere—or maybe I heard my father talking about it once with a business associate. The storage of memories through virtual reality technology. It's not yet widely used, but it's also not surprising that Gravelle would already have a fully realized version of the technology.

I dig in the back of my brain, trying to remember. Gravelle made his initial fortune starting an augmented reality company nearly twenty years ago. This is his field.

Though there are hundreds of folders, only a few are high-lighted. The unhighlighted ones don't open when I click on them, so I assume I don't have access. I select the first highlighted folder in the group—"Memory: Early Darkwood." The room darkens like inside a movie theater. Images swirl around me, not in one static spot, like the flowers, but all over. I'm transported from the bed in this white room to a dorm room, much like my room at school. I take in my surroundings, knowing full well I'm not there, not really. I'm still confined to this bed. Yet this dorm room feels so *real*. Real, and entirely frightening, because I know in my gut there's no way out until the memory is over. For the foreseeable future, the past is my very real present.

THE MEMORY

A BOY LOUNGES on one of the twin beds, leaning back against the wall, his laptop computer on his knees. The laptop is my first clue that we're a couple of decades in the past. It's oversize and clunky, a relic you'd see in a pawn shop. The boy is typing furiously, the grin on his face half-hidden by the long brown bangs that fall in his eyes. He is so wrapped up in his typing that he barely notices when another boy walks in, hesitating awkwardly at the threshold. This second boy carries a beat-up duffel and a weathered paper shopping bag.

"Um, hi?" says the second boy.

The boy on the bed glances up from his laptop, an impish smile still on his face. He's good-looking. He has an ease about him that's magnetic, and I'm immediately drawn to him. It's almost like I *know* him, but I know that's silly. This memory probably took place before I was born.

"Hey," says this boy on the bed. He studies the boy in the doorway, noticing the boy's too-short khaki pants and threadbare shirt. His clothes are ill-fitting and worn, but they look like they've been ironed. There's not a wrinkle on them.

The second boy fidgets, his angular face etched with discomfort. His jet-black hair is greased unattractively behind his ears, yet he has strong, attractive, even intelligent features.

The boy sitting on the bed grins and hops up, extending a hand.

"Welcome to the rest of your life." He waits for the second boy to shake his hand. After a moment, he does.

"John Underwood," says the second boy. "Everyone calls me Johnny."

"Colin," the first boy answers jauntily, stuffing his hands into his pockets. "Colin Chance. Nice to meet you."

The air goes out of me like I'm a giant balloon. It's the first time since I entered this memory that I've even thought of myself, of my own body.

This boy, Colin Chance, is my father.

I'm watching my own father when he was a student at Darkwood.

But I don't have time to process this. I turn my attention back to the scene. I don't want to miss a second of it.

"That's your bed," my father—I mean, Colin—tells his new roommate. "Where's the rest of your luggage? In the car?"

"The rest?" Johnny says. "No, this is it." He sets down his bags, then sits stiffly on his bed.

"That's all you brought with you?" Colin stares at the duffel and paper bag in confusion.

Johnny grabs the handles of the paper bag and dumps its contents on the bed. It's all textbooks. They're used, and not gently. Some are missing covers. Johnny unzips his duffel and removes the contents: a few clothes, one extra pair of shoes, and a Ziplock bag containing his toothbrush and medicinals.

"I like to travel light." He places the clothes in a dresser drawer, slides the shoes under his bed, and sets the toiletry bag on his desk. My father looks from the dresser to the bed, something clicking in his mind.

"Good call leaving the rest of your stuff at home," Colin says generously, even though Johnny quite obviously doesn't *have* other stuff. "Half the junk the kids here bring is a big waste of space, if you ask me." I let out a breath, relieved my father has chosen, in this situation, to be kind.

Johnny shrugs, surveying Colin's side of the room, which has everything from snacks to a mini-fridge and even a bike, propped up on one wheel by the window.

"Where're you from?" Colin asks as he flops back onto his bed, picking up a soccer ball and lazily passing it back and forth between his hands.

"New York." Johnny watches the ball. "Not the city. Upstate."

"Sounds…nice?"

"Sure, if you like cemeteries. Our house was built on one. When I was a kid, I used to watch the hearse bringing the coffins up the hill. Once, there were sixteen funerals in a twelve-hour period. There'd been a fire at the local pub. That was a pretty interesting day."

I focus on Colin's face. Johnny's finally made an impression, and not a good one. He drops the soccer ball.

"Oh," he says quietly.

A voice rings out, cutting through the silence. "You made it!"

Colin and Johnny turn. A skinny kid stands in the doorway, his hair tousled like it's been brushed once, ages ago, his clothes mismatched and wrinkled. He grips a messy notebook under his arm. Clunky, tortoise-shell glasses with thick lenses sit on his nose.

Johnny springs from the bed. "Hey."

"What's up, Al?" says Colin, who welcomes the distraction.

"Albert," mumbles the kid. "I prefer Albert."

"Yeah, sorry." Colin laughs. "I forgot. Al—I mean, Albert, this is my new roommate. Johnny Underwood from New York."

"He knows my name," says Johnny to my dad, though he looks straight at Albert.

"Oh." Colin looks between the two boys, confused. "You two met already?"

"You could say that," says Johnny, his voice measured.

Johnny and Albert stare at each other another beat. Then, out of nowhere, Albert throws open his arms, his notebook falling to the ground as he pulls Johnny into a bear hug. Albert's glasses hit Johnny's shoulder and knock askew as he embraces him. Johnny doesn't hug Albert back. He just stands there, stiffly. But he doesn't push Albert away either.

Albert breaks the hug. Now I can clearly see his face. He's grinning, pushing his glasses back up the bridge of his nose.

"Johnny, my man! Long time no talk. Wait till you see what I've been cooking up in the lab. I don't want to get anyone prematurely excited, but the cafeteria food is gonna taste a whole lot better once I get my beta enhancers in it..."

Johnny shrugs. "Sure. Whatever you say, Albert."

"Show me a little enthusiasm, buddy. I'm going to vastly improve that mush they call dinner—"

"I haven't tried the dinner yet, remember?" Johnny says, sounding agitated. "I just got here. A year later than you. Because I couldn't—because this is my first year," Johnny amends. I know what he was going to say. Because he couldn't afford it.

"How'd you two meet again?" Colin asks, and I want to tell my father to butt out, but I don't because he can't see or hear me. This is only a memory, after all. I'm an invisible bystander.

"We didn't *meet*. We've known each other our whole lives. We're brothers, okay?" Albert snaps. The blood drains from Johnny's face at the revelation.

"Half brothers," Johnny says carefully. "We're half brothers."

My father looks from Johnny to Albert, and back to Johnny. The impish smile creeps over his face.

"Brothers!" he says excitedly. "Why didn't you say so, you big dweebs?"

"We aren't that close," Johnny says quietly.

Albert grimaces, collecting his notebook and papers from the floor. "We're close enough."

"We didn't grow up together, is what I meant." Johnny walks to the window and stares out. I see a hint of Dark Lake through the glass. It's twilight.

"We have different mothers," says Albert matter-of-factly.

"Different lives," Johnny adds, his back to Colin and Albert.

"Well, I think it's neato," says Colin. "You should've told me you've got family here, Johnny. It'll make Darkwood homier, won't it?"

Johnny turns on his heel, his eyes flashing as he stares down Colin.

"Didn't I just tell you that Albert and I didn't grow up together? That our lives, up until this point, have been as different as they could possibly be?"

Colin stares at Johnny, taken aback by the sting in his voice.

"You don't have to freak out on me, man. I was only saying…"

"I should get back to the lab," Albert says evenly. "It's good to see you, Johnny. I'll look for you at dinner, okay?"

Johnny shrugs. "Sure. See you later."

Albert leaves as quietly as he came.

"I take it your brother—sorry, half brother—didn't grow up on a cemetery?"

"No," says Johnny Underwood. "He didn't."

◇—⊢—◇

The scene in front of me changes, and I have to remind myself that none of this is real. It *was* real, but it's not actually happening right now, and not to me. That was my father in his dorm room, years ago, with his roommate. And not just any roommate: Johnny Underwood. Now Augustus Gravelle—Oliver's biological father. It's all so surreal.

Before me, the scene shows the Darkwood cafeteria. It's dark outside, so it must be dinnertime, the first dinner of the semester. I can tell from the "Welcome Back" banner hanging over the entryway. It must still be the same day.

My father—Colin—sits at a table with a polished-looking crew. An overly confident brown-haired boy flips some playing cards on the table, slapping them down like it's part of a game. A thin girl joins in, and she reminds me of someone else I know. That's when I realize it's Bianca Huxley—Madison's mother. She was Bianca Kravitz back then. I focus on the brown-haired boy playing with the cards and decide it's Zeke Choate—Jake's father. Another kid sits across from Zeke. He's on the scrawny side but has striking features. It takes me only a moment to figure out it's Jaeger Stanwick, Pru's dad as a younger man.

I don't know why I'm so surprised to see them all here, sitting together. I knew they were all part of the Ten. I guess I didn't realize they were good friends too.

"Half brothers?" Zeke jeers, slapping down another card. I can see more clearly now. He and Bianca are playing war. "And here I thought the most interesting thing about Albert was the potion he made that helps me lie without giving myself away."

"How does it work?" asks Bianca.

"Don't you want to know."

Bianca doesn't take her eyes off the cards. "When you lie, you sweat like a pig, Zeke, so I'll have to assume the 'potion' Albert gave you was a good old-fashioned stick of antiperspirant."

Zeke laughs. "Too bad you'll never get close enough to

find out. I win, by the way. Look at my pile. Way more cards than you."

Bianca frowns. "Cheater."

Zeke howls with laughter.

I focus on Jaeger, who clearly isn't interested in this conversation. He looks like he's still thinking about Colin's news.

"All this time, Albert never told us he had a half brother," Jaeger says. "Are you sure you heard right?"

Colin shrugs. "They have different mothers. It was all very clear."

"Didn't you say this new boy's on scholarship?" Bianca asks, spitting out the words like they might contaminate her tongue. I feel my blood boiling.

"I didn't say that," Colin snaps. "And what's it got to do with anything?"

Bianca nudges Colin in the ribs. Johnny approaches their table, awkwardly balancing his tray and his school satchel.

The four teens stare as he approaches, not one of them saying a word in greeting. When Johnny reaches the table, he stops, unsure of whether or not to sit.

Finally, my father speaks. "Johnny Boy! I was just telling my friends about you. This is some of the crew. Zeke, Bianca, and Jaeger."

"Hi," Johnny says, still frozen.

"I'm gonna let you in on a little secret, Johnny Boy." Colin leans in conspiratorially. "They'll never actually invite you to sit down."

Bianca pops a fry in her mouth. "If we invited everyone to sit

with us"—she gestures, indicating the rest of the dining hall—
"how would anyone be able to tell who's actually important?"

Johnny's jaw tightens. His shoulders square. Without hesitating, Johnny squeezes his tray onto the table, directly between
Colin and Zeke.

"You're going to make room for me, right?" says Johnny
evenly.

Zeke looks annoyed, Colin proud. "Sure thing, roomie!"
Colin scoots over, giving Johnny space on the bench. "Cheer up,
sour faces. This new kid might give us all a run for our money.
And I don't think that's such a bad thing. Do you, Zeke?"

Zeke shrugs. "Not if he can keep up."

Bianca spears a piece of melon with her fork. "Keeping up
requires a certain image." She eyes Johnny. "I doubt the new boy
has what it takes."

"You don't know anything about the new boy," says Johnny.
Bianca's hand freezes midbite. Her eyes narrow. Then she laughs.
"He's got a sense of humor, that's for sure." She leans back in her
chair, studying Johnny like a specimen. Then she shrugs. "Guess
you'll have to prove me wrong, new boy."

That's when I notice two other students approaching in a
whirlwind of energy. The girl is stunning, with strawberry-blond
hair, blue eyes, and the kind of smile that doesn't come from
good dental work. She's laughing as a boy next to her makes
a joke, gesturing with his hands. He has a friendly face, dark
skin, and curly black hair that he runs his hands through. I can't
hear myself over the simulation, but I gasp at the sight of them.
It's Jane Porter and Booker Ward. They are Oliver's mom and

stepfather, some twenty years ago. Of course they are. They were here too. They were part of the Ten.

"You two look like you're having a rollicking good time." Bianca smirks, forgetting all about the new boy as the duo approaches. "Want to let us in on the joke?"

The girl giggles. "Booker was just telling me the funniest story about…" She stops talking when Booker shoots her a look. It's clear he doesn't want her sharing his joke with the rest of the group.

"Oh, never mind," she says, and I'm certain she is who I think she is. She has the same relaxed, happy expression I've seen on Jane's face a thousand times. Only not since *the thing that happened*.

Jane flops down at the table next to Jaeger and across from Johnny.

"Jane Porter," she says to him, holding out her hand for him to shake. "Resident bookworm and miscreant extraordinaire."

Johnny appears surprised by the gesture, but quickly composes himself. "John Underwood. Everyone calls me Johnny. Except for your friend Bianca," he adds. "She's dubbed me the 'new boy.'"

Bianca snorts. Zeke smacks her leg. They both laugh.

"That's right," Colin says as Jane smiles at Johnny, then digs into her dinner. "Johnny New Boy joins us from upstate New York."

"What the—!" Jane shouts after swallowing her casserole. "What's in this glorious mess? Dead snails?" She pushes away her tray. "Who wants to sneak down to Bertie's Diner for some real food?"

"Count me in," says Booker as he slides an arm around Jane. "Any of you kids wanna join? Or are you too chicken to play hooky?"

"It's not that we're chicken. We don't want to watch the two of you make out any more than we have to," scoffs Bianca.

This is all too painful—watching Jane and Booker so happy and carefree together. That changed after Oliver's death. And yet, I want to watch. I have to.

"I'll go," says a quiet, determined voice. Everyone looks over at Johnny. "To Bertie's. I'm in."

Booker scowls. Jane grins. "We'll pick you up at your room tonight. Nine p.m."

"You know you'll be breaking about ten school rules, right?" Zeke says.

Johnny shrugs. "So?"

"So you could lose your scholarship," Zeke replies.

Johnny tenses at the word. "Who says I'm on a scholarship?"

"An educated guess," Zeke says, staring at him.

"Hey," says Jane. "Would you two shut up? They're about to announce our strata." With that, the view goes blank.

◇──┤├──◇

It's dark. There's enough light to see we're outside, no longer in the dining hall. I squint to take in the scene. We're behind one of the Darkwood dormitories. Two figures walk down the dimly lit path. As they get closer, I see it's Jane Porter and Johnny Underwood.

Johnny walks with his hands in his pockets. He's standing taller than before. His clothes fit him better, and he's more confident. I wonder how much time has passed. Weeks? Months? I don't have long to wonder.

"You can't take half of what Zeke says seriously, you know," Jane is saying.

"I don't," Johnny replies defensively.

"Then why do you care so much what he thinks? I've seen the way you act around him. Around all of them."

"They're my friends," he says. "So I humor Zeke. Or tell Booker what he wants to hear."

"Or compliment Bianca every chance you get? 'Oh, B, you look really nice today,'" Jane mimics. "You know they're not all that, right? They're regular people, like you and me."

"Like you, sure. You're one of them."

Jane stops and looks Johnny in the eye. "I guess it's time," she says.

"Time for what?"

"For me to let you in on the secret that no one else at this school will ever tell you, but that you desperately need to hear."

She's got Johnny's attention now. "I'm listening," he says.

"Ezekiel Choate, Colin Chance, Bianca Kravitz, and Booker Ward all have one thing in common." She pauses dramatically. "They are the biggest bunch of insecure babies I've ever met in my life."

Johnny scowls. "Thanks. I thought you were going to share something useful." He kicks at a rock with his scuffed sneaker.

"Don't you get it? They are clueless. They've been polished

like precious gems but have never left the vault, except to be paraded around by Mommy and Daddy. They don't have any idea what it's like to live. Not like you do."

"Why? Because I grew up poor?" When Jane doesn't respond, Johnny speaks for her. "That's what you meant, isn't it? My mother cleans houses for a living, Jane. Have you ever stopped to consider what that means to someone like Bianca Kravitz?"

"I think it's noble," Jane says softly.

"I detest that word, that tone. You're really saying you pity her." His next words are barely audible. "And me, by association."

"I could never…"

"You absolutely could. Because you're one of them."

"Somehow I don't think you mean that as a compliment," Jane responds.

"It isn't."

The two are silent for a moment as neither one knows what to say. Johnny appears sad. Heartbroken, even. And Jane's no better. I sense she's on the verge—of crying? Walking away?

Then Johnny grabs Jane's hand. But his voice isn't sad, it's full of passion. "You're one of them, but you aren't the *same*."

"You just said…" I notice tears filling her eyes.

"You have empathy. Zeke and Bianca and the others don't."

"They care about you, Johnny," says Jane. "You're their friend, even if you won't let yourself believe it."

His voice is tight. "I believe I'm the friend they keep around to feel good about themselves. I'm their charity case. We all have our roles to play. I know what mine is."

"Then what's mine?"

Johnny drops Jane's hands and stuffs his own into his pockets, not looking at her directly. "You know," he mumbles.

"Sorry, Johnny New Boy. I don't."

"You're the one they covet. The one those guys want to call their girl. The one Bianca wishes she were."

"Please," Jane answers, her voice ringing with laughter. "If they all like me so much, why am I alone?"

Johnny leans on the wall separating them from the woods and Dark Lake beyond. "Because you have your whole life ahead of you. Because you know you don't have to choose any of them. Not yet. Maybe not ever."

Jane moves to stand next to him. Side by side in the moonlight, they breathe as one.

"Maybe I'll move to the country, live in a shack, and teach kindergarten to a bunch of snot-nosed kids."

"I could live in a shack."

Jane laughs.

"But I could get us something better. Way better," Johnny says, reveling in the fantasy.

Jane smiles. "Can you imagine what my family would say? If I left all this?" She indicates Darkwood, but I know she means more than the school, and so does Johnny. She's referring to all that a Darkwood education affords beyond graduation. "They'd drag me kicking and screaming back to their penthouse on Park Avenue."

Johnny stares off into the distance at Dark Lake. It's shining like a black pearl.

"I wonder what they'd think of me."

"Johnny…" She reaches out, but he jerks away.

"Don't."

"I was just going to say…"

"What you always say. That I'm as good as them. That this is my legacy, if…"

"It is, isn't it? Darkwood was started by your ancestors…"

He spins on her, fire in his eyes.

"Ancestry only matters if you're acknowledged in the family tree. My father got my mother pregnant, abandoned us, and left us destitute. Then he went on to have a real family. Albert is his son. Not me."

"You are still his son."

"Semantics, Jane. He's never even spoken to me. That doesn't exactly make him father of the year."

"Well, he's missing out. I think you're brilliant. Zeke and the others don't have an ounce of the scrap you have."

"Good for me," he snaps.

"It's good for me too," she says. "I'd be worried if the boy I was with didn't live up to my expectations. Luckily, he's got the number-one stratum."

Johnny turns to her.

"But I have the number-one stratum?"

Jane smiles. "Exactly."

⟡⊷⊣⊶⟡

We're in a science lab. The equipment and white countertops all gleam like they've been wiped down with antiseptic spray. It only takes me a moment to recognize this as one of the abandoned research labs. Huddled in the corner are three figures.

"Punch in the code," says one of the guys. "Come on! It's not that hard!"

"Why don't you do it yourself if it's so easy?"

The person who spoke first doesn't reply. As I get a better look, I see that it's Jaeger Stanwick. Even now, watching this fourth memory, it's still surreal seeing them—our parents—as young Darkwood students.

Jaeger squats, his knuckles white as he clamps his fingers into nervous fists. The second figure, the one fiddling with a keypad, is Johnny Underwood. Next to him is Zeke Choate.

"Got it," says Johnny as a loud *beep* rings out. He's unlocked a steel box.

A metal door swings open, and three animals peer out of a cage. I can't tell what kind of animals they are at first; they look like a strange cross between a dog and a fox. They have foxlike snouts and bushy tails, but their ears lie flat like golden retrievers'.

"Hey, little guys," Zeke coos at them. "You're free. Go on! You're free!" The animals simply stare at him and sniff.

"If anyone is having second thoughts about this, the time to voice them is now," Jaeger says under his breath.

"Too late," says Johnny as the animals emerge from the cage tentatively. "I don't know about you, but I'm not shoving them back in there. Let's go! We'll open the main door and let them out. Then I'll double lock the front door from the outside, put the override code on, and we'll make a run for it."

"Why are we doing this again?" Zeke whines as he prods the animals toward the door. They are docile and not particularly eager to run away. Now that they've made it out of their cage, they don't know what to do.

Suddenly, an alarm rings out. The three boys freeze in their tracks.

"Run!" Zeke shouts to Johnny and Jaeger. Then the scene goes black.

◇──┤├──◇

We're in the Tower Room of a Darkwood dormitory. Several stern adults—two men and two women—sit at the end of a mahogany table. At the other end, Johnny Underwood sits in a blazer and tie looking like he hasn't slept in weeks. Dark circles rim his eyes. His hair is greased back behind his ears. A few other students sit along the perimeter of the room, also looking serious. I immediately recognize Zeke Choate and Jaeger Stanwick. Jane Porter is there, and next to her, Booker Ward. My father is noticeably absent.

"We've reviewed your classmates' account of the evening of March fifteenth, and there were no discrepancies in your stories." I'm stunned to see it's none other than Headmaster Ransom talking. Gone is his gray-flecked hair and laugh lines. He is a relatively young man. "However," Ransom continues, "there is one account of the night in question that we would like to review again. We've asked Albert Seymour to answer a few additional questions for the board. Albert?"

There's a shuffling at the back of the room, and I scan the room to find him standing up from his chair, dropping a notebook, and bending nervously to pick it up again.

"Here," Albert mumbles. "I'm here."

"Have a seat at the table, please," Ransom instructs. "Next to your brother."

There's a noticeable buzz in the room as that word is spoken. *Brother.*

Albert drops his satchel on top of the shiny wood veneer. Johnny doesn't look at him.

"Thank you for joining us, Mr. Seymour," says Headmaster Ransom. "Is it true that on the day and the evening of March fifteenth, you were not present on the Darkwood campus?"

Albert shifts in his chair. "Yes. That is correct."

"And where were you at the time?"

"In New York City," Albert says quietly. "On a trip."

"A trip?" Ransom presses. "What was the nature of that trip?"

Albert purses his lips before answering. "It was a family matter. I was in New York visiting my father."

At the mention of their father, it's as though Johnny has been punched in the gut.

"You were visiting your father," Ransom repeats, making a note on the pad in front of him. "Ms. Fleischer? Do we have proof that Mr. Seymour was absent that day?" I turn my head to Ransom's left, surprised I didn't notice her before. Though she's a good twenty years younger in the memory, and judging from the way Ransom just addressed her, probably still a Latin teacher and not yet the principal of the school, she is still every bit the Principal Fleischer I know. Her face retains that weathered, perpetually stern look I've always known. Maybe she never looked young.

"Definitive proof," she barks. "Albert missed a midterm exam. World history. Made arrangements to reschedule it for the next afternoon."

"Thank you," Ransom says. "Mr. Seymour? You produced a train ticket for the administration, dated and time-stamped for March fifteenth?"

"Yes, I did."

"And so, we can assume that it was *not* you who punched in the code that gave access to the animal laboratory on the eve of March fifteenth? The laboratory where you—and only you—were conducting an experiment by special permission from the science department. Can you tell us about this experiment?"

Albert fidgets in his seat, shooting a look at Johnny, who continues to stare at the table. "I was working with those animals—the ones that were set free—on a lengthy study that had begun one year earlier. Because that laboratory houses top-secret experiments by Darkwood faculty and visiting scholars, it is usually closed to students."

"But your research was compelling enough to prompt the science department to give you a small grant to work in the east wing during after-school hours?"

"Yes." Albert is shaking.

"What animals were you working with, Mr. Seymour?"

"*Canis vulpes canis*," he whispers, his voice barely audible.

"Domesticated foxes. A cross between a wild fox and domesticated dog."

"And what were you attempting to accomplish with your research?" Ransom presses.

Albert pauses a beat, his knuckles going white as he wrings his hands together, presumably to stop them from shaking.

"I was attempting to clone them."

There's a complete hush in the room.

"And were your attempts successful?" Ransom continues.

"Yes," says Albert. It's only now when he glances over at his brother that Johnny meets his gaze.

"But you did not free the animals from the lab?"

"No," says Albert, never taking his eyes off Johnny. "It wasn't me."

"We've already established that Albert wasn't on the school premises at the time of the violation!" pipes in Fleischer. "It couldn't have been—"

"Mr. Seymour, one final question. It was your personal access code that was used to open the laboratory. Did you willingly give this information to any student?"

The two brothers' eyes are locked. I can sense an understanding pass between them.

"No," Albert says quietly. "I did not willingly give this information to another student."

The room is silent as everyone waits for Ransom to respond. My pulse pounds in my ears.

"Is all this really necessary?" Fleischer interrupts. "Johnny Underwood was caught freeing those animals. It's clear what happened. He stole the access code from his brother and released those animals as a childish prank. I'd recommend we proceed to the punishment portion of this session."

Ransom nods, shuffling through his notes.

"Does anyone else have anything they'd like to add?" Ransom addresses the other adults in the room, the members of the Darkwood board.

A woman to Ransom's left—gray-haired, stiff, matronly—surveys Albert and Johnny. "The two of you are brothers?" she asks.

Albert nods. Johnny remains silent.

"They are half brothers, Helena."

"Ah yes. Mr. Seymour, you are a descendant of the Seymours who founded this school—am I correct?"

"That's right," Albert mumbles.

"And you, Mr. Underwood. You are also a descendant of those same Seymours?"

Johnny clenches his fists, unclenches them. "Technically? You could say that."

"And yet," Helena presses, "you are on a scholarship, while your brother comes from some of the greatest wealth in this school's history."

"Your point, Helena?" Ransom interjects. "The boy's background has no bearing on how this offense was committed, and certainly no bearing on the punishment."

"Respectfully, Ransom, I disagree—"

Ransom cuts her off. "It is protocol that the defendant has one last chance to speak. Mr. Seymour, you can return to your seat."

Albert mumbles something I can't make out, grabs his

notebook and satchel, and gets up from the table, retreating into the shadows of the room. He doesn't sit with Zeke Choate, Jane Porter, and the others.

"Mr. Underwood," Ransom goes on. "Are you prepared to speak?"

"If you require it, sir." Johnny looks over at Zeke, Jaeger, Booker, and finally, Jane. He meets her eyes, and only then do I see the desperation on his face. Jane shakes her head.

"I don't have anything to say beyond what's already been reported by my friends," says Johnny, looking Ransom in the eye. The acidity in his voice—especially on the word "friends"—is not lost on me. "I slipped out of my dorm room at eight p.m. on March fifteenth after telling my friends what I had planned. They thought I was joking, which is why they didn't try to stop me. I used the laboratory key code I got from Albert without his knowledge, sneaked into the east wing, and liberated the animals in question. It was my idea, and I worked alone."

I hear a tiny gasp from the sidelines, and Jane has her hand over her mouth, stifling a sob.

Ransom's voice is stern. "So you don't deny that you committed the infraction alone? And that it was solely your idea?"

Johnny looks at Jane. Booker is at her side. Next to him are Zeke and Jaeger, who looks like he's about to be sick to his stomach. He whispers something to Zeke. Zeke shakes his head sharply. Then Jaeger stands. I'm wondering whether he's about to confess that he and Zeke were, in fact, there that night—but he doesn't. Instead, he strides out of the room.

Johnny sags. "No," he says, resignation in his voice.

"Wait!" It's Jane. She stands, her whole body trembling.

"Sit down, Ms. Porter," Fleischer barks.

Ransom puts up a hand for decorum. "Was there something you wanted to add?"

Jane and Johnny lock eyes again.

"No," Johnny says quickly. "She doesn't know anything about that night."

"But..." Before Jane can say more, Booker grabs her by the arm, pulling her down into the seat next to him. "This is wrong," she murmurs.

"Jane doesn't know anything," Johnny reiterates. "She had nothing to do with what happened. I'm ready for my punishment now."

"So be it," Ransom says, and I can tell he isn't happy about this outcome.

There's a hush in the room. My whole body tenses. I'm being held captive by the very man—then a teen boy—who's awaiting his fate. How will the outcome of this memory influence mine?

"John Underwood," Fleischer announces, "you committed four Darkwood infractions: breaking curfew, trespassing, breaking and entering, and interfering with a laboratory experiment. Though the administration has chosen not to press criminal charges, that does not lessen the serious nature of these crimes. We have no choice but to insist upon your immediate, and final, expulsion."

I hear weeping. Jane is hunched over, her head in her hands, sobbing. Booker puts a hand on her back, consoling her. I can't see Albert.

I only get one last glimpse of Johnny Underwood's face before the memory cuts out. He is devastated.

REALITY

THE NEXT THING I know, I'm in an armchair in a vast room with skinny glass windows that afford an expansive view beyond the compound—the rolling green down to the blue waters that meet the azure sky.

Across the room from me, Levi is probably ten or fifteen feet away. I make a move to go to him, but apparently whatever force field there was on my bed is at work here too. I slam back in my seat.

"You're okay," I choke out as I meet Levi's eyes. I'm surprised by how emotional I sound.

"So are you," Levi points out defensively.

"Wow, even being locked up by a tyrant hasn't stripped you of your need to argue."

Levi smiles. "Never."

I let out a little laugh. It feels good to joke. I was beginning to think I might never see Levi, or leave that room, again.

I spot two guards standing by the door, a reminder that we aren't alone. "Did Gravelle make you watch them too?" I ask Levi.

"The memories? Naturally," Levi says.

"He's an outsider." I'm anxious to fill Levi in on what I learned. "Gravelle—he was an outsider his entire life. At Darkwood, he hoped he'd find a place to fit in. But then they betrayed him." I recount what I saw—the discipline hearing, the expulsion.

"What I saw was later, then," Levi says. "Gravelle graduated from a local high school. Never made it to Harvard like he wanted, but he married Jane. It was the one dream he couldn't let die. Jane stayed true to him, even when everyone else cast him off as a liar and a cheat. But then his personal life fell apart."

I listen as Levi fills me in on the rest of Gravelle's life story. How he made billions investing in an early version of the virtual reality technology he used to show us his memories.

"He and Jane *were* happy," Levi explains, "for a time. But Underwood was cold, cynical. Perhaps he never felt loved enough, so he sabotaged the one good relationship in his life. I don't know. Whatever the reason, Jane began to long for someone who didn't take her for granted. Someone like Booker.

"When they had trouble conceiving a child, they sought fertility treatments, which eventually worked. But Underwood was already losing her. They grew further apart until she *did* seek out Booker. He had never stopped loving her.

"Jane and Underwood divorced when Oliver was two.

Underwood had become hardened, angry even. She had seen outbursts of this anger; he'd even directed it at Oliver. She was worried about her son's safety, so she petitioned for full custody, and she won. Later on, after Underwood faked his own death, he watched as Booker Ward legally adopted his son. He was never the same again."

"How did he do it? Fake his death like that?"

"I don't know all the details—that memory was hazier than the others. The car accident wasn't planned. He was driving too fast, too recklessly. His face was nearly destroyed by the fire. That's when he decided to reinvent himself. To change his name from John Underwood to Augustus Gravelle and make everyone believe that Underwood had died."

I'm about to ask a thousand questions when Gravelle's voice booms through a sound system.

"It's remarkable technology, isn't it?" says Gravelle. "Amazing how easily I could introduce you to my thoughts, my memories, my world?"

I respond icily. "If that's your most advanced virtual reality simulation, I wasn't all that impressed." Levi's eyes widen, but before he can jump in to apologize for my impertinence, Gravelle walks into the room.

"Oh dear, Emmaline," Gravelle shakes his head, leaning on his cane. "I'm afraid I've given you the wrong impression. *That* is not my most advanced technology. No, no. We've improved the system light-years since we created the demo you saw. That was the first iteration, my dear. But since you asked…" He punches a code into a virtual panel. "Please. Take the latest model for a spin."

A guard strides toward me holding a syringe, and I prepare myself for the inevitable haze brought on by the injective.

◇━┤ ┝━◇

I'm back at my house in San Francisco. Light streams in through twelve-foot-tall windows. I recognize my room, though it looks different from how it is now. An intricate dollhouse with gables and turrets and period furniture inside sits in the corner. There's a child-size desk with crayons and construction paper strewn over it. Everything in the room is pink.

I'm in the corner, facing the ornate, wrought-iron bed. A child lies in it, her small frame nearly swallowed by white pillows and a puffy pink comforter. The child's eyes are closed, her face pale. It's me as a little girl. I'm witnessing a scene from my past. But this isn't like earlier, when I watched Gravelle's memories. That felt like I was observing from afar. This feels different. Immersive. When I reach out to touch the dollhouse, I can feel it. I see its every vivid detail. And I see *her* in vivid detail too.

The girl's face—my face—is sickly. The stuffed monkey I used to take with me everywhere is cuddled beside me. My throat catches at the sight of him.

A woman comes and sits gingerly at the edge of the girl's bed. She places her hand on the girl's forehead. She's startlingly thin, with straight brown hair pulled back into a tidy ponytail. I watch as she fusses with the pink comforter and moves the stuffed monkey closer to the girl. The woman is obviously my mother. I know she's isn't real—this is virtual reality, after all—but it's the first time I've ever seen her like this, full of life and not a photograph. It knocks the wind out of me.

"Mama?" The girl—*me*—has woken up.

My mother clasps the girl's hand. She is memorizing every detail of her face.

"Yes, sweetheart?"

"I don't like that place. It smells yucky. I missed my room."

"I know, sweetheart."

"Can I stay here? I don't want to go to the hospital."

"Yes," says my mother, her words coming out breathy, strained. "Yes, you can stay."

"I go to sleep now, Mommy. I'm tired."

"Of course, baby. Sleep tight."

My mother presses her cheek to the girl's—to mine—then begins to sing.

"Hush, little Emmaline, don't say a word. Mama's gonna buy you a mockingbird…"

Just as my breath catches in my throat, I'm transported to Oliver's room, at his house.

He's on his bed. He isn't moving, isn't breathing.

I stand over Oliver's body. I'm not just observing a scene; I *am* the scene. And I know with certainty, I'm about to relive every excruciating moment of what happened. There is no way out of it. I can't extricate myself from the memory or stop the feed from playing.

"Oliver?" I hesitate, as I lean over him. "Oliver?"

I shake him a little, willing him to wake up.

"Ollie!" I shout. I lean over him, profoundly helpless.

"Emmaline?"

I spin. It's Jane.

"Oliver! It's Oliver! He isn't breathing!"

The look on Jane's face is one of horror, but also of accusation and blame.

"He told you how he felt about you," says Jane. "He told you he loved you. You crushed him."

"That's not what happened. It wasn't like that! I loved him! That's why I couldn't risk it. Why I could never…"

My words fall on deaf ears, because Jane has turned and walked out the door, urgently calling the paramedics on her plum. I feel my insides twisting, as though a hand grabbed my organs and won't let go.

Suddenly I'm back in my house again, in the living room this time, watching as my father, dressed in a dark suit, speaks with other somber adults. They mill about, nibbling on tea sandwiches and scones. Their faces are bleak.

"We're so sorry for your loss," says one of the men.

"Katharine was…" says the woman next to the man. Her voice breaks. "We're heartbroken for you and your little girl."

My father thanks the couple and excuses himself. He walks away, steadying himself on a table. His eyes meet mine. It's clear what's written there. Recrimination.

I shake my head. *No.* This isn't real. It didn't happen like this. I was only three when my mother died. I wasn't in this room. I was sick. Too sick to attend her funeral. Too young to understand.

Breaking my father's gaze, I sprint to my room. I know I

wasn't there. I find the little girl—me—lying in a hospital bed, not the wrought-iron bed I saw before. Hospital-grade machines surround her, swallowing her up. The girl's eyes are closed, and she looks thinner than before. The stuffed monkey lies beside her, his fur matted where she—where I—loved him.

A nurse walks briskly into the room and presses a compress to my forehead. Another nurse follows.

"I put in an urgent call to the doctor," says the first nurse. "I'd give her two days. Three at most before she's on her way to join her mother."

My throat tightens.

"I think it was selfish," says the second nurse as she fiddles with the machines. "Taking her own life because she couldn't bear to watch her daughter die? Leaving that man to bury his wife and then his child?" The second nurse shakes her head. "Poor man."

"I wouldn't exactly call him poor," says the first nurse as she repositions the compress.

"Money can't buy health, now can it?" asks the second nurse.

I close my eyes, tuning them out. *This isn't real, Emmaline*, I remind myself. It's only a memory, and not even that. This is clearly a fabricated memory made up of the bits and pieces of stories I'd heard from my childhood. I don't remember this conversation.

I breathe slowly, trying to calm myself. This vision will end. This, too, shall pass.

Suddenly the steady beeping from the monitor turns to a long continuous beep. My eyes fly open to see the nurses urgently leaning over the girl's bed.

"She's flatlining," says the first nurse.

I focus on the little girl's face, willing this moment to end.

I squeeze my eyes shut and try to banish the image of the dying child from my mind.

The doctor in Sweden saved you, Emmaline. You didn't die. You lived. You're still alive.

When I open my eyes, I'm not in my room at home anymore. I'm standing at the edge of Hades Point. The wind is howling, and my face feels frozen, as though I've been standing out in this desolate spot for ages.

I look at my feet planted mere inches from the edge, and peer down at the sheer cliff below me. I can't get those images out of my head. My father's blame. Jane's reproach. Logically, I know Gravelle distorted those moments and used them to manipulate me. I know my dad and Jane don't blame me for my mother's death, for Oliver's death. But still.

The wind slaps at my face, and I begin to sob. I stare off Hades Point, knowing it would only take a second for me to stop the noise and calm myself forever.

The toe of my right foot skims the edge of the rock. I scoot forward. I'm about to leap. To my death? But I don't actively wish to die. Not now. Not at all.

I don't want to plummet to the rocks below. I don't want the earth to close in on me like a giant fist, crushing every bone in my body. I don't want my life to be over. I may be without my mother and Ollie, but everything I still strive, love, and hope for…

And yet, I can't stop. Some force greater than myself pushes me forward. I take in a deep breath and air fills my lungs for what might be the last time. I resign myself to my fate.

I am free-falling. As my body hurtles toward the rocks below, I wonder how long it will take for the pain to cease, for my body to break. I close my eyes, bracing for impact.

It doesn't have to be like this, a voice—my voice?—says.

I open my eyes, confused. The rocky crags are below me. I'm still falling. Time has slowed, but the rocks grow closer. Surely they will devour me.

You don't have to do this. You can live. You will *live.*

I can't tell if this voice is mine or someone else's, or some-*thing* else entirely—but it gives me pause.

You are in control. You can stop this, Emma. You can change your fate. You can change the course of your life.

Without warning, without knowing how, I stop, hovering in midair. Inexplicably, I'm no longer careening toward my immi-nent demise. I'm floating. I'm *flying.*

It's impossible to understand, but somehow my body is being carried upward. I'm rushing toward the sky, toward the clouds—away from death.

I stretch out my arms, hesitant at first, then with more con-fidence. I raise my face to the wind and let it carry me up. Up to safety, to something otherworldly. I am flying. *Flying.*

I'm not a bird; I'm still me, and yet I'm soaring through clouds. I look down at Hades Point, taking in its majesty. From this angle, it's not ominous. It's beautiful. I see trees, Darkwood. I can see the whole world from here, and it is glorious. I'm not afraid. I close my eyes, and this time, I feel powerful. I feel free…

I wake with a start. I'm back in the chair in the compound. My heart is racing. I'm panting, bowled over by an acute pain in my chest.

I take a minute to catch my breath, and when I do, I try to catch Levi's gaze. It is such a relief to see his face. But he looks ineffably sad.

"*That* is our latest technology, Emmaline," Gravelle says, coming up beside me. I don't like how he's looking at me. It's different from when I first arrived. Goose bumps flush over my arms. I'm shivering.

"Congratulations," Gravelle continues. "Only a handful of select and very lucky candidates have had a chance to demo the VR Obsidian."

"Did he do this to you, Levi? When you lived here? Was this part of your…education?"

"Yes," Levi says, his voice hollow. "He hoped to strengthen our minds the way he'd trained our bodies. Make us tough enough to withstand emotional torture."

I take that in, my mind reeling. "What did he show you just now?" I ask. "All the worst moments of your life?"

"Not exactly," Levi says.

"What?"

"The only way to explain is to show you," Levi says. He looks so lost—so *sad*—I want to wrap my arms around him to reassure him. But I still can't move.

"Oliver?" Levi says, raising his voice. "We're ready for you."

OLIVER

A TEENAGE BOY enters the room. He strides deliberately toward us. He looks exactly like my dead best friend. He looks like Levi too, of course, but he is more Oliver. He has Oliver's hair, Oliver's slightly thinner build.

"Why are you doing this to me?" I ask as I look from this Oliver look-alike to Levi, and then to Gravelle, who appears to be enjoying this.

"Doing what, Emmaline?" Gravelle asks cordially.

"Torturing me."

"Ah," he answers. "I would call it entertainment. But semantics…"

"First, you showed me all those horrible memories. And

now you bring in another apparition to remind me that my best friend is dead?"

"Emma," Levi says quietly.

"What kind of trick is this?" I struggle to get out of my chair, but I can't.

"It's not a trick, Emma," Levi offers.

"No, Em," says the boy, and I startle. *Is he talking to me?* I look at him. "Levi's right," he says in a voice that sounds completely Oliverian. "It's really me."

I stare at this boy, certain I'm back in the virtual reality simulation again. I must be. The serrated knife slides into my chest.

"You aren't Oliver." My voice cracks. "Oliver *died*. You *died*!" I turn to Gravelle. "And you! You brainwashed him or tortured him. You did this. You drove him to suicide. Why would you do that? To your own son? Are you that heartless, Underwood?"

"Of course not," Gravelle says. "I never would have wanted *that*, Emmaline. Which is why the dead boy in Oliver's bed was not Oliver Ward—'my son,' as you call him. He was a clone, created for the sole purpose of assisting my grand plans. The real Oliver Ward is alive and well and standing in front of you."

I stare at Gravelle, not comprehending. I look to Levi. Why do his eyes look so…hollow? So weary?

Out of the corner of my eye, I notice the Oliver-clone looking at me, taking me in. He closes the gap between us, kneeling so his face is level with mine.

"I know it's hard to believe," he says quietly, smiling at me, his eyes crinkling the way they used to, exactly the way I remember them. "But it's really me."

I stare at him, disbelieving. "No," I say softly, shaking my head. *Impossible.* "The real Oliver would be yelling. Or fighting to get me out of this chair," I insist. "You can't be him. It doesn't make any sense."

Gravelle hobbles toward us. "I've given you the moon, Emmaline, and you're complaining because it's full of craters! Give Oliver a break. If he's slightly more relaxed than usual, it's because he's on a low dose of pharmas. A few mood enhancers to guarantee that his time here at the compound is nothing short of delightful."

I whip my head around to glare at Gravelle. "So you've been drugging him?" I turn back to this Oliver and take in each detail of his face, his hands, his body. Tears of confusion, exhaustion, and flat-out fear pool in my eyes. *Can it be?*

"My guess is the pharmas keep him docile," Levi explains. "They make him more agreeable. Less prone to excitement. Without them, he might have attempted to escape."

"Why would he try to escape, Levi?" Gravelle purrs. "I've given your original everything he could ever want. A library stocked with books. A room full of the most hi-tech cameras and editing equipment available. All Oliver's wanted is at his disposal."

"I'm sure Ollie's really motivated to make films when he's been practically lobotomized," I mutter to myself.

"So you believe me, then?" Oliver says, his voice eerily calm.

"You died," I insist. "You left me your key. That note…"

"I did write that note," Oliver says, his voice drifting off. "But from the compound. I've been here since last summer."

"Gravelle killed an innocent clone," Levi explains. "He

wanted you to think Oliver was dead. Not just you, of course. You, Jane, Booker, everyone. It was all a trick. We fell for it. Can we get up now?" Levi indicates the force field.

"Certainly." Gravelle manifests a touch screen and presses a few buttons. I feel the force field around me dissolving. This time, when I try to stand, I can. As I stretch my legs, I notice the two guards stationed by the door tensing. I'm still trapped. There'd be no point in running; I'd never get away. Instead, I walk up to Oliver, desperate to make my brain understand what I'm seeing. It still makes no sense, none at all. Even under the influence of pharmas, the real Oliver would share more of an explanation… Wouldn't he?

"You were gone," I choke. "For almost a year." The serrated knife twists in my chest.

"This isn't a trick, Emma," says Levi, who now stands next to me. "You know I'd be the first person to question this. All of it… Why my guardian did what he did. Why he made you all think Oliver was dead. Why he created us in the first place," he says darkly.

"It was him all along," I say. I turn, enraged, to Gravelle, feeling so angry I could rip off his face with my bare hands. "What did you *do*?"

"I simply righted some wrongs," he says with a smile. "I enlisted my brother, Albert Seymour, to help me create the Similars so I could leave a legacy. Make those who betrayed me understand certain…things."

I must look confused because Levi elaborates. "He wanted Jane and Booker to feel the pain of losing a son, just like he did all those years ago when he lost custody of Oliver. So he made them believe, for nearly a year, that Oliver had died. And then he sent me to rub it in their faces. I'm a pawn in this whole situation. We all are."

I look at Oliver—is it really Oliver?—wondering if it could possibly be true. "Ollie?" I ask, afraid to say his name out loud and jinx this, whatever it is.

"Ah, young love," Gravelle says, grinning. "So wonderful for you, Oliver, to finally have the reunion with Emma that you deserve." He claps his hands merrily. "Doesn't feel good, does it?" Gravelle addresses Levi. "Now you understand what it was like for me, when I was so cruelly abandoned by my wife and child."

"You can't turn me against her," Levi snaps, and I understand why he looked so sad before. But I can't think about that right now. I have to deal with this. I have to be rational.

"If it's really you," I say forcefully, for everyone's benefit, "prove it."

"My mom's cookies," the Oliver likeness says.

"What?"

"You loved the lemon meringue the best, but you didn't want to hurt all the other cookies' feelings, so you always ate a chocolate chip and a sugar cookie, so they wouldn't feel left out."

"What else?" I whisper, hanging on to his every word.

"Fifty years, fifty years—I'll be your best friend for fifty more years."

"And after that?"

"You have to reapply."

My whole body tenses. *It's really him. It has to be. No one else would—no one else* could *know those things…* I stare at Oliver's face, his expression dulled by months of pharmas. *Oliver. Oliver!* I could stare at him all day. It isn't long before panic consumes me. What if the pharmas have altered his personality irrevocably?

"Where's Prudence?" I demand. "We've been waiting long enough."

"You certainly are an impatient one, aren't you?" Gravelle tuts as he hobbles toward the far wall with the skinny windows. He calls up a virtual control panel and begins typing commands into it. As he types, I notice the opposite wall beginning to open. There is space behind that wall. A long, narrow compartment, or room of sorts.

There, chained to the wall in shackles, is Prudence.

ESCAPE

"THE GANG'S ALL here," says Gravelle, surveying Pru with satisfaction. "Together again, and all that jazz. Don't you just love happy reunions?"

I run toward Prudence. "What have you done to her?"

"I'm okay," Pru says bravely. But from the look of her, she's anything but.

"You were never a good liar," I tell Pru as I suppress a sob. Pru is much thinner than when I last saw her all those months ago, and the shackles binding her wrists to the wall are abrading her skin. I feel like I will be physically sick.

I turn to Gravelle, my body heat rising as my ire grows. "Why is she in that—that contraption?"

"Emmaline, Emmaline," Gravelle chides. "You do tend toward the dramatic. Pru paid me a visit, and it turned out to be quite convenient timing for her to assist me in some research." Gravelle comes over to fiddle with some wires at Pru's feet.

"He means I've become a human lab rat," Pru says.

Gravelle laughs. "Prudence has been a useful, if uncooperative, subject."

Peeling my eyes off Pru for a moment, I take in the room. So much was hidden from our sight before the wall was opened. The space is filled with equipment, shiny and metal and foreboding. I see monitors, sharp instruments gleaming on aluminum trays, and rows of test tubes and beakers.

"You're impressed by my laboratory," Gravelle notes. "It's quite extensive, as you'll soon see. Oliver, Levi... This can, and *will*, all be yours one day."

"As if we'd ever want any part of this," Levi mutters.

"I'd advise you to speak only for yourself, son." Gravelle moves through his lab, absentmindedly stacking some glass jars. "Oliver's spent the last several months enjoying all this compound has to offer. Seeing just how powerful he might become by my side. You'd be surprised to hear that he disagrees with you..."

"I don't," Oliver snaps, and I glimpse my best friend again, deep below the surface of the pharma haze. "I want to go home to my parents."

Gravelle's face ripples with anger. "Too bad. You're both staying here for the foreseeable future. Levi's had years of training on this compound. You have a lot more to go, son. Levi, have you forgotten what awaits you back at Darkwood? You're still a suspect in dear Prudence's attack. Here, you're safe—"

"Levi didn't do it," Pru interjects. "It wasn't him. Emma and Levi saved my life. If it weren't for them, my attacker might have done me in. She was scared she'd get caught and left the boat-house before Emma found me."

"She?" My heart pounds wildly. "But it wasn't Madison. She was meeting her tutor, if you can believe it…"

"No, not Madison. Tessa Leroy. She bludgeoned me with a rowing oar and left me for dead in that canoe."

"Tessa?" I'm bewildered. "But why?"

Pru sighs. "I knew about the experiments Ransom and Fleischer were going to be running on the Similars. I found out over the summer, from my dad. Someone in the Quarry gave him a tip. I'm not sure how they knew. But I confronted Tessa so I could stop it all before it started. I asked her to meet me at the boathouse, warned her that they wouldn't get away with it, that the Quarry would stop it, that she needed to get on our side. But it quickly became clear that Tessa wasn't going to see reason. She said the Similars deserved the treatment they were getting. She said Theodora ruined her family, and it had all started with me. With my father."

"Your dad? What did Jaeger have to do with—?" That's when it hits me. He wrote that exposé about Damian, made his fraud national news. "The news story. About his crimes."

"Yes," Pru answers. "That, and the fact that my father is unabashedly pro-clone. Tessa's on a mission to destroy each clone personally, if she can. But she started with me."

"That's crazy," I sputter. "Your father's a journalist. He was doing his job. And it isn't *your* fault he wrote that exposé. Shouldn't her dad take responsibility for what he did?"

"I hate to interrupt this happy reunion," Gravelle says, "but this is *quite* the interesting tidbit. Damian Leroy's daughter has a bone to pick with your father, Prudence?"

"Apparently," she says, wrestling to get out of her shackles, but to no avail.

"Well, well. She's in good company, then," Gravelle muses.

"And what's *that* supposed to mean?" I ask.

"It means that Jaeger Stanwick hasn't changed much in the two decades since we were classmates. It means that he likely isn't sorry about how he treated me back then…"

"You're talking about the foxes, letting those animals loose from the lab, aren't you? Your expulsion."

"She nails it, folks," Gravelle says, his face deadpan.

"You're still angry about that? It was more than twenty years ago! You were kids. You became a freaking billionaire. You married Jane Porter—"

"Don't pretend to understand what it's been like to be me," Gravelle says, all humor gone from his voice. "As a child, I was denied my legacy and true parentage. It took everything I had to fit in at Darkwood. The day Jaeger Stanwick refused to come forward and acknowledge his role in that fiasco set my life on a devastating trajectory, one I could never course correct."

"Did you know all this, Pru? That Gravelle hates your father so much?"

Pru shakes her head. "Of course not. I came here to talk with him, to try to work with him to protect the Similars from people like Ransom. The Quarry believes—"

"The Quarry, the Quarry. Such noble motives you all have. Let's be honest, Prudence. You sought me out because you were curious about the Similars. About why they exist. About why you have a twin in Pippa."

"Of course," Pru says softly. "Of course I was curious…"

"It was all for revenge," Levi says quietly. "That's why we exist. To be pawns in Gravelle's sick scheme…"

Gravelle guffaws at that. "You underestimate me, Levi! My plans are far more complex than simple restitution. You and your friends have only begun to help me accomplish my goals. The legacy I will leave on this planet before I die—"

"You've made your point," Levi interjects. "Now let Emma and Prudence go. Oliver and I will stay. You can continue your research—or whatever it is you're doing—on us. You've been studying Pru's mental control, yes? Let me guess: you want to compare her brain to Pippa's. Study me and Oliver, instead. We can handle it," he says stubbornly.

"You and Oliver are too important to be prodded and poked," Gravelle says, staring me down like prey. "You will all stay here for the foreseeable future." Gravelle nods to the guards. "And if you're thinking of contacting your father, Emmaline, I think you'll find your plum doesn't work. He may love to come rescue you, but he doesn't know where you are or where this place is, does he?"

"The other Similars," Levi says. "They'll come for us."

"They'll do what I tell them," Gravelle says. "In the meantime, guards? Prepare three more beds."

Two guards grab me and Oliver.

"Sorry, old man," says Levi under his breath. "But everything I know, I learned here. From you."

Levi flies through the air, kicking and twisting as he knees the gun out of one guard's holster and kicks the weapon out of the other's. As the guards fumble, Levi flips his body in the opposite direction, taking out the third guard, knocking him unconscious. He can't get to the fourth guard in time. That man fires a shot at Levi, narrowly missing him, hitting a table full of glass beakers that shatter into a million pieces. Levi rolls on the ground, grabbing one of the guns from the floor and shooting it at the guards. The bullet strikes one guard in the foot. He crumples in agony. Levi steps over him, dodging another bullet. Adrenaline courses through my veins. I reach for the cuffs binding Pru's arms and pound frantically at the latch with a piece of equipment. It's a struggle, but I finally get it bent enough for Pru to slide out. Once unbound, Pru's arms slip to her side like noodles, and she collapses on me, in agony. Were her arms dislocated from her shoulders?

"The girls!" a guard shouts, noticing that I've freed Pru. I hear a shot ring out as two of the guards beeline for a glass case on a counter in the lab. I hadn't noticed it until now. It's full of rows of injectives.

"Inject the subject!" Gravelle shouts. "We can't lose all that data!" he bellows.

A guard lunges toward us, injective prepped and at the ready. I push Pru to the side, thrusting my own body in the way.

I feel the familiar prick as the injective pierces the skin of my upper arm. I know I only have moments before I'll be at the mercy of whatever memory or darkness is to come. Before the injective takes hold of me, I scan the room for help, but I'm on my own. Levi has picked up Pru and is carrying her toward the exit, while Oliver tries to run interference. At least preserving Gravelle's precious data means not killing us. The bullets have stopped flying for the time being, though the guards are wholly focused on keeping us in this room.

No one's concerned about me anymore. I'll be compromised in seconds. As soon as I'm thrust into the virtual reality, I'll be helpless. I fight the sinking feeling in my gut that tells me I'm as good as dead because I won't be able to defend myself. That's when I notice the case of injectives. The guards have left it open. I drag myself over to pull two of the syringes and shove them into my pocket, then muster all my energy and concentration to follow Levi toward the door.

Pru insists that she's regained her strength, and Levi sets her down.

A guard comes from the side, blocking the door. Pru surprises him with a kick to his groin. He bends over in pain, and we push past him into the hallway. Pru takes the lead, shouting that she knows the way out. Just before the injective overtakes me, a bullet strikes Ollie in the leg. I pray that when I finally return from this memory—if I ever return from this alternate reality—we'll both still be alive.

INJECTED

I DON'T KNOW what I expect when my vision returns. My childhood home? Hades Point? Instead, I'm right where I was moments ago—in the hallway of the compound.

Oliver is only a few yards away, gingerly testing his weight on his injured leg and wincing in pain. Pru is farther down the hall. Is this real or just a memory?

A bullet flies past my head.

I don't know if it's possible to die in a virtual reality, but I don't want to find out. I have to *move*. I need to get out of here.

I reach an arm out to Oliver, urging him to lean on me. He does, and we make our way with Levi toward Pru, who holds open a door at the end of the hallway.

"Come on," she urges. "I left a small boat anchored to the dock. We can take that back to the mainland."

I assist Oliver through the exit and wait for Levi and Pru to pass before going through it myself. The door shuts behind me, and I exhale. Even though we're still not in the clear, I'm relieved. My friends and I will make it out of here—out of this vision I'm experiencing, and in real life too. We will leave this island for good. We have to.

My friends. Suddenly, I'm in a dark hallway. *They aren't here.*

"Pru?" I cry out. "Ollie? Levi?" I turn around, squinting in the dark, praying that they're up ahead or around a corner. But from what I can see, the hall is empty. They're gone, and I'm entirely alone.

Fueled by my desperate need to survive, I jog down hallway after hallway, losing myself in the heart of the compound. When I reach the end of a long corridor, I pause, wondering whether to go left or right. Two guards grab me. Before I can resist, they carry me off. I try to free myself from their grasp. It's a futile effort. They are too strong, and their grip is as unmovable as a vise.

Within moments, we are back in the big room where Gravelle kept Pru. The room looks the same as it did when we left it, only the floor is covered in blood. New terror grows in the pit of my stomach. They are bringing me here for a reason. That reason must be to kill me.

The guards strap me into the manacles that bound Pru to the wall. They yank my arms to the ceiling and handcuff them into the shackles. They bind my feet too, then hook me up to electrodes. I scream, and they poke needles into my veins. I imagine myself trapped here indefinitely—my friends gone and unable to save me. That's when I realize there are worse things in life than death. Like this. Definitely this.

No! I scream in my mind, as the guards stab me with more needles, conversing in a language I can't understand. *No,* I plead, tears pooling in my eyes.

Someone appears in front of me, pacing back and forth, surveying his handiwork. I blink out my tears, expecting to see Gravelle—the madman himself. But it's not him. Instead, Headmaster Ransom is the one studying me. He watches from a comfortable distance as the guards finish their work.

"Emmaline," Ransom booms. "It's a pity things had to end this way. But you always were so…fascinating. My research on the Similars is plateauing. I need a new subject. Someone with potential. Someone like you."

"Never." I grimace, the pain of the needles and the throbbing in my shoulders beginning to make me woozy. "I'll sabotage the data. You'll never get anything from me."

Ransom sighs. "I do wish duty had taught you a lesson, Emma, but I can see it had little effect on you. Guards? Can we see how her body reacts to the drowning sensation?"

"No!" I shriek. I won't let him torture me. I wrench my hands and my body against the binds that hold me. In one excruciating motion, they pop. The handcuffs release.

Wait—how…?

And that's when I remember: flying from Hades Point. Floating, freezing in midair, and flying upward, not falling down onto the rocky crags. Saving myself.

This isn't real, Emma. It's only a simulation. A fabrication. A fiction.

I'm free. I'm no longer bound by the chains, and I've propelled my body high in the air. I'm flying again. The view in front of me is out the long, rectangular window at the top of the wall. Outside there are trees, then water as far as the eye can see, and endless blue sky.

A decorative picture hangs on the wall below me, and I swoop down and grasp it, yanking it off the wall and pushing my feet off the Sheetrock, propelling myself toward the window like a human battering ram. I angle the picture frame at the window. It cracks the glass, which shatters around me. I slip through the opening, straight to the outside.

Now I'm flying toward a grassy clearing, where I see them—the Similars. All six sit motionless in their chairs, staring straight ahead, looking comatose. I notice blood flowing out of their bodies through IVs. Their faces are pale, so pale. With frightening clarity, I understand why—their bodies are being *drained.* They won't live through this. When this simulation is over, they'll be dead.

Panicked, I fly toward the Similars, about to land between Pippa and Maude when I hear the snarl. An attack dog crouches behind me.

I spin to face the dog. With razor-sharp canines and bright red gums, he lunges at me, snapping. I spring into the air, channeling the power I felt when I burst from the manacles, when I flew to safety off Hades Point. I aim my body toward Pippa, who is directly below me. I will pull out her IV and save her—

Chomp! The dog leaps several feet in the air and sinks his teeth into my ankle. I fall to the ground as more dogs appear, surrounding me. Moving in for the kill.

No! I shout in my head. *This isn't real. Gravelle—it's all part of his sick virtual reality. It's not happening, not really…*

But the pain in my ankle feels more than real. I crawl forward, reaching to yank the IV out of Pippa's arm. Seconds later, the dogs have converged around me, snapping and growling. I make a move to fly into the air again, out of their reach, but I can't. They have me now. One dog knocks me over as another set of teeth clamps down on my calf, and two more dogs jump on top of me, one sinking his canines into my shoulder, the other into my neck. The end is surely in sight.

Then I remember Hades Point.

The injective. You are in control. You don't have to be here. You can leave, Emma. You can leave…

"No!" I scream, my voice raw and primal. "No!"

My body is different now. It's made of metal. Or maybe I'm wearing armor, I can't tell. It doesn't matter. All that matters is that when the dogs go to bite, their teeth hit a hard surface. I hear the scraping of their teeth. Frustrated, they scratch and scratch until they lose interest, backing away from me. My pain is gone, and I am healed. Stronger, even.

I look at my hands. My fingers are made of individual pieces of metal attached by joints that give me fluid range of motion. My torso, my legs, and my arms are also covered in this aluminum material. It clangs when I tap a metal finger on it. I don't bother to explore my body any more than that. I don't need to. In this virtual reality, I am strong. I know what I can and must do.

I run toward the Similars, who are confined to their chairs. I move from one to the next, yanking out their IVs one by one and detaching the electrodes and other needles.

"You're free!" I shout, but no one moves or responds. Their eyes are still glazed over. "You're free," I say desperately.

Still, the Similars don't react. I rush to Pippa. I know she would acknowledge me if she could. She doesn't. Her eyes are blank. I will Levi to look at me. He doesn't.

Frustrated and angry, I shout, "Wake up!" I push him with my metal hand, but as it connects to his body, his torso breaks open. Dust and feathers pour from his shell. I stifle a sob. He isn't real. He's fake. A dummy. A doll. None of these Similars are real. This was all another trick.

Leave, says a voice—my voice. *Stop letting him manipulate you. Stop it now, Emma!*

In an instant, I'm on Gravelle's man-made beach. I see Prudence working to untether a motorboat that's tied to a dock. She's screaming out my name, calling for me to get in. Ollie hobbles over on his injured leg, blood flowing freely from the wound.

I look down at my body. It's no longer metal. My armor is gone. I am just me again. I may have finally escaped the virtual reality test, but I am still vulnerable.

I hear a shout and turn. Two guards pin Levi down. I move to help him, but Gravelle blocks my way.

I look into his face, the face of a madman. He motions for

the guards to release Levi, who stops struggling. Levi stands slowly, trying to communicate something with his gaze. I don't know what.

"Welcome back, Emmaline," Gravelle purrs. Even over the rumbling of the boat's motor, I can hear him clearly. "I must admit, I'm surprised. That simulation should have kept you out of commission for hours."

"How long was I in it?" I ask, my voice sour, tinged with disgust. I'm aware of the tightrope I'm walking, standing here, conversing—provoking—this man when all of our lives are at stake.

"Fourteen minutes," Gravelle answers.

"Oh," I say, feeling defeated. It felt far longer than that.

Gravelle circles me, and I look to Levi for help. *What does this man want from me?*

"I am convinced," Gravelle says, "that you would benefit from training at the compound. I'd give a lot to study that mind of yours…"

I reach in my pocket for the only saving grace I have left. The injectives I grabbed from that glass case. My fingers close around one of the syringes, and I pull it out, lunging at Gravelle. I catch his arm through his sleeve.

Surprise registers on Gravelle's face, and I back away from him, tossing the needle aside, as Pru rushes up and grabs my hand, dragging me back toward the boat.

Gravelle grimaces. We both know the injective will affect him soon. Within moments, he'll be transported to an alternate reality to relive every misery he's ever faced in his life.

"Enjoy your reality—alone," I shout over my shoulder.

"Don't you think I've relived those moments every day of my life?" he responds.

I stop. "Then it won't be hard, will it? To exit the memories? You created the technology. Surely you know how to end it. How to overcome it. How to do what I did."

"What you did wasn't possible," he says, his eyes becoming unfocused. The injective is starting to work. Pru pulls again, but I put out a hand to stop her. *Wait*, I silently beg her. *Wait*.

"It *was* possible. But I'm not surprised someone unworthy like you has no idea how that kind of mental control works. You have to care for someone else more than yourself."

"I am not unworthy..." he mutters, and for the first time ever, I see a man behind that scarred face. A man who has lost everything—and lashed out because of it.

Trembling, he falls, the injective rendering him helpless.

"Now!" Prudence shrieks as she ushers me to the motorboat.

"Levi," I cry out, struggling against Pru.

"Save yourself, Emma. Please!" Ollie shouts from the safety of the boat as I fight off Prudence.

"We can't leave him here," I choke as I watch the guards starting to drag Levi away. Gravelle lies on the ground, his eyes closed, his body seizing. I don't have time to wonder what he's facing in the portal. I hope it's as horrifying as the dogs. I hope it's worse.

"LEVI!" I cry out again.

"Go," Levi says in return. "Please. I've never asked anything of you, Emma, but I am now. Please, go."

"But Gravelle. He'll torture you!"

"And I'll survive it," Levi says. With a yank, the guards make it clear that it's time for him to go.

"No." I sob as Prudence pulls me away from Levi, and Oliver hoists me over the edge. Pru knows how to operate the boat—I had no idea she could do that—and within moments, we have left the shore and are headed out onto open water.

I get one last look at Levi as the guards drag him off into the compound. I have never missed a living person as much as I do now.

◇——┤ ├◇

On the ferry ride home, Pru and I stand at the stern of the ship, looking out over the vast ocean. On the boat to Queen's Harbor, Pru applied an emergency medical patch to Ollie's bullet wound. He can have it properly cleaned and stitched when we get back. Now, he naps, his head resting on the seat next to him. The ordeal has left us all exhausted, starving, and ragged. As the adrenaline begins to drain from my body, I feel the full weight of what's happened.

We left Levi at the compound with his guardian—a monster.

I have Oliver back, but I have lost Levi.

After a while, I go and sit next to Oliver. A piece of folded paper falls from my sweater pocket and flutters to the ground. Confused, I pick it up. This isn't mine, or at least, I don't remember it. I unfold it and start to read.

Dear Emmaline,

I very much enjoyed your surprise visit to my island. It tickles me beyond measure that my former roommate's daughter has become such a valued player in both of my sons' lives. Do tell your father that I took good care of you while you were here. He'll be pleased to hear that.

Emma, I do not wish to disrupt your life, but it is time you learned exactly who you are.

When my brother, Albert, cloned the originals all those years ago—when DNA samples were taken from Madison, Tessa, Jake, Prudence, Archer, and Oliver and embryos were implanted in artificial wombs—there was another little girl, a sick little girl, who was cloned along with them.

Fortunately for that family, I learned early on of the child's dire situation and was able to offer a solution: a clone. A new daughter who would look exactly like her original. One who could replace the little girl after she died, offering the girl's widowed father a second chance at being a parent. The original little girl, the one who was not saved by experimental treatments in Europe, who, in fact, died in her father's arms, was named Emmaline Chance. You, my dear, are her clone. Your birth certificate says Eden Gravelle. I'd be happy to send along any paperwork that will give you the assurance you need that this is the truth.

What matters now is that you understand who you are, Emmaline. Or should I say, Eden. After all, that is your given name. You were born on my island, but you didn't grow up there. You had a more "normal" life, and I hope you appreciate that you had what the others didn't. I'm sorry if your father couldn't properly love you. I suppose he may have resented that you took the place of his first little girl, the daughter he adored more than life itself. Pity he couldn't appreciate what I did for him—cloning you as a surprise gift and delivering you to the bedside of his dying daughter. I suppose you made it hard for him to love you.

If this is a lot of information to process, I apologize. I simply wanted you to know the truth. You are a Similar, Eden, in every sense of the word.

With all due respect,

Augustus Gravelle

THE CLONE

THE NOTE FROM Augustus Gravelle no longer exists. I tore
it into a thousand pieces and threw them over the ferry's railing
into the endless ocean. No one knows about the letter, because I
haven't told anyone. And I won't. Not ever.

I won't think about what it said either. I won't dwell on the
fact that my father has never really loved me because I am me,
not *her*. I won't think about how my name isn't my own. How I
am an imposter, a stand-in, a replacement for a little girl whom
everyone loved. I can't think about how my father knew—and
lied to me all these years. So much for family. But I keep this all
to myself. Now is Oliver's moment. His turn, finally, to see his
parents again.

The three of us have ridden the bus back to the station where Levi and I started our journey. We are fatigued and numb, but that does not stop us from being joyful.

Oliver called Jane and Booker before we boarded the ferry, breaking the news gently. I'm quite sure Jane didn't believe him, just as I didn't—couldn't—believe the news at first. But now, in the middle of the bus depot, she holds her son in her arms. Her frail, ravaged frame grasps him like a lifeline. Booker's tears run down his cheeks unabated. I feel myself smiling. This is right and good. There will be time for explanations later, about how and why Underwood did this to them. For the moment, a son has been returned to his family. Jane can breathe freely again.

Tears pool in my eyes as I watch the happy reunion. There was a time when seeing Oliver alive, like this, was all that mattered to me.

But now—now, there is Levi. Levi, who has never had a chance at a happy reunion like this. Levi, who has only ever known suffering. Levi, whom we left behind.

I check my plum for the millionth time, hoping I'll get a buzz from him. A note, a one-liner. Something that will tell me he's all right.

"Dash," I whisper. "Is there anything from Levi?"

"No, Emma," Dash responds. "I'll let you know the moment I get an update."

The update doesn't come.

◇⊷⊶◇

Time passes. Two weeks, to be precise.

I only let myself think about Gravelle's note in the middle of the night, during the witching hours when I can't sleep.

Is he lying? I've asked myself that question a hundred times, and I still don't have a good answer.

Is it true? I've asked that question more often, but the mere asking sends my heart to my feet like an anvil.

If I am not who I thought I was... If I'm not my father's original daughter, but a stand-in, a replacement...

I know nothing about who I am. My past isn't what I perceived it to be. My future is a question mark.

Only one thing remains constant: Oliver is alive, and for that, I am grateful. Back at Darkwood, he sits next to me at the long, rough-hewn table, and we eat lunch. He is back. He begged Jane and Booker to allow him to return for the last six weeks of school, explaining that the normalcy of his life at Darkwood would serve as a much-needed salve to heal his wounds. They were reluctant but ultimately didn't argue. Having him back here is a dream come true, but that doesn't change the fact that the serrated knife is still lodged in my chest.

If I am honest with myself, Oliver is not the same. Gone is the carefree and spontaneous boy who viewed the world with such enthusiasm and wonder. Pippa has assured me that this is simply a side effect of the pharmas, that in a few weeks' time he will be back to his old, chipper self—but I worry.

Today, I try not to. My father is visiting. He felt the need to check on me after the news of Oliver's return. I've held a spot for him next to me. Prudence sits on the other side of that. Pru has been on the receiving end of her fair share of squeals, hugs, and screams. She is alive, she is well—and she remembers who attacked her. Tessa Leroy hasn't been at school since our return. Pippa sits with us too, and the rest of the Similars. It's unfamiliar and strange, yet it feels easy, like it always should have been this way.

Pru points to the feeds. We all look up to see the latest report on clones' rights. We aren't the only ones paying attention; nearly everyone in the dining hall stares up at the view space. Judging from the fragments of conversations that I hear, some are pleased with what they see, others unsettled.

"What's happening?" I murmur. "What did I miss while I was gone?"

"Clones without updated paperwork will no longer be allowed across the border into the U.S. And that paperwork, even if it *is* current, can be challenged by any U.S. court. Which means that individual judges can deny a clone's citizenship," Pippa explains.

"But that's unconstitutional," I say, my eyes traveling from Pru to Pippa, to Maude, Theodora, and the others.

"Not if the Supreme Court decides that clones aren't human," Pippa says.

"We can't think about that now," Maude says evenly. "We need to lie low. Not give anyone any more reason to dislike or distrust us or question if we belong here."

"And what happens when Headmaster Ransom calls you back to the research lab? Are you going to go?" I press.

Maude nods. "For now, yes."

I'm frustrated, but I know I won't change her mind.

"We have to tell someone," I appeal to Oliver. "We have to report what Ransom's doing to them. The research. It's a violation of their human rights… Maybe you can make a documentary?"

"But not if they don't want me to. This isn't our battle, is it? We're not one of them…" Oliver says.

But I am, I think, before I can stop myself. *Or am I?*

When my father arrives in the dining hall, I wave to him. He gathers a tray of food, then sits next to me, squeezing awkwardly between me and Prudence. It takes all the willpower I have not to ask him, right here and now, if the original Emma died, like Gravelle said in his letter. If I was cloned to be a replacement. If that's the reason he has never really loved me.

I don't. I won't, especially not here.

"I got you chocolate cake," my father says. "You always liked that as a kid…" It's not lost on either of us that he has no idea what I like anymore, what my tastes and preferences are.

But then, maybe I don't either. I was raised as someone else. How can I be me?

"We're so relieved you're home, Oliver," my father says, neatly folding his napkin over his lap. "You too, Prudence. How is your mother?"

"She's stable again. Thanks for asking."

The table goes noticeably quiet. My father hasn't acknowledged that Levi isn't here.

Maude nods from across the table. Her eyes are kind. She understands. When it comes to Levi, Maude is as disturbed by his absence as I am.

"He'll be back," she says quietly, as the others return to their chattering. They're all looking across the cafeteria at the originals' table, at the empty chair where Tessa would have been sitting. Madison sits there now without her sidekick, flanked by Archer and Jake. They notice us watching them and look away.

"How do you know that?" I ask.

"Because Levi is a fighter. He survived sixteen years with that man. He'll find a way to give our guardian what he wants, and then he will return to you."

To me. What does that even mean? The idea of having Oliver back, safe and sound, and Levi here too, makes me giddy with relief, joy. It also terrifies me.

I look over at Oliver as he chats with the Similars, so foreign and strange to him. He is respectful in his curiosity, not overdoing his questions. Ollie catches my gaze, smiling. In that smile, I think I see him, the real him, breaking through whatever Gravelle did to him. He grabs my hand, squeezing it.

"Em? You okay?" Oliver asks me quietly, so the others can't hear.

"More than okay," I say. "You're home. Everything can go back to normal now."

For the first time in my life, I lie to him.

ACKNOWLEDGMENTS

This book would not exist without a handful of core people I would clone this very instant if I had the technology handy to pull it off. Thanks to every single one of you who supported, advised, and encouraged me on the most thrilling ride of my writing life. Do not be shocked if your exact DNA copy tracks you down tomorrow at Whole Foods. You've been warned.

Endless thanks to my agent, Sasha Raskin, who is the definition of fierce. I am forever grateful for your guidance, your all-hours responses to my frantic emails, your editorial instincts, and your steadfast belief in this story from day one. You are an excellent human, and you helped me realize a lifelong dream, which is a roundabout way of saying *I heart you*.

Thank you to my brilliant editor, Annette Pollert-Morgan. Your insights are simply astonishing. I am beyond thankful that I get to work with an editor as experienced and thoughtful as you. Thank you for loving my characters and pushing me, and them, to be better.

Many thanks to the Sourcebooks family—from sales, marketing, and publicity to Sourcebooks Fire's talented copyeditors and design team—I am so grateful for all that you have done to make this story come alive. Special thanks to Kathryn Lynch, Heidi Weiland, Valerie Pierce, Stephanie Graham, Stefani Sloma, Cassie Gutman, Sarah Kasman, and David Curtis for your eternal support and patience.

There aren't enough words in the dictionary (I checked) to adequately thank my best friends and critique partners, Bill Hanson and Winnie Yuan Kemp. This book would not be what it is without your eternal patience, expertise, and willingness to read 849 (or was it 850?—it felt like it!) drafts. Stanford housing assignment gods, whoever you are, when you paired me with these two back in FloMo, you forever altered my life's course. You are two of my favorite people on the planet, which is why I have already stolen samples of your hair and plan to recreate you in a lab. Stay tuned.

Thank you, thank you, thank you, Victoria Frank, for holding me accountable, and for always being willing to geek out with me over YA. Emma and Levi only made it to Castor Island because of you, which is why you are now permanently on the hook to read everything I send you within an hour of receipt. SORRY!

To Alexa Gerrity Johnson, my productivity partner in writing and in life, thank you for spending an entire weekend curled up with my book, which was only a sliver of a dream when we were neighbors on Ninth Street and I wore that hideous suit to Stanford Networking Night. Thank you for sticking by me ever since that first bubble tea.

To my manager, Matt Sadeghian, THANK YOU for believing this book could be so much, and more.

To Jill Hurst, David Kreizman, Donna Swajeski, Chris Dunn, Kimberly Hamilton, Danielle Paige, Brett Staneart, and Ellen Wheeler, thank you for taking a chance on a newbie writer, and for teaching me everything I know about storytelling. To Nidhi Mehta, you are the butterbeer to my hippogriff. Tammy Camp, Celeste Oberfest, Caitlin Crawford and Andy Lurie, Stephany Gabriner, and Allison Manzari, thank you for being my San Francisco family.

Thank you, Mom and Dad, for your undying support, from *The Sound of Music* to *Suburban Revenge* to now. Mom—that phone conversation you and I had where one of us wondered out loud, "What about clones?" changed everything. I love you both so much. To Jessica Hanover, categorically the best sister in the world (a statement backed up by heaps of data), you assured me that clones were plausible—and even possible. Thanks to you and Nicholas Priebe for putting the actual science into my science fiction. And for being the only people I would call for help if anyone ever tried to mind control me.

Thank you to my father-in-law, Ray Kurzweil, for being a sounding board and confidante. Sonya Kurzweil, you have always been so enthusiastic about my endeavors. Thank you for all the years of love, laughter, and biking the Ashuwillticook. Amy Kurzweil, sharing our love of writing is such a gift. To many more years of "writer talk" (plus or minus wine). Jacob Sparks, thank you for the dinner table discussions that never fail to grip and challenge me. I think we (i.e., humans) are gonna make it.

Leo and Quincy, you inspire me on the daily to write as many stories as I can fit into one extremely busy lifetime. Thanks for understanding, and even looking a little proud when Mommy disappears into her black hole to write. Leo, reading Harry Potter and countless other books with you has been one of my greatest joys. Quincy, there are books beyond *Maisy's Tractor* (although that's a great one). We have so much reading fun yet to come!

Colossal thanks to Laura King for all the hours you spend nurturing and caring for my kiddos so I can write, write, write. This book would still be a work in progress without you.

And, finally, to my husband and partner-in-crime, Ethan. You provide the rock from which I can leap to the most far-flung places in my mind (with my life jacket strapped securely on, of course). Thank you for everything.

ABOUT THE AUTHOR

Rebecca Hanover is a television writer, sandwich lover, and young adult author. She earned a bachelor of arts from Stanford University in English and drama and was awarded an Emmy for Best Writing in 2008 as a staff writer on the CBS daytime drama *Guiding Light*. Rebecca lives in San Francisco with her husband, Ethan, and their two sons. *The Similars* is her debut novel. Follow her online at rebeccahanover.com.

DON'T MISS THE
THRILLING CONCLUSION

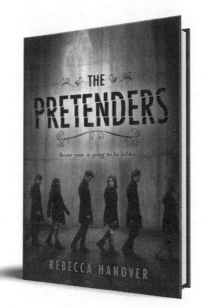

COMING JANUARY 2020

Emma must figure out who she really is and, alongside her friends, stop a dangerous plan that could destroy everyone she loves.

To: levigravelle@darkwoodacademy.edu
From: emmakchance@gmail.com
Date: August 29
Subject: Can't

…not write you anymore. It's been ninety-nine days since I left the island, and you, and I told myself if I let it get to a hundred without doing something—anything… I wouldn't.

So. Levi. I hope you're safe.

I hope you receive this, and not Gravelle.

I hope when you eventually get off that island, I'm one of the people you want to see. Of course, you miss Maude and Ansel and Thea and Jago and Pippa like crazy, but—

I miss you too.

Can you figure out what I'm not saying? Because what I'm not saying is really kind of everything.

Yours,
Emma

RETURN

I DREAM ABOUT Levi every night.

I'm still an insomniac. That won't ever change. But when I do catch a few hours of fitful sleep, Levi is the first thing I see. His face. His hair, too long and scraggly around the edges. I hear his voice and the accent that used to sound so wrong in his mouth. I see his gray eyes and his solid arms. Those arms carried Pru to safety, and I long for them. For him.

I sent him a message five days ago.

Nothing.

Nothing to let me know that the boy who made me feel *all the things* last year is okay. Not that this radio silence on Levi's part is anything new. I haven't heard from him all summer.

Which is why I've spent the last few months running every possible scenario through my head. *Is Levi okay? Is Gravelle torturing him? Has Levi thought about buzzing me? Has he even tried?*

Yes, I've considered that Levi's silence isn't Gravelle's doing at all. That maybe he just doesn't want to talk to me. Because maybe what we had—maybe we *didn't* have it, after all.

I anguished over every line of that email. Wrote fifty-seven versions before I finally sent it, then instantly second-guessed every word choice. What I said, and what I didn't.

But I don't regret sending it.

I miss Levi with an ache that takes my breath away. It's why he inhabits my thoughts even when I'm sleeping. I don't dream of Oliver. No need; I have Ollie back. He's beside me now, napping on the cool leather of the Lexus Earth that's delivering us to our senior year at Darkwood. I look over at him—at his head propped up on his hand, on the armrest—and my heart does a familiar flip. Ollie is home. Ollie is *back*.

We spent the summer together, but it wasn't the carefree reunion I'd imagined. Ollie's been different since he returned. I don't think he's changed fundamentally, but I'm still struggling to work out what's off about him on a cellular level. What's the pharmas, and what's *him*.

My father rides in front. I've placed myself strategically behind him in the back seat. It's better if we can't look at each other. Ever since I read Gravelle's letter—the one where he revealed that I might not be me, but another girl, Eden, the replacement for the daughter my father originally loved—it's been hard to face the man I call Dad. The gulf that already existed between us is now wider than ever. Every time I think about him, I wonder: Is this why he's never loved me? Why he's tolerated me, at best? Because I might not be me, but another girl? One born on a remote island. And if what Gravelle claims is really true, and my father's kept this secret from me for all these years, how can I ever trust him again?

"Darkwood campus in five! Four! Three!" chirps the virtual driver of our car. She's so peppy. Why can't bots be programmable to fit your general mood? In this case, "utter relief that your best friend is alive, with a side of total despair over the boy you love."

I know how lucky I am. Oliver is back. And for the most part, well. He's listening to music through his earbuds, dozing in and out after our flight from California, a look of contentment on his face. He shouldn't even be here right now. I spent nearly a year mourning his death. Believing he'd committed suicide. At the end of the school year, when I learned it had all been a trick, that he was alive… I fully appreciate that what I've been given is a precious gift: more time with the boy who befriended me in the third grade. Who knows I like to layer chips inside my sandwich and who teases me about all the right things: my sarcasm, the way I eat pizza—crust first—and never about the wrong things, like the fact that I'm always overcompensating. That my mother's death left a permanent scar, its edges still raw. If only Ollie's return weren't inextricably tied to leaving Levi on Castor Island, at the hands of Gravelle.

"Emmaline," the familiar voice of my bot, Dash, cuts through my tangled thoughts. "You have an incoming call. Do you wish to answer it?"

I look down at my plum. There's no number listed, but it's definitely ringing.

Could it be him? Levi?

The thought of it sends every nerve in my body tingling.

Is he okay?

That question sends fear coursing through me.

"Yes!" I whisper, frantic, as I shove my earbuds in. I don't want to wake Ollie or tip off my father, whose head is bent over a work memo. But if there's any chance this is Levi, there's no way I'm not answering.

I take in a breath. "I'm ready," I tell Dash. Then, after a click, "Um, hello?"

"Hello, Emmaline," says a familiar voice, infiltrating the quiet space in my head. "Long time, no talk."

I instantly bristle, feeling my skin growing clammy, my heartbeat quickening. I know that voice, would know it anywhere.

It's the Similars' guardian. The man who created them, and who wrote me that note back in April breaking the news that I'm a Similar.

It's Gravelle.

In seconds, his face pops up on the screen of my plum. I shiver at the sight of his sagging skin. His thin lips. His eyes that seem to bore right into my heart, squeezing it dry.

"Yes?" I'm testy, on edge. Why is Gravelle calling me? Why *now*? I have nothing to say to this man, except to rail at him for all the suffering he's caused. To demand to know why he insisted on holding Levi on that island. "What is it?" I ask, not bothering to keep the venom out of my voice.

"Emmali—rather, *Eden*." His pinched lips curl into a half smile. "You did get my letter, did you not?"

"Of course I got it," I snap at him. "Excuse me for not writing back. I didn't think your *note* warranted a response. Especially since there's a good chance you're lying to me. You didn't exactly provide proof that I'm a..." I don't say the word out loud. *A Similar*. "So who's to say you're not making the whole thing up?"

"I can see I hit a nerve." Gravelle's lips drop the pretense of a smile. "I can understand how *traumatic* the contents of my note must have been to you. But that's not the letter I'm concerned with. Not today."

It's not? Heart pounding in my chest like a brass band, I glance at Ollie. Thank goodness he's still asleep and hasn't heard a word of this conversation. My father's wearing the noise-canceling headphones he always uses while working. Good.

"Surely you know what this is about?" Gravelle prods, bringing my focus back to his soulless face.

"Of course I don't—"

"I intercepted a certain...email of yours. Not five days ago, I believe."

My heart lurches to my throat. He means my email to Levi. He read it. *He* got it. Of course he did. How could I have ever thought he wouldn't see it? The man sees everything. Controls everything.

"That jog your memory?" Gravelle asks, humorlessly.

"Where is he? How is he? What are you doing to him?" I choke out in a strained whisper.

"Ah yes, young love. You would want to know, wouldn't you?"

"Tell me what you've done to him. Or I swear—"

"What, dear Eden? What would you, what *could* you possibly do?"

I don't answer, because I have no idea. What power do I hold over Gravelle? Absolutely none at all. He holds all the cards, and he knows it.

"Don't hurt him," I whisper. "He's never done anything but try to please you. If you do, I'll tell the world what you did to us last year. Holding Pru hostage. Killing an innocent clone so you could pretend Ollie had died and destroy the Wards."

Gravelle sizes me up. "Two can play at this game, Eden. I don't suppose my other son, Oliver, would have any interest in seeing your email to Levi—would he? Because I'd happily forward it along. If you'd like."

I freeze. Forward that note to Ollie? I sneak another look at him, my pulse thudding. *No, no, no.* He can't see that note. I haven't told Ollie about Levi, except to say we were friends. All summer I struggled with how to explain that Levi's arrival at Darkwood rewrote my entire narrative. It's impossible, and it would only hurt him.

"No. Don't send him that."

"I didn't think so," Gravelle answers silkily.

"Put Levi on the phone," I demand.

"That's impossible."

I feel my stomach lurch. Sweat forms on the back of my neck, and I feel faint. Impossible? Why—because Levi's hurt? Or worse, *dead*?

"What have you done to him?"

"Always so dramatic. It's not what *I've* done. It's Levi. He's asked me to tell you not to contact him again. I know this won't be easy to hear. Such is life... He doesn't want to see you. Now, or ever."

"I don't believe you," I snarl.

"Levi's made it clear he'll be quite content finishing up his senior year here, with me. Darkwood never was a good fit for him. He felt he was always in Oliver's shadow."

"But...but..." I stammer.

"But what about you?" Those narrow lips curl up into the first full smile I've seen on his face since he called me. "Must I spell it out? *You* were never a good fit for him, Eden. And if you need a reminder that contacting him is not in your best interests, or his—check your email. Until next time," he grins at me, and his face vanishes from my plum screen. The call cuts off.

Hands trembling, heart in my throat, I'm about to ask Dash to open Gravelle's email when I hear voices outside the car. I look up from my plum, past the leaves and branches that brush against my window as we glide up the hill to school. We should be pulling into the circular drive right now. Why are we stopped?

I press my face to the glass. A cluster of students blocks the entrance to the driveway. Eight, maybe ten kids stand in our way, holding up signs: CLONING IS A CRIME, AND SO ARE CLONES.

Your hub for the hottest young adult books!

Visit us online and sign up for our
newsletter at FIREreads.com

 @sourcebooksfire

 sourcebooksfire

firereads.tumblr.com